# THE PURPLE THREAD

## John Broughton

Dedicated to Maria Antonietta Valente
my patient wife who shares many characteristics with Leoba

Special thanks go to my dear friend John Bentley for his steadfast and indefatigable support. His proofreading and suggestions have made an invaluable contribution to *The Purple Thread*.

Cover design: *Piero and Marialuisa Corno*

TABLE OF CONTENTS

**CHAPTER 1**

**CHAPTER 2**

**CHAPTER 3**

**CHAPTER 4**

**CHAPTER 5**

**CHAPTER 6**

**CHAPTER 7**

**PART TWO**

**CHAPTER 8**

**CHAPTER 9**

**CHAPTER 10**

**CHAPTER 11**

**CHAPTER 12**

**CHAPTER 13**

**CHAPTER 14**

**PART THREE**

[CHAPTER 15](#)

[CHAPTER 16](#)

[CHAPTER 17](#)

[CHAPTER 18](#)

[CHAPTER 19](#)

[CHAPTER 20](#)

[APPENDIX](#)

[GLOSSARY](#)

[ABOUT THE AUTHOR](#)

# CHAPTER 1

*April 733 AD*

A murder of rooks flapped heavenwards startling Begiloc while he sowed beans in the Near Field. In the trees edging the woodland, they perched, cawing while he marvelled how the tender branches bowed but did not break under their weight. The earthy smell of the harrowed soil pleased him as he sought to discover what had startled the sullen sentinels.

*'Ealric!'*

Was something wrong? A command to stop the headlong rush before he broke a limb died when his son skidded to a halt on the ox-trail before a rainwater-filled rut. The boy, heedless of the mud, dropped to his knees.

Constant and fierce this love, because Gerens, his father, drowned when he was Ealric's age and the wound never healed. Setting these thoughts aside, Begiloc stepped over the furrows and strode down the path.

A whitethroat hushed its song when he passed and the sun slid behind the clouds to cast a shroud over the land, but Begiloc, taken with Ealric, did not care about the bite in the April air. What was he up to? A sleeve rolled up, he plunged an arm into the puddle. What's slithering from his upraised hand?

*'Frogspawn!'*

With a smile, Begiloc bent over and ruffled the mane of wavy hair, different from his own chestnut curls. How it spilt down like ale froth! A gift of his Saxon wife. His hand lingered.

Ealric jumped up and took a deep breath but Begiloc dammed the flood of words.

"Why would a man risk his bones for a dollop of frogspawn, is what I want to know?"

Squatting next to him, he stared into his face. Amused, he watched the boy take in his meaning and the pale blue eyes change to solemnity. Under his hand, the skinny shoulder shivered.

"Come, let's walk!"

The words tumbled out, "Mother says come at once. Meryn's waiting at the Monks' Trail. Be fast! she said."

Why was Meryn not digging the ditch by the Far Field? Why the Monks' Trail?

At the entry to the village, he squatted, face level with his son's. Ealric leant forward pressing his nose against his father's, who rocked back and tweaked the impertinent snout.

"Here, take the basket home. Do you think you can get there without stalking beetles? Don't stop for anything. Tell your mother I'm off to meet Meryn. Got that?"

Another ruffle of the tousled locks and he rose. Ealric eyes wide, grasped the handle with both hands and set off on his mission. The boy's straight back and earnest march warmed his heart and he left, whistling, to meet his friend.

*'Better not be another of his foolish jests.'*

Propped against a tree, Meryn said, "What held you up? Our Lady Abbess will not be pleased to wait on two labourers. Before you ask, *no*, not a joke."

"The abbess? What's all this?"

Hands on hips, Meryn stood elbows raised.

"All I know is two monks came asking for Meryn from across the Tamar and when I confessed, they told me to bring you to the Abbey."

"Men like us don't enter Wimborne Abbey, it's not done. Let alone meet the abbess..."

A careless shrug and Meryn inspected his hands before wiping them on his breeches. "Don't worry, old friend, she may want to reward us for hard work – or make monks of us!"
Up the track they trudged toward the religious settlement.

"Did they say why?"

"No."

A mystery.

The walls of the abbey compound made a familiar sight since the villagers brought their harvest tithe at Lammas. Yet, Begiloc never passed through the heavy gate where he and his comrade stood exchanging lowered glances. Did his companion share his longing to be elsewhere? Not that Meryn struck him as a deep thinker – his beard the only neat thing about him, plaited with wooden beads. Nobody else in the kingdom of Wessex wore such an arrangement. As for the rest of him, he looked like he had been dragged behind an ox.

*'Typical Meryn!'*

A fine pair to stand before royalty! Why would a warrior like Ine give up the throne for a pilgrimage to Rome? Seven years past. Abbess Cuniburg was Ine's sister and sister-in-law to the new king, Aethelheard. The year after he, Begiloc, was born she founded the abbey. A thumb stuck up to represent God and a finger for the royal family serving Him, thus he ticked off a chain of service on his other fingers: earls and thegns, ceorls and slaves.

"The likes of us are a long way off God," Begiloc murmured.

"What? This isn't the Pearly Gate?"

Trust Meryn to ease the tension. At odds with his wiry frame, his friend's deep laugh rumbled as Begiloc pummelled the barrier. A panel slid back and blue eyes studied their faces. Purpose stated, a monk admitted and invited them to follow him. Arranged like two villages, to the left of the compound nuns went about their tasks and to the right monks led a separate existence. In the centre, topped by a cross, stood a large thatched building.

*'The abbey church!'*

Twenty times bigger than the one in the village, Begiloc reckoned a thousand trees had gone into its construction. Passing by, they approached a well where Meryn seized the monk by the sleeve.

"Brother, I dug ditches all morning. May I have a drink?"

The brother lowered a bucket and Meryn poked Begiloc in the ribs, gesturing toward the monk winching up the pail.

"When I get back home, I'm going to take a vow of silence. Not that anybody listens to me overmuch..."

Stifling a laugh, Begiloc bit his lip. Meryn, wordless? As likely as silent rooks at seeding.

*'Those scavengers! Why are we here with work to be done?'*

The proffered ladle in hand, Meryn slaked his thirst while Begiloc contemplated the scattered stones around the base of the well. Offered the tin scoop, he shook his head.

*'Let's get on with this!'*

The monk led them to where seven buildings ranged in a row. The aroma of fresh-baked bread wafted from the second. Between this and the next, they glimpsed nuns weeding between rows of onions. The monk indicated the way to the smallest house. The roof was covered by dried sods not thatch and the structure appeared no larger than Begiloc's own home.

*'Can it be the Abbess lives here? The Mother Superior in so humble a dwelling?'*

The monk knocked.

"Come!"

The brother indicated to step into the room, where with difficulty in the dim light, Begiloc discerned two nuns stationed either side of the door. Mixed smoke of wood and tallow made him want to pinch his nose. On one side, a pallet served as a bed over which hung a wooden cross. Nearby a table bore a leather-bound book. On the beaten earth floor a fire burned inside a ring of stones and his eyes followed the wisps of smoke to a hole in the roof and back down to a table covered in documents, beakers, bottle and food, some spices and another tallow candle. The spices were the only luxury in this austere setting.

Nor had he seen anyone like Abbess Cuniburg. Though small, she seemed to fill the room. Judging by the lines on her face, she was fifty but the wrinkles were gentle and added to her beauty. Under no delusion, Begiloc caught the shrewdness in the deep eyes weighing up the two men from Dumnonia.

*'Can she read our innermost thoughts?'*

No trace of wealth about her in spite of her regal bearing. A wimple covered her head and a hood draped her shoulders. Under it, a burgundy cloak overlaid a grey tunic, at the waist, a wooden cross tucked in a belt.

Cuniburg smiled and a dimple formed.

"Welcome, my sons. I thank you for the haste with which you responded to my summons. After your work, you must be hungry and thirsty."

A wave of her hand and the two nuns glided to cut bread and cheese and pour ale from the leather bottle. The abbess murmured words in Latin and made the sign of the cross, the gesture imitated by Begiloc while Meryn's eyes moved from one to the other before making his own clumsy attempt.

"It is plain fare, but God provides for our simple needs."

Her throaty voice bore no hint of pride.

Curious, Begiloc bit off a piece of cheese, appreciating its tangy saltiness. The eyes of the women never left him as he tried not to devour the food. No such inhibitions for Meryn. Tearing at his bread, he reached for his beaker, a series of gulps, smacked his lips and wiped his sleeve across his mouth. Instead, Begiloc savoured the malty taste of the ale, likely twice brewed, not watery like that of the village. When he looked up he read approval in the lady's eyes. Even so, he refused another measure. In spite of the kindness of the Mother Superior, he was tense and needed a clear head.

*'There must be a serious reason behind our presence and it bodes ill.'*

Not sharing his reserve, Meryn rubbed his hands together when a nun refilled his cup.

*'He sees no trap in anything it'll be his ruin one day.'*

Meal over, the abbess reached across the table to select a parchment.

"A messenger bore this from overseas." She moved nearer the candle, her eyes roving over the Latin script, she translated: "...Holding you above all women in the innermost vault of our hearts we desire your graciousness to know that, after the death of our parents and other relatives, we went to the people of Germany, were admitted into the monastic rule of the venerable archbishop, Boniface, and have become helpers in his labours in so far as our humble incapacity allows..." The abbess halted but her unwavering gaze admonished them for attention. She resumed, "...we beg also that you will send on by the bearer of this letter two young freedmen, named Begiloc and Meryn, whom I, Lull, and my father released on our departure for Rome and entrusted to my uncle for the welfare of my soul – if this should be their free act and if they are within your jurisdiction. And if any one shall unlawfully attempt to impede their journey we beg you to protect them..." Cuniburg paused, "Well, the rest of the letter does not concern you. The sender is Denehard, the son of your late lord."

The colour drained from Begiloc's face and his head pounded. Heels close together and head bowed, he frowned. A flippant remark occurred to his comrade, but from under his brow, Begiloc noted the gravity of the situation dawn on him, hence Meryn crossed his arms, planted his feet apart and stared at the nun.

Tone imperious, she said. "Prepare for your departure after daybreak on the morrow."

The air heavy, his head began to spin, but Begiloc found the courage to say, "In the letter is writ, *'if this should be their free act,'* My Lady..." he lifted his head and stared into the grey eyes. Had they grown darker? "...I have a wife and son and land to—"

"Fear not on that score, the Abbey will tend to their needs till your return. The brothers will work your land and your family will be safe here. Your boy will study and she will serve. As for you, you will be answering God's call, so rejoice!"

Her face shone and Begiloc understood that Meryn, he and his family were of no importance to the abbess other than as teeth in the cog of a mechanism he did not understand.

*'Like motes, unseen until a beam of sun illuminates them.'*

Breaking off his reverie, Begiloc's voice quavered, "M-may I not take my wife and child with me?"

"Indeed not! Among pagans? Must I repeat myself?" her tone sharpened, "They will be safe here till your return."

Careful to keep his voice reverential, Begiloc made one last effort at defiance.

"And should we refuse this *'free act'*, My Lady?"

No sign of the sweetness that had greeted them, "Need I remind you that you were a slave?" Her voice rang like the knell of the convent bell: "You were raised to a freeman, as I hear tell, because of your prowess in battle eight years ago on behalf of my brother against Ealdbert of the South Saxons. Still, it is a simple act to return a man to slavery." The eyes of the abbess were iron, but she lightened her tone and the dimple reappeared, "Come, we need not disagree! Your warrior's arm is needed once more and Our Lord's will is you shall go to the German lands. Your family will be here to welcome you on your return. God blesses those who labour in His name."

The regal woman, like a whirlpool, drew him into the depths of her will. "As for you," she turned a cold gaze on Meryn and placed a forefinger to the tip of her chin, "you have no family to leave behind. There are no objections I presume?"

A tug at his beard, Meryn said. "Far away across the Tamar, My Lady. I'll be a slave no more."

"Wise! Hark, these are my plans. In addition to the request of Denehard, after prayer for guidance, I acceded to the supplications of my sister in the Lord, Leobgytha." The voice of the abbess mellowed. "Since her seventh year she is with us and will leave for Franconia to be Abbess at Bischofsheim under her cousin, Archbishop Boniface. They corresponded and I consent to her departure with some sisters and brothers."

The abbess placed a hand on Begiloc's sleeve, "The Lady Leobgytha is as a daughter to me. Your task is to deliver her. Protect her with your life," her gaze switched to Meryn, "both of you."

Such skill in blending plea and authority, Begiloc marvelled – she the potter, we the clay. "Do this for God and our Lord Jesus Christ and your reward will be great. Kneel!"

The Mother Superior blessed them, adding: "Go home, ready your weapons, gather warm clothing and sleep well. Be here at dawn to meet your charges. There will be ten armed men at your command."

"At my command? Forgive me but will Saxons be led by a Briton?"

In silence, she scrutinised the scar over his left eye. At last, Cuniburg said, "I chose well. God has guided my choice and my men are sworn to obedience. Until the morn!" A hand waved in dismissal. Dazed, Begiloc hesitated but Meryn tugged at his arm, pulling him toward the door. "Out! While we can," he whispered.

Outside, Begiloc squinted against the brightness his head reeling at the bite of the air. In silence, they hurried to the gate.

On the Monks' Trail, he slowed. Shaken by the reality of the charge placed upon them, trembling with repressed anger, he halted. Unaware of this, Meryn strode on, stopped, spun round and glared. Curious, Begiloc approached him, his chest tight. Head pounding, he stared at his friend. What of the usual cheerfulness? In its place a flat, sour look. A finger pointed and jabbed the air with every word.

"We must go and the sooner the better."

In return, Begiloc gave him a blank stare. "You heard the Lady, we leave at dawn."

Eyes narrowed, Meryn bunched a fist, "I mean we must go *home*, to Dumnonia. Now!"

"Home?"

"Yes, home, to our people."

Eyebrows meeting, Begiloc said, "Never make it. My home's here."

Challenge in his eyes, Meryn said, "Think about it. They won't miss us till morn. A day's start–"

"Impossible! With a woman and boy. The Saxons have horses–"

"Well, I'm going with or without you."

The edge to Meryn's voice, unrecognisable as that of his happy-go-lucky childhood friend, shocked him. Born of an awareness of future bloodshed cloaked in the Lady's command?

Begiloc's shoulders sagged and he rubbed his forehead. Meryn's words plunged into his entrails like a seax and his stomach clenched.

*'Does he mean to flee without me?'*

On a wayside marker, he sat head in hands but Meryn shook his shoulder, words distant as from the next valley.

"Come! Don't waste time! We can be three leagues away by nightfall."

With a glare, Begiloc clamped Meryn's wrist, "I listened to you once before and it cost me my brother's life. Victory turned into humiliation, remember, Meryn? The battle at Hehil when we drove the Saxons back across the Tamar, tails between their legs? Look! Here's a reminder," he pointed to the scar above his eye. "And Keresyk, only sixteen. Dead these eleven years. Death and enslavement. Our reward for heeding you. Did you learn nothing?" Head bowed, he muttered, "We followed you – ever headstrong – straight into a trap–"

"We were all young and foolhardy. Not only me," Meryn let his hair fall forward to cover his face. "Nobody's forcing you to come."

Temples pounding, Begiloc jumped to his feet, "No, and I didn't have to save your wretched life eleven years ago, it cost me Keresyk."

No sooner had he spat out the words than he regretted them. Wounded, Meryn stomped off down the trail.

"I didn't mean that!" Begiloc called.

Damage done, words cut deeper than a knife and having struck, he sagged back down on the stone, once more head in hands.

A while passed before thrush song invaded his consciousness. A soothing balm, he absorbed the lilting notes. By instinct, Begiloc clung to the belief of his forefathers – the interweaving of everything in nature in a community of being. Hence, the birdsong, the yellow ox-lip next to his foot, the limestone marker, the earth, the sun, the scudding clouds melded to connect in fellowship with him. This – other than the demanding God of Abbess Cuniburg – raised his spirits. At last, he set off home.

In no hurry, he considered Meryn's scheme. Even if the four of them reached the nearest port, they had nothing to offer for passage. A Saxon crew would never risk mooring in Dumnonia. Overland, they were sure to be captured and enslaved. Not for nought had he shed blood to gain his freedom and win a bride.

*'The devil take Meryn!'*

He must consider Somerhild and Ealric and what had the abbess said? *'Your reward will be great.'*

Overcome by regret for those harsh words to Meryn; nonetheless he had made up his mind. No doubt he would miss his friend, his humour, his fine singing voice and his interest in everyone and everything. In the abbey, his family would live well while his land would be farmed without the sweat of his toil. The thought brought a wry smile.

Why had God freed him from slavery? There must be a purpose. Trust the Mother Superior.

Irresolute, he surveyed the house Meryn and he built and they must leave. Twelve trees felled. The crucks next to the door frame pleased him, more so the shuttered window with its transparent scraped pig-skin pane. Somerhild kept it closed today because the wind was sharp, but with such a fine fit little draught entered. The thatch would last for years yet. Satisfied, he pushed in through the door.

On her knees, his wife stirred a pot over the fire. The smoke made his eyes smart and he coughed. With a cry of joy, she leapt up to hug him. How he loved the smell of her hair – rosewater and smoke. Burrowing his face into the fine strands, he kissed her and embraced her tight. She gazed up into his eyes.

"What did they want up at the abbey?"

Her concern upset him as he released her. The necklace of glass beads he had given her sparkled – Talwyn, his mother, had pressed them on him against the day he found a bride – Somerhild, conscious of his scrutiny, smoothed down her blue dress, creased from kneeling at the hearth.

"Well?" Instinct warned her of bad news.

Voice even, he said, "Fact is..." he studied the upturned nose over her full lips.

*'How I love you.'*

"...you and Ealric must go and live in the abbey–"

"The abbey? Why?" Her eyes widened.

"I have to go away. Overseas. Only for a while..." her stricken expression tugged at his heart, "...I-I'll come back...maybe a year–"

"How can–"

"There is no choice, my love, the abbess needs me...I mean...she *commands* me. No more to be said."

"A year? A year! You make it sound like a week!"

No more than a twelvemonth, he hoped as he held a rush taper over a chest by the wall where his face did not betray his feelings. Out came a linen cloth with ties attached which he spread on the floor. From the tail of his eye, he regarded Somerhild. Still, she stood hands over her mouth. Out followed a woollen cloak to fold for his bundle. At last, she unfroze.

"Here, let me do that! Where is it you go?"

"To the German lands."

"You'll need warm breeches."

Nose in the box, she began to sob. Folk told fearsome tales about the 'German lands'.

"We're a-feared of settlers as close as yon side of the river, so why risk your life for others a world away?" she said.

Dismayed at her tears, he held her for a while till she calmed but did not meet her eyes; instead, his gaze fixed on a tiny pulsing vein purple at her temple until she buried her head in his chest.

"Hush!" he implored her, voice catching, "Not for ever." For all he knew, it might well be for ever – the irony – warrior of the Church for an early meeting with its saints.

"Where's Ealric?"

In a whine hard to understand, she said, "Gone to check the eel trap, but there's bean soup in any case..."

"Be brave for Ealric, he can't see you like this. A boy doesn't know how long a year is." Raising her to her feet, Begiloc smeared her cheek with his hand. "Tell him I'm off to the coast. Three leagues or so. The truth, up to a point. That's all he needs to know."

The bundle of clothes occupying her, Somerhild nodded.

"Can't I stay here with Ealric? I don't want to go to the abbey."

"Enough woman!" His voice harsh, "It's dangerous here for a man. What of wolves or raiders? Do not disobey your husband and worse, our Lady Abbess. Cease your prattle before the boy gets back. Ah, here he is!"

Someone knocked, so not Ealric. Curious, Begiloc lifted the door latch to find Meryn, his expression strange.

"I thought you gone to Dumnonia."

The familiar grin creased Meryn's face. "What leave all those pretty nuns to you? Oops, only joking Somerhild! You know me...but..." he noted the red-rimmed eyes and his face fell, but the impish smile returned, "Mixed up Saxon, you should be jumping for joy to be rid of the old bear for a while...and I'll wager you shed tears. I could tell you a story about ..." he saw she had wept, so he picked her up by the waist and swung her, her feet clearing the soup pot by an inch. Everyone was laughing when he put her down.

First to speak, Begiloc said, "I was wrong–"

"I'm sorry. Say no more! You're my best friend. I won't let you down. I came to say that – and I'll be off. See you in the morning."

Begiloc seized him, "I'll give you old bear..!" and they were all laughing again. Meryn had the gift of turning disaster on its head. At that moment, Ealric came in holding an eel snare.

"Did you get one?" Somerhild took the elongated willow basket.

"Clever boy!" she passed the trap to her husband who reached for a small axe.

"Well done!" Meryn said, "I once showed my father a clean pair of 'eels!"

A laugh at the joke and Begiloc insisted on his friend staying.

To his relief, no more work awaited except to feed the dark-skinned, bristle-haired pig. Heat from the decomposing straw in the pit under the floorboards and from the clay-lined hearth made the room cosy. After they had eaten stew washed down with cider, Begiloc reached for the hearpe he had carved from yew wood.

"Come, Meryn, recognise this?" After strumming a few notes, he said, "The tale of Drustanus and forbidden love for his brother's wife, the queen?"

"Course I do!" Meryn's rich voice blended in perfect harmony to sing of the tragedy that tore apart the royal family of Dumnonia two centuries before. Preoccupied, Somerhild packed their belongings, caring not for the melancholy song of a race not her own.

At daybreak, they made a strange sight on the Monks' Trail: Somerhild with a pack on her back leading the long-legged pig on a rope; Ealric with his mother's dog skipping and yapping beside him; spear and shield in hand, Begiloc tramped with helm and seax at his belt, his six-stringed instrument strapped across his back and in his other hand a roll of clothing.

As they approached the palisade enclosing the abbey, the oak gate swung open. A different scene greeted Begiloc from the day before, confusion reigned, including Meryn gesticulating to a monk leading off his pig and goat. Opposite them, at the well, a band of armed warriors exchanged banter over the water ladle.

*'My men.'*

The Abbess shouted orders to servants and pointed toward the stables. There, a group of monks, Begiloc counted six, stood around a cart on which two men were piling packs. A few paces apart, seven nuns whispered and smiled among themselves and the eyes of a young nun bored into him. When he met her gaze she lowered her head and stared at the ground.

Unkempt as usual, grumbling about damned monks, Meryn ambled over. In greeting, Begiloc threw an arm around him.

"Uncle Meryn! Uncle Meryn, can I hold your axe, please, please?"

Dour expression melting, he unslung his double-headed battle-axe, handing it to Ealric. The boy seized it with both hands but to his dismay, he could not hold it upright. The axe head sliced into the ground and Begiloc laughed.

"Men! Typical! Ealric could have chopped his foot off!"

"Ay, Somerhild, as well he didn't – though if he had, there'd be one left! Eat up all your food, young man so as you can wield a battleaxe," Meryn ruffled his hair and reclaimed the weapon hoisting it back into its harness, winking at his friend's son.

"Have you chopped many heads off, Uncle Meryn?"

"Hush!" his mother said as a monk approached. The brother invited Begiloc and Meryn to load their packs on the cart before backing an ox between the shafts and yoking it. Two horses were brought for a couple of nuns to mount. Curious, Begiloc noted one, in her twenties and the other twice her age hoisted into their saddles. The Abbess, a warrior in her wake, hurried to halt before them, bestowing a smile on Somerhild and Ealric.

"Welcome, soon we will have you settled and happy," she stroked Ealric's cheek. Her warmth made Somerhild smile though her heart ached. Cuniburg became brisk and efficient, addressing Begiloc while half-turning to the huge Saxon beside her. The Mother Superior indicated the man, "This is Caena," she said, her tone firm, "he will be your right hand. He obeys you and his men follow him."

The Saxon, stood three hands taller than Begiloc, his beard and moustache long, the latter covering his upper lip. In spite of the cold, his shield arm, bearing a livid scar, was bare under his leather jerkin. The man's eyes, hard, scrutinised him.

The abbess passed Begiloc a document with a wax seal. "Keep this for your safe conduct in the Frankish lands. Today you travel four leagues to Werham. Spend the night at the Priory. In the morning, board the ship to the Frankish lands." Out of her mantle came a bag of coins. "Take this!" The shrewdness returned to her eyes. "Do not give the steersman more than three scillingas, the sum agreed." A nod of the head. "There is more money for the journey. Come! I shall present you to your charges."

The abbess led him to the younger woman on horseback.

"Sister, this is Begiloc who will lead the men."

With raised hand, she indicated the nun in a black cloak. "The Lady Leobgytha. Obey her in all things!"

Hazel eyes in a pale, oval face appraised him.

*'Like an angel.'*

The nun smiled at him, smiled a greeting and lowered her gaze at once. Dumbstruck, he forced his gaze from the lovely countenance.

"Go, make your farewells for it is past Prime," the abbess said, "you must be away soon." The Mother Superior approached the horse, "Leoba, this parting tears at my heart, child. But it is a sin, for the Lord means it to sing with joy, for you take the Word to the heathen ..."

*'Leoba? The abbess's name of endearment?'*

"Leoba", he repeated under his breath. Joining Somerhild and Ealric, he planted his spear in the ground.

"Somerhild, my love," he approved of her brave face, "pray for my wellbeing, as I shall for your happiness." He embraced her while Ealric attached himself to his thigh. She whispered, "How can I be glad without you, husband?" Leaden-hearted, he kissed her, stroking her hair.

"Sing every day. Your love will speed my return. A warrior cannot march with a boy clinging to his leg."

Lifting Ealric level with his face, his stomach tightened at the sight of wet eyes.

"I'm counting on you Ealric. While I'm away, you're the man. Look after your mother, behave for her!" Resolution chased away the boy's tears, satisfied, he lowered him and kissed his head, took his shield and spear and turned his back on them.

*'God willing I'll see them again.'*
Voice harsh, he called Meryn.
The Briton left off stroking the ox behind its ear and strolled over.

"Find Caena, the one with the scar down his shield arm. Tell the lumpen oaf to fetch his men to the abbess."
Accustomed to Begiloc's descriptions, Meryn hurried off grinning, looking back and calling, "The Saxon's a big 'un, even for you!"
Not looking at his family, Begiloc strode to the Mother Superior. The Saxons arrived and he said to Caena, "Choose three men. The four of you will lead our party."
The warrior spun on his heel and called out three names in rapid succession.

"Get here and quick! Slow bastards, move I say!" A steely glare born of brutal campaigns fixed them and they leapt to form up in pairs in front of the two horses. Begiloc cajoled the monks and nuns into line behind the armed men. While he organized the servants behind the animals, the abbess exchanged a glance of approval with the Lady Leobgytha. That done, he shouted orders to the other warriors.
The sour look and gesture did not escape him as one of the Saxons, a shifty-eyed, skinny fellow spat on the ground. The man's face he would remember – *'weasel-eyes'*.

"Flank the horses to the left, Meryn. I'll take the right."

With a wave, he ordered the cart to the head of the procession.

Abbess Cuniburg sketched a blessing as they moved off while Begiloc searched for Somerhild and Ealric, who waved and, trying to imprint every detail of their faces on his memory, he raised his spear in salute.

Lady Leobgytha leant toward him from her horse, "Be not sad, for the Lord smiles upon us." Wide hazel eyes full of tender compassion, like the voice, beguiled him.

*'She cares!'*

Beyond her black hood, the sight of the ashen sky wiped away his smile.

# CHAPTER 2

The cows in the meadow below the abbey grazed tails to the east and three geese flew low overhead. Weather-wise it bode ill. The Saxons, resentful at being led by a Briton, disturbed Begiloc too. No doubt to win respect he must prove his worth in combat. The journey, skirting marshland, fording the river toward Corf proceeded as dull as the day. Clouds scudded darker and the breeze had teeth like a wolf. He worried that it would freshen into wind but the weather held and the cart kept a decent pace on the dry ground while the nuns and monks bore the march in high spirits, singing psalms and chanting prayers along the deserted road. At the mill on the Stour, Begiloc calculated they had travelled more than a league, about a third of the way. Refreshed, they should reach the priory well before nightfall.

In exchange for coin, the miller closed the sluice gate and let them water the animals at the mill race. For Lady Leobgytha and the older nun, he placed a table and chairs in the shelter of a wall. The others sat on the grass.

Natural circles formed of monks, nuns, and warriors so Begiloc lowered himself down next to Caena with Meryn on his other side.

"Hey, Saxon!" Meryn said, "Don't mess with yon warrior at t'other side of me – he's known to slice men's throats from ear to ear if he don't get on with 'em." A finger drew from right to left lobe as a demonstration. Damage done. Menacing under his breath, Caena made a point of staring the other way, creating an effect on his men.

Monks came handing out bread and dried meat. Chewing hard, Begiloc glanced to where Leobgytha sat with a nun standing next to her. No meal for that one, holding a book from which she began to read aloud.

*'I wish I could read.'*

Words set down on parchment spanned the sea. If he could write to Somerhild ... he sighed ... shook off the thought, no use being as heavy as the clouds above.

After a draught from the ale skin, instead of passing the bottle to Caena, Begiloc wished to make a point by handing it to Meryn who seemed surprised but did not hesitate to seize it. The huge Saxon stared at the ground but did not react, though some of the others muttered and exchanged glances. A long swig later, he offered the vessel to the warrior next to him, teasing him again about Begiloc's 'violent nature'.

In a voice hard to hear, the Saxon said: "I won't drink from the same skin as slaves."

Meryn thrust the container into Begiloc's chest. Seax drawn, he leapt up and three or four Saxons did the same.

"Say that again, so we can all hear it and so I can rip out your filthy tongue!"

Caena rose but Begiloc held him back, his deep voice rang out: "Does any man here doubt the wisdom of our Mother Superior? Let him speak! For she has entrusted us with a task that may yet cost blood. Let's not spill it among ourselves."

His gaze roved from man to man and each one met his eye. Gladdened, he had neither use for cowards nor fools.

"Put up your weapon, Meryn. If any man here wishes to call me *slave*, I, who won freedom on the field of battle, let him do so." The man who had spat on the ground at the abbey failed to meet his eye and looked at the ground.

*'Trouble there!'*

"That's settled!"

The ale-skin, he passed to Caena, "Drink!" The Saxon drank. Not caring more for lunch, Meryn walked over to the mill race, where he stared into the water. Instead, Begiloc decided to stay with the Saxons, whose brawn and courage were sure to be needed in hard times ahead, but his heart went out to his friend. The drink found its way, man after man, back to him. Weighing it in his hand, he turned to Caena.

"One silver pening says you can't down the rest in one go."

A smile spread across the warrior's face.

"You'll be wasting your coin, let me tell you. I always said Britons were born stupid!"

His grin widened as he seized the skin and rose his feet, planted them apart and glared round the group in defiance. A deep breath and he held the vessel to his mouth, chin up-tilted, his beard moved up and down. At last, he tore the flask from his lips, upturned the container and two drops dripped to the grass. A roar went up from the Saxons and Caena grinned.

"A silver pening! I warned you, didn't I? Like stealing an oatcake from a babe!"

"A Briton always pays his debts."

Tone flat, Begiloc intended the subtle threat but held out a hand in peace and waited. The corner of Caena's mouth twitched upwards. Seconds of stillness passed like the instant on the battlefield before the death blow is struck, but at last, the Saxon clasped his hand. They remained like this for a moment, each man weighing up the other, before Begiloc shook a pening from his purse. As he did so, he sensed avid eyes on the bulging leather bag, but Saxon cheers greeting the coin falling into the outstretched hand of Caena distracted him.

"See your leader drink! I'll better any man at supping ale!"

Under no delusions, Begiloc had achieved an armed truce – until the next challenge emerged.

From an unsettling quarter arose another, different, for the young nun who had stared at him in the abbey courtyard, gazed at him anew.

'*I know her not. She isn't of our village.*'

Between stares, she turned to speak with her companion, the older sister with a horse.

'*A nun eyeing a married man! It's unseemly.*'

Troubled, empty ale-skin in hand, Begiloc walked over to the mill race to rinse and fill it afresh from the river. With this excuse, he approached the scowling Meryn.

"With that banter of yours, you'd provoke a saint, but why give them the satisfaction of knowing they've wounded you?"

Meryn's shoulders sagged.

"Why let them see your wrath?"

"Anger is indeed a sin."

The gentle voice made them start. The nun with the angelic face raised a hand toward Meryn, but replaced the gesture with a smile, in turn, ousted by pursed lips.

"Sage to avoid bloodshed and soothe turbulent spirits, but you ran a grave risk that might have finished in death and eternal damnation," said Leobgytha.

"No, My Lady, no peril. Caena can drink twice the ale in one go."

At once, he regretted his rude tongue. How best to address a noble lady?

The nun shuddered, "Wise to placate him with a coin," she smiled again, "should we move on?"

"Yes, it is time."

Begiloc bowed and waited for her to turn away before giving his attention to the ale-skin.

On his return, finding Caena readying everyone gladdened him.

"Load that sack, and today would be good!" the Saxon bellowed at his men making Begiloc believe the sarcasm in his voice matched a ruthless temper.

Displeasing, he found Meryn threatening the man who had offended him. Their mutual glares presaged strife. Later, he would warn him off. As he passed by to take his position, Meryn said, "Did you note the frogs? We're in for a drenching."

Nonplussed, Begiloc paused, "I did." So, his comrade had observed them too. The loud croaking meant rain on the way. Better to set off at once.

Half a league farther, Leobgytha dashed hopes of swift progress. Within hailing distance of the village loomed a wayside cross where an old woman knelt in prayer. Leobgytha's voice rang out like a bell summoning everyone to prayer. The ox-cart halted and forced those behind to stop.

"My Lady?" said Begiloc.

"The hour of Sext. This holy place serves instead of a church for the villagers."

To his dismay, she dismounted and likewise the other nun.

"My Lady, the sky foretells bad weather."

"Our psalms will please the Lord and rain will hold off."

The hazel eyes brooked no discussion, no point in wasting time in futile protest.

"I beg you, My Lady, short psalms."

At her bell-like laugh, again he regretted pitting his earthy wit against her spirituality.

"Come, Begiloc," he started at the use of his name, "the Lord will not be pleased if we treat Him with less respect than we give the weather."

The monks and nuns recited six psalms.

"Thank God, Sext is shorter than Vespers or we'd never be away," he whispered to Meryn. After what in his impatience, he deemed an eternity, they moved on. Out of the village his spirits lifted when they came to the Roman road to Werham. Raised on an embankment, it ran straight as his seax blade and to his relief, the wheels of the ox-cart rolled with ease over the hard packed stone and gravel surface. Steering round potholes, they kept a decent pace. At the top of the Beacon Hill, Begiloc knew they would reach the Priory before Vespers.

At last, the forest gave way to marshy plain between two rivers, where the road leading towards an island ran in a spine-like ridge preventing them from sinking into the rough waterlogged grass. Peering through the gloom, Begiloc cried, "A huge church!"

Leobgytha murmured, "Built sixty summers ago under King Cenwalh."

The name meant nothing to him. Those of the Dumnonian kings from Caradoc to Geraint, often enough heard in song and rhyme, he could recite but of these Saxon invaders he knew two – Ine and Aethelheard – he'd fought against the former and for the latter. The nun interrupted his reflection,

"Lady St Mary Church dedicated to the Mother of Our Lord. The Priory is attached, on the right. None we chanted on our way but Vespers will be on consecrated ground. Will you come to the service, Begiloc?"

Did he detect amusement? Mixed with – determination? None had eluded him because they'd cantillated all the way from Wimborne and he didn't know a None from a Sext nor one psalm from another. The wind was freshening – that he could tell.

The approach to the church had no defences, he considered, but easy enough to hold the causeway. Constructed of local stone, unlike Wimborne, the building inspired him. Except for ancient ruins, he had never seen a structure of that material.

The Prior, wearing a black habit, his tonsure circled by white wispy hair, met them at the entrance. Formalities ended, Leobgytha instructed her party to clean up before meeting outside the church.

Once gathered there, she sent the nuns inside, before a procession of brothers from the priory shuffled past chanting in Latin without raising their heads as they filed into the building. Leobgytha ordered her monks to follow.

"Now," she said to the ten armed men, "leave your weapons outside and come into the church to attend Vespers," her tone challenging, but duty-bound, Begiloc consented, he was charged to obey the lady.

Incongruous, high in the awesome interior, a chirping sparrow flitted from one roof beam to another. The warriors, ushered by Leobgytha to the benches, obeyed her whisper, "Sit down! Copy the monks." Last to be seated, Begiloc sat next to the nave.

Altar candles cast shadows in the gloomy church. Small square windows conceded little light: none, on a dull day at dusk. Instead, tallowed tapers flickered in iron holders, the reek of melting fat overlaying incense.

Meryn dug Begiloc in the ribs, "Pfaw! What a stench, glad I didn't eat lunch ..." When he looked past his comrade to the glum Saxons, Begiloc's smile widened because he guessed they would prefer to fell trees or hump rocks. Somerhild apart, as a Briton, he despised the invaders of his homeland.

His gaze wandered along a solid, round column up to the capital, to its carving of a mounted knight holding a spear and huge pointed shield. The other facet depicted a rutting ram.

Caena sighed and his head drooped. Disrespectful, this cheered Begiloc who jumped up with the brothers as the priest entered. *"Deus, in adiutorium meum intende ..."* chanted the cleric and the nuns and monks joined in.

When the clergyman began the oratio, Begiloc, who knew no Latin let it wash over him while he studied the tub-like pulpit. Its intricate centrepiece was topped by a stone lectern in the shape of a book. The volume, was supported by an eagle perched on the head of a bearded man, standing on the back of a ferocious beast with the face of a cat.

*'About to devour a pagan!'*

Unaware of the substance, he'd sat and risen through a sequence of hymns, psalms, canticles, antiphons, preces and oratio. At the end of it all, he ate a piece of bread, the body of his Lord.

Still seated the warriors watched the nuns file down the nave. The fair-faced one smiled at Begiloc. Disturbed, he sighed, grateful the others had not noticed.

*'Report her to Leobgytha? Where's the sin in a smile?'*

But he felt guilt at his stirring desire.

At supper in the refectory, he found the ale did not match that of Wimborne. However, hunger and thirst slated, they were led to a dormitory with pallets spaced at regular intervals around the walls. No guest dormer at Werham, they had to share with the monks.

A bed near a corner suited Begiloc where he propped his spear and shield. There, he sat and strummed a sad tale of lost love on his hearpe. On the next bed, Meryn began the daily ritual of removing the beads to comb out his beard. A copper disk reflected his handiwork in its bright surface.

*'Vain creature!'*

Meryn started to rethread.

*'When ever did a beaded beard win the heart of a maid!'*

"Jealous of my fine bristles? Of course, with yon corn stubble on your chin!"

Ready to rest his aching back and feet, Begiloc grinned and leant his hearpe next to his shield. The flames of the torches on the walls guttered from the draught swirling about the dormitory floor so, grateful for the rough woollen cover, he pulled it up over his clothes. Setting his burnished copper disk down on his blanket, Meryn said, "A cock crowed after Vespers, didn't you catch it? Another sign a storm's brewing." At the sound of the wind whipping around the Priory, they agreed it would be folly to sail the next day. Respectful, they ended their conversation when monks entered to kneel in prayer before their beds. Orisons over, one went around the cressets putting out the tapers to plunge the dormitory into darkness, leaving the air sour with pungent smoke. Soon, snores and regular breathing lulled Begiloc to sleep.

In the night, he woke, a weight on his chest. A hand clamped his mouth while a finger and thumb nipped his nostrils. In vain, he tried to thrash about, his arms pinned under the blanket.

*'If I don't get air soon I'll black out!'*

A hand groped at his belt as he strove to raise his knee, but it too was blocked.

*'So that's it!'*

The thief sought the bag of coins.

*'I must open my mouth. Not going to let me live. Break the grip. Bite his hand.'*

Try as he might, the grasp held firm. Growing weak and sliding into blackness, there came a footfall followed by a groan and a throaty gurgle. The hand slackened, the attacker went limp and slumped sideways. Head pounding, Begiloc gasped for air while a stickiness seeped through his blanket on his arm; revolted, he heaved upwards and the body rolled and landed with a thud on the floor. The only sound discernable was the wind lashing the priory until whispered words: "Are you all right?"

*'I know that voice!'*

In truth, the only person he could exclude was Meryn.

"Ay, just about."

"Good. Sleep. We'll see to the corpse at daybreak."

"Sleep?"

Another footstep but no reply.

*'How can I?'*

In an attempt to sit up, he fumbled at the cover wet with blood. Disgusted, he threw it off and reached down, groping for the body, found it and followed an arm to the shoulder and thence to the neck: no pulse.

Appalled, he rolled back on his pallet but ignored the blanket. Better chilled than covered in a dead man's blood. Shivering, but not from the cold, he began to think. How, with no light, had his attacker found his bed?

*'Of course, the corner!'*

All his assailant had to do was find it and he had the right man.

*'Who was he? Weasel-eyes, I'll wager. Did he not ogle my purse at the mill? Who do I thank for saving me? Not Meryn. The dozy lump's asleep. Who? Not a monk. One of the Saxons! Odd. None of them would mourn my death.'*

With this flurry of thoughts, his eyes closed and he did not wake until a hand shook him. In the feeble light, he discerned Meryn's face.

"Bad habit, taking corpses to bed!"

*'Typical Meryn ... one day he'll come up against something he can't turn into a merry jest.'*

"Arise everybody! Morning's come and all's not well!" Meryn exclaimed.

Men struggling to rub sleep from their eyes coughed and swore.

*'The voice in the night?'*

Begiloc struggled to remember.

*'Whose?'*

A group formed around his bed and a monk knelt beside the bloodied corpse. The brother made the sign of the cross and recited a prayer in Latin. Another dashed toward the door, calling, "I'll fetch the Prior."

Light filtered through the nearest window sufficient for Begiloc to discern some details. The tunic had a single slash angled up through the ribs. The blade had pierced the heart. How was such a blow possible without light?

When the monk finished his prayer, Begiloc rolled the body over. No surprise – sightless weasel eyes, whose lids he lowered, not out of respect for a Saxon he'd taken an instant dislike to but out of deference to the dead.

One of the Saxons pointed: "The Briton's killed Paega, seize him!" Three men thrust monks aside to rush at Begiloc. One monk, a burly, red-haired fellow – one of their party – stuck out an arm.

"Wait! A body next to a man's bed and blood on his blanket does not mean *that* man struck the blow. Let's hear what the Briton has to say!"

The bearing of the brother, one of a man experienced in conflict, struck Begiloc. Later, he would discover more about this monk.

"Well said, Brother. It may seem I killed this man, but on my oath I did not. Someone saved me. Whoever he is, step forward, tell it true – for I am innocent of this death."

At that moment, the Prior came in, his face pale and anxious, the messenger scuttling at his heels.

"Desecration! Murder!"

Caena held up his seax. "Still blood on the blade." When he spoke, Begiloc started. Of course, the voice. "My arm trailed out the bed, hand on the floor, when he, Paega, stepped on it. I rose and followed him knowing he meant to rob and kill the Briton in his sleep. The coward. I slew him. May the cur rot in Hell! Mind, I should have let this one die…his lot have been a thorn in our side over the years…"

"I thank you, but –"

"Save your thanks. I am Saxon and fight with honour. If I slay you it will be well done, man to man, not like a serpent in the night."

The warning, he absorbed since he had seen allegiances dissolve in an instant, why should this Saxon be different?

The Prior, his face mottled and twisted, tight around the eyes, clutched at the cross hanging at his chest. Scowling at Caena, he held it, white-knuckled.

"How dare you utter those words on sacred ground? Is it not enough to have slain a man? Still your tongue or better, shape those utterances to beg Our Lord's forgiveness."

With his shoulders hunched over his chest, the Prior seemed to age as he turned to his monks. "When did this happen? After Lauds I presume."

The brothers shrugged.

"Well, you," he waved at four of them, "carry the body down to the church! Wait there for me and pray for the man's soul. Brother Octha and Brother Selwyn, clean the blood from the floor and wash the blanket!" The monks hurried off to fetch what they needed for the task. "The rest of you prepare for Prime."

The Prior turned to Begiloc, "I have decided. Under the circumstances, we shall take no action. The man was a would-be murderer and a thief. As such he will be buried in unhallowed ground outside the abbey." When he addressed Caena his tone softened, "I suppose you did the right thing. You saved an innocent life. Set down your weapon. Come kneel, here!"

The warrior stared around at the faces of the men.

"Kneel? Kneel! We don't kneel even in defeat…"

Their expressions grave and expectant, he knelt as ordered. The white-haired monk breathed through his mouth, shook his head to clear away the horror and raised his right hand, *'Et ego te absolvo a peccatis tuis in nomine Patris, et Filii, et Spiritus Sancti.'*

The Prior lifted his head in a gesture to stand. Tall enough to look Caena in the eye, his gaze did not waver, "Be loyal to your leader, be faithful to the Lord." Although Begiloc appreciated the monk's intervention, the sullen face of the Saxon made him doubt the admonishment had any effect on the warrior. A suspicion confirmed when the Saxon moved away muttering, "I kneel! Me, Caena! To a fellow who gibbers in tongues!"

Turning to the red-haired monk, Begiloc enquired, "Brother, how are you named?"

"Robyn."

"My thanks to you Brother Robyn for your words."

A bell began to chime.

"Prime!" the Prior pointed to the door then led them out into the rain to the blessed shelter of the church.

After the liturgy, Begiloc stood toe to toe with Lady Leobgytha. To an onlooker the difference in demeanour was clear: he bit his lip, shook his head and thumped his fist against his thigh; she held her chin high and peered down her nose at the Briton.

"My Lady, the weather is foul. We'll drown if we take to the sea."

Pointing to the black sky, he said, "What difference will a day make? Let's shelter here and set out tomorrow. The storm will be spent by then."

Leobgytha pursed her lips. "We leave now! On the Lord's mission. He will protect us. His precious time is not ours to waste. Go, fetch your men and belongings."

To a small group of monks and servants she issued orders while Begiloc hesitated. Faith was one thing, but the might of the ocean? The Church had snatched him from his family, did this foolhardy woman intend to lead him to his doom? The words of Abbess Cuniburg came to mind: ' ... *Lady Leobgytha, you will obey her in all things.*' Further challenge quelled, he fell silent.

The Prior, head bowed against the rain strode over to join the nun, calling to two monks and giving them instructions. To grasp the gist of their orders, Begiloc hung back, learning of preparations for a second ox-cart laden with hides and tin ore for merchants in Frankia. The Briton headed for the dormitory.

At his approach, Meryn ceased whetting the blade of his axe. A glance at Begiloc's face and a joke died at birth.

"What's up?"

Arms folded, Begiloc said, "The woman's taken leave of her senses."

"Who?"

"Who do you think? She'll have us all drown."

"The Lady Leobgytha?"

"Ay."

Alerted, a couple of Saxons wandered over. Caena joined them, eyebrow raised.

"We must set off, get your things together!"

"Hold, I order you!" The Saxon stepped in front of him. "Have I the right of this? The fool nun wants us to take a ship for the Frankish lands in *this* weather?"

"Ay, about the measure of it."

On their feet, everyone talked at once. One, named Hrothgar, said, "I'll be damned if I set foot on board a–"

"Silence!" Caena glared around then addressed Begiloc, "Madness, with a storm raging," he folded his arms and stared from one to another. "I say we stay here until the morrow. In any case, it's a woman would send us to our doom! Since when do we follow the orders of a mere woman? Just because she wears a fucking wimple!"

The warrior's narrowed eyes challenged Begiloc to a chorus of assent from the circle of Saxons.

Unsure whether the contempt in Caena's voice was directed at the Church, womankind or at himself as a Briton in command, Begiloc harboured no illusion – to impose authority his wits would be tested to the full. Fingers running along his scarred brow, his eyes locked on those of Caena but with no challenge in them.

*'Of course, I can tell Leobgytha the men refuse to obey. She will think me no fit leader – or ...'*

"I am with you Caena. It is folly but the Lady will not be gainsaid," he said, to a growl of dissent from the men. Wrathful faces surrounded him, so he needed a quick solution. "Hold! Hear me out! Let's take her to the harbour. She can witness the rage of the sea for herself. When we are back, we shall not have disobeyed her command."

A moment passed while his words took effect.

"You speak well, Briton," Caena said, "the holy woman will

not have the spirit to argue with the might of the waves."

Caena grasped his axe and the others their weapons. Two miles to the harbour, the rain whip lashes, the going hard, they plodded along the sodden track next to the river. What a task to keep the carts rolling! The iron-rimmed wheels sank deep into the earth causing the men to swear and the brothers, cowls flapping in their faces, to scold them. Soaked to the skin, hands numb and raw, they spent a miserable morning until they reached the harbour.

Three ships bobbed at anchor in the bay of brown water where two marshland rivers dumped silt. Under the dark sky, the surface neared blackness but for the strong contrast of the white-crested waves. Aware the sheltered harbour bore no likeness to the open sea, they made a forlorn group, the nuns and monks shivering and huddled close together, the armed men glum. Only Meryn grinned and he pulled Begiloc aside.

"Our luck is in."

"How so?"

"Count the sailors."

"There are no sailors."

"No sailors, no sailing!"

True! Their group the only sign of life around the harbour, even the gulls had flown inland. Unconcerned, Leobgytha rode over.

"Our ship is the middle one of the three."

The one she indicated had a carved prow in the form of a purple dragon."

"My Lady, there is no steersman, it's the weather you–"

"There will be a helmsman soon," she said, eyes half-closed against the driven rain. "Tell the men to gather their possessions from the cart. As to the rest, it is my concern." the noblewoman wheeled her horse toward the monks and nuns.

Mystified, Begiloc frowned at Meryn who shook his head and muttered, "The best acorn goes to the worst pig," leaving him more puzzled. Heads bowed against the weather, they made for the cart, but voices raised in song caused them to look up. The monks and nuns intoned another psalm.

"The Devil's wildest storm can't save us from the curse of the psalm!" the irrepressible Meryn laughed.

In spite of the wind, the thin chanting served its purpose. On the ship, a head appeared above the gunwale and its owner clambered into a boat to row across to the shore. Lady Leobgytha dismounted and walked over to the sailor, a swarthy fellow with knotted arms before gesturing to Begiloc to join them.

Uneasy in the presence of a highborn lady, the sailor dry-washed his hands.

"My Lady, I didn't reckon on you being here this morning." Leobgytha eyes narrowed and she raised her chin. By now, familiar with that attitude, Begiloc's heart sank.

"Why? We have an agreement, do we not?" Her jaw set and her lips pressed together.

"Ay, My Lady, but the weather–"

"What of it?"

The sailor flapped his hands, "Lady, there's a gale! How can we leave the shelter of the harbour–"

The nun lowered her voice but kept it forceful: "We can and we shall."

"But–"

"Pay the man the sum agreed, Begiloc."

When he reached for his purse, the man clutched his stomach and leant away from the nun. "I can't risk my ship and my men for three gold coins," he whimpered, " Give me three scillingas on the morrow, My Lady, and I'll take you." Again he wrung his hands. "I-I'm sorry."

"Give the man double!" she tapped her foot.

"Forgive me, I cannot. Our Lady Abbess instructed me not to pay more than three gold scillingas."

Greed in his eyes, to Begiloc's dismay, the sailor peered from one to the other.

"I shall pay the other three scillingas with my own coin. The nun reached into her soaked mantle and drew out a purse of purple cloth rich with embroidered scrolls.

*'She'll have us all drown!'*

Into her hand, she shook three gold coins and gave them to Begiloc.

"Add these to yours."

The helmsman grasped them waiting for instructions.

The two Britons stood apart and spoke of the folly of the young nun and the avidity of the steersman. The noblewoman walked over to Caena and they broke off their discussion to stare from a distance at the heated exchange between the Saxon warrior and Leobgytha. "Listen to me, Lady, you can't...but I swear...it's madness!" but they only caught snatches of the argument borne on the wind. Meryn asked, "Do you think he will change her mind and save us from an 'orrible death by drowning?"

With dread and trepidation, Begiloc eyed the purple-black clouds and shook his head in despair.

# CHAPTER 3

On board, the steersman huddled with his crew, whose angry gesticulations caught Begiloc's eye. Did he detect a resemblance between two of the crewmen and the helmsman? Likely they were brothers. With aggressive gestures, they browbeat those reluctant to sail. The discussion ended and the crew set about their duties, weighing anchor to row the vessel along the reed-lined channel.

The wind thrashed rushes in all directions and the occasional pig-like squeal of a water rail issued from a reed bed, but few other sounds rivalled the roar of the gale until a flash in the distance triggered the first crash of thunder. In the prow, Begiloc studied the clouds and the sea; as yet the water of the sheltered channel was not rough, but the distant lightning filled him with foreboding.

The red-haired monk interrupted his thoughts.

"You are troubled, my friend."

"Brother Robyn! Are you not?"

"Ay, by what awaits us beyond that isle, well named Brunoces – *'brown sea!'* "

A pleasant deep laugh warmed Begiloc to his rescuer of earlier, who pointed at the isle, "On yon mount lives a hermit said to help sailors in distress."

"Today we may well need his aid."

A silver spear lanced the black clouds to the east and thunder echoed across the ocean as their ship passed the isle and reached a curved headland. The rowers pulled the oars in and raised a small sail flapping with whiplash cracks until it billowed so taut Begiloc feared it must rip asunder. The open sea filled him with dread. An endless horde of huge relentless waves rolled from the east. In battle, prepared for his doom, a man might succumb to enemy blows but his skill in combat provided a chance of survival.

*'Damn the Church and all her servants!'*

Convinced of his ill fate, in his mind, Begiloc berated Leobgytha's stubbornness and the steersman's lust for gold while clinging to the gunwale of the insignificant piece of driftwood that passed as a vessel. Through half-closed eyes, he cursed the man struggling to keep the craft on course. Like Begiloc, the other passengers grasped any part of the ship to stay upright while a cut above an eyebrow left one monk with a crimson mask. The ship rolled, rose and sank into the deep troughs between waves. She plunged to the seabed only to shoot skywards an instant later.

Lashed by the salt spray, soaked, Begiloc expected the craft to capsize, reviving thoughts of his father's death. Gerens saved a boy and his mother from the voracious sea off the Dumnonian coast only to die attempting to rescue the woman's husband. Was his wyrd the same?

A wave smashing over the bows, sending him crashing into the gunwale. Had he broken a rib? Shaken, in pain, he hauled himself up and saw Brother Robyn, soaked like himself, rising to one knee. Fighting to keep his balance as the ship lurched, Begiloc rubbed his arm and swore at the crashing thunder.

The white faces of the passengers and the angry expressions of the crew struck fear into him. How come such obedience led them to risk their lives, overcoming their obvious reluctance to sail? When with reason might a man challenge authority?

*'The woman ordered us with resolute trust in her God, ignoring advice not to ride the waves. What sort of faith can this be?'*

Clinging to the ship, he peered through the rain. A headland! The waves were sweeping them due east. In a matter of minutes, their craft would be reduced to fragments. A hand grasped his shoulder, lightning illuminating the wide-eyed Leobgytha who tugged at his sleeve.

"We must pray," she said and pulled harder as she knelt, dragging him to his knees.

"My Lady, I know not how."

Once more he wondered at her belief.

The rain ran down her face as she turned to him.

"Ask Our Lord to stop the storm, is all ..." she said, joining her hands in a steeple under her chin and closing her eyes, "...and I shall beg the Virgin Mary to intercede." Her lips moved in silence.

Head bowed, he tried to plead with God not to leave Somerhild a widow. But, his thoughts drifted away faster than their ship, would he be united with his forefathers in the afterlife? This thought comforted him more than the forlorn supplications of the Lady next to him.

The storm continued, the gale howled unabated, spray slapped him across the face and the ship plunged down into the foaming abyss. Why should God help those whose folly and stubbornness defied the laws of His Creation?

A man used to hardship, working the earth, sowing seeds that at times failed to produce crops and rearing animals that might perish before their time of slaughter: Begiloc was a man to cope with the land, not with the icy depths. Eyes closed, he resigned himself to a saltwater grave.

A cheer not drowned by the wind arose. Leobgytha hauled him to his feet.

"The Lord has answered our prayer," she said, emotionless, turning, lurching from one support to another back to her nuns.

The day brightened and the wind dropped, the rebellious waves still high but no longer vicious.

*'Saved! A miracle!'*

The helmsman steered south-east sending the ship rolling and dipping as Begiloc clung to the side in alarm. To starboard, the headland in plain view, drew an involuntary wince. How close their vessel had come to being reduced to driftwood! In awe, he gazed at Leobgytha and voiced his earlier thought, "A miracle!"

Brother Robyn at his elbow said, "Ay, friend, yonder is St Aldhelm's Head, one with sharp teeth."

The bow of the ship ploughed through the ever lowering waves and the timid sun appeared as a shaft of light between breaks in the purple clouds.

"Is it possible a storm can end so?"

Brother Robyn's eyebrows met in surprise.

"Do you have so little faith, Briton? The disciple tells us Jesus stood in a boat on the Sea of Galilee, rebuked the wind and ordered the waves, *'Quiet! Be still!'* The wind calmed. Today He did the same for his beloved Leoba."

Motionless, Begiloc pondered on the enormity of Robyn's explanation.

"Only a nun like any other," he muttered.

"In your heart you know it isn't true." The monk shook his head, "Her mother dreamed of delivering a church bell, which chimed merrily. So she changed the name of her baby to Leobgytha and called her 'Leoba', which means 'beloved', and dedicated the child to serve Christ. I will tell you more another time. The monk stumbled and swayed over to join the others.

Begiloc stared back at the English coast. What he had witnessed disturbed him. It should not be possible. The gale must have blown itself out, simple as that.

*'If the nun can ask the Lord to quieten the storm, why did she not do so back at the harbour? Didn't it make more sense? We didn't need to risk our lives.'* Again, he pondered. *'If I ask her will she challenge my faith? What did Brother Robyn mean when he said she's no ordinary nun? Apart from her beauty, what's so special about her, unless it's her stubbornness? The monk said there's more to tell. She's remarkable right enough, else how was she able to convince the Saxon to get his men aboard?'*

Bemused, he shook his head, more pressing thoughts troubled his heart. The coast of his homeland dwindled to a thin purple line every moment carrying him farther from the woman and child he loved.

Before nightfall, they reached the land of the Franks.

*'O for the warmth of my hearth, the laughter of my son, the idle chatter of our neighbours!'*

Yet, the more he thought about it, the happier he felt that Somerhild and Ealric were safe in the Abbey. Women had hard lives, fearing death by childbirth and counting the number of babes who died in infancy. A typical day did not take Somerhild beyond the confines of the village, at most as far as the stream to wash clothes or to the well for water. The walls of her home were her prison, goats, lambs and dogs her companions while she prayed for her man to come home safe at night. Sure, they were better off in the Abbey. There'd be company for them and no fear of hunger, rats, trolls or witches. Comforted, he settled down for the night.

The mewing of innumerable gulls woke him and it took him a moment to realise he was not with his family. The ache in his bones and the rocking ship set him straight. Groaning, he clutched at his bruised ribs before pulling himself up to peer across the harbour. Several ships with furled sails, traders from

Hamwic or Wessex, rode at anchor in what he later discovered to be the port of Rouen at the mouth of the main waterway flowing through Paris.

Not long afterwards, the monks and nuns at morning prayers, the crew took to their oars to nose the ship into the river. The sailors, muscles bulging, battled upstream to the rhythm of a chanted psalm.

Mid-morning, Begiloc, struggling to tune his hearpe in the damp air, looked up into the face of a a nun.

"My Lady would speak with you," she avoided his eyes and fidgeted with the sleeve of her habit. Before he could reply she slipped away and he followed to the prow where the nuns and monks were gathered.

"My Lady?"

The hazel eyes, irises flecked with amber, appraised him.

"I asked the steersman to stop at the Isle of Saint Denis where we have an appointment at the quay with the cellarer. Did you know there is an abbey nearby?"

Begiloc shook his head.

"The provisioner will supply us with food and drink for our journey. He arranged for us to meet a merchant. In exchange for our hides and bales of cloth, he will provide us with two river boats and a guide for each." Leoba paused to assure herself he understood, "I intend to pray at the tomb of the saint – Denis. As you know, King Dagobert had the monastery constructed around a chapel rebuilt to house the sepulchre."

Mute, he refused to display his ignorance.

"Now," she pouted, "we shall arrive later than I hoped. You see the problem?" She widened her eyes.

Was it her beauty that made him so dull-witted? Confused, he shrugged, hoping for elucidation while she turned to gaze from the straining backs of the sailors to the dense woodland lining this stretch of river. She sighed. Exasperation would not move the craft any faster and he had not found the reply she sought.

"Well, I do not wish for myself or my nuns to spend the night in the abbey, far from the quay and this ship will be no longer with us ..."

Once more, the upward tilt of the head, a clear warning, put him on his guard but he found no reason to contradict her.

"... instead, I want you to find a suitable inn for my sisters and I by the river. When we return from the abbey chapel we will retire early since we shall have a long day ahead. The hostelry must be clean. The monks and your men will sleep in tents ready to leave straight after Prime."

The nun still peered down at him but a radiant smile rewarded him when he said, "Caena and the men can escort you to the monastery." Strange to tell, he was beginning to have faith in the Saxon who in other times would have been his sworn enemy. "In the meantime, my friend and I shall seek a suitable place for you, My Lady."

On time, they moored at the Saint Denis quay and the ears of Begiloc rang at the hubbub of a bustling market.

As the crew unloaded the goods onto the quay, Begiloc joined Meryn to disembark into a flurry of activity. Planks on trestles with poles and canvas canopies flapping, the stalls were laden with leather ware, fish and meat. Countrymen drove pigs and goats among traders whose shouts betrayed their Frisian and Wessex origins. Ears ringing from the shrill cries and whistles, their noses wrinkled at the slime of entrails and rotting vegetables at their feet, Begiloc and Meryn ventured among the Frankish merchants, who wore their hair flowing at the shoulders over otter skin cloaks but cut close at the forehead. On the river at their backs, boatmen called to each other about the weather as their vessels crossed. A skinny cur with a bone in its mouth flashed past and a heavier dog in pursuit skidded and crashed into Meryn's legs, earning itself a kick to help it on its way.

Back on the quay, the gesticulations of a rotund figure in a black habit threatened the unwary amid the press of bodies.

"Must be the cellarer," Begiloc murmured as the plump monk clasped his hands and bowed to Lady Leoba. "Come on," he took Meryn under the arm, "we should get organised."

"What? With me entering into the spirit of a Frankish market! I was going to move on from dogs to kicking Saxons!" Ignoring him, Begiloc gave orders to Caena for the escort and entrusted his spear and hearpe to Brother Robyn but slung his shield over his shoulder. In a distant land in dangerous times, no point in being unprepared.

Leaving their party on the quay, they proceeded through the market. Intent on finding accommodation for the sisters, Begiloc was not as sharp-eyed as usual. Meryn tugged at his sleeve, pulling him closer he whispered, "Don't turn round, but the fellow in fine apparel – the one by the fish stall. Since we left the ship he hasn't taken his eyes off our group."

With time, Begiloc had learned to respect Meryn's rare serious moments so he looked around in a natural way when his friend bent down to adjust the thongs around his breeches. The man's flaxen hair was tied up into a kind of tuft above the forehead and fell behind his head like the tail of a mare. Clean shaven except for long moustaches, the man wore a close-fitting grey tunic, enhancing the muscles of a warrior and at his waist, a sword and a dagger hung from a broad belt.

'A wealthy man of high rank. Why such interest in us?'

"I see him. Let's go!"

Beyond the market, they chanced on a Breton well disposed toward his 'cousins' from Dumnonia. Forthcoming, the trader advised them of an inn not far from the quay, where the ale sold at a decent price. Nowhere better on the isle, he swore. To the question of its suitability for nuns he laughed – "as long as they stay out of the tap-room!"

The inn was a large, squat, wooden-built hall with a roof of thatched reeds. The commotion in the gloom of the tap-room shocked them. Men slammed down and spilt ale from earthen pots, sang bawdy songs and belched. One farted and guffawed along with his drunken mates. Others, arguing and mouthing oaths at every throw, played dice for coins. The Britons decided to leave when a balding man with bandy legs, tunic covered by a stained leather apron, accosted them in their own tongue, though with a strong accent.

"Good men, I can offer you the finest ale on the Isle, in the whole of Neustria."

"I seek not drink, landlord, but clean beds for holy women. Rooms where they will not be disturbed. This inn does not suit."

Begiloc turned to go, but the innkeeper caught his arm.

"Not so hasty!" A tilted head towards a door, "Come wi' me, see you do not err."

Into a spacious room, he led them where wooden casks were stacked in one corner. At a table, two women were cutting bread into similar-sized chunks. Over a hearth where a fire blazed, another woman stirred dried herbs into a cauldron hanging from an iron frame. A waft of vegetable soup from the pan reminded Begiloc of his hunger but he pushed thoughts of food out of his mind and followed the host through another door into a corridor with five doors on either side.

"The first two are mine," the ruddy-faced landlord said, "there're two fine gentlemen in the next rooms. No worries on that score – one's a merchant from Aanwerp an' t'other's from Quentovic–"

"Show me the rooms!"

Simple, floors swept clean, each room contained three beds and a small table bearing a stout candle. On inspection, Begiloc grunted approval.

"I only need four, but I'll take six. This one night. If the price pleases we'll stop on our return."

"What's more, this evening we'll bring you nine thirsty oafs to quaff your ale," Meryn added.

The innkeeper's face grew redder.

"Well, all six rooms, but as you say ..." he stuck his tongue between his teeth and began to calculate. "I suppose I'll ha' to charge twelve denarii," his eyes shifted from one to the other.

"Show me a denarius!"

The landlord dug deep under his apron and pulled out a silver coin, but when Begiloc reached to examine it, the man's fist closed around it.

"How can I weigh it if you won't let me hold it?"

Eyes two pinpricks of suspicion, the innkeeper passed the silver piece to the Briton who tested its weight before holding out the coin to be snatched and stuffed away whence it came. Crossing the room, Begiloc took out his money bag, holding it poised over the table.

"Ten denarii, no more," and with a trace of a smile noted the greed flicker in the man's eyes.

"Ten denarii's good."

"I don't have denarii, but these are sceattas from Wessex. By my reckoning, two sceattas make one denarius. Coins fell onto the table and the innkeeper's eyes grew as round as the largest gold one among them and twice as bright. The small silver pieces separated, he counted them out "... eighteen ... nineteen ... there you are ... twenty."

The man snatched up a sceat to weigh it, adding another and grubbing inside his clothes for the denarius. Hands moving up and down, he balanced the two against the one and a crafty smirk vanished in an instant. The landlord thrust the denarius away and bit a sceat. Contented, he swept up the coins.

"The rooms are yours. The women can come in through the back door."

Outside the room a thumb indicated a rear entrance.

"Nobody will see 'em enter an' they won't be bothered."

Satisfied, Begiloc smiled.

A solid bone key appeared from his apron, "Here, use this! Leave it i' the door when you go."

"Let's use it now!"

With that, he slid in the key and it turned in a well-oiled lock.

"We'll bring the women after Vespers," he turned to Meryn, "and we'll find out the worth of his ale, what say you, old friend?"

"We'll test it right well!"

All three exchanged satisfied grins, but outside with the door locked, Meryn said, "Old fox! I'll wager two sceattas are heavier than one denarius, am I right?"

"Ay, but not much. Come on, to the quay."

Late afternoon, seated on a half-rotted upturned boat, Begiloc pulled his cloak closer against the damp river air. Next to him, Meryn, as usual fiddling with the beads in his beard, nudged him and pointed to their party making its way down to two boats on the far bank. From this notable distance, however faint, they heard Caena's bellow.

"In the boats...get in, get in! Idle whoresons! Useless, the lot of you...!'"

In spite of its roughness, the Saxon had a manner, an authority that those under his command respected. The men rowed across to the quay where the Britons noticed two Franks with their group.

"Frankish guides! Know their job too, they found the right island!" Meryn jested. "So, my leader, and all we need to do is make sure they don't poison the ale, steal our money or murder us in our beds. Nothing to worry about!"

Begiloc led the nuns to their lodgings while Meryn took the men to the place they'd chosen in the afternoon for their camp where they pitched tents. The monks settled to pray and sleep whereas Caena and his men were eager to follow the Briton to the promised ale. Caena, his capacity for drinking beer renowned, sought an opportunity to surpass previous feats.

They soon added to the clamour of the rowdy inn. Once again, Meryn proved the more alert of the two Britons. Drawing his companion aside, his eyes indicated a table by the ale counter where the man in grey and white conversed with a wealthy-looking Frank, by appearance a merchant.

"I've watched him as much as he's watched us and, believe me, that's a lot of watching!"

With a wink, he said, "Here's what I'll do. I'll feign drunk, stagger over there and pretend to pass out. Trust me, Begiloc, I've practised this over the years!"

He raised his jug and downed in one, letting the vessel drop with a crash, drawing the attention of the Saxons around him. The pretend drunkard lurched away in the direction of the counter, barged into a couple of drinkers who swore and pushed him away, before bouncing off the bar into the table in the corner, where the two men grabbed their ale as Meryn appeared to slide unconscious to the floor. The Frank in grey and white half-rose to his feet, sat down again and bent down to peer at the prone Briton. The fellow who had quarrelled with Meryn at the mill jumped up and pointed.

"My sister's girl is only ten and she can hold ale better than the Briton! My dog can hold ale better and it pisses less too!" Caena encouraged the Saxons as they howled, whooped and banged their jugs.

"A Briton's bladder is weaker than his brain, an' that's sayin' something!" yelled Caena. The oaf needed little persuasion to ridicule anyone not of his race, as Begiloc well knew; unperturbed, under lowered brow, he watched the men in the corner relax. The unwitting contribution of the Saxons proved effective since they resumed their close conversation.

An emptied jug of ale later, the two men made to leave. Tense, out of the tail of his eye, Begiloc watched their suspect slide the table back and push Meryn with his foot. The limp body half-rolled and dropped back like that of an unconscious sot.

*'Well done Meryn!'*

Satisfied, the man pointed to the door and they left before Begiloc went over, opened it a crack and assured himself they were strolling away.

The nimble rise and steady step of Meryn drew surprised glances and the odd comment from the Saxons. Begiloc gestured to Caena to come over before leading the two men outdoors far from indiscreet ears.

"What news?"

"Grave, old friend. The man in the fur coat is a merchant out of Marseille, a dealer in slaves, selling Christians to the Arabs in Iberia. Heed this! The one in grey is a Frankish nobleman. The two guides are in his pay to betray us. Their plan is to lead us downriver into an ambush late in the afternoon. The place chosen for overnight camp is where they will seize us, chain us and take us through woodland to Quentovic and thence by ship to Iberia."

"The devil they will! If they think they can get me like that, in a snare, they are mad. I've survived a score of traps and all better than whatever they can throw at me. Ambush! The isle is small. Let's find them and flay them like swine," Caena said.

Unconvinced, Begiloc laid a hand on the warrior's arm.

"Hold! We know neither who they are nor their strength. Meryn, how many will attack?"

"They've counted our warriors and reckon twenty men is sufficient to win the day."

"Heed me well, this is what we will do ..." he spoke at length and Caena assented, his rage extinguished by the Briton's cool demeanour. As the plan unfolded, Meryn's grin widened and reached its full extension when Begiloc suggested another ale.

"I thought you'd never ask, spying is thirsty work, Briton!" he mimicked Caena's voice to perfection, drawing a thin-lipped smile from the Saxon.

After leaving them to their drink, Begiloc drew the innkeeper aside to press two sceattas into his chubby palm.

"Do you recall the two men sat over there? One is a merchant and the other?"

A flicker of fear showed in the eyes before they settled on the two coins in his hand.

"A leud from the region known as Champany."

The landlord lowered his voice. "They say he's not to be crossed, a vassal of the Bishop of Rems. Everyone knows the bishop is the most powerful man in Neustria, close to the Mayor of the Palace. Steer clear o' him," his voice nothing more than a whisper, "he strangled a man with his bare hands, they say."

The Briton stared unmoved, "Do you have a name for this leud?"

The innkeeper confirmed, jowls wobbling, "A comitis, Donatus by name."

"Most helpful, friend," he grasped the man's shoulder, "I charge you, do not talk of this."

No mistaking the relief on the face of the landlord, who scuttled off in response to demands for ale. Reassured his curiosity would remain a secret here, where walls had ears and an idle comment could cost them dear, Begiloc made of slyness a virtue. Whatever his own vices, those of the Bishop of Rems stuck in his mind more... *'he strangled a man...'*

Early in the morning, they gathered on the quay. Overhead, the gulls relinquished their substance, ghost-like, in the morning mist while Begiloc's breath rose like a wreath in the damp air.

The two long boats had twelve seats and space in the belly. There would be, he considered, three oarsmen either side of each boat if all were counted, including himself, Meryn and the two guides. Cloak pulled tighter against the damp, he divided the Saxons and the scouts between the two boats, putting Caena in charge of the second one that would carry the monks. Instead, he placed the Lady Leoba and her nuns in his lead boat and with the Franks as the respective first oarsmen, they set off upriver. At first, some of the men had difficulty keeping rhythm but they improved until moving at a satisfactory pace. Like those of the other rowers, Begiloc's arms ached but his hands did not blister, thanks to callouses from work in the fields. The weather was kind and, unimpeded by clouds, the sun emerged.

A nun sat on the bench next to Leoba and read to her from the holy book. The noblewoman never tired of religious tales like he never wearied of the tale of *Geraint mab Erbin*, though it was best told around a fire with scrump cider in hand.

Around midday, they came to where the river forked and the guide nosed them to the left along the Marne. They passed scattered villages, stopped for food, where the pretty nun spent her time eating and casting glances at Begiloc. This insistence unsettled him, for he told himself, man is a hunter – not only of deer and boar.

Refreshed, they moved on through a landscape of dense woodland, the mixture of hazel, oak and alder occasionally broken by flatter marshy grassland.

The height of the sun promised its presence for another two hours but the guide indicated the left bank of the river and called to make camp. The Frank pointed to an area of flat grass used for pasture though at present without beast or dwelling. The loss of rowing time confirmed the suspicion of Begiloc. Heart beating faster, he knew why the guide had chosen this place so he pulled his oar aboard, picked his way past the seated passengers to the front bench. There he drew his hand-seax, seized the guide's oar in his other hand to prevent it from falling into the river, and held the knife to the man's throat. Inboard with the paddle, his other hand grasped the guide's long hair and tugged it downwards, forcing the man to the floor of the boat and pinning him there with a knee. Realisation dawned in the Frank's eyes and Begiloc sneered with satisfaction. Meryn brought rope to bind his hands and feet, before ramming a cloth in his mouth and gagging him.

"Better than a trussed goose on a thegn's table at Yuletide. Carve him later brother!"

The success of his plan depended on the seizure of the

guides unobserved by the foe, but the latter would be well hidden. The gloom might help their cause since they were still a considerable distance from the woods even for the most sharp-eyed scout. Glancing back at the other boat, he grunted his satisfaction at Caena's swift action in securing the second guide.

*'A lumpen Saxon, but he gets things done!'*

Leoba tapped him on his shoulder, "What is the meaning of this?" She frowned.

*'Not now!'*

He looked from her indignant face to the rowers. Urgent to hold position on the river not to overshoot the grassy area with two pairs of oars light.

"Excuse me, My Lady. Meryn, take up your oar again and get the rowers to back-paddle."

Order given, he turned his attention to the nun.

"Last night we discovered betrayal. Soon we will be attacked and we must be ready. My Lady, forgive me, but I shall explain later. I must row. For now I beg you to keep your sisters calm. Act normal. Sing a psalm?"

From her pinched expression and folded arms he could see this woman disliked not being in control, but to his relief her eyes softened and she picked her way back. Soon, the nuns intoned a psalm and it pleased him when the monks in the other boat joined in.

Aware of precious daylight dwindling, Begiloc gestured for the rowers to take them to the bank. In a hushed voice, he gave orders and they hauled the boats out of the water to impose a semblance of normality.

"Brother Robyn, over here! Take charge of the monks, get the tents pitched, light at least three camp fires and keep on singing those psalms."

Robyn hastened to do his bidding and Begiloc gathered the fighting men close to outline his plan.

First, they bundled the two guides into the woods away from Lady Leoba. The last thing this situation called for was compassion. Indifferent, Begiloc knelt beside the younger of the guides.

"Here's what's going to happen ..." he beckoned Meryn over, "... take your axe!"

Fear gripped the man as the Briton sliced through the rope binding his arms before pressing his hand-seax to his throat.

"If you cry out it will be the last sound you make. Clear?"

The guide nodded so he removed the gag and cloth from his mouth, grasped his right arm and pinned it outstretched on the ground.

"Meryn, when I give the word lop off his hand..!"

"I'm handy with an axe and I take pride in my handiwork!" Meryn joked.

The man struggled to move the limb, but the far stronger Briton held him firm, face so close to that of the scout, he could almost smell the terror from the captive's pores.

" ... unless you tell me what I need to know."

The words came tumbling out with Begiloc hard-pressed to understand the foreign tongue. To his surprise, Wybert, one of the Saxons, helped him: "The enemy awaits fifty yards back from the edge of the trees and at three hoots of a clay whistle they will attack from the woods."

In all haste, they bound the Franks to trees.

With gestures, Begiloc ordered his men to move in a wide arc to the rear of the foe. The weak afternoon sun filtered through the tender spring foliage as they picked their way, avoiding every dry twig and briar. Through the trees, he caught his first glimpse of movement and raised his hand.

"Our seven spearmen," he whispered, "will spread out and lead the attack. Each will drive a spear into a back before they realise we are on them. The four axemen will follow."

"A vile act!" Caena hissed "It's not many moons since I told you what we think of cowards, is it?"

"Ay, but with seven dead they still outnumber us and there'll be no place for faint hearts. Surprise is our only chance. Move with stealth, together."

"Agreed!" said Caena, his tone grudging: the tactics beyond dispute.

Ten feet away from their backs, Begiloc chose the tallest of a group of three Franks. Raising his spear, he gestured to his companions either side. The iron-tipped ash pole flew from his hand with all the force he could muster. The weapon thudded home, screams and cries of alarm filled the air as he bounded forward. A thrusting spearhead forced upwards with his shield, he rammed the boss with all his might against that of his adversary. His other hand moved with the speed of an adder to drive his blade between the exposed ribs. Pain and helplessness dulled the man's eyes as he fell away.

Two more Franks rushed them. Wolf-like, Meryn howled his fury swinging back his axe while Begiloc snatched up his shield and bent to grasp the sword of the fallen Frank in time to parry a mighty blow. The clash of iron vibrated up his arm as he fended a shield thrust with his own. A gamble – throwing his shield to the ground, he held the weapon two-handed. A wager – a gain in mobility against greater vulnerability. The Frank advanced, sensing victory, aimed a mighty slash at the Briton's exposed flank, but spinning to his left, Begiloc thrust the blade up under the armpit of his assailant. Disbelief filled the warrior's face when his arm fell useless to his side and his sword dropped to the ground. Behind the shield that faced him, the man squinted against the sweat that trickled into his eyes, pain etched in his face. The shield covered him well, but his leading foot and leg were exposed. Short-seax drawn from his belt, Begiloc slashed down with the sword in his other hand, slicing into the warrior's shin. The man screamed and as he fell forward the knife found his throat with a backhand slash.

Chest heaving, Begiloc saw Meryn leaning on his axe, a Frank dead at his feet. Countenance pale, blood stained his comrade's tunic at the waist and he swayed. Flinging his sword to the ground, Begiloc rushed over and grasped him in time to prevent him falling.

*'No, not this! I lost my father and brother. I can't lose Meryn too.'*

As a precaution, he took the axe from the hand of the wounded man, just as well, for there came a footfall behind. Letting Meryn sag to the ground, he spun, the axe rising in a vicious arc.

"Steady Briton!" Caena, streaked in blood, studied the carnage with appraising eye, "I took out four of the bastards ..." he looked at Meryn, "... our friend is hurt!"

"Nought but a scratch," Meryn said and forced himself to one knee. A hand under his comrade's arm, Begiloc hoisted him to lean against his body.

"The others?"

"The day is won, Briton."

"And the cost?"

"I know of one dead and one wounded."

The real price would be counted in oarsmen. Still, he was relieved, his plan had worked and had not the Saxon called Meryn, *'friend'*? Had he misheard? Saxons hated Britons...always had, always would.

"Let's get back while it's light, for the sun bids farewell to the day."

"Beasts will feast here tonight," Caena scanned around at the dead foes again, "not that they're in a state to complain."

The grating laughter of the Saxon irritated Begiloc who had more important matters to concern him, such as staunching Meryn's blood. With this in mind, he passed the Briton to Caena and taking his knife to the tunic of a fallen Frank, hacked a large square of cloth, folded it and fixed it over the wound. Together, they hoisted Meryn's arms over their shoulders and walked him back to the camp. There they found three monks knelt in prayer by the body of a dead comrade.
Halting, Begiloc stared, "His name?"
Caena replied in a flat voice, "Hrothgar. A brave warrior, one like me and I bow to a true fighter. Wimborne has another widow and children to mourn the loss of their father."

"When we return we will honour them but his burial must be far from home."
Caena freed himself of Meryn.

"See to your friend and I'll see to mine. We have our own ways with the dead. Send me the red-haired monk, will you?" he said, calling orders to his men who came at a run. Instead, Begiloc took Meryn over to the camp to be met by Leoba, nuns in train.

"I await an explanation." Her tone was cold, her eyes full of worry on Meryn. "First we must tend to your friend."
They left him to Sister Theodilde, the infirmarian, and sent Brother Robyn to the Saxon gravediggers. Satisfied, Leoba drew him aside. She turned, "What happened today?"
Begiloc explained.

"Why did you not inform me this morning? The archbishop could have had the merchant seized."

"My Lady, if you will, we had no names, no proof. They

would have melted like snow on the river only to fall upon us in another place. Far wiser to use their own trap against them."

The noblewoman frowned, "It may be true, but henceforward I insist on consultation. Take no important decisions without my consent."

She tilted her head to one side like a rooster set to attack.

*'Not if you put our lives at risk.'*

With a bow, he said, "My Lady."

"... and the guides," her voice trembled, "... are they dead too?"

"No, not yet."

"Not yet. What do you mean? Where are they?"

"Bound to a tree, awaiting justice."

"Bring them to me!"

*'She spits like a wildcat when her ire's roused!'*

Caena, busy helping dig the grave for Hrothgar, looked up at his approach. Without spades, it was tough work to use axes, swords and pointed staves, but they had made it deep enough to deter scavengers. The sun was nigh on set as Begiloc led Caena away.

They untied the guides from the trees to push them before Leoba.

"My Lady, say the word and I'll take off their heads. Trust me, I know how to deal with these imps – let me, my Lady!" In a gesture of beheading Caena chopped one hand with his other.

The nun, although amused by his calling the foe *'imps'*, gasped and narrowed her eyes at the Saxon, her tone imperious, "Unbind them."

Obedient, Begiloc drew his seax and hacked at the bonds of the older man. The Saxon did not move.

"Unbind him, I said!"

Caena leapt forward and sawed at the ropes. The men stood

heads bowed before the nun.

"Look up! Look up for the Lady! And I pray her punishment is half as painful as what mine would be! A fighter's end should be honourable...yes, honourable but painful as Hell," Caena growled.

Leoba threw up her head at his words and Begiloc would not have been surprised if her anger had been diverted to Caena. When she spoke, her words came hesitant but in the language of the guides.

"So, you betray fellow Christians and would sell them into slavery ...?" Her voice was icy with repressed rage, "...handmaidens of Christ and monks on their way to convert the heathen. Would you lose your immortal souls for thirty pieces of silver?" Leoba clenched her fists till her knuckles were white. "My men wish to take off your heads and I am tempted to let them. But I believe your souls may be saved."

Hope flared in the face of the younger man but when his eyes locked with hers, her demeanour grew colder.

"A lifetime ago your Queen Balthild, herself a slave in childhood, abolished the practice of trading Christian slaves in all the Frankish lands. She strove to free children sold into slavery. What you did is against the laws of God and man. You must perform penance." Leoba paused then said, "Are you willing?"

"Ay, Lady."

Caena snarled. The Saxon, Begiloc guessed, sensed Leoba's judgement might not be what he hoped. In fact, he made to address her but refrained, deferring to her eminence.

The older Frank stood silent, head bowed.

"And you?" the nun said, exasperated.

The man did not look up, but Caena swung a backhand blow across his face.

"Speak! Answer the Lady!"

The prisoner's lip split and seeped blood. The guide put his hand to his mouth, dabbed it and spat on the ground. The hand of Caena went to his seax, but the man looked up.

"I'll serve penance," he muttered.

Satisfied, Leoba called, "Aedre!" A tent flap opened and Begiloc started as a nun hurried over – the sister who had stared at him so many times.

*'Aedre.'*

The newcomer looked at him from the tail of her eye.

"Fetch me the Bible, child!"

The nun hurried off returning with the heavy book familiar to him. Leoba held it out before the older guide.

"Place your hand on the Holy Book and swear to God you will serve me two years to the day until your penance ends."

Caena brought his head near to Begiloc and said, "Trust is a fine thing. Keep a close eye on them Briton! Forgive them at your peril. I've met church folk like her before and they are too soft...yes, that's it, *'soft'*...I'm not good with words and it doesn't help when she talks in foreign talk...but you'll see."

Their eyes met in silent accord.

She had not heard him, but Leoba stared at Caena as though she read his thoughts. Her next words made his prediction seem well founded: "See they are fed! To practise forgiveness does not mean accepting wrongdoing. Compassion gives meaning to our lives, never deny it to any of God's creatures for only when we defeat the darkness within may we walk in the light."

# CHAPTER 4

The stars appeared when Begiloc went to Sister Theodilde's tent to check on Meryn. The nun explained, "The spear thrust missed vital organs and I washed his wound with vinegar, covered it in balm and bound it. Cowslip root made him sleep, but fever rages and he lost much blood, he is in God's hands."

"Will he pull through?"

The infirmarian pursed her lips. "I cannot be sure. The gash must not fester and the fever break in the night or he will not see the new day."

The words gripped Begiloc's heart like hands of ice. Poor Meryn sweated and murmured while Theodilde dabbed his face with a cloth.

"Pray for him."

Not trusting to speech, a lump in his throat, he preferred to concentrate on the man wounded to the shoulder, in the next bed.

"And him?"

The nun dipped her rag in cold water and wrung it. She paused, "Ina is strong and sleeps easy. As I said, pray for your friend."

"Win another battle, old comrade," he said, laying a hand on Meryn's scalding brow.

Outside, he gazed at the sky. The stars pulsed like the blood in his veins and he sought out twin points of light.

*'Thiassi's eyes – are they staring now into those of Somerhild and Ealric?'*

The vastness of the heavens made him feel small and alone. The firelight cast dancing shadows around him and he could sense the brooding mound with the rough wooden cross lying at the edge of the camp.

*'May God spare us the task of digging another grave.'*

The wolves were active, a barred owl whooped and he picked out the mewl of a lynx, the constant flitter of bats swooping around their fires: much like the forests of home, yet so far away. Wherever he laid his head, he mistrusted the night, thick with demons and evil wraiths. Shuddering, morose, wondering how to find the words to beg God to save Meryn, he strolled toward the fire where Caena and his men sat.

*'I must try.'*

At his approach they made space for him, Caena saying, "Sit with us Begiloc ..."

*'He used my name!'*

"... sup with us, old beast!"

For the first time, he found acceptance in their faces as they drank to their victory with beakers of cider. A Saxon and a Briton sitting together in friendship. A rare moment for both men and one that might bode well.

After their meal, the oldest of the men, Alfwald, flushed from drink, called to Begiloc.

"Fetch your hearpe and I'll sing to honour Hrothgar!"

On his way to his tent, he passed the nuns, Leoba clapping her hands, "Come! Come sisters, time for bed. Lack of sleep makes for dull minds and slowness in reading!"

On his return, Alfwald asked, "Briton, do you know *The Wife's Lament*?" By way of reply, he plucked the tune and the men cheered. "Let's sing it for Hrothgar and his widow..."

The Saxon intoned, *"I ever suffered grief through banishment ...*

and they sang on into the night, *The Wanderer* and *The Seafarer* until the drink ran out and they staggered to bed.

Alone, his head spun from rough cider and he felt maudlin. A hand laid on his shoulder caused him to look up into the smiling eyes of Brother Robyn.

"May I sit with you for a few minutes?"

"The cider's finished."

At once, Begiloc regretted his churlishness.

"It's late for drink."

"Ay, with a long row ahead in the morning."

"The reason I want to talk to you ..."

"How so?"

"With three rowers light, you can use my strength."

Brightening, he grasped Robyn's forearm. "A warrior's arm I'll wager."

"In my youth, no more than eighteen springs, I fought with King Ine at Woden's Barrow. A crushing victory against the Mercians. Well, it changed me. What is war if not the utter lack of respect for life? A mother suffers childbirth to bring a babe squalling into the world after nine months yet one blow, one instant, is enough to end that existence. Of course, I came to realise life does not begin in the womb and does not finish in the grave. Though the years pass us by, Begiloc, they are but a moment set against eternity."

The silence between the men lingered as they stared into the flickering flames until Robyn stood, but Begiloc said, "Stay! Tell me about Leoba."

The monk sat again.

"Ha, Leoba! To this day, people talk about her dream at Wimborne, in which a purple thread issued from her mouth. When she drew it out there was no end. It grew to a huge length filling her hand and still it came out of her mouth so she rolled it into a ball."

Diffident, Begiloc stared into the fire before meeting the monk's eyes and muttering, "Only a dream."

"God speaks to us through dreams or through the words of others. Our task is to understand the meaning."

"There's a meaning?"

"Of course. At Wimborne a sister with the gift of prophesy explained it: Leoba, with her teaching, will confer gifts on many people. The thread from her mouth is the wise counsel she will speak from the heart. The hand full of thread means she will carry out in actions whatever she speaks in words."

"That I can believe!"

The monk laughed and said, "The ball of thread turns earthwards through active works and heavenwards through contemplation. By these signs, God shows she will profit many by her words and example and their effect will be felt in far off lands wherever she will go."

Begiloc lowered his head, "As I said, it was only a dream."

The monk's voice hardened, "Believe what you will, but you can see for yourself she is no common woman. I follow her for this reason. It is late, good night until the morn."

The fire, flames dwindling, held his gaze.

"Remarkable Leoba might be, but why did God take me away from my family? They're special too," he said. But Robyn had gone. Following his example, he retired.

Next morning, with Meryn on his mind, he rose early. Dawn upon them, the feeble light revealed movement among the nuns and monks. The warriors were asleep when he hurried to the tent of Theodilde. Hand on the flap, Begiloc hesitated suffused with guilt. Instead of finding the words to talk with God, he'd fallen into a half-drunken sleep. Seeing the haggard infirmarian sitting on the floor next to his comrade, deepened his remorse. He should have sat with his friend instead of carousing by the campfire. Eyes closed, Meryn lay face the colour of parchment, chest motionless. Anguished, Begiloc groaned and knelt beside the sister.

"What troubles you so? The fever broke in the night."
The words of the nun slow to penetrate his misery, he turned his face in disbelief.

"He lives?"
A smile replaced the weariness in the lined face of the infirmarian.

"God in His mercy has so decreed. For a day or two he must not be moved but he will survive. Go! Give thanks to the Lord!"

"Bless you sister for what you have done."

Back at his tent, the need to relieve himself became urgent, so he grabbed his spear and set off into the woods. Among the trees, a woman's cries for help startled him, making him change direction to find a nun clutching her habit above her knees running toward him, chased by a grunting boar.

"This way!" he yelled at the terrified woman, charging past her at the animal with lowered spear. Intimidated by the sharp point, the beast swerved away in a flurry of twigs and leaves, crashing off through the undergrowth.

Relieved, he stuck his spear into the ground as the nun threw herself into his arms with a sob, pressing her head into his chest.

*'This is wrong!'*
Hands by his sides, hesitating, he embraced her as a comfort. The warmth of her body and its softness stirred him. Perturbed, he detached himself, only to recognise the tear-streaked face of Aedre.

"I needed a private place and I disturbed it. it was f–" her voice choked, her body wracked with sobs, "... it was horrible...it, he–"

"Hush! Feeding on a dead man? Come!" Grabbing his spear, he put his hand under her arm and urged her back to the camp. At the edge of the woods, he halted, "Go ...we cannot be seen together ..."

"Begiloc," she breathed his name and again he flinched, "help me. I beg you, save me. My mother...I-I do not wish to be a nun. I'm an oblate. There is time–"

The distress and urgency on the upturned face chilled him. What could he do? Take on the Church? Did he not have troubles of his own?

"Now is not the moment. Go!" he hardened his heart against her pleading face, spun her round with a push towards the camp, "Go!"

It explained the behaviour of the young woman. As the lay leader of their party, her approach to him was natural. Why was her mother a nun? Why make her daughter take vows against her will? Shaking his head, he strode back to the encampment.

To his dismay, Leoba and Caena shouted orders to dismantle the tents and to gather up belongings – the noblewoman authoritative, the Saxon bellowing expletives. The nuns packed supplies and the monks carried them to the boats along with the spoils of the skirmish. Hurrying over to Leoba, Begiloc said, "My Lady, we cannot leave!"

The nun bit her lip, her eyes narrowed, "Why ever not?"

"Meryn..." he coughed and sought the right words, "... Sister Theodilde advises he may not be moved–"

"As I told our infirmarian," she pushed back her shoulders and raised her chin, "our mission will not wait. Faith and prayers will suffice if it be the will of Our Saviour."

"But–"

"My last word on the matter. Collect your belongings!"

With undue haste, Begiloc rolled up his tent.

*'Is the God she worships so demanding, so unbending? Or is it she, the noble nun, pride and determination driving her and everyone she commands?'*

"If we lose Meryn, I'll hold it against her and her religion," he muttered.

*'The old gods of our forefathers made no such demands. They wove fate and the wælcyrge chose the warrior to be slain and accompanied him to the hall of the dead. All so simple. No prayers – only offerings.'*

In apostate mood, he stomped toward the boats.

They had nine able-bodied oarsmen, but at Brother Robyn's suggestion the other monks, though unused to rowing, agreed to take frequent turns among themselves at an oar. Each boat had five rowers, meaning one oarsman light on the previous day. With the camp site diminished by distance to the size of a kerchief, Begiloc sighed with relief. While Hrothgar was a grievous loss, the astuteness of Meryn at the inn had prevented worse.

At the thought, he glanced at his friend's pale face. When they laid him in the boat – Begiloc smiled at the recollection – the Meryn of old informed them the wound was worthwhile to avoid rowing. A short-lived smile, for Theodilde knelt beside the patient, shaking her head, muttering, "He bleeds afresh." The infirmarian clicked her tongue, peeled back the dressing and set about her work. Slick with sweat, Meryn groaned and

Begiloc bit his lip, driving murderous thoughts from his mind to concentrate on rowing.

Snug in a meander lay a settlement the guide named Meldi, but at twilight it lay many miles behind. At the chosen campsite a sharp discussion flared. The infirmarian would not allow the wounded man to be moved from the boat. Theodilde called for extra blankets and refused to leave her patient, while Leoba ordered Begiloc to his tent when he offered to relieve the nun of her vigil during the night. The lady herself agreed to alternate with her infirmarian and quelled the protests of her sisters with a call for obedience. Whether her sacrifice was out of care for Meryn or to ensure he, Begiloc, should be fit to row the next day he knew not.

They set off early for the town of Catalauns, where the defeat of Attila had stopped the advance of the Huns many lifetimes ago or so Leoba informed Begiloc – not that the names meant anything to him. Their guides promised arrival before nightfall with hard rowing.

Two boats heading downriver hailed them otherwise the day proved uneventful. Begiloc checked on his friend, whose dark hair made his sallow skin appear paler. Every pull of the oar became more urgent to him as the never-ending day wore on with the persistent thought of the promised care for Meryn at destination. To his relief, he sighted the citadel of Catalauns an hour after None.

This town marked the end of their river route. From here they would travel overland, making more arduous and much slower progress.

On the bank, Leoba joined Begiloc and pointed up beyond the citadel.

"See, on the hill, the monastery of Saint Valerian. Carry your friend to the monks where the infirmarian will tend him," she said, eyes gentle, full of commiseration. "Once healed, he can join us in Austrasia," she continued, "the brothers will instruct him how to reach us. On the morrow, I will visit Bishop Bladald in the town to deliver a letter from Wimborne. Also, I have the matter of the boats," her captivating smile, "so, you will have time to bid farewell to our brave Meryn." In an encouraging tone, she said, "Pray for him and all will be well."

Mute in her presence, he returned her smile, but how to find the words to talk to God, when he found it so difficult to express his sentiments to his fellow man?

They were welcomed by the claustral prior, a lantern-chinned monk, the affable deputy of the abbot. A crooked nose, broken in a fight as a hot-headed youth, lent him a distinguished appearance.

"Our Abbot cannot greet you ..." voice conspiratorial, "... an issue with the bishop about immunities, tiresome matters. Come," he bowed to Leoba, "tell me, whatever your requirements we shall attend to them."

There followed a long discussion on the sale of the boats, their basic needs and those of Meryn, concluded to everyone's satisfaction.

The next morning, Begiloc asked directions to the infirmary where he found Sister Theodilde in conversation with the infirmarian. Next to them, Brother Robyn greeted him with raised hand. Disappointed to find Meryn asleep, pallid as before, he inquired about his condition to the healer-monk, a man with grizzled beard and rheumy eyes who replied, "We must pray for him."

"Yes, but how *is* he?"

The monk spread his palms upwards, "The patient lost much blood. Hen broth and red wine are the cure, but...above all prayers. God willing, he will pull through."

Sister Theodilde gave Begiloc a weak smile, saying, "They should not have moved him, not with a fever."
Her dismay brought an inward curse at Leoba's stubbornness.

In vain he waited, his friend did not wake and Begiloc could muster few words for God, his mind straying to home and family.

*'Denehard and his accursed letter! Without it Meryn would have finished the ditch around the Far Field and I'd have made the new rake I never got round to.'*
Dwelling on Somerhild and her soft skin, on Ealric and his pranks...he listened to the rasp of Meryn's breath and noted the blackness around the eyes, the sunken cheeks and the sheen on his brow. Pray, he could not, but a blessing for healing used by the folk of Dumnonia came to mind. Glancing around, he made sure they were alone before reciting:

*'Your pain and illness*
*Be in the earth's bowels,*
*Be upon the rugged stones*
*For they are everlasting.*

*Fly with the swallow high,*
*Fly with the bees of the hill,*
*Swim with the sea-going seal,*
*For they are the swiftest.'*

The blessing made him feel better, but would it benefit Meryn? Wary of fever since his mother, Talwyn, died of it soon after the loss of Keresyk, his hand strayed to a reminder of her, the brooch pinning his cloak. His friend lay feverish and although prayer would not come, he could unpin the clasp. When would he part with it if not now? Fastened the breastpin to Meryn's tunic, he stared at him taking in every line of his face including the twelve small beads in his beard. Smiling, he compared his friend's vanity to that of Thunor's wife.

*'Sif's golden tresses!'*

The goddess was the prey of Lôgna. Was Meryn the victim of Leoba? Anger flared in his breast, his comrade must not die! May the brooch serve as a healing amulet – the Devil take the Church's condemnation of them! With this thought, he ran his hand over the damp hair of the patient before leaving.

The next morning, Begiloc considered the moss on the sunless side of the oak trunks and concluded their guides were leading them north-eastwards. The fresh-leaved trees stood tall and close, the morning sunlight falling dappled through an overarched canopy. The dry spell, unusual for late April, made the going along the ill-defined, undulating forest trails easier underfoot. The men with their heavy packs welcomed monastic routine determining longer breaks for prayer in the wearisome journey. The nuns travelled light, their only burden a change of clothes, books and parchments.

Late in the day, they camped beyond trees fringed by wood violets next to a trickle of a stream, where no bushes might shelter the advance of an enemy intent on surprise attack, given the avid leud Donatus, pride scalded, was sure to seek vengeance.

The older of the guides, reserve close to surliness, when pressed, said, "About ten miles to the east beside a small river lies a village. We should get there by mid-afternoon, thenceforth the going along the valley is easier but too close to the lands of Donatus."

The fear in the man's voice confirmed the remorseless enmity of the leud.

They awoke to a sunny day marred by a breeze from the east. Even so, they made good progress through the forest. The Saxons changed positions to keep fresh eyes for any danger hidden among the trees. Soon after midday, the lead man warned of a clearing with a woodman's hut, sty and store, a tethered goat, heaps of charcoal and a fellow with a blackened face and muscular frame who greeted them. A slight palsy compromised his speech so Begiloc failed to understand his coarse Frankish tongue. The woodman pointed past his kiln through the trees and gestured downwards, all this accompanied by a flood of grunts and spittle interpreted by the guides to mean the source of the river Auve lay below in the village they sought.

Beyond the trees, two fields stretched, brown and furrowed, with ten houses between them grouped around a larger building. No smoke rose from the dwellings but it spiralled from embers in their midst to form a feather-like cloud, tugged along by the wind. The shouting and arm-waving in the village puzzled Begiloc. All the villagers gathered he guessed as he squinted at the crowd.

Drawing nearer, the cause of the commotion became clear. The men formed a ring around the fire while the younger women chanted an invocation as the older ones kept the children at a distance. Youths with sticks drove pigs and goats, berserk with fear, squealing and bleating over the ardent embers. Their hooves and trotters cast showers of sparks into the air as the onlookers covered their faces, coughed and beat at their clothing – a pagan rite.

The travellers were closing on the village when disaster struck. The breeze carried sparks to the thatch of the nearest house, fanning them so in an instant, the dry straw caught fire. Women screamed and children cried as men, ritual abandoned, shouted, dashed around, yelling orders and seizing buckets. Dropping his pack, Begiloc called to his men to help because the flames spread to two other dwellings, threatening the whole village with destruction.

"Come, Brothers and Sisters," Leoba waved, "kneel here in front of the houses! Pray the Lord save these poor homes!"
In frustration, Begiloc shook his head; how could fine heavenly words extinguish the voracious flames when they needed more hands to fling water?

The men formed a chain to pass buckets hand over hand where a nearby spring gushed to form a stream flowing through the village. Nothing served to save the first house, so they threw water on the next two, but this proved inadequate as the insistent wind wafted the flames. The thatch of a fourth building ignited, the one behind the nuns and monks, surrounding them in fire.

"My Lady!" yelled Begiloc at the kneeling Leoba, at the apex of a praying echelon, "Move away, you are in danger!"
The heat and the smoke intense, the nun, unperturbed, continued her prayers. About to abandon the chain to run and tug the noblewoman away, Begiloc hesitated when the breeze changed direction.

"Throw the water at the fourth thatch!" he shouted to the men next to him. In moments, the fire extinguished and the property saved, they channelled their efforts to the homes in front of the fiery-faced, nuns and monks. The light wind held its course long enough for them to dowse the flames. Three skeletal houses smouldered as the breeze, from the east again, drove smoke into the faces of the kneeling figures, making them cough and splutter.

Black-faced and angry, Leoba pushed past Begiloc to confront a bear-like, bald man with grizzled moustaches who, judging by the respect he received, must be the village elder.

"What is the meaning of this?"

The man, towering over the nun, quailed before the fierce hazel eyes.

"W-what – there's been a fire – that's what!"

"I can see, I'm not blind nor stupid. Why were you driving animals through the fire?"

The man licked his lips, swallowed hard with everyone staring at him and began to sweat, not from the heat of the seared beams. With a wry smile, Begiloc looked on. Was it possible this woman could intimidate anyone she chose?

"*Need-fire*. Our beasts are sick and *need-fire* is the remedy."

"How do you suppose driving creatures through fire can cure them of sickness?" Leoba took a menacing step forward.

"It's not just any fire – as I said, it's *need-fire* from kindling oak by–"

" I have no wish to hear! It's a pagan rite! Are you not Christians? Were you not baptised?"

Leoba's fury swept round to include the villagers. She did not wait for an answer, "Was it not thanks to our prayers the Lord changed the wind to save your homes?"

In the silence some hung their heads, but a woman dashed forward, knelt before Leoba and grasped her dress.

"God bless you holy lady, you rescued my home!"

She pointed at the house with the charred thatch and her tear-streaked face turned to the man, "Freyr doesn't listen! When did the old gods do anything for us? They're deaf to our needs. God has punished us for lack of faith."

Begiloc wandered over to the group of men who had rounded up the pigs. Bending over a sow, he inspected it. The animal, still trembling, struggled and squealed from its ordeal so he took care not to distress it further as he lifted its ear. Satisfied, the Briton strolled to where the nun and the man were in discussion. The fellow dropped to his knees before her.

"...well, I can start over. You can baptise me anew."

"I'm not a priest. Nobody can be baptised twice. Repent of your sins! Work together to build three new houses. Each day at sunrise kneel and pray to God for the wellbeing of your village and its animals. Do you understand? If you fail to do this," her lips pursed, "you will bring down God's wrath but if you fulfil your penance, in His mercy He will shine His light on you. All of you would do well to join this man in prayer." With a smile at the assembled villagers, her beauty shone through the mask of soot.

"My Lady, may I speak?"

"Begiloc?"

"The swine have the mange. They can be cured."

To the villagers, he said, "Prepare a lotion from garlic, elder and violet leaves, wormwood and clover. Wash the animals three times a day and take special care with the suckling pigs. If you do this, the disease will pass. Oh, and another thing, do not put ash from this fire in their feed – that's pagan nonsense too!"

To his gratification, Leoba beamed at his words.

Their moment of shame past, the villagers crowded round the travellers eager for news of the wider world and keen to offer hospitality. Their leader, Amalric, bade them sup and stay the night offering them use of the hall, the large building, to share with those who lost their homes in the fire. First, they needed to wash at the spring. The pretty daughter of Amalric, Ingitruda, spoke to Caena, "It becomes a river and I've heard tell it flows into a greater one to the east and one day I hope to see it! In the old days, our forefathers worshipped the goddess of the spring, but of course ..." she added in haste, "... before we were baptised into the true faith."

After a simple meal of legumes and weak ale in which all the villagers participated, came a raucous demand for song. Leoba imposed silence on them all, "We will sing a psalm," and nobody dared gainsay her. "Begiloc, will you accompany the nuns and monks with your hearpe?" A short, wiry villager hurried over bearing a bone flute and sat next to him while another brought a tambour. "Psalm 44," Leoba said.

The Briton and the other two musicians waited, following the voices before joining in. Wondering what the words meant, Begiloc enjoyed the vocal harmony unaware of the reproval her choice intended for the unsuspecting villagers, who like himself knew no Latin.

The notes died away and Leoba called to Begiloc.

"Remember the sad song the night of the attack? Will you sing it for us?"

She referred to *The Wife's Lament* and the Saxons were glad to take it up again and afterwards to join in with local lays. Begiloc missed the mellow voice of Meryn and it darkened his mood, in spite of the others in good cheer and seeing Caena giving much attention to the daughter of Amalric.

The Saxon leant over and in an uncharacteristic low voice, said, "Begiloc, that girl ... er ... Ingiter ... no, In-*grit*-uda, yes that's her name. She's worth more than a minute of my time! I can tell you! What do you think of her?"

Contemptuous of the other man's carnal desires with brave Meryn struggling to cling to life, Begiloc shrugged.

Early next morning, they followed the brook out of the village until, as the sun rose high in the sky, the stream became a river. At the point where a tributary flowed into the Auve,

Leoba hurried over to Begiloc trailing a flustered nun. The Briton recognised her as Williswind the mother of Aedre.

"Aedre is missing!"

"Missing?" he stared at the noblewoman.

Williswind brought her hand to her breast, "I rode beside Theodilde and we – I – failed to notice she wasn't with us. My own daughter! How is it possible?"

All the nuns dressed alike so it was more than possible thought Begiloc.

"Nobody left our group along the course of the river," Leoba said, "we would have noticed."

The older woman threw up her hands, saying, "Do you suggest she stayed in the village? Why would she do that?"

Again the warrior kept his counsel.

"How far are we from our next stopping point?" Leoba asked the guides.

The two men debated as Caena joined the group.

"Your directions had better be good today. No wrong turns, understand? Get it right or you'll answer to me and I'm not as forgivin' as the nuns."

The older guide, less surly after the evening entertainment, ignored the Saxon and bowed to the nun before he spoke.

"At the confluence with the Aisne is the fortress of Sanctá-Menehilde. We shall be there by mid-afternoon."

"Go back to the village," Leoba said to Begiloc, "find Aedre and bring her to me. You will have time to reach Sanctá-Menehilde before Vespers."

"The dangers then? Come on, out with it! What perils hereabouts?" Caena demanded.

"None, I believe. At Sanctá-Menehilde is the castle built by Dreux ou Drogon and his son Girard rules this area with an iron fist. The keep has a dank dungeon and they say whoever ends up inside never emerges. It stands on the only rock amid a vast plain. Soon we should sight it."

"Since there's no danger," Caena said waving toward the group, "I'll come in case a strong arm be needed."

"There's nought wrong with mine," Begiloc said, but in truth, having Caena's company pleased him.

The two men made haste back to the village where a cluster of women were wailing, scratching their faces and pulling their hair around the lacerated corpse of a villager, a smith's iron in his limp hand and his blood thick on the beaten clay. Amalric strode over, his face grey and haggard, "My brother's son, more courage than sense," he shook his head, "the nun warned me. God has punished us, they took my daughter–"

"Ingiter? When did this happen?" Caena clenched his fist.

"See, the blood is fresh. They took your nun too."

"Aedre!"

Kites began to circle overhead and crows cawed nearby. Amalric pointed skywards addressing the other villagers, "Don't stand there, idlers! Carry Bertmund into the hall."

"Do you know why Aedre stayed behind?" Caena asked. The Frank said, "Ay, she told Ingitruda she didn't want to be a nun so they planned to go into service at Sanctá-Menehilde."

"And you encouraged them in this?" Begiloc said.

Anxious, Amalric replied, "Me? No, you know what young women be like–"

Caena muttered, "I've never been able to fathom 'em. I've tried but they're beyond me! I take 'em as I find 'em. Ay, as I find 'em."

Begiloc interrupted Caena's attempt at wisdom, deflecting sword thrusts not fine speaking, the Saxon's strength.

"Who did this?"

"There be no justice..." Amalric frowned and spat on the ground "...there be witnesses, but there be no wergild...not when there be a comitis and a bishop ..."

"A comitis?"

"Ay, from the north east, from the Ardennes–"

"Is there a name for this comitis?" Begiloc asked to confirm his suspicion.

Bereft, the village chieftain replied, "What use be his name? If it's Donatus you can do what you like. Unless the bishop or the duke beat him to it."

Murmurs of agreement came from two of the villagers.

"You should protest to the bishop," Begiloc said.

"Milo? He'd take my daughter and your nun for concubines if he knew Donatus had them. They wouldn't be the first either."

"Concubines!"

"Even the dogs know about the Bishop of Rems." Amalric spat again, "Brother by marriage to the Mayor of the Palace. Together they drove Bishop Rigobert – a real saint – from the city. Charles appointed Milo his successor, and him already Bishop of Treves like his father and grandfather before him–"

"Two bishoprics?"

"Ay, two, so as he can better pillage the Church! One thing's for sure, we won't see the day when men like Milo and Donatus leave poor folk in peace."

The villagers growled in agreement.

"Which way did they go? How many of them?"

Amalric screwed up his face and muttered something about wailing women.

"About a dozen, two on horses and the others on foot – all well armed," he said, pointing to the woods, "beware, the comitis questioned your nun, wanting to know about where

your party was headed. Sanctá-Menehilde, she told him and ..."
he shook the Briton's arm "...he told the other rider they'd
follow and seize you after you left the castle. I swear by my
own ears."
Caena and Begiloc exchanged glances and the Briton spoke,
"Did you pray at sunrise as instructed?"
The shoulders of the village chief dropped.

"My Lady warned you. You brought God's wrath upon this
place! Kneel tomorrow and hope God heeds the prayers for
your daughter. Come, my friend, it is time to leave."

Begiloc hated himself for entreating others to prayer. The
concept filled him with dread, inadequacy, in spite of his
growing confidence in its power.

They set out along the brook and after only a few paces, he
realised Caena was not with him. The Saxon was standing, feet
apart, staring at him. He sighed and strolled back. "What is it?"

"This is not the way!"

"Well?"

"So...we should trail them. It's obvious, isn't it? Besides,
I'm growing a liking for these sweet, pale-faced nuns. But, I
jest ..." he said at Begiloc's frown. The Briton thought it
probable Caena was revealing his true nature and not jesting,
but on reflection, he accepted that like himself, the Saxon did
possess a core belief in right and wrong."

"Two against a dozen?"

Caena's nostrils flared. "We can't leave Ingiter and Aedre to
the mercy of those savages!" Begiloc considered his comrade,
hidden behind the coarse exterior and bluster beat a steadfast
heart. Unconvinced, Begiloc said, "Agreed, but they will not be
best served by raven carrion. First, we must warn the others
and avert capture. *Then* we shall move. Donatus is the leud

who set the trap on the Marne – there's a score to settle and when the day comes the might of your arm will be needed."

Caena contemplated this for a long moment before saying, "I'm up for a damn good fight! I'll settle it all right by ripping the innards out of the bastard with my bare hands."

# CHAPTER 5

A wooden wall with two towers flanking the gate surrounded the keep of Sanctá-Menehilde, built on rock. The inanimate mass brooded and challenged malefactors to breach its defences. Yet as Begiloc and Caena approached, the entry swung back and the sentry jerked his head toward the tower.

A variety of timber and wattle and daub houses clustered in the shadow of the castle, where women of all ages went about their tasks; Begiloc and Caena had passed the men at work in the fields outside the sheer stone walls, whose parapets offered a view for miles in every direction. No unseen approach was possible.

The gloom of the entrance served to sharpen other senses assailed by aromas from the kitchen and the clamour of servants shouting and receiving orders. One indicated to leave their weapons and follow him up a winding staircase to a hall where a fire blazed.

Two hounds sprawled by the hearth and back to the flames stood the lord of Sanctá-Menehilde, a man the Briton guessed to be his own age, younger than presumed. The man with the reputation of an iron fist possessed a frame to match while exquisite sword and dagger pommels contrasted with the plainness of his garments. Leoba sat conversing with a woman in a fur-trimmed dress, whose thin head-veil of blue silk brushed against the wimple of the nun. From the grey at the temples, lines around her eyes and fine features, Begiloc judged the woman to be fifty and of noble birth. Her clear skin was pale and her nose long and straight. The amethyst necklace at her breast caught the firelight, casting purple flames across her white throat. A smile played at the corner of her mouth as she observed the Briton studying her. The nun followed her gaze and letting go of her companion's hand, rose to her feet.

"Ah, Begiloc, Caena, come! I must present the Lady Albemarle de Roussillon, the dowager comitissa and Lord Girart, Comitis of Sanctá-Menehilde." Formalities over, Leoba pressed them for news of Aedre and faces grew grave at Begiloc's words. The comitissa took her hand once more, her expression hardening.

"Whoever this man is, he has no respect for the sanctity of your calling and as the village lies on our estates, he may not act with impunity ..."

Thick black eyebrows met over the hooked nose of the leud and his eyes flashed. They bored into Begiloc, "Do you have a name for the slayer?"

"Ay, my lord, Donatus. The same whose men attacked us at the Marne."

The dowager gasped and said to Leoba, "The Comitis of Grandpré! These are ill tidings. The man is as wild as the Ardennes whence he comes and he enjoys the protection of the Bishop of Rems. His reputation for cruelty and avarice is well merited."

Wide-eyed, Leoba stared at the comitissa. The older woman pursed her lips, "At Verden, within his domain, he encourages a slave market. Oft-times our Christian brothers finish in slavery. And worse," she shuddered, "parents in need are urged to sell their children. All manner of wickedness takes place there. A steady stream of slaves flows through Bavaria, over the mountains to Venice and thence to Byzantium." The dowager squeezed the hand of the nun. "My dear, things that happen at Verden a woman may never utter."

She grimaced and shook her head.

"Mother, the Comitis of Grandpré can be as cruel and avaricious as he wishes on his own land, but Auve is my village and the girl, Ingitruda, is my property."

Caena's eyes bulged on hearing her described as a mere chattel, prompting him to take a step toward Leoba and drop to one knee. "My Lady, let me hunt this craven and bring you his head."

Girart put his hand on the shoulder of the Saxon. "Time presses. We shall pursue him together." For confirmation, he turned to Begiloc, "From your account, they travel on foot except for two who, perforce, keep the slower pace. Donatus has a stronghold at Somepin near the confines of my estates. It serves also as a hunting lodge where he is likely to spend the night before leaving for Grandpré. With a forced march, we will arrive before sunset." The comitis clapped his hands and servants hurried over. "Fetch my coat of mail, helm and spear. Gather your men and meet me outside," he said to Begiloc and Caena.

"Take care and bring Aedre safe back to us," Leoba said.

On the way to muster their soldiers Caena said, "So, Briton, we'll have to guard each others' backs on this one. I'll watch for you, and you do the bloody same for me! Understood?"

"Ay, let's go!

*'A new friend then!'*

The shadows lay long before them when they pitched camp before the palisade of Somepin. The stronghold stood on a rocky white outcrop and Begiloc asked himself how Lord Girart meant to take it with the score of men at his command. A problem for the morning.

Not long after daybreak he had the answer. Weapons at the ready, he formed up with the others. The blast of a war horn nigh rent his eardrums. A lone figure appeared on the rampart and called, "State your purpose!"

Lord Girart moved a step forward and his barrel chest rumbled, "Girart de Roussillon would speak with your master."

"Our lord is not here."

"We shall see for ourselves."

For a moment, in the silence, Caena pushed to the fore, his rage at the abduction of Ingitruda uncontainable. By way of reply, the defender gestured and by instinct, the men outside raised their shields. No need, the gate swung open.

"Beware a trap, my lord," said Caena, expressing the thoughts of each man, "they're none to be trusted. None."

They advanced with the nobleman at their head, but before they reached the entry one man, no armour, sword at his belt, came out to meet them. The slight inclination of his head passed for a bow.

"Sigibrand de Somepin, at your service."

The comitis inclined his head with a tight smile, "So, Sigibrand de Somepin, your master is not here?"

"No, my lord."

"Am I to believe that?"

"See for yourselves," he said, leading them through the gate. Inside were a dozen men, two lounging against a wall, one sitting, legs swinging, on a cart and all with weapons undrawn and faces sour. The limestone-built stronghold contained three levels. Pulling out his sword, Begiloc mounted the steps and shoved the door with a foot. The few servants the place afforded glowered, sullen, as a search of the first two floors proved in vain.

Their footsteps on the stone drowned the weeping of a woman in a third-floor bedchamber. On the floor propped against the wall, she sat with her head on her knees, her long locks a veil, back heaving with sobs. At their approach, she cowered but her hair parted to reveal a bloodied tear-streaked face.

"Ingitruda!" Caena pushed past Girart, and made to lift her to her feet, but she cringed away from his touch and whimpered. Seeing her dress torn and her throat marked livid purple, the Saxon roared, "I'll kill the devil who did this! How dare the bastard ill-treat an innocent like her!" Girart pulled him aside and spoke to the young woman, "You are safe and we will take you back to your home. First, you must help us catch your attacker."

Using her tresses as a shield, Ingitruda lifted her shoulders to hide her neck. Her voice was feeble and the words little more than gasps, "H-he ... killed the ... cat ..." she pointed a quivering hand to the corner of the chamber, where a kitten lay, its head twisted at an unnatural angle to its body, "... h-he threw it ... a-against the wall!"

"When did he do this? Was it last night, this morning, when..?"

Ingitruda swallowed hard and her words came out as a wail, "This morning ... !"

The vein at his brow corded, Caena with thunderous voice said, "He's still here. In hiding. Find him! Bring him to me!"

The men hurried out off in all directions. Begiloc bent down, "Fear not, we will avenge this wrong." Drawing Ingitruda to her feet, he supported the shivering woman. Her eyes never left the dead kitten until they passed out of the chamber and he cursed under his breath, for the violation of the woman was evident in the intensity of each tremble and start of her body. Every illusion of happiness, goodness and rightness she held dear was shattered, he had no doubt, and he swore vengeance.

With the vague idea of finding water for her to drink and to tend to her wounds, he took her to the kitchen. A cook, tut-tutting and clucking, gave Ingitruda the care and comfort of a woman.

No trace of Donatus. In appearance the compound had one entrance, Begiloc considered, so either the leud was in hiding in the building or had used another way out. In that case, a hidden passage at ground level, but not the kitchen – too cluttered and in plain sight. From above came the muffled sound of his comrades searching. Where would he conceal an exit?

Next door seemed a likely place though his eyes needed a moment to adjust. Light filtered in from a small barred window, sufficient to reveal the game birds hanging from the beams beside two cured hams. Sacks bulged in a pile in a corner while of the barrels by a wall one out of line alerted Begiloc. Seax drawn, he squeezed between two casks and hit the masonry with the hilt. The sound was dull, he moved to one side and struck again, hollowness. How to open the passage? His hand pressed over the stonework and he cried out in surprise when one stone ceded with a groan as part of the wall swung back. The poor light made it hard to discern detail, so he ran to the door shouting for the others. One of his men dashed off to fetch a torch and its flame lit up a ladder down to a narrow passage.

"We must follow!"

Caena frowned at the nobleman, "Ingitruda?"

Seizing the firebrand, Begiloc scrambled down and said over his shoulder, "She is tended by the cook until our return. Come, make haste! The rapist has Aedre!"

In the limestone tunnel, they moved bending forward to prevent their heads from hitting the roof. It was wide enough for Caena's broad shoulders but as the tallest of the company he suffered most, slithering on the damp floor until his patience snapped.

"Shit! What sort of a burrow is this! I fear no man, but I can't bloody take being in tight spaces … by Satan's arse, how much farther, Begiloc?"

They hurried on for a long time, Caena's oaths worsening, before the air freshened against Begiloc's cheek. A chink of light revealed three steps carved in the stone where half-rotten tree branches covered by twigs blocked an opening.

They struggled out into the undergrowth of ferns, briar and holly among the broad-leaved trees. Nearby a brook gurgled and in front of them crushed and broken bracken betrayed recent trampling that led to a track, over which Begiloc pored.

"Footprints!"

Two sets of prints in the damp soil.

"They are new and one set is large and deep, the other smaller and lighter," he said, "Donatus and Aedre! Come on!"

"Hold!" Girart grabbed him. "I leave you here. The trail leads westwards where I cannot follow. The coward makes for Rems for he is a leud of the bishop and under his protection. The craven knew if he headed for Grandpré we would capture him. Believe me, once he leaves the forest with the nun he will be impossible to take." The comitis shook his head. "You will move better without me. This coat of mail slows me and your number is sufficient to overcome one man. Your best chance is to seize him in the forest. Do so, and bring him back to Sanctá-Menehilde. I shall return to Somepin to escort the woman, Ingitruda," he clasped Begiloc by the arm, "remember it is perilous to leave the woodlands. God speed!"

They hurried along the trail, hurdled fallen trees, snagged their breeches on briars and slipped in the mud. Like the others, as he ran, Begiloc wondered how far behind they lagged in pursuit. Caena matched him stride for stride, the one spurring on the other.

Into a glade they burst where uprooted beeches lay criss-crossed. The nun, Aedre, sat on one of them, a dagger under her chin. Donatus, spattered in mud, sneered as they fanned out in a slow encircling approach.

"No closer or she dies!"

With his other hand, he unhooked a horn from his belt, its shrill note silencing the persistent birdsong.

"A trap! To the trees!" Even at his command, Begiloc saw the surrounding spearmen. Outnumbered at least three to one, resistance was useless. The ring of iron points drew closer.

Sheathing his dagger, Donatus said, "Place your weapons on the ground. Do it!"

What choice other than to obey?

"Bind them!"

Rough hands pulled their arms behind their backs to carry out the order before they encircled their waists too until they were all trussed in a line. Only then did Donatus approach to stare at the lead man, Caena.

"Did you take me for a fool? To be hunted like a stag in the forest?" The edge of his mouth curled, "Did you think I have only the few men you found at Somepin? You underestimate me!"

Caena spat at the leering face and the fist of the leud split his lip. Blood stained his beard, but the Saxon remained defiant.

"Kill me now Frank, because if I live I will castrate you for what you did to Ingitruda! Rely on it, you bastard!"

"Why? Is the whore your woman? She was poor sport, cuckold!"

"If he doesn't geld you, I will."

"What have we here? A Briton!" Donatus drew his sword and held the point to the groin of Begiloc. "One sharp push and you will rue your empty threat. Want to know why that thrust will never come ... ?" His sneer matched the malice in his eyes, " ... what use are you dead? I need you hale to sell at the slave market."

"My lord! Over there!" one of his men called.

The comitis spun round and from the trees appeared a man on horseback. The jaw of their captor dropped and once more from the woods emerged spearmen, this time in greater numbers. Farther behind them servants carried a boar trussed and hanging from a pole.

*'A hunt then!'*

The leud sank to one knee before the horseman. "My Lord Bishop!" he bowed his head. The prelate reined his horse a yard in front of his vassal. A doeskin-gloved finger pointed at Donatus and a red jewel sparkled in the sunlight. Bulbous eyes and fleshy face did nothing to soften the hostile glare directed at his leud and Begiloc reckoned this was a man who cared nought for Christian mercy.

"Why are you on my land with armed men? Stand!"
Donatus rose and bowed his head, his tone sycophantic.

"Your Eminence, beg pardon. We pursued these Saxons to avenge a wrong–"
The bishop glowered at the captives and turned in his saddle to scrutinise the oblate.

"Enough! We return to Rems where I shall have the truth of the matter."
The mounted ecclesiarch delivered his orders with venom, a skill honed by years of dominance, and even Begiloc, battle-hardened as he was, felt a rush of fear along his spine.

Weary, they trudged into Rems after nightfall. The last hour of their journey undertaken by moonlight across the flood plain. By the silver light, they marched along the filth-strewn, winding streets. In their midst, the cathedral in appearance lurked squat and huge ready to pounce and gorge on its prey. On the Marne, Begiloc recalled they had passed the town, according to Leoba at less than a day's march north of the river. It pained him to think he had failed her. How much she wanted to visit this place! There, in her words, the archbishop saint, Remigius, had ordered the barbarian king *'to bow his head and worship what he had hitherto destroyed, and destroy what he had hitherto worshipped.'* He needed to call upon similar bravery but his fate was out of his hands.

Thrust through a huge oak door into a room of stone with high slits through which the faint moonlight relieved the darkness, Begiloc caught the glimmer of a blade. For a moment, he feared the worst until a man hacked at his ropes. The blood flowed to his numb fingers, the door slammed shut and a key grated in a lock. Curses abounded but they fell silent when a metal plate in the door opened. A rough voice said, "Take this bread – if it was up to me yer'd have none."

Begiloc woke with the feeble light of morning, body aching in every limb. In the corner of the room at a stone seat with a hole one of his companions sought relief to the accompaniment of crude laughter. At least spirits were high for the moment, but what would the day bring? Aware of the menace in the bishop's tone the night before, fear had been replaced by frustration at being unable to defend themselves.

At last, the door creaked, men brandishing swords led them unbound since unarmed men posed no threat. They proceeded in the shadow of the squat cathedral to an ancient and splendid villa, Roman in appearance. These buildings made Begiloc uneasy, they didn't bring him luck. Give him timber any day, like the home he had built for his family. The fate awaiting him inside might mean never seeing Somerhild and Ealric again.

The walls of the entrance vaunted painted gods and cherubs. Were the wings and haloes fresher and cruder, Begiloc wondered, added as a Christian afterthought?

In stark contrast, trophies of the hunt, bear, boar, and deer heads, hung in the great hall. At the far end of the room sat the bishop and though the day was young, he drank wine from a cup. Behind him, stationed four guards, two at either side of the throne where six scantily-clad women, no more than girls, waited on him. Next to the seated prelate stood Donatus and beside him, Aedre.

A click of his fingers and a woman approached the prelate with a dish, curtseyed holding the delicacy aloft in both hands.

"Exquisite! Fried horn of young stag," the clergyman enthused. He helped himself to a slice and rolled it around on his tongue, savouring the taste, taking another before waving the woman away, crooking a finger for more wine. The prelate swilled the drink before dragging a sleeve across his mouth in a blur of jewelled rings.

Under the effects of good living and the finery bedecking him, Begiloc noted the warrior. The silk cloak over the broad shoulders intrigued him. What use was it? No protection against the cold nor against the grasp of branches on a hunt. On the chest of the prelate hanging around his bull-like neck from a thick chain of the same metal lay a gold cross the size of a man's hand. His stature, Begiloc suspected, had been broadened by boyhood hours spent in mock combat later tempered on the battlefield. The face muscles showed signs of slackness, but the protruding eyes, bloodshot and shrewd, conveyed the hostile nature of the man. They fixed on Caena.

"Who is your leader?"

The voice of the bishop was as hard as a crucifixion nail.

"I am."

"I am."

Begiloc and Caena stared at one another.

"Two leaders! The Church should adopt the method – two Holy Fathers in Rome to cancel each other out!" A wink at Donatus elicited a forced laugh from the leud. The prelate waved at the guards, "Take them away but for the *two* commanders!" He waited until the clatter of footsteps died. "So," he said to Donatus, "I repeat my question, why were you on my land with armed men?"

Donatus's stare fixed the woman beside him for a moment, before turning to the bishop, "Your Excellency, this woman goes by the name of Aedre," his voice was suave and respectful, "she is a nun from the Abbey of Wimborne in my service for six months–"

"It's a lie!" Caena said. "I tell you it's a lie!"

The bulging eyes switched to the Saxon, "Silence! Speak when ordered!"

The leud bowed, not that it was a concession to him, "...she is the sister of the tall warrior..." Begiloc gaped at the shamelessness of the falsehood. What did the Frank hope to achieve? "...he wishes to carry her back to Wessex, where she must wed against her will."

The ruby ring on his fourth finger seemed of more interest to Bishop Milo. He toyed with it for a while, letting the silence endure.

"Is this the truth, child?"

Aedre nodded her lowered head. The prelate spoke to her in honeyed tone, "Look at me, my dear. Do not fear to speak. I repeat the question, "Is what he says true?"

The nun lifted her head but her gaze reached no higher than the gold cross at his chest before darting to one side, to Donatus. At last, she replied, "It is, My Lord Bishop."

A single eyebrow arched and his head cocked, the prelate placed a bejewelled finger to his lips. His tone was sarcastic, "Reprehensible! To seize a bride of Christ and marry her against her will. An example must be made ..." With a gesture to the guards his voice, weary and slow, ordered, "... take them away. Hang the lot of them!"

The triumphant smile of Donatus vanished and Aedre gasped.

"No, wait!"

Different emotions passed across her face as she wrestled with inner demons. She backed away from the leud and said, "This is not what was supposed to happen." With a sneer, Milo leant forward on his throne. The oblate, in panic, knelt and clasped her hands in supplication.

"My Lord Bishop, I have sinned," she swept an arm behind her, "these men are innocent."

Tears ran down her cheeks and she babbled her tale of woe.

Milo heaved his bulk off his seat and stepped toward her. Raising her, he said, "You have been sorely tried, my child," he devoured the form of her body, "it is clear to me you do not wish to be a nun. Have I the right of it?" Like prey beguiled by a serpent, the woman nodded.

"There is place for you in my palace. I shall treat you most kindly. Would you like that?" Still holding her, the bishop turned his head toward the two captives. "As for your friends, you can spare them a hanging, say the word."

Begiloc stared at Aedre with revulsion, but their lives depended on her next words; judging from her face, alight with joy, he needed not worry.

"Your Excellency does me much honour," she bobbed a curtsey and still he held her, "I shall be pleased to stay in your palace."

At last, he released his grip, "It is settled." He clapped and the women scurried to him. "Take your new companion, bathe her and see to her arrayment. Guards, take these men back to their quarters!"

The Briton reached inside his tunic. "Your Eminence, if I may..." he pulled out the parchment he bore from Wimborne and held it out to the bishop. The prelate frowned and took the document. "It requests safe passage–"

"I can read!"

The reading was cursory and he tossed it on the floor.

"Take them away!"

"But–"

"Enough!" Guards marched them away while Milo turned to Donatus to speak in a low voice. Begiloc, bringing up the rear, was in time to see the animated conversation end in a handclasp.

The next day, on the trail through the Ardennes forest into the mountain foothills, Begiloc reflected on the events at Rems. That Bishop Milo had betrayed them was clear from the rope binding him and his men and from the hubris of Donatus. What was unclear was how a man of God might live such a life of sin without being brought to account. To disregard the request of Abbess Cuniburg in a display of unbridled arrogance meant the Bishop of Rems and Treves felt secure in his power. To defy God, Begiloc shook his head, mock the Pope, flaunt his concubines and exult in riches was to spurn the teachings of Christ. Why had the bishop allowed Donatus to get away with his deceit? What did he gain from letting the man go with his captives? Why did Donatus not kill them in the forest?

Before the gate of Somepin, three long and two short blasts of a horn responded to the same signal from Donatus. Led into the hall, their guards pushed them into a ring and forced them to sit while Donatus gave orders to a broad-shouldered, stocky warrior before retiring to his bedchamber. Servants brought logs for a fire, a welcome relief after the damp of the forest. Their captors let them speak so Caena vented his frustration by telling Begiloc what he intended to do to Donatus when he got free. To what purpose? To no avail had Begiloc chafed his wrists raw in an attempt to loosen his bonds.

Servants lit tapers on the walls as daylight faded. Food arrived for their captors and Begiloc reckoned they would not eat. He tried to ignore the growl of his stomach. To his surprise and relief, when the Franks ended their meal, the Saxons were permitted food two at a time. They left Caena and Begiloc for last so until he sank his teeth into the meat, he did not allow himself to hope. What pleasure to move his arms! Begiloc marvelled at this treatment, not only was the stew of tasty flesh unknown to him that Caena identified as squirrel but he washed it down with decent ale. Meal over, the guards bound them so they endured a sleepless night, how could they slumber tied together in this way?

The May morning brought a sunny day in Champany, a foretaste of summer. They tramped along the valley of the Aisne in unseasonable heat and Begiloc, who loved Nature, would have traded the swathes of lavender, lilac and purple wild flowers and all the butterflies and dragonflies for a beaker of water. Near the point where the Aire ran into the Aisne they passed a small stone church with a thatched roof that Begiloc thought as old as the valley itself. A spring gushed from the rock not far past the building but Donatus rode on.

"Water, for pity's sake!"

Donatus placed his horse between Begiloc and the fountain.

"Remember the chapel back there, Briton? Dedicated to St Oriculus who lived in it with his sisters." The Frank's expression awed, his hooked nose and long face displayed unsuspected fervour. "Ages past, when Attila led the Huns, they beheaded the three of them. Legend says the corpse of Oriculus picked up its head and carried it to the fountain to wash away the gore, before taking it back to a tomb prepared beforehand and lying down."

"I want a drink."

The lips of Donatus curled, "You'll go thirsty, for only the worthy may slake their thirst at this spring. Only the blessed few who see a cross of blood on the rock above the fount, otherwise the drinker falls sick for a year and a day–"

"I see the cross of blood!" lied Begiloc, desperate for water. He cared nothing to deceive the Frank and as for the rest, it was superstition and foolishness.

"Liar!" Donatus leant down from his horse to strike him across the mouth with the back of his hand. "You see no cross and I cannot risk you falling sick for a year. I need you in prime condition at the next moon for the slave market at Verden. We drink at a nearby spring."

Marching to the fountain, Begiloc dwelt on those words. Donatus meant to trade them as slaves: his original plan of St Denis. What about Bishop Milo? Why would the prelate let Donatus take away Christians and sell them to the infidel? It defied belief.

Thirst quenched, they trudged along the rising valley of the Aire and on the third day they entered the castle at Grandpré, where their captors replaced the ropes with shackles and they exchanged the fresh air of the forest for the vileness of a dungeon. The most notable contrast was between the comfortless cell and the wholesome food and drink supplied to them. Under no illusion the Comitis of Grandpré meant to sell them in prime condition, for Begiloc the days of imprisonment dragged by to the scansion of twenty scratches on the wall, measured by the weak light he glimpsed through a grating. Begiloc remembered the words of Donatus – *'in prime condition at the next moon'* – so, the slave market must be held every month. The night sky of their last encampment came to mind, then the moon was a waxing crescent; again he counted the scratched lines, twenty days, the full of the moon was due.

As calculated, their cell door ground open and Donatus came in flanked by guards, swords in hand. The Frankish leud looked around and bent to pick up a shackle, which he turned in his hand examining it like a precious artefact, before letting it drop with a clatter. Strolling over to Caena, he stood feet apart hands behind his back, saying, "In the morn, we leave for Verden," he mocked the Saxon, "my prize bull, I expect a good price at the slave market."

"Rot in Hell, bastard!"

With a smirk, Donatus kicked Caena in the ribs.

"You, I can understand," said Begiloc, "but the Bishop of Rems, I cannot. A man of God would never permit the sale of fellow Christians to the Moors. What tale did you spin to get us here?"

A hard, half-laugh-half-grunt, "How little you know, Briton. The only way to get gold into Neustria is through the slave trade. My lord, the bishop, loves gold more than any living being. His e-mi-nence ... ," the leud's voice was laden with sarcasm, "...did not hesitate to insist on half the profits from the sale. Indeed, he wants you all castrated. Castrati bring a higher price at auction."

The Frank loomed over Caena, and in a silky voice sneered, "When my lord bishop made his suggestion, I thought of your insolence. You will remember your empty threat in the forest when you were angry about your whore. How ironic! As it happens, you shall be the one castrated. Strange the weaving of fate, what you Saxons call the way of the wyrd, I believe. Your destiny, if you are lucky..." he paused for effect, "... is to end up in a harem or to stack bricks under a taskmaster's whip. Do not fret, they tell me the castration knife is sharp." The harsh laugh came again, "A prize bull that cannot be put to stud, oh, I pity you!"

A stream of curses from Caena failed to drown the slam of the door. The fear of emasculation filled hardened warriors with dread, causing them to swear, threaten and make futile plans to flee. The night brought tortured dreams of the horrific ritual – not one among them slept easy.

# CHAPTER 6

Three days through the Ardennes forest brought them to a wooded gorge, where they slithered down to a river of green water to which Verden owed its name.

The watercourse led to the town where they tramped through the filthy streets, rife with vermin and scavengers. One captor laid the flat of his sword across the back of a boy whose curiosity brought him within striking distance; stolid indifference met the ensuing string of obscenities.

Amid the bustle of a crowded square, two men hauled trimmed stones stacked on a wooden sled and cursed a man trading glass beads who impeded them. Another lugged a sack of turnips, tripping over a goose, causing it to honk and clatter into its companions, scattering them, the drover blaspheming.

While the armed men thrust through the crowd, Begiloc dwelt on the stark contrast between innocent commerce and the dark purpose behind their presence. The lack of curiosity in the captives meant slaves were a common sight.

Herded into a side street, they halted and Donatus gave orders to the thickset thegn who strode to the door, beating on it with his sword pommel. After a delay, a huge, muscular, bald-headed, swarthy-skinned figure filled the frame. Stripped to the waist, he wore purple silk pants laced at the ankles and emanated menace. This man fitted tales heard of giants from the east although Begiloc had never seen men from Constantinople. The thegn passed on his message and the colossus vanished to reappear with a man half his size with dark, oily hair and beard who, pressing his hands together in a steeple, bowed over them as he approached the leud.

A curt nod and arrogant tone greeted him, "Shmuel ben Chofni, here are eight slaves I intend to sell within two days–"

Changing his hand gesture to a clasp in front of his chest, the Jew, his voice as greasy as his locks, said, "...you come to Shmuel to increase their worth." On the hook-nosed, narrow face, Begiloc glimpsed the glint of greed reminding him of a raven set to alight on carrion.

The leud and the castrator haggled before Shmuel snatched the proffered money bag.

At the same instant, a shout of alarm alerted Begiloc who spun to see Caena had broken rank, running for all his worth down the narrow lane. A guard raised his spear, but Donatus thrust the man aside.

"Fool! I want my bull alive! Take my horse!" he yelled at the thegn. "After him! Bring him back sound of limb!" The Frankish horseman rode down Caena, hampered by arms bound behind his back. A collective groan from the captives greeted the blows that brought the warrior to his knees. The rider passed a rope between his wrists to drag him on his heels, bloodied, behind the horse through the mud and filth to his companions. Face a mask of spite, Donatus took leave of the Jew, with the recommendation to castrate Caena first.

"To assist at your little operation would be my pleasure, prize bull," he sneered, "but there is pressing business to attend to brooking no delay." One eye swollen and closed, hair matted with blood, the warrior said, "The day will come when I kill you and it will be a cruel death."

Begiloc believed the pain would mean nothing to Caena; indeed, the prospect of being castrated would daunt him less than the humiliation of being unable to strike back. The Saxon's next words confirmed as much: "By Christ, I will slay you! I swear I will!"

"Empty threats!" the Frank mocked wheeling his horse. Driven like cattle through the door into a dim interior, Begiloc peered around and despaired at the sight of six Turks, built like bullocks, carrying crescent-shaped swords held by a sash at the waist. Added to the men of Donatus, they swelled the number of guards to a score. Escape, as Caena had discovered, was impossible.

Shmuel ben Chofni clapped his hands. "We shall resume," he said, raising a finger to three men holding down another, the lower half of his body naked, face contorted in terror. Tears trickled over the high cheekbones of a Slav and though he tried to struggle his efforts proved in vain against the combined might of the Turks. Two, either side of a raised clay bed shaped to keep the victim in a reclining position, grasped a thigh, keeping the legs well apart. The third behind him, his arms wrapped about the waist of the Slav, pinned him back. A vertical groove ran along the centre bed under his buttocks and the dark stains and dried blood of the runnel betrayed its purpose. At the foot of the platform, a charcoal brazier smouldered, where an iron with a flat head glowed in the flames.

Shmuel ben Chofni strolled over and turned the youth's head to the left. Three fingers, he placed on his neck, pressing down on the jugular vein. After a moment, the Slav lost consciousness and the Jew picked up a small bronze sickle. With a deft sweep of the wicked blade, the youth became a eunuch. Horror gripped Begiloc at the sight of the seeping blood. There came a knock as Shmuel reached for the iron in the brazier. The Jew waved one hand at the huge Turk to answer the door while with the other he seized the handle of the flat implement. With care, he offered the ardent metal to cauterize the wound. The smell of burning flesh turned the stomach of Begiloc and he tasted bile in his throat. Above all, humiliation devoured at his entrails, a fight ending in manful defeat was one count, but to be demeaned, to lose one's manhood and be condemned to live on, made him fear for his reason. Somerhild wanted a brother for Ealric. It would never happen. The captor released the waist of the young man to carry him to a clay recovery bed. The sickened faces of the Frankish guards nonetheless promised no hope of aid.

Shmuel ben Chofni moved two men holding curved swords close to Caena.

"You shall be next according to the wishes of Lord Donatus," he spoke fast and clipped with a strange accent, "but you will experience the whole operation, for I will not press down on your neck."

The reaction of the Saxon was a slight widening of the eye not swollen by the beating.

"Remove his breeches and leggings," the castrator gestured to two other guards.

"Do your worst, Satan's turd!" Caena spat at the Jew.

Their move to obey was their last movement in life. A black-fletched arrow passed through the throat of the first Turk and another buried into the chest of his companion. No time to react. The guards fell to arrows loosed without respite from the gloomy recess of a doorway. Two of the Franks raised a shield, but soon, thighs transfixed, they dropped to their knees. Men, knife in hand, leapt forward to slit their throats, but one rushed over to Begiloc and cut his bonds.

"Meryn! How–?"

"Later! We must get away. Come on, bring your manhood with you!"

Stunned by events, Begiloc could only gape at the number of archers in action. The short, dark men severed the ropes binding his Saxons and urged them to gather all the weapons of the fallen. The archers' features suggested South Britons – almost kinsmen. How he longed to embrace them! Not a suitable moment, the frantic retrieval of arrows from their victims revealed their urgency. In haste, Begiloc wrested a weapon from the hand of a dead Frank as Meryn tugged at his arm, "Let's go!"

"Not so fast!" Caena boomed, curved sword in hand, "...unfinished work," he strode over to the beds by the wall, to a corner alcove covered by a drape. Sweeping it aside, he reached into the dark recess and hauled out the trembling figure of Shmuel ben Chofni.

"Please, please, I beg you! I'll give you coin, lots of money. Don't hurt me!"

"Servant of the Devil! Do you think I need your foul silver? You'll get the same mercy you reserved to me."
Sword raised above his head, the warrior sought revenge for himself as for the countless wretches subjected to emasculation over the years.

"Stay, Caena!" Begiloc hastened to grasp the arm drawn back for the blow.

"This wretch can show us the safest way out of town."
Hope surged in the face of the Jew who said, "Nobody knows the secret paths like Shmuel ben Chofni...," he rubbed his hands together under his chin, "...our people learned to live in shadows, for envy rots the bones and we must elude the green-eyed–"

"Enough! Your words weary me. It is decided. Lead us out of Verden!"
"How do you know we can trust this cur?" Caena spat, "Are we fuckin' dolts! I expect better judgement from you, Begiloc...the Jew lies!"

"What choice does he have? Betray us and he dies. Bind him! Give me his money bag!"

The resentment on Caena's face as he obeyed the order troubled him. Gaining the Saxon's acceptance had been no easy task.

*'He almost treats me as an equal! I'd better be right about the Jew.'*

A back door gave out on a narrow alley where Shmuel ben Chofni hurried them up strait steps, past buildings so close a man needed to turn his shoulders to pass until the maze of houses ended in nothing more than crude huts near a retting pond. The stench of decaying stems of flax assailed them. Hens clucked and pecked at the ground among the ragged women who heaved bundles from the slimy water and laid them out to dry. Nearer the dwellings, with flaxen sheaves draped like horsetails, some threshed dried stalks, others scrutched straw from the fibres and behind them, two more hauled a coarse wooden heckling comb. Next to them, dogs, all ribcage and little flesh, dozed in the sun.

Close to Shmuel, Begiloc surveyed the scene: beyond the pond three men sowed beans, woodland lay past the field, but how to reach its dense cover without being seen? Caena pushed forward to join him, "We can take them out with arrows."

"How so?"

"Dead men tell no tales."

"Dead women, neither," Begiloc hissed. "Do you mean to kill them all?"

"Dead bodies shout loudest," Meryn said, "whereas silver coins still wagging tongues. You should pay greater attention to my proverbs … sometimes they come in handy."

Shaking money from the Jew's bag, Begiloc handed them to the philosopher, "Send the nearest woman to the men in the field with these. You know what to tell them."

Deep in the woodland they picked up a trail. Luck was with them since Shmuel ben Chofni had led them to the west of Verden so they kept the direction intent on reaching Leoba at Sanctá-Menehilde.

Toward nightfall, they came to a clearing where the surrounding hornbeams dripped catkins. The dry ground sprouted ferns and Begiloc considered it as suitable a place for encampment as any, given an archer had found a stream not far away. The Britons kept themselves apart from the Saxons but shared what food they had, though they exchanged hard glances and few words owing to the entrenched enmity of the two races. Curiosity drove Begiloc to hear Meryn in spite of the tense situation.

"How did you find us in that hellhole?"

"The Church in Frankia is beset by problems what with false priests and all. It's like this ..." he said with the air of a man with a lengthy tale to tell, "... some of the bishops are not happy, including Bladald at Catalauns. They are tired of Bishop Milo, his whoring and his greed," he grinned, "men of God aren't supposed to revel in flesh ... mind, a revel appeals to me ... such a long time ..." the Briton decided to be serious, "They say he likes to hunt and his love of gold is common talk."

Begiloc stared into the fire and through clenched teeth said, "As we know to our cost."

"More than one bishop keeps a spy at his court to record his wrongdoings and report to their masters. It is said," he grimaced, "someone betrayed an agent and Milo had him flayed alive – the evil bastard!" Meryn played with the lowest bead in his beard. "It appears our Bishop Bladald keeps writing to Archbishop Boniface about Milo. The problem is, since his father and grandfather were bishops before him, he has influential friends.

"When a message arrived about your capture, Bladald sent the Lady at Sanctá-Menehilde a warning. Brother Robyn took money to Catalauns and our dear bishop hired these archers, on their way home to Britain. Mercenaries. Fought the Moors at Tours last year. And, what of this? Milo was one of Charles Martel's warriors. Word has it, a victory that saved us all from the infidel..." he half-rose, "... I must get one of them to tell us the tale of the battle. You never know, Begiloc, you might learn something and–" Begiloc seized him, pulling him down. "Now's not the time. Finish your story, we must plan for the morrow."

Sullen, Meryn's tone sharpened, "There's little to tell. I left my sick bed and led them to Verden. By the way, I'm still weak and shaky," but finding no sympathy, continued, "the best place to get news is an inn, that's where we found some of the men of Donatus," His voice mellowed, "drink loosens a man's tongue – they like their ale, I'll say that for them. They joked about the leud's prize bull," he flashed a wary glance at Caena, but the warrior heeded him not, "and laughed at how the Saxon with the big moustache was to be made eunuch that day ... it had to be him ... couldn't be anybody else, could it? Nobody else round here's so whiskery, Caena–"

In spite of apparent disinterest in the conversation the Saxon's gruff voice cut in, "Who else is worthy of that description? Only I'm built like a prize bull!"

"How did you find out where we were held?" Begiloc asked, ignoring the Saxon and growing impatient with his friend's drawing out of the account.

"I'm coming to that ... easy... a knife to the throat when one of them stepped outside and he was only too keen to tell us where to find the Jew... and you know the rest. Ah, one more thing..." Meryn unpinned the brooch from his cloak and handed it to Begiloc. "I know why you gave me this and I thank you," his eyes twinkled, "but keep it pinned as a charm to protect your bodily parts!"

The warmth he felt for his friend shone through, as he turned his mother's breastpin over in his hand, but then his face clouded.

"What's up?"

"Can we trust them?" he indicated the South Britons.

"You and I have nothing to fear, but there's little love lost between the men of Glywysing and the West Saxons. See how they keep themselves apart. While there's promise of gold there should be no problem. The Lady pledged more coin on our safe return. That's their leader, Cyndrwyn, the tall one in the yellow léine. Fought at Garth Malog he did, and at Pencon when the South Britons were victors over the Mercians of Aethelbald."

Relieved, Begiloc sighed at Meryn passing on details of the event without the usual digressions.

"Go, Meryn, fetch him over...no, wait! Better *we* go." Begiloc stood, stretched, yawned and in a casual manner sauntered over to Caena. The eyes of both groups on him, he clasped the warrior by the hand, lifting him to his feet. Heads close, Begiloc murmured a few words before all three walked to where Cyndrwyn and his men sat.

The subtle movement of hands positioned near knives did not escape Begiloc. The leader of the British mercenaries, a tall broad-shouldered man whose years of tensing a bow sculpted the muscles of his arms, laid a finger on his lips to suggest this visit gave him pause for thought.

In turn, Begiloc studied Cyndrwyn: the well-fulled cloth of the man's cloak, among Britons, such a braught was a sign of status and this green garment had a border of fine needlework in spiral pattern. Five-folded and pinned at the right shoulder with a silver brooch – it was worth at least two full-grown pigs.

Right hand raised in greeting, he spoke a blessing Gerens taught him as a boy:

*"Power of storm be yours,*
*Power of sun be yours,*
*Power of moon.*
*Goodness of sea be yours,*
*Goodness of earth be yours,*
*Goodness of heaven.*
*Each day be joy to you,*
*No day be sad to you,*
*Honour and gentleness."*

Begiloc and Meryn placed hand flat against the chest with Caena quick to copy. The effect of his words instant, the tension melted from the glade as an icicle vanishes in the sun.

The tall archer rose and clasped forearms with Begiloc, no hint of menace in his manner.

"Brother, welcome, from your speech you are from Dumnonia, am I right?"

The bonds of blood as tight as the rope binding them of late.

The Britons made room round the fire and though without strong drink, their lively exchanges were cheerful. Even Caena relaxed and the talk centred on the next day. Donatus would be in pursuit of revenge and while safe in the forest, the evident danger of the open plain before Sanctá-Menehilde troubled them. There, the Frank with his greater numbers, should overcome their resistance.

The South Britons had never been there so Begiloc explained the lie of the land and as he spoke an idea struck him. The Britons had retrieved their arrows at Verden, there was a chance Donatus knew nought of the presence of the mercenaries. Also, he hoped the flax workers remained silent. He outlined his plan and since no man could think of a better one, they retired for the night. For the first time of late, he slept a sound sleep, relieved they had a way forward.

Around mid-morning, they placed stones in a line across the track twenty paces ahead of their position. Next, they gagged Shmuel ben Chofni so he should not cry out a warning. The eight Saxons, Begiloc and Meryn waited, weapons ready, in a valley. Sharp-eyed Meryn noticed a glint of sun reflecting half a league back, with a nod conveying the tell-tale sign.

The enemy closed with two score men on foot led by Donatus on horseback. According to plan, the Frankish leud reined in, halting his men before the stones, scanning around, suspicion contorting his features. Satisfied, he called, "It is over, prize bull! How considerate of you to bring the castrator with you! Lay down your arms and we'll make a eunuch of you; otherwise, you will feed the ravens before night sets in."

"Mine is a better offer!" Caena stepped forward, voice confident, "Turn about and take your men home unscathed. Do not pass the stones or *you* will be carrion before nightfall."
Donatus turned in his saddle to smirk at his men, "Hark at him! I named the bull well! All muscle and no brain," he turned back to face Caena, "you can count, I suppose? See, five to your one ... better a live eunuch than a dead hero! Why spill blood?"

"Go home while you can!" The Saxon shouted.

With a roar, Donatus kicked his heels into his mount and charged. Archers rose up on either flank as they crossed the line to the hiss of falling arrows. Men screamed and Donatus's horse pierced four times, stumbled as its rider struggled to free himself. A second and third volley followed in quick succession and death from above only ceased when the survivors reached the Saxons, who were still outnumbered, but not when the South Britons, laying down their bows, poured down from the shallow ridges concealing them. The Franks found themselves penned in on three sides and the close fighting favoured the shorter swords of the Britons.

Over the din, a mixture of screams, the clash of iron, war cries and the wail of the dying horse, the voice of Caena rang out. "Leave him! He's mine!" The Saxon thrust aside a comrade and parried a blow from Donatus meant for the other. Donatus brought skill and nimble-footedness to contrast the might and fury of the blond warrior. The two men circled, Donatus skipped over bodies. Moving like a goaded bear, Caena stumbled over a dead Briton. The ensuing stagger should have been fatal to the Saxon, but he caught the leud off guard by spinning into an ungainly lunge. The Frank managed a half turn to protect his stomach. Even so the sword impaled his side. To free the blade, Caena kicked him away and scenting the weakness of the enemy redoubled his onslaught. Bloodlust pounded in his head leaving him unaware the battle was over.

"I've waited too bloody long for this hour! Prepare to die bastard!"

The words forced through teeth clenched tight in rage.

His companions, exhausted, leant on their swords but cheered every blow delivered by Caena. With grim satisfaction, Begiloc watched the energy of Donatus ebbing with his loss of blood, the slowing reactions, the movements of a beaten man. The end came when the shields locked and the might of the Saxon prevailed. The knees of the Frank buckled and to a roar from the watching victors, he sprawled on his back as Caena swooped merciless as a wolf on its prey.

"For Ingitruda!"

His sword transfixed the genitals of his enemy and buried into the earth. The blood-curdling scream was lost in the deep roar of vengeance from the throats of the Saxons, followed by swords beating against shields and "Caena! Caena! Caena!"

The face of the Comitis of Grandpré wracked in agony.

"Better a dying eunuch than a live Frank!" Caena mocked the leud's own words.

Placing a boot on his enemy, he tugged out the sword and plunged it where his foot had been a moment before. Donatus, deaf to the roar of the Saxons and Britons, writhed twice, blood coursing from his mouth.

Begiloc strode over to Caena, "Friend, it is well done. You made his end swift with more mercy than some threatened at Verden might have shown the cur. A fine victory! Two lost with four men wounded." With the dead on his mind, he turned to Cyndrwyn. "What of the bodies of our brothers? But stay! Cyndrwyn, you too are hurt!"

Pale, the tall Briton held his left arm to his chest, blood seeping through his fingers. "Nought but a scratch. Let us build a cairn over each," the archer said, "there are stones aplenty and custom is to show our dead the respect they never gained in this life."

The men hurried to gather rocks while Begiloc removed the gag from Shmuel.

"We should staunch the wound for he loses much blood. I possess no little skill in these matters but you must unbind me."

The Briton's eyes widened when having cut the bonds of the castrator, he asked for the knife.

"Have no fear..." the Jew said, "... cloth for bandages."

"I can do that," Begiloc bent over the nearest body and began to slice a long strip of the man's tunic.

"Good, a shorter length, to stem the flow of blood."

This he took as a tourniquet.

"Make a fist!"

A brief inspection of the wound and Shmuel beckoned Begiloc, "Come, help me, hold the cloth," he drew the gash together, bind it tight, just so," he pinched the cut, "here, again." Once tied off the bandage, Shmuel removed the restriction. "No sudden movements until we get to ..." he shrugged, "...wherever we are going."

"You'd better tend to the other wounded," Begiloc said, eying progress on the cairns as ravens and raptors wheeled lower, a kite alighted on the body of a Frank, beak plunging into an unseeing eye.

Not long after noon, Begiloc, Caena and Cyndrwyn stood in the great hall of the keep in Sanctá-Menehilde before Leoba, Girart and the dowager comitissa. The nun shook her head eyeing Begiloc with an expression of bewilderment and sorrow, "... and you say Aedre *wanted* to stay in Rems?" A decision inconceivable to her, "... you are quite sure?"

Begiloc spread his hands while Caena confirmed, "It's true, My Lady."

The gaze of Leoba clouded and she seemed distant, she bit her lip. "The wicked, foolish child! What words may I find to comfort her poor mother?"

"Do not fret so, the girl stayed of her own free will. No harm will befall her," said Lady Albemarle.

The nun tossed her head, her tone testy, "No bodily harm. Aedre is seduced by Satan. We should worry about her eternal soul. Alas! The Evil One takes on many forms, even that of a bishop."

"That false priest!" Lord Girart said, "One of many wrongs in this land. King Theodoric is a prisoner in the Abbey of Chelles, the Mayor of the Palace does as he wishes and like Milo, his favourites are free to abuse their power." Frowning, he peered at Begiloc, "Tell me, what happened on the way back from Rems."

When he recounted the battle and the death of Donatus, he caught the exchange of glances between the comitis and his mother. Leoba spoke first, "I expect the torments of Hell await the Comitis of Grandpré. We must pray his successor will be a better man. What is this," her gaze fell upon the blood-soaked bandage of Cyndrwyn, "you are hurt?"

"It is nought. The Jew patched it up."

"The Jew?"

So Begiloc, with no little shame, recounted the meeting with Shmuel ben Chofni and details of the place of castration, to the outrage and horror of the dowager comitissa and the nun.

Lord Girard raised a fist, "For his sins, the castrator will hang from the gate tower."

Leoba laid a hand on the arm of the nobleman.

"Stay, my lord, I beg you, let him be brought here. I wish to speak to this man."

Acquiescing, Girart beckoned a servant to fetch the captive. Grave and apologetic, he said, "You must understand, much as it would please us were you to remain longer, it would be far wiser for you to leave in the morning."

The fleeting expression of relief on the face of the dowager did not escape Begiloc.

"How so?" asked Leoba.

"You made an enemy of Bishop Milo, liege lord of Donatus," said Girart. "No-one defies him with impunity, he chases down enemies as remorselessly as he hunts boar," he said, ill-concealed admiration in his voice, "he insists on being alone to finish off the beast. That's the measure of your adversary. The death of Donatus means any friend of yours is an enemy of Milo."

The words of the comitis captured the attention of Begiloc. Unsurprised the bishop was an inexorable foe after their encounter in Rems, neither did he underestimate him, given the arrogance he displayed casting aside Abbess Cuniburg's sealed letter. So the ingenuousness of Leoba's next utterance astounded him. The nun folded her arms across her chest and lifted her chin.

"My cousin, Archbishop Boniface will protect us from the wrath of this Godless priest. Indeed, I denounced his sinfulness in a missive to his eminence."

To Begiloc, the nun's faith in her Church was breathtaking.

*'Does she think a letter has any force? She can denounce his sinfulness till all her quills are blunted, but it won't change a thing.'*

Lady Albemarle fiddled with a silver brooch set with garnets and as she spoke she stared past Leoba into space.

"Sister, your cousin can be of no succour hereabouts. The best course of action is to flee. A few precious days will pass before news of the death of Donatus reaches Rems. Use this time well. Heed me now," at last her eyes, full of concern, met those of Leoba, "move with all haste."

Two guards entered the hall with Shmuel to stand in front of Lord Girard. Of his own volition, the Jew knelt.

"For my part," Girart's voice was gruff with menace, "you would swing for your crimes, but this lady will speak with you, so get up!"

"A simple hanging's too good for the vermin," Caena muttered.

Trembling, the castrator rose still looking at the floor, but at the words of the comitis, from under his brow, he squinted at the nun.

"How came you to practise so loathsome a trade?"

At the sound of her gentle voice, Shmuel found the courage to raise his head.

"I fear it is a long tale, Lady."

"Then the sooner you start the better."

"My age is measured by thirty and nine summers and I was born in Toledo when King Egica ruled. My mother was a *musta'ribun*, an Arab Jew, and her father a physician who owned many texts." At this, Leoba smiled in approval and the castrator continued, "My father learnt to read Arabic and taught himself to be a healer so we were comfortable in Toledo. All was well until the king brought in harsh laws against the Jews, citing a conspiracy. Many were enslaved, above all those who had converted to Christianity."

Shmuel's wary eyes darted to Girart. Reassured he had not given offence, he continued, "I was a babe in arms when my parents fled Toledo and made a home in Narbon. The brother of my father instead went farther north and took his family to Verden."

"The connection with Verden," murmured Leoba.

"In Narbon, the Christians tolerated us because of our knowledge of healing and I worked as a physician with my father up to his death. In my twenty-fifth year, Umayyad troops under Al-Sahm ibn Malik al-Khawlani took Narbon. It is still part of the Emirate of Cordoba."

"How did the infidel Arabs treat you Jews?" Lord Girard's tone was laconic and Begiloc was sure that without the interest of Leoba, at this hour the tongue of Shmuel would be swollen, purple and lolling from the mouth of a corpse.

"At first, the Jews greeted the Arabs as liberators, but soon they introduced the jizya ..."

"Ji-zya?" Girart stumbled to form the sound of an unfamiliar word.

"A tax, to be paid by hand and brought on foot so he who pays lowers himself, accepting the humiliation of the conquered. Easy enough for Jews but hard for Christians. The jizya began as a fifth of our coin, rendered by the new moon, soon a third and the Arabs overestimated what a physician could earn. My mother, may she have a long life, pressed me to leave Arbūnah—"

"Arbūnah?" Leoba frowned.

"Arab for Narbon. I left by night for Verden to the family of my uncle ten springs past and—"

"Did you bring those texts with you?"

"No, mistress, they are in Arbūnah. I had to move in haste, the books are heavy."

"Of course," Leoba pouted.

"Well, in Verden my practice began well, but as often happens, they blamed the Jews for a disease that took hundreds of people. The persecutions started and they captured me as I sought to escape, so they took me before Bishop Milo and I believed my end had come, but he showed interest in my skills. Many slaves died at castration and it cost him. In short, he promised protection if I agreed to work as a castrator – eunuchs are worth double ..." Shmuel held out both hands palm upward in front of him and bowed his head, "What choice had I?"

"Milo doubled his money by sending slaves to you," Lord Girart said.

The Jew explained, "I have ... er ... *had* ... not to charge for those he sent, but to pay a tithe on my earnings from others," he looked from Leoba to Girart, eyes pleading. "The rest you know."

Lord Girart said to the nun, "Now we have heard the tale of this wretch – all gall and wormwood – what will you have me do with him?"

Leoba stared at Caena. From the attitude of the warrior, he had not forgiven what happened at Verden, malice in his tone, he growled, "I await your orders, My Lady."

One word from her, Begiloc was sure, and the Saxon would send Shmuel to meet his God. Instead, she smiled, "Cyndrwyn, hold out your wounded arm."

Surprised, the Briton obeyed. "Shmuel, remove the bandage!"

The Jew paled, "B-but it is most unwise, mistress."

"How so?"

"First we must prepare scalding water and a basin of wine, to clean and to wash out the wound and honey to soothe it, fresh bindings to staunch the blood so it may begin to heal ..."

"There!" cried Leoba, "There speaks the physician!" She pleaded with Lord Girart, "We cannot kill this man, his knowledge is precious. No nonsense like drinking the water used to wash a saint's skull...or eating a candle burning at his shrine! I beg you, let me take Shmuel ben Chofni into my service."

The Jew sank to his knees and bent his head. To the surprise of the nun, he kissed her shoe.

"Shmuel ben Chofni is your loyal servant, mistress," he crawled backwards and rose, bowing several times.

The noblewoman turned to the Frankish lord, "Well?"

"Let it be so!"

Leoba clapped her hands in delight and bestowed a smile on Girart for his wonderful gift: a soul saved, good supplanting evil.

"There will be much to discuss about medicine and those texts. Though I shall not force you to take our religion, I insist on your knowledge of it. Your first task is to heal the arm of Cyndrwyn and tend to the other wounded."

Lord Girart gestured at the two soldiers, "Provide everything he needs."

The Jew bowed his way backwards until the guards spun him round and out of the chamber. When the door closed, the dowager *comitissa* embraced Leoba, "You are beautiful and wise, little sister."

"You are kind, Lady, but what wisdom I possess tells me we must leave at dawn. We cannot endanger you. Such would be poor thanks for your hospitality. The servant of Satan will seek notice of our whereabouts and we must be long gone when he comes."

# CHAPTER 7

Fearful of the reputation of the nun entering the kitchen, the scout pushed a maid off his knee. The young woman, her face red, adjusted her dress and scurried off to work. Ignoring the two women clearing wood ash from the huge ovens, Leoba scowled at the fleeing girl. The ten flat barley loaves lined up on the table filled the room with a delicious fresh-baked aroma but did nothing to improve the mood of the noblewoman.

"They told me I would find you here."

At her sour tone, Begiloc and Meryn exchanged a grin while Caena stared wolf-like at the bread.

"My Lady, how can I be of service?"

"What way does our journey take us?"

"Through the forest to the north-west runs the ancient paved way. At sixteen leagues lies Valleroy–"

"Would you take us whence we came?" Begiloc interrupted, "What of the danger?"

Leoba raised an eyebrow.

"Well, the road passes through open countryside to the south of Verden, with no place to hide." He looked from one to another. "Should we strike out in that direction, I and my companion...where *is* the layabout?...do not know the lie of Burgundy and beyond in Swabia. The journey is much longer."

"Ay, seeing off an untrained band of robbers is one thing, another is facing troops from Rems," said Caena.

"What's at Valleroy?"

The guide glanced at Begiloc, "The river, the Orne, and it will take us to the east where it joins the Moselle and on north to Remich–"

"Sixteen leagues, a three-day march," Meryn said to Leoba, "we can arrive before Milo. The news of Donatus cannot reach him before two sunsets and he knows not what direction we take."

"Ay, but he will have spies out," Caena cut in. "How far is it from Rems to the river?"

"The bishop will use horses," the guide sighed, "he can catch us."

In the sudden silence, Leoba tapped her foot, clapped and issued orders.

"Everyone out until we finish and close the door behind you!"

They scampered to obey, except a plump woman in a stained white dress, who stood her ground, a bunch of purple wild carrots in her hand.

"You are the cook, are you not? And what wonderful food you prepare! Your kitchen will not be occupied for long, my child. A matter of a few minutes."

A radiant smile from the nun removed the surliness of the woman, who grinned, her eyes almost disappearing into chubby cheeks. She bobbed a curtsey, an ungainly affair, before laying down her vegetables and closing the door with exaggerated care.

Leoba lowered her voice. "Nobody must hear this. Only Lady Albemarle need know. On the morn, we leave at first light to the south-west."

The guide made to protest, but the nun held up a hand.

"Out of eyeshot of Sanctá-Menehilde, we shall double back."

Now Leoba held their attention. She turned to the Frank, "Know you the abbey in the Argonne forest?"

"Ay, Beaulieu Abbey. A mile over two leagues away."

"You will lead us," her eyes shone. "When I knew we should come to Sanctá-Menehilde, I determined to visit the hermitage of Saint Rouin. Chrodingus, a virtuous Irish monk at the monastery of Tholey, they elected him superior and–"

"My Lady, we cannot lose time visiting a religious house," Begiloc cut in.

Leoba raised her chin.

"As I said, we must be astute and you will hear me out!" She continued unperturbed, "...visitors from all parts disturbed the saint for consultation so he went to Verden to the holy bishop Paul–"

"No relation to Milo, then," Meryn quipped at once wondering if he had overstepped the mark with the venerable lady, though her smile and shake of her head indicated he need not worry, she had warmed to the light-hearted Briton.

"Indeed not! After two years with the bishop, Chrodingus went to Rome," she sighed, "oh, how I would love to visit *caput mundi* and the Holy Father ... no matter! Upon his return, the saint gained permission to establish a house in the forest and founded the abbey. We shall go there!"

Begiloc nudged Caena and, in unspoken accord, the Saxon tried to dissuade her, "We'll lose precious time lingering at a monastery, to the advantage of our enemy. My Lady, I, Caena, have fought near to home and far away. I understand the mind of a soldier...if you will hear–"

She turned her back on him.

"King Childeric protected the saint," the nun continued serenely, "he governed the abbey for thirty years before retiring to a solitary place. At this hermitage, I shall pray for his intercession." Their bemused faces made her smile, "You see, as simple as that!"

The mouth of Meryn dropped open and Caena rolled his eyes.

"We will make our devotions over his bones. Thus will the servant of Satan be confounded. So that's settled!" Leoba strode to the door, but stopped, a thoughtful expression on her face, "Should we take the Britons with us?"

Meryn looked doubtful and Caena leant closer to their leader to speak in a quiet voice, receiving agreement before Begiloc said, "No sense to it! Our hope to get to Austrasia depends on evasion as we cannot fight the bishop. A band of British archers will not save us, let alone the cost of keeping them on."

"Then it is decided!"

The nun pushed the door open, "You may all come in!"

Upstairs in the hall, awed, Begiloc admired the personality of the noblewoman dwarfing that of the battle-hardened Cyndrwyn as she paid him off. In spite of the mercenary towering over her, haggling, the sum lowered sending him away beguiled and discontented.

Later in the day, she gathered her nuns and monks and dispatched Brother Robyn to fetch Begiloc. The red-haired monk wore an enigmatic expression, "The Lady Leoba summons you and all your men to the chapel. This evening she decides for Compline." He smiled at the ill-disguised irritation on the face of the Briton. "Begiloc I believe you are more than half-pagan! I reckon Leoba wishes us to recite *In manus tuas, Domine* for our safekeeping in the days ahead."

"By Thunor's hammer! I'll go along with that!" he said with a hearty laugh and a clap on the back of the monk.

On the second day of their stay at Beaulieu, much to the consternation of Begiloc, Leoba said, "I am going alone to the hermitage. Father Abbot tells me it is deserted with no material comforts. Better so. Mortification of the flesh aids prayer and we need divine assistance. I shall return in three days."

"My Lady, is that wise? The forest harbours wild beasts and worse ... let me accompany you as a guard," Begiloc protested.

"Alone. That's an end to the matter!"

For hours, he imagined her mauled by savage creatures. Had Brother Robyn chanced by at the right moment, he would have been surprised to find him attempting prayer.

On the third morning, the rain beat down. A messenger from Sanctá-Menehilde arrived at Sext, his cloak sodden. In the absence of Leoba, he reported to Begiloc with news as bleak as the weather. The men of Bishop Milo had taken Lord Girart to Rems to answer in person to his Eminence while horsemen had followed the false trail. Lady Albemarle de Roussillon sent a warning to trust no-one and to remain hidden.

Leoba returned pale and fatigued before Vespers, her clothes dripping water on the stone floor of the abbey.

"Sister, off with you to the kitchen to dry out and to break your fast," said Abbot Aubert.

After the service, Begiloc, Caena and Meryn received a summons to the abbot's cell where Leoba, the abbot and his chamberlain awaited them. Distinguished from the others by its size, the room boasted a corner hearth, the fire unlit. A bed covered with a sheepskin ranged along the wall, at its foot a prie-dieu, on it a curled parchment with writing in Latin. Above this, a cross hung from a nail. On the other side stood a solid wooden table with a jumble of papers, bottles, wax and candles and around it, chairs with woven straw seats where they sat. Leoba spoke first, "My prayer and contemplation in the hermitage inspired me."

In spite of her confident words, she frowned, worried.

"My Lady?" Begiloc sensed her unease.

The nun stared in his direction but her eyes focused beyond.

"Do you think, Begiloc, Donatus ever told the false bishop about the nuns?" She did not wait for a reply, adding, "Sure, he has Aedre, but she'd never betray us."

Whatever her meaning, he failed to grasp it.

As of habit, tucking stray hair into her wimple, Leoba said, "Father, we shall require help to escape the clutches of our enemy."

"My child you need but ask," said Abbot Aubert, a man in his fortieth year with a voice in harmony with his mild features, a weak chin and fleshy lips under a straight nose but with large blue and gentle eyes.

"Well, the loan of two monks," she ticked off on her fingers, "the statue of Saint Rouin, an ox-cart, a sarcophagus, eighteen habits, a score of candles – I shall pay for them ..." her voice tailed off.

The abbot appeared nonplussed, "My word, quite a list, but the effigy of our Saint ...?"

"A procession by the light of tapers. At night."

The eyes of Leoba glazed over but then, all briskness, she said, "The nuns shall wear the habit of a monk. Do you see why I worry about Milo knowing? The cowls will hide their long hair. Also, Begiloc, you and your men and the guides will put on the clothing of the brothers, but you will carry knives, hidden away, in case...to scare off robbers. Weapons, shields, clothes, the nuns' vestments, my books, in the stone coffin ...," her words came in a torrent, "... the sarcophagus and the Saint go on the ox-cart and we travel along the old road. The way will be easy to follow by candlelight and the light of the moon. How is the moon?"

At first, no-one answered, because the abrupt silence came while thoughts dwelt on her plan.

Meryn fiddled with his beard as though the threaded wisps were seers of the weather.

"It is waxing, My Lady, so if the rain ceases there will be moonlight, but what of the daytime? At ox pace, Valleroy is three days away."

"By day, we must remain concealed."

"But the statue," the abbot frowned running his tongue over his lips, "is the Saint necessary?"

Leoba placed a reassuring hand on his arm, "The effigy and the habits of the monks will be back after seven sunrises. The Saint will protect us in heaven and on earth. Should the so-called bishop learn of a night-time procession and send men to verify, with the Saint and the stone coffin we have an excuse to be travelling. We shall say we are transferring the Saint's bones to another monastery for some reason," she ended on a lame note, opening her eyes wide in a silent plea to Abbot Aubert. "Father, may we bear a parchment with your seal? We can show it if challenged!"

The scheme of Leoba astonished Begiloc – so improbable it might work – seeing the doubt of the abbot, he added his voice to forestall a refusal.

"Father, we cannot lie here like a fox in his den. All these mouths to feed, we must not profit by your goodness." The abbot inclined his head at the compliment and the Briton asked, "Is there a religious house near Valleroy?"

After a hesitation, he said, "A double monastery, Comitis Villa, nearby to the south. My cousin, Himiltrude is in charge of the nuns. Close to Auboué, less than a league to the east of Valleroy."

"Perfect!" murmured Leoba.

With a thin smile, the abbot regarded her, "We exchange messages, I am in regular contact. I can inform her of your needs."

"Thank you Father, and the parchment...put down we are taking the bones of Saint Rouin to cure your relative who is ill. Is it not a fine idea? May the Lord keep her in rude health and pardon our deceit! In this way, we have the ideal excuse for our journey. In your message, will you ask the monks to find us two river boats for four days hence? They must be discreet at all costs."

The abbot sighed, "All this will be done," his face solemn, he said, "on no account may you translate the bones of our Saint, whose rest shall not be disturbed. The statue is another matter."

"In any case, the sarcophagus must be empty. I have stated its purpose. Father, I offer you my gratitude, my prayers and blessings on this House. We must gather everything we need. Prepare the men Begiloc, we leave before Matins. Come there is much to do!"

Leoba rose, as ever graceful, turned to the chamberlain but he anticipated her, "I shall arrange for the habits and the candles to be brought to the west range as soon as possible," he bowed, "we will take the statue of Saint Rouin to the cart and..." he turned to the warrior, "... you can bring six men to the crypt, to choose a sarcophagus and thence carry it to the stables."

"I shall prepare your parchment and a message," the abbot rummaged through the clutter.

Next day, they set off before Matins, the air heavy with damp but no rain. The Franks used the stars as a guide, making slow progress through the forest, since the moonlight, when not obscured by passing clouds, filtered through the trees and the light cast by their candles only served to avoid crashing into the cowled figure ahead.

A while before dawn, they came upon the prey of a wolf pack. Bloody, shredded meat the remains of a red deer calf and many in the procession averted their eyes. At dawn, still in the forest with no idea of how far they had come, Leoba called a halt in a clearing and gave instructions. The scouts would determine the way and the distance to the Roman road, the soldiers would hunt for fresh meat while the monks and nuns would carry out tasks such as bringing water from the nearest stream, gathering firewood and making the camp as comfortable as possible, because they would have to sleep in the afternoon.

Before noon, the guides returned with the news they were two hours from the road. Soon after, Begiloc returned with a doe over his shoulders, ordering it skinned and cleaned. They spit roasted it while monks carrying brim-full water skins led back the ox from drinking at the stream.

The weather improved as the day lengthened, not that many of the group were awake to appreciate it. After nightfall, they set off, pleased to reach the paved road and to follow its undulations through open countryside. Candles lit, the weak moonlight sufficient to ease progress, the monks and nuns chanted psalms.

In high spirits, Meryn grinned at Begiloc, "It's not fair! The sisters get to dress as brothers and you don't get to wear a wimple. You'd make a fine nun, Sister Begiloc!" For a while, the banter and laughter from the warriors accompanied the creaking cart with its painted wooden statue swaying like a sailor on a gentle sea, but soon the cowled figures, the candles and the psalms took effect. The Saxons lapsed into silence, impressed by the immensity of the sky, the infinite stars and the incantation of the sacred song. Overwhelmed by the mystery of existence, Begiloc felt minuscule.

At dawn, the scouts reported woodland south of the road and led the party across rough ground, in spite of the hard going for the ox-cart. Across a small valley, where a stream cascaded over its rocky bed, lay meadows. As the sun rose over the horizon tinting the land with delicate hues, a pair of labourers appeared on a pasture. Judging by the outstretched finger, he had spied the strange procession.

"Hellfire!" Begiloc cursed, "Another minute and we'd have been hidden among the trees. We've travelled this far and only they have seen us." As the day wore on and nobody came to pry in the woods, his assurance grew. Time passed in prayer, hunting, cooking and sleeping until at night, they regained the road.

Well into the march, above intoned psalms, came the sound of hoof beats and the sight of bobbing torches. Overtaking them, the riders fanned out to surround the party. As arranged, Brother Munderic, one of the two Beaulieu monks, threw back his cowl and halted the procession. The lead rider dismounted and approached him, firebrand held aloft to examine the features of the brother, voice harsh and heavy with suspicion, saying, "Who are you and where are you bound?" The next few moments would prove critical.

The Frankish monk was not cowed, "Who wants to know?"

The others in the procession, heads bowed, did not move. The hand of Begiloc sought out the weapon under his habit but it was futile.

*'What use a knife against armed horsemen?'*

"These lands fall within the jurisdiction of the Bishop of Rems. You must account for your presence at night."

Brother Munderic gestured to the red-haired monk and said to the commander, "You will need this."

Robyn handed the rolled parchment to the officer who studied the seal with narrowed eyes. Making no attempt to break it open, he thrust the document at Munderic, then drew his sword, "I am a soldier," he said, "I can remove your head with one blow but I cannot read. Now..." he raised the point of the blade to the throat of the monk, "... answer my question."

The brother shrank back and swallowed hard.

"We are from the Abbey of Beaulieu, near Sanctá-Menehilde, on our way to the abbey at Comitis Villa."

He raised a finger over his shoulder careful not to make a sudden movement, "As the parchment explains, these are the mortal remains of our founder Saint Rouin and his statue. With God's grace, they will cure the Mother Superior at Comitis Villa, who lies ill; the Abbess Himiltrude is a relative of our Father Abbot–"

The Frank sheathed his sword and grabbed Munderic by the arm dragging him to the cart. In the flickering torchlight, Begiloc peered around, noting some of the horsemen had drawn their swords, steadying their steeds with their knees. Their leader passed the torch to the monk before hauling himself up on the cart.

*'Damnation, if he decides to open the sarcophagus we are lost!'*

The officer reached down to regain the brand before holding it close to the coffin lid. Begiloc considered action, but what? In spite of the freshness of the night, he felt the sweat on his brow. What happened next shocked him.

The voice of Brother Munderic rang out deep and strong. "Open it! Let Saint Rouin greet the air of his beloved Neustria!

For more than two score and ten years, he has lain undisturbed since his death. Kneel brothers, let us pray!"

As he knelt with the others, head bowed, Begiloc indeed prayed, supplicating the scheme of Munderic should work – that the Frankish warrior would not open the coffin.

With a creak of the wagon, the officer jumped to the ground, hoisting Munderic to his feet. "I shall not be the one to disturb the slumber of a saint," he crossed himself, "but answer to my satisfaction."

"Ask, my son."

"At dawn, you were seen entering the woods. Why do monks travel at night and not by day?"

Begiloc caught his breath but Brother Munderic smiled.

"Know you not the life of our holy founder? A hermit who vowed never to see the light of day in penance for the sins of his youth. The last years, he spent deep in a forest and only left his cell at night. To honour his wishes, we travel by night and by day we seek the cover of trees as was the wont of the blessed Saint," he smiled, "sure, it slows us no end, but what *can* we do?"

He spread his arms and sighed.

The Frank frowned, "It explains why monks would hide in woodland," his tone still suspicious, he stepped forward two paces, "You," he pointed to a brother, "Reveal your face!" The monk turned, Begiloc bit his lower lip, but then relaxed.

*'The Saint is indeed our protector!'*

None other than Brother Theodard, the other Beaulieu monk, stared at the officer who asked, "Where are you from?"

"From Beaulieu Abbey, but in Sanctá-Menehilde was I born."

No mistaking the tongue – Frankish.

The soldier approached his steed grazing by the road near the head of the procession, but stopped, spun round and pointed, "You!" he indicated another monk, "Where are you from?"

No time for Begiloc to worry, the firm reply came in a Frankish accent, "I was born in Quentovic and entered Beaulieu two winters past," thus spoke one of the two guides.

*'Thank God he doesn't betray us – he swore on the Holy Book.'*

The officer mounted and spoke to another horseman, "All Franks, we must search elsewhere."

Munderic raised his hand to make the sign of the cross.

"Bless you, my son. May the Lord be with you."

The warrior wheeled his mount and the others followed whence they came.

Meryn nudged Theodard next to him, "Is it true about the Saint only coming out at night?"

The monk laughed, "Badgers come out at night! A hermit Rouin may have been, but we must thank the quick wits of Munderic for that tale!"

The guide turned to Meryn, "... and express our gratitude to the Blessed Rouin the officer did not ask me to uncover my face ... a monk without a tonsure!"

Another cowled figure stepped forward, flinging back her hood in a flurry of golden hair, Leoba revealed her beauty without a wimple. She ignored Meryn muttering about werewolves and said, "Let us rejoice in our salvation! Psalm 94 ... 'Come, let us exult in the Lord. Let us shout in joy to God, our Saviour ...' " and the monks and nuns raised their voices in song: *"Venite, exultemus Domino, iubilemus Deo salutari nostro..."*

Though Begiloc had no Latin and he listened without understanding, he shared the sentiment of the line the nun had translated.

Early morning found them safe inside the monastery of Comitis Villa. As much as Leoba must have longed to put on her own clothes, she took the time to instruct Munderic and Theodard to wait one day before journeying back to Beaulieu, there to bear testimony to the miraculous recovery of Abbess Himiltrude thanks to the intervention of Saint Rouin. The object of the spurious miracle beamed at Leoba. She had pale, clear skin and the blue veins in her delicate hands stood out as she took those of Leoba.

"My dear child, what an adventure! Come!" The lines around her light grey eyes crinkled, "The prior awaits us and I believe he has news." She linked arms with the nun and led her through the cloister to that of the monks, where a rotund, ruddy-faced monk conversed with Brother Robyn.

They fell silent when the nuns approached, the prior bowing to Leoba.

"Welcome, our poor house is at your disposal."

He stared at the nun in her oversized monk's habit, head uncovered, and at the warrior brothers.

"I am sure you will all wish to change, refresh yourselves and rest and though my news can wait, I cannot. I suffer from the sins of over-keenness and impatience!" his face lit up.

*'Like a huge pompous cherry.'*

"I received a fulsome message from our dearest brother at Beaulieu, in which he asked me to provide for two boats to undertake an arduous journey. Well, this man in Valleroy..." and he continued to explain the arrangement, causing the Briton to think if the prior had other sins they paled before his pride. In the end, the patience of the saintly Leoba snapped. She pursed her lips and tapped her foot.

"Are you telling me the boats are being *built!* When *will* they be ready?" Begiloc flinched at the sharp-honed voice.

Hurt, the prior murmured, "These things take time–"

"My Lady," Brother Robyn intervened, "Our Heavenly Father moves in mysterious ways. Who knows whether it's for the best? We are safe and as the days pass our enemy will grow more confounded and less vigilant so when the time comes, we shall move away safe in the boats."

The prior beamed, "All is well! Off to the lavatory followed by the refectory, you will feel better, ready for Terce."

The days turned into weeks and months while summer slipped away to the calm but demanding rhythm of monastic life. In contrast, Begiloc insisted on twice-daily weapon training outside the monastery gates, by no coincidence held at the time of Sext and None. The chance to escape liturgy for any length of time made the knocks and bruises, the sweat and fatigue worthwhile to the Saxons.

On the morning of 14 August, between Prime and Terce, a dragon ate a slice of the sun – so Begiloc believed as a child. Now, he stared in awe as the world around him grew dimmer. Nobody in the monastery would free the sun with wild and mad actions to scare away the wyvern, but as he told Brother Robyn, who joined him to stare at the sky, it bode ill. True to his Celtic blood, in hushed tones, the superstitious Begiloc stated the eclipse foretold crop failures, maddened livestock, caused outbreaks of pestilence and war and the demise of a ruler.

Robyn laughed. "Anything else, Briton? Haven't you forgotten the end of the world?"

"You can laugh," Begiloc ran his fingers over the stubble on his chin, "but believe me, it's a harbinger of doom," his voice trailed away as grey gloom shrouded the earth and the sun disappeared.

Brother Robyn said, "One of the Church fathers, Gregory of Nyssa, tells us the whole universe is full of darkness and light and this obscurity is made to cast its shadow by the body formed by the earth ..."

"Well, that's as may be, my friend, but I hope our fate depends not on its foretelling. I want to be as far from Bishop Milo as possible and we are trapped in this monastery."

"Sure, there are worse places to be confined ..." and as he spoke the sun revealed a segment of light, "... see, a promising sign for us," he clapped Begiloc on the back, "be of good cheer, we shall be on our way in no time."

In truth, the monk did not expect his words proved true so soon. After two days, news came from Valleroy that the boats were ready. Preparations made, the next morning, they attended Prime, then partook of a light breakfast of bread and mead.

This time, no ox slowed them. Content to shoulder shield and spear, Begiloc strode through the monastery gates. The boats awaited them at Valleroy and he should have been cheerful; instead, he reflected on the words of the abbot about pluralism. Their route would take them upriver toward Treves, the seat of Milo's second see. It bothered him.

As they pushed off from the bank of the River Orne, Begiloc spotted a lone rider watching from a hilltop before he vanished. This glimpse of the foe brought to mind the eclipse. Bishop Milo too blotted out light, casting a long shadow of misfortune that threatened to pursue them to the very confines of Christendom.

# PART TWO

## CHAPTER 8

*Anno Domini 736, March*

Leg dangling over the wall, the other bent at the knee, Begiloc sat against a stone arch staring at the cloister well.

*'Why me? Three years away! Bloody missionaries. Abbess Leoba. Resolute? Nay, stubborn! Thought I'd find Denehard and Lull, plead my case and be back in Wimborne. They're away evangelising, sending demons back to Hell.'*

An idle brush of his hand swept a centipede off the wall.

*'All this Church business – new bishoprics in Thuringia. Archbishop Boniface behind it. Consecrated another monk, Burchard, like Robyn from Malmesbury. Made him Bishop of Würzburg. Typical bad luck! Bishop's a close friend to Denehard. Made him his chaplain. So I'm here and he's there!'*

Drawing his hand-seax from his belt, Begiloc sighed.

*'What about Lull? Off to a monastery up north at Fritzlar. Robyn says the abbot's a saint. Wigbert! Another flaming missionary from Wessex – as if I bloody care! I'm trapped here. Why does everyone get what they want: Leoba, Denehard, Lull? But not me!'*

He picked at a piece of loose mortar.

*'Is it their relationship with God? I can't pray but I've done my duty. The word of Christ, taken to the villages of Hesse at sword point, with Meryn's axe and the might of my Saxons, an iron ring around the missionaries to defy the heathen gods and desecrate their groves. Conversion by coercion not conviction!*

*Village elders baptised under threat from landowners, their faith determined by allegiance.'*

The piece of mortar came away and he tossed it on the grass.

*'I've done everything asked of me. Helped erect churches. Escorted workmen to build monasteries in the wild. Fought off raiders. They keep me here those young men from Wessex. All ardent faith. Come to convert their German "cousins". The irony! Most of them bereaved of family. Their passion in their mission but no-one cares about my wife and son. What I'd give to hold Somerhild!'*

Another sigh and he pinched the bridge of his nose.

*'How are they? Ealric will be ten.'*

Only natural to worry about them since hereabouts the winter had been hard on the villagers working the land around the River Tauber. Without succour from the monastery more would have died. In desperation, owing to the poor harvest some had eaten damp grain tainted by fungus. The results, men and women paralysed, dead with stretched blue skin after fever wasted the limbs and burned the internal organs.

Acorns destined to swine instead ground for bitter bread. When you're starving there's little choice, he supposed. Without them, few of the villagers' pigs survived, weakened by lack of food. When the ague scourged the valley, the old and the very young were the first souls to leave their earthly remains to the winding sheets.

Wispy clouds reminding him of home swept by high over the cloister. So little news of his family seeped through from England. His gloom deepened.

*'At least I got new breeches from Somerhild. She couldn't have spun and sewn were she not well. God willing, the fever rife here in the Tauber valley spared Wimborne. Spring's here, the worst's behind us.'*

Begiloc sighed.

*'What prospects of a return home? The Abbess lectured me on the importance of the work of God compared to my selfish desires! Two years for her and her God–'*

A hand laid on his shoulder ended his brooding and he looked up into the cheerful face of Brother Robyn or, rather, Father Robyn, ordained three months past. A better priest Begiloc could not imagine. Not many clergymen put a man at his ease by sharing a laugh and a companionable ale. All his toils and troubles, he would confide to him if only the day came when he might unburden himself, but he had never been secure with words when it came to his feelings.

"Father!"

"What then Briton, all the cares of the world on those broad shoulders?"

Shaking his head, Begiloc jumped down from the wall.

"My thoughts wander at times, is all."

"Your legs too unless I'm mistaken."

"How so?"

The priest sighed, "Our Lady Abbess calls for you. Sister Williswind lies ill."

"Aedre's mother?"

"She asks for her daughter, begging to see her before she goes to embrace Our Lord."

"Aedre's in Rems," he frowned, "fourteen nights away."

The red-haired cleric tugged him along the cloister, "Best not waste a minute then, the abbess awaits you."

Brisk and efficient, Leoba said, "Travel with Meryn since I cannot spare other men. The task is simple. Escort Aedre back to Bischofsheim without delay. Here is a sealed document to be delivered to Bishop Milo. There is a boat waiting as I speak."

Gazing into the gold-flecked hazel eyes, he hesitated. How to find the right words?

"My Lady, the prelate is no respecter of documents nor seals and he has old scores to settle with Meryn and I. We shall not be welcome messengers. Is there not another who might succeed where we will fail?"

"Fail?"

Where he expected her chin to rise and her face to harden, the smile of an angel met him. When she did that she held him in thrall, but had she heeded his words?

"How can you not succeed? On an act of mercy in the name of the Lord? He will be your guide. Seek his protection in prayer and all will be well."

Radiant, she passed him the parchment.

"Make haste Begiloc, if it be Our Father's will, our prayers will keep Williswind with us until she embraces her daughter for the last time."

Later, at the prow, he brooded as the hull sliced a wave and the boat ploughed along the river. Their speed, aided by the wind filling the square sail, proved the only positive event to come to mind although it meant drawing closer to his enemy.

A coiled rope served as a seat for Meryn, cheerful and convivial in adversity, he hummed a lay about a brave warrior. Familiar to Begiloc, he noted the expressive brown eyes of his friend. As ever they sparkled with amusement.

"I know that tune."

"God bless the scop that sang it at your wedding feast! I thought you'd never speak to me again. Go on, mope some more if you will!"

"It's that woman!" the words forced out through gritted teeth.

"Who, Somerhild?"

"No, Leoba."

Choosing the anchor stone opposite Meryn, he sat and peered at him. How could he not smile at the one person capable of dispelling his dark mood?

"That's better," his comrade tossed back his head, "tell me what she's done?"

"When I complained about being sent into the lion's maw, do you know what she said?"

"I will, soon."

"We are on an act of mercy in the name of the Lord, she said, and He would be our guide. Our prayers would protect us. Two breaths later she said if it was God's will her intercession would keep Williswind alive. See what I mean?"

"Not exactly."

"Well, what if God's will is *not* to shield us from Bishop Milo? In any case, I can't pray. I'm no good at it."

Meryn flipped a finger under his moustache, "Nah, me neither. Never could, mine never get answered. Wouldn't be here otherwise ..." he grinned "...we'll have to rely on tried and tested methods, my brain and your brawn – as ever was and ever will be, amen."

"That's settled then!"

Begiloc unslung his hearpe and plucked at the strings while Meryn sang but whenever he forgot the words of the tale, he invented so the story grew more outrageous until fits of laughter halted them.

The last stage of their journey began: two days on foot to Rems from the second boat from Catalauns, moored at Tours.

Inside a tavern within the walls of Rems, a serving maid placed two jugs of ale at a nearby table, "By Satan's foreskin!" Meryn said, staring at her, "A comely one, what do you think...? She'd scrub up well!" In spite of her ragged dress, grubby face and lank hair, Begiloc nodded distracted, dusty and weary. This being the first tavern they reached and needing to wash away the dust in their throats persuaded them to enter this insalubrious hovel. Grimy from travel, they would not stand out while they sat over their ale – or the watered down brew that passed as such.

In spite of his weariness, Begiloc decided to move on as he would rather sleep next to an open cesspit. After the boat, they had striven to reach the town in haste and having trudged with heavy packs or been jostled on ox carts, their bones ached for a bed.

The squalid tavern behind them, they followed the road to a more acceptable place for the night. When they settled down on their pallets he discovered tiredness compromised his thinking, but he needed to work out a way to get their message to the bishop without risking arrest.

The next morning, the quandary tormented him the moment his eyes flickered open to the insistent accompaniment of chiming bells. For an instant, they dwelt on the plastered ceiling of the room and swept down to the simple wooden cross hanging on the wall. The moment of disorientation passed as he remembered choosing the small priory near the town centre. The idea to ask for a bed by showing the seal on his document came to him while they searched for an inn as the sun dipped. An ideal solution, this religious house, since they were on church business and it ensured them a safe and clean haven for the night. But it served only to put back the problem as they could not justify a delay in consigning their message.

To solve the predicament, Meryn took out his copper disk and bone comb and made an effort to resemble normality.

"The fat swine won't recognise me now from what little he saw of me two years ago," he said, "he might well remember you and Caena, but to him, I shall be another messenger, a Briton, but so what? There are many Britons in Neustria, but only one has a beaded beard."

"It is so." Begiloc chuckled, "No other is so weird! Without beads, there is no reason to suspect you."

Outside, he handed the document to Meryn, clasped hands and said, "Go to it, find me near the gate where we entered the town."

The wait was short.

"He did *what*?"

Begiloc gaped at his comrade as they met up again at the appointed place.

"Tossed the parchment to the ground like a bone for the hounds."

"Then what?"

"The fat swine said to tell Abbess Leoba he sends his greetings to his Sister in Christ and it pains him, but he cannot spare Aedre from her *ministrations*."

"Ministrations? He said that?"

"Ay, leered when he said it. I had to kiss his fucking ring too. What do we do now?"

Meryn, the most optimistic of persons, sounded defeated.

A glance toward the squalid inn and Begiloc said, "Quaff an ale and think. I won't drink puddle water, though."

In search of a better brew, they stumbled on a street market where Begiloc clicked his fingers.

*'The bishop's palace must serve itself of produce from here.'*

Grabbing his comrade by the arm, he led him among the stalls, between one selling linen dyed different colours, where he ignored the woman's strident cry for his attention, and another where eels wriggled in wicker baskets and perch and carp lay in lines attracting flies to be flicked away in a desultory manner by the back of the stall keeper's hand. They passed tubs containing powders crushed from madder root, woad leaves, walnut shells and murex snails for valuable red, blue, brown and purple dyes.

A few quiet words with a man who traded in fox furs, coins for information, and they fought their way to the stall of Emmon, who sold the meat of hare and goose. Tied to the aprons of the counter, geese honked and gabbled. One hissed at Meryn who hissed back but kept his limbs out of range of avenging wings. Under the trestles, three hares floundered with their legs trussed. Begiloc took care not to tread in a pile of offal surrounded by dried blood and swarming with flies: a creature had been gutted and sold not long before. Without a word, he held out a silver piece in the palm of his hand and at once, the desire showed on the round face. The viander stretched out his hand, but the fist of Begiloc closed over it.

"We need to speak, Master. Far from pricked ears. Oblige me in this."

Opening his purse, he put back the coin and withdrew a larger one.

"This is yours if you walk a way with me. My friend here will guard your fare."

Emmon reached for a cloth and wiped his hands. Tossing his stained apron over a cask used for a seat, he admonished Meryn, "Anyone wanting meat, tell 'em I'll be back anon. Don't sell anything, mind."

The bustle and stench of the market street behind them, Begiloc found a quiet corner and peered up into the tradesman's good-natured face.

"When do you next take your goods to the palace of the bishop?"

The smile faded into a frown. Emmon was bluff, "What's that to you?"

By the change in the man's mood and the way he tensed, Begiloc sensed he must tread with care. This tradesman, he guessed, in common with many, lived in fear of Milo.

"Fret not, friend. The task is simple and, what's more, an act of Christian charity. I need to get a message to a person in the bishop's household and I learned you have a sister, handmaid in the palace, is it not so?"

The large silver coin glimmered between his fingers as he turned it over. Reassured and tempted, the stallholder became amenable, so Begiloc explained the errand and made him repeat the message for Aedre until word perfect.

"Tomorrow at noon remember," he handed over the coin.

A little before midday the next day, an angry merchant and his retinue caused commotion at the gate. Three horse-drawn wagons, one covered with canvas, made up his assemblage. The trader, red in the face, yelled and waved in protest. Impassive, the captain of the guard, six armed men at his back, waited for him to calm. Formed up in line to leave the town, others, less patient, voiced their frustration with hoots and jeers. The source of contention was the toll the bishop had imposed; it obliged every layman travelling in land within his jurisdiction to pay a levy.

Distracted by the fracas, Begiloc and Meryn did not see the hooded woman in the mouse-grey mantle sidle up to them.

"We must leave at once!" she whispered into the ear of Begiloc.

"Aedre!"

"Hush! We must set off." when she tugged at his arm, he could not fail to note the heavy bejewelled rings.

"Hide them," he hissed under his breath, "we're in enough danger. Wiser to have left them behind. They provide the bishop two reasons to hunt for you."

Aedre bridled, "They're his gifts to me. They're mine!"

"Ay, and *you* are his!"

He heaved his pack on his back, linked arms with the woman and steered her to the line of travellers. They shuffled forward when the merchant conceded defeat and inched nearer the gate. Aedre pulling off and pouching her rings pleased him. At their turn, he paid three copper trientes without question and tossed a fourth into the tin of a blind beggar sat on the ground by the wall.

"Poor wretch," for once Meryn was sombre. "It must be cruel never to see the light of day."

Forks in the road, the different pace of the various horsemen, horse-drawn wagons, ox-carts, and people of assorted ages on foot led to dispersion until they walked alone.

When pressed, Begiloc did not reassure Aedre about the condition of her mother, but stressed the need for haste. For her part, she assured him she would not be missed until later in the day since Milo had risen early and set off with his goshawk, two of his sons and cronies for a day's falconry. The bishop, once noted her absence, would send out mounted search parties so they agreed it wiser to leave the road and head for the river sheltered by woodland. On foot, they could reach the Marne in two days, but still, they must not take risks, the fewer people to notice them the better their chances of making the boat – at the cost of adding a day to the journey time.

Where a trail led southwards, they took it, first ensuring nobody up or down the road might see them. The well-lit track ran through a mixture of birch, aspen and oak, the ground among the trees being covered in ferns, mosses and lichen meant they made steady progress, Begiloc satisfied they held a southward direction, because wherever the path forked he used the ever more western position of the sun as a guide. The light began to fade, so he called a halt, content they had not encountered anyone in the woodland.

In the morning, Begiloc groaned on his bed of bracken. Having ceded his sheepskin to Aedre for the night, for this consideration, he paid for it in aches and pains. Above the treetops, the lightening sky free of clouds, boded well for a fine day. Around the top of the oaks, he glimpsed the purple sheen of flittering hairstreaks feeding on honeydew. Grateful for the weather and the firm ground, pleased to avoid a wet night in their situation, by mid-morning his mood changed.

An hour before, they had been forced to skirt a gorge and after that, the trail petered out into impenetrable thicket and undergrowth of thorns and nettles. They backtracked to a clearing with several narrow paths leading in different directions. The one they had chosen, at first sight appeared right, only to deceive. The others, little more than tracks made by animals, left them no choice; they would have to take one of them or face the prospect of turning back around the gorge which would cost them precious hours with no assurance of success.

"Let's save time," Meryn shrugged off his pack, "I'll go ahead unburdened marking my way," he pointed at his seax, "if I'm not back by the time the shadow reaches here," he scuffed a line on the ground with his shoe, "you follow my marks. I'll be straight back if it leads nowhere."

Glad of the rest, Begiloc used the break to recount to Aedre the fate of Ingitruda and Donatus and the other events of the past two years, before he gave rein to his curiosity.

"What about Bishop Milo?"

She bit her lip and peered at him from under lowered brow, "A man of great appetites, he takes what he wants, generous, but quick to anger and...and...he's a cruel man...better not to cross him..." a tear brimmed over to trickle down her cheek, "Oh, I'm such a fool!" Once more the bowed head, she sniffed, "I fear what he will do if he finds us."

The more Begiloc pressed her about the prelate and his activities the more his unease and foreboding grew. The revelation of a vulnerable side and desperation to flee from Milo meant she was not the self-seeking woman he imagined. Their meeting in Rems the day before, she assured him, gazing deep into his eyes, was a response to her earnest prayers.

The shadow reached the line drawn by Meryn. Aedre insisted on carrying Meryn's pack so Begiloc helped it up on her shoulders. How long her frail frame could bear the weight remained to be seen. Reassured by the fresh marks scored at intervals in the bark, they trudged along the trail. After a little way, it widened and the undergrowth no longer whipped their ankles. The ground became firmer, less an animal track and more one used by man. This encouraged Begiloc as he ascertained by the position of the sun they were heading south. They stopped where the terrain dropped in a gentle slope down to a lane of beaten earth. Wide enough for a cart, it wound off, disappearing in a curve among the trees in both directions. Off came their packs.

"What now?" Aedre asked.

By reply, a tightening of the jaw and shake of the head, for he saw no sign to indicate the direction his comrade had taken.

For a hundred yards, he scoured the lane and its verges while she waited. Before retracing his steps, at a certain point, he bent to study the other side of the road. A mark left by Meryn? His wiry figure straightened and went on as far as the curve before he turned back scanning the trackside to no avail. Up the bank, he scrambled and grimaced, "It doesn't make sense, he was sure to leave a mark, unless ..."

"What?"

"... he saw something. Say he followed someone and wasn't able to make a sign. Suppose he didn't want to draw attention to this place here – to us."

"Shall we wait?"

Begiloc unpacked bread, cheese and water, which they ate in silence. An hour passed and he grew more uneasy, getting to his feet and staring along the track for the hundredth time. The only signs of life came farther down the trail, where first a vixen and then two jays darted from one side of the lane to the other.

"Let's go!" his voice reluctant, he said, "We can't take the track. It would be folly. Also, the shadows tell me it runs east-west and we must head south."

"Can you manage that?" he pointed to the pack. Without waiting for an answer, he unfastened a full water skin from Meryn's bag and tied it to the opposite side of his own, unlaced the sack and transferred more bread and cheese.

"We can't do better," he murmured, "we need the sheepskin and the rest is his belongings. Meryn must make his own way to the boat."

Voice assured, he hid the worry. This disappearance so unlike Meryn meant something must be amiss.

"It's all right, I can manage," Aedre said.

Glancing up and down the lane, he led her to the place where he had bent over. At that spot began a narrow but definite trail, so he helped her up the bank. Reassured they had not been observed, they pressed on through woodland of birches and alder interspersed with oaks growing amid much undergrowth, which hampered their passage. They kept on south and by mid-afternoon the vegetation changed, the ground becoming mossy with a single ash tree dominated each clearing.

With a cry of delight, Aedre pointed through the trees at a small lake. The water clear and inviting, she dumped her pack and rushed to the edge. Begiloc followed, not letting up his guard, but only Aedre disturbed the birdsong and – *'what's she doing?'* – he gasped as the Saxon woman shed her clothes, untied her blonde hair and plunged naked into the water.

*'She can swim.'*

She bobbed away before turning and calling him to join her. The lure of washing away the grime of travel and easing his aching body prevailed over his hesitation. Stripping to his breeches, again he wavered, but more practical to dive in without them, he tugged them down and blushed. In spite of the iciness of the water, they swam for a while until she emerged nymph-like on the shore. The Briton stared rapt at her beauty but dipped under the surface before she noticed his admiration.

Their sheepskins overlapping, Aedre sat and Begiloc lay naked to dry off. From Meryn's pack, she pulled out the comb and tugged it through her long hair. Raised on one elbow, he studied the rise and fall of her breast as she combed. Resistance melted, his hand fluttered down the line of her spine. The shiver and smile under his touch encouraged him. He stroked her cheek with the flat of his hand and rested a finger on her lips, which parted to take it between her teeth and flick her tongue against the tip. Pulse hammering, he leant forward, withdrew his hand and replaced it with his mouth.

His tongue battled in sweet combat with hers while his hand slid up and down her thigh enjoying its silky smoothness. Lips unlocking from hers, they moved to a dark brown nipple, causing her to shudder and breathe his name. Heart beating fit to burst, he pressed his leg between her thighs. Aedre opened to him and he fell into her with hard urgent strokes. It had been so long and she kissed his face, panting his name as he plunged deeper. In that instant, he felt himself part of the forest around them, the soft ground beneath them, the sky above and the whole of creation. Most of all, he felt one with her as he groaned and shuddered, so she grasped his face, green eyes full of joy staring into his while he clasped her tighter before lying still, his cheek next to hers as she stroked his damp hair.

Sighing, he pulled away to roll on his back by her side. Gazing up at the sky, flecked with small white wisps of cloud, he hated himself for what he had done.

"Begiloc?"

By way of answer, he took her hand, kissed it and let go. A mask of practicality cloaked his self-loathing, voice hoarse, "We should clothe ourselves and move on. Get as near to the river as we can before nightfall." Without a word, she pulled on her dress and stockings and braided her hair. All thoughts dismissed from his head, he put his mind to rolling up and tying his damp sheepskin. Like him, Aedre tied the skin to her pack and they skirted the lake in silence before finding a trail in the right direction. Leading the way, he dwelt on what had happened.

*'I didn't mean it to happen. I didn't want to betray Somerhild. Two years without touching a woman ... damn! Not all my fault – the Church is to blame too – Abbess Cuniburg, Leoba, Denehard, Lull, Burchard and all the rest of the flaming missionaries keeping me apart from my Somerhild ...without their fervid beliefs, I would be tilling and sowing the land at Wimborne never having met Aedre. No doubt about my attraction to her, but what of my marriage vows?'*

Distracted, he tripped over a tree root and the weight of his pack pitched him forward.

"Damnation!"

"Are you all right?"

Looming over him, the delicate face, the wide eyes full of concern and something more...

"Ay, there's nought broken."

Her lips pressed to his and in spite of himself, he responded in a long passionate kiss.

Throughout the afternoon, they trudged on until they found a dell with a stream and grassy hollow, ideal for the night. Aedre collected twigs and he lit a fire. First, they placed their damp sheepskins as near to the heat as possible to dry out, then he surprised her by bringing two fish from the brook. While he gutted and spitted them, he explained he learned the skill of tickling trout as a boy in Dumnonia. After a drink from the water skin, her voice hard to hear, she said, "I suppose you think me the bishop's whore."

Swallowing his fish, he stared at her unhappy face. Since Rems, she had been seldom without a smile. A long silence followed, at last, he spoke in a soft tone.

"How can I judge you? I am a married man as you well know and it takes two to trespass."

"Our forefathers, not so long ago, thought not of sin."

The deep green eyes flashed at him in the firelight.

"The goddess Freya smiled on one who coupled with his friend or neighbour," she said, "The Christian God is so demanding and makes life wretched. Where is the harm in loving and giving?" She cocked her head to one side.

"Ay," Begiloc dwelt on the word *'demanding'*.

*'Would I be miserable far from Somerhild but for this 'demanding' God and His servants? Why am I here? Are we*

*not fleeing from a prelate of this God? With the old gods, an offering was enough to gain their favour. Why not take pleasure with Aedre?'*

A wild thought came to mind – a sacrifice to Freya.

Still hungry, he spurned his half-eaten fish, sighing and throwing it on the fire.

"A gift to Freya," he explained to the shocked Aedre.

Her throaty laugh inflamed him and he grew more excited when, like him, she tossed her trout into the flames and said, "To Freya."

Adding a few more branches to the blaze, Begiloc went over to the now dry sheepskins, which he placed next to each other before starting to pull off his clothes. Aedre did the same, her body flickering red in the firelight. Pulling her down next to him, he began to kiss her mouth, throat and breasts. His hand ran down her side and felt her ribs and the slender waist widening to her hips before it traced the line of her groin from where his fingers passed over her stomach and back down between her thighs. He murmured her name as she clung to him, drawing him deeper inside. Pulling her to him, he squashed her breasts against his chest. For her part, she crossed her ankles over his back, pressing down with her hips until he groaned and shuddered and loosened his grip, laying her flat on her back. Soon, his breathing grew quiet followed by a long sigh. Energy returning, he rolled away, drew their cloaks over them to lie together exchanging caresses and kisses until she straddled him before they fell, entwined, into a deep sleep.

Strident birdsong greeted the cool light of early morning and Begiloc sat up to gaze at the serene face of Aedre asleep. An attractive woman, but he felt confused, emotions isolated. A wave of hopelessness swept over him at the thought of how he yearned for her last night and satisfied his lust. Aware he did not deserve the sweetness and tenderness of her body, yet he wanted more. The distant Somerhild trusted him and he had betrayed her. With no intention of hurting either woman, his weakness had prevailed. The unimaginable risk, now upon him, of losing the life he had worked so hard to build with his wife, he made a fist and struck his thigh leaving a red imprint. Sinner that he was, how could he ever forgive himself?

*'What kind of man am I? An adulterer! A trespasser among Christians who enjoy an easy relationship with God. I offended Him and He'll punish me. In a few days, we'll be at the abbey. How can I look Leoba in the eye?'*

# CHAPTER 9

Below them, the River Marne glistened like a winding, silver snake: a lifeline, an escape route, a projection of their desperate need to find Meryn. Heaps of white clouds meant their journey should be rain free, against that, their desire for the safety of cover had cost them their comrade and the whereabouts of the waiting craft. They needed to skirt the woodland along the river to plunge into the trees at the first sign of danger. With no landmark to help orientation should they turn left or right? Their captain, paid to wait for seven sunrises, had moored at the village of Tours so three remained to find the vessel but Begiloc hoped to find it in hours rather than days by going down to the river, hailing a passing craft and seeking information. While he did this, Aedre stayed in the shade of the trees to prevent reports of a man and a woman seen together.

They reached their boat an hour upstream but lost the faint hope of finding Meryn there, abandoned him to his fate and left for Catalauns. After two nights, they reached the River Orne where another vessel awaited them for the five-day voyage to Bischofsheim.

From the prow, Begiloc sighted the village and calculated his absence at twenty-three days. Would they find Williswind alive?

Inside the gates of the abbey, Caena stood beside a pile of split logs, axe in hand. Dropping the tool, he wiped his brow and cried, "Aedre!" He grinned at the Briton, "So you brought her back! I didn't think you'd make it." Searching for the right words, he paused then continued, "I … I mean we … were starting to worry about you …"

Never before had Caena expressed any warmth. Respect, but not affection, hardened warriors did not show their feelings.

"… it's a miracle and we've had one here too."

"Let me guess. The well water turned into Bischofsheim ale?"

"Ha-ha! Better than that! Or not, now I think on … but come, give me that weight, Aedre–"

"How fares my mother?"

The Saxon murmured something incoherent. Ignoring the brimming tears, he took her pack, steering her toward the priest's house.

Outside the church, Father Robyn, squatting and talking to two boys, ruffled the tousled heads and at a word from the priest, they scurried away.

"Aedre! Welcome, child," he said with a firm embrace, "you look well."

"Father, my mother is she … is she …"

"Well! Praise the Lord!" The face of Robyn lit up with joy – exultation, indeed. "Our Lady Leoba performed a prodigy," he directed his smile at the Briton, "*another* miracle, I tell you, Begiloc. Did I not say she is special?" The priest turned to Aedre, "Our beloved sister Williswind lay close to death when Begiloc departed to fetch you, but our abbess, with the grace of the Holy Spirit, restored your mother to health through prayer and by feeding her with milk off her own silver spoon. How blessed we are to have a miracle-worker among us!"

With a cry of happiness, Aedre flung herself into the arms of Begiloc and the bittersweet memory of their illicit adventure flooded back. But, this time, she showed understandable joy, born not of lust, so he returned the gesture.

"My mother is well!"

"Come, the abbess is with her. I shall take you to them!" Robyn said.

Returning to his work, Caena called to Begiloc over his shoulder, "An ale together later, old beast?"

Inside a small cell Leoba was reading to Williswind on her pallet. A flush of pleasure tinged the pallor of the patient at the sight of her daughter.

"I shall leave you Aedre but I expect you in my chamber after Sext."

The voice of the abbess came crisp and sharp.

*'Rather Aedre than I.'*

"You and I will speak now, Begiloc," she said, interrupting the Briton's thoughts. Closing the holy book with delicacy, she stood, "Come Father!"

The corridor led to an oak door with an iron ring, which the abbess turned ushering them into her chamber. The number of books and parchments impressed in an otherwise austere room. New calfskin covers bound many of the tomes, but Begiloc ought not to be surprised, Leoba spoke often enough of the *lectio devina*, the deep meditative reading of the Scriptures she insisted on for her nuns. Shafts of sunlight from the narrow round-arched windows picked out the tooled lettering on the spines of the volumes – the heavens indicating the path to illumination.

Leoba arranged three chairs and bade them sit. Elbows placed on the chair arms with one hand over the other in her lap, she said, "So, Begiloc, you return with Aedre but not with your friend?"

Was it possible this holy woman knew all about him, his innermost thoughts? How did she know about Meryn? The Briton might be out in the yard for all she knew because without forewarning, they had gone straight to Williswind's room.

She cut short an explanation of their separation in the forest north of Tours.

"You have done the Lord's work, Begiloc. As well as any man could ..." his guilt flushed in his face, but the abbess could not read minds, "... you brought Aedre to her mother and I hope back into the fold of Christ. Her presence will speed the recovery of Williswind." She paused, her expression sad. "I pray the price will not be excessive. You see, I must send you away once more." A hand raised stayed his objection. "Two days ago, a message came from our brother abbot at Beaulieu containing information received from Bishop Bladald at Catalauns – do you follow me? – in turn obtained from the monastery of Saint Basle at Verzy. You know, where Basle built his oratory and converted the pagans?"

Begiloc turned to Father Robyn and shrugged.

The priest smiled, "Mother, Church history may not be the strong point of a layman and a warrior."

By way of reaction, a tinkling laugh – her perfect teeth and matchless beauty overwhelmed him. Sure, he blamed her more than anyone for his continued absence from Wimborne, but her presence compelled him to accept whatever she wanted of him.

"You are right, Father Robyn! I shall be concise, the message bore ill news," and her face clouded, "it concerns Meryn. I fear he is afflicted ..."

"*Afflicted?*"

The abbess frowned and touched the cross lying on her dress.

"That is the wording. Monks of Verzy found him *'sore afflicted'* on a woodland track while returning to the monastery." Her speech slowed, "I know not what the words mean for poor Meryn–"

"He is hurt?" Begiloc's heart and brain worked at different speed. Chest pounding, he jumped to his feet.

"Please sit, Begiloc, we have much to discuss. Of course, you will leave for Verzy to seek out your friend, but heed this, you have another task. Three years ago, our Holy Father in Rome, Pontifex Gregory, the third of his name, sent the pallium to my cousin Wynfryth. Named Boniface after Bonifatius of Tarsus the martyr ..." she smiled at Robyn in recognition of his warning glance, "... the archbishop is addressing the ills of the Church in Bavaria, Hesse and Thuringia. False priests roam the countryside from Neustria into Hesse. One, in particular, a certain Aldebert ..." the hand of the abbess strayed again to the cross at her breast ... this *heretic* began to preach in Soissons and moved thence eastwards and this is how you can help, they last reported him near Tours."

"Where we moored our boat?"

"Verzy is not far from there. Of course, go succour Meryn and afterwards seek out this Aldebert. The charge is simple – listen to him twice or thrice, return with our brave friend if he can travel and tell me what this man preaches." She paused, "Is something the matter, Begiloc?"

Frowning, he leant forward, "My Lady, I'm sure I can track him down, but ... as to telling you what he says, I don't think–"

"Worry not, friend," Father Robyn said, "this Aldebert speaks to the people in their tongue. I doubt not he has a smattering of Latin but local speech serves his purpose."

Leoba walked over to a table where she pulled open a central drawer.

"You are a loyal servant Begiloc and I wish to make you a gift."

She came over to stand before him. A carved rood in ivory, the size of a hen's egg, hung from a leather thong. The abbess slipped the loop over his head then slid her fingers under the cross lifting it.

"See, here at the base is an angel holding a hearpe, as you do."

The radiant smile shone again.

"The cherub will keep you safe and at the centre is an ox, the symbol of Saint Luke and of the sacrifice of Our Lord to remind you everyone makes sacrifices in His name."

She smiled up at him and he flushed a deep red. The ivory was the fine work of a master carver and worth much money.

"My Lady, I cannot accept. I am a sinner."

These last words bitter and full of remorse.

"We are all sinners, Begiloc," Father Robyn said, "but what's in our hearts matters."

"Keep it with you always."

*'If I wear it, will it stop me sinning?'*

"Leave at first light on the same boat that brought you," Leoba said, " I'll send a messenger at once to pay the captain to carry you tomorrow. Take Caena, for we live in perilous times when even bishops are enemies of the righteous. Guard one another. Archbishop Boniface, on my recommendation, wrote to the pope about Bishop Milo, so stay away from Rems."

No need for a warning!

She blessed him and his mission, adding with a smile, "Go to the refectory, you are in urgent need of a meal."

Hungry, indeed, passing through the empty canteen for the kitchen, the aroma of stewed meat hastened his step.

On learning the abbess had sent the Briton, the cook sat him down in a nook by the fire and began to beat two eggs, taking a glass bottle, the monk poured a green liquid into the bowl.

"Verjuice," he replied to Begiloc's interest, "the juice of sorrel stems. I'll add this mixture to the water where I boiled the flesh," he stirred it into the steaming pot, "and now the stewed meat ..." His stomach rumbled. Without a hot meal for days, pork was a rare treat to savour with every mouthful. Caena and he would be back on bread and cheese on the journey and the thought gave an edge to his appetite. The skeletal cook beamed approval at such appreciation and rummaged around in a cupboard for slices of oven-dried apple to press on Begiloc. The monk put a finger to his lips before pushing the Briton out of his kitchen.

Much hungrier, thirteen days later, he and Caena stood in the presence of the abbot in the monastery of Saint Basle at Verzy. On their way, they came across a track through the woodlands leading to the building which, startled, he recognised as the same lane where he'd lost Meryn's trail three weeks before and, he supposed, the road where the monks found his friend. A sense of foreboding overcame him and his fingernails dug into his palm.

On entering the monastery, a monk led them to the abbot, a short, voluble man with notable ears and contrasting small, sharp nose. A South Saxon, he told them he had lived at Verzy ever since he came to Neustria twenty-four years past. In a few minutes, they learned about the trials and tribulations of running a monastery and the flood of words drained to reticence only when Begiloc interrupted with urgency asking after Meryn. The watery eyes of the abbot filled with pain and rather than meet those of Begiloc and Caena, flitted from one face to the other.

"Alas, poor Meryn," he sighed, "Meryn is sore afflicted." Reaching for a bronze handbell, he shook it with vigour.

*'Those same words!'*

A monk, bowed with age, came into the room.

"This is our infirmarian who will explain the condition of your friend and take you to him."

A wave dismissed them and a shaken head increased their unease.

Outside the door, the brother halted and laid a tremulous hand on the arm of Begiloc. Unlike his abbot, the elderly brother, eyes so dark the pupils and irises seemed one, met his gaze. In contrast, his voice matched his quavering muscles.

"Meryn heals well in the body but the wound to his soul festers. I fear he has no will to live."

The walls closed in on Begiloc and he swayed on his feet.

"What have they done to him?" Caena growled.

The infirmarian turned and stared at the warrior.

"They have put out his eyes."

A howl of pain and rage from Begiloc echoed in the empty corridor and the Saxon seized him in time to prevent him smashing his fist against the stone wall.

"The wounds ..." his voice faltered but the white-haired monk went on, "... are clean. They used a red-hot blade so the flesh cauterised. I treat the patient twice a day with a salve of comfrey."

Words choked in the throat of Begiloc, but he managed: "I beg you, lead us to him." In his time, he had witnessed the bloodiest carnage, the worst suffering and deprivation, but nothing matched the dread he felt at greeting Meryn.

The infirmary contained six beds. The wall by the door bore shelves full of pots and bottles. From the two beams hung bundles of herbs and below stood a workbench laden with pestles and mortars, books, jars and phials of coloured liquids. Scattered dried lavender bloom lay in purple puddles and crunched underfoot releasing its fragrance. Oblivious of his surroundings, Begiloc hurried past a bed where an elderly, sallow-skinned monk stared at them full of curiosity. On the next bed sat their comrade, a linen cloth bound around his head under the brow and across the bridge of his nose. Back resting against the wall, his knees were drawn up.

"Meryn, you have visitors," the infirmarian turned to them. "He is weak after his ordeal," he whispered. "I'll leave you while I prepare fresh salve, do not overtax him."

Begiloc felt the hand of Caena press his shoulder.

"Strength, Briton."

His heart, fit to burst with sorrow, was grateful for the gesture. Tears welled and he fought them back. When he spoke, his voice did not seem his own.

"Meryn, we are come."

The head turned in the direction of the voice.

"Begiloc, is it you?"

A raised hand wavered, which Begiloc caught and squeezed before sitting on the bed and pulling his afflicted comrade into his arms.

"Ay, with Caena."

Rage mixed with pity at the body racked with sobs. Clinging to his friend, he forced the words through his teeth.

"Who did this?"

At last, Meryn pushed him away and slumped back.

"I don't want to think about it," he said, voice scarcely audible.

Frowning at Caena, Begiloc tilted his head back and spread his hands.

"We'll find them Meryn, I swear on all that's holy," Caena said, "We shall find and slay them. Give us the names."

The Briton remained in stubborn silence and began to rock backwards and forwards from the waist. His hands went up to his bandaged eyes then the whispered words came in a rush though they strained to catch them.

"When I left you and Aedre I found a track and saw riders coming to the monastery. I followed them and spied on them from the edge of the trees, but others on foot in the woods – I – I didn't know, they seized me from behind and bound me ..." The moving to and fro became insistent, "... they took me to a clearing and they – they had a fire and, well, they were cooking. The riders returned and he recognised me from Rems–"

"Who?" – he asked, but knew the answer.

"The fat bastard, the bishop." Meryn stopped the rocking and reached out for Begiloc to take his hand. The voice rose to a frenzy. "Why ... why not slay me? It were better!"

"Not so," he said, "I can take you home, to your family. They will be glad you are alive. They love you."

"Let them see me like this? Never!" he let go and his tone pitched higher, "I stay here. That's an end to it! If you want to do something for me, hear me out. Find him and avenge me. Do it with care – in such a way you live to tell the tale."

"I swear it. We both do."
Meryn resumed after a long silence.

"Milo questioned me about Aedre – wanted to know where I'd hidden her. Was she in the monastery? Was she in the woods? I told him I'd never seen her, but he didn't believe me and wanted to know why I was prowling amidst the trees. The ones who seized me, they – they told him I was spying." He fiddled with his bandage and hit his forehead three times with the heel of his hand. "The vermin laughed and asked if I knew what they did with spies – well *I would*, he said, but I must not delay his lunch. Capturing a spy gave him an appetite, he said, sneering and – and he laid his spearhead in the fire..." Meryn began to rock again. "...he sat and fed his fat face and licked his fingers. Stood. Belched. Told them to hold me. Took the spear from the flames. Blade red hot and, and ..." his voice rose to a scream, "... and he drove it into my eye." Meryn's frame shook with soundless sobs causing the infirmarian to hurry over.

"Enough, enough! Go! You must leave him."

"Ay," Begiloc swept the frail monk off his feet and handed him to Caena.

"First I must say farewell to my friend."
Unpinning Talwyn's brooch, he pressed it into the hand of Meryn.

"This is my pledge. The Bishop of Rems dies. Return it when I have fulfilled my oath."
Meryn closed his fist over the breastpin, opened it again, and traced the brooch with the fingers of his other hand. For the first time, a half-smile flickered and he whispered, "Stay safe, friend!" He brought the ornament to his lips and kissed it. Caena squeezed the patient's shoulder in a silent gesture while Begiloc said, "We leave now Meryn, but I swear I will die sooner than let your torturer live."
The Briton spoke not a word.

"Come!" the infirmarian called. They obeyed following him out of the room. In the corridor, he turned to Begiloc. "We will do our best for Meryn. The loss of his sight leaves him grieving. Only time can help." The monk frowned, "He's stubborn, but he must learn to lead a new existence. When he feels in control of something – anything to latch on to – he will begin to heal."
Muttering his thanks, Begiloc dipped into his purse and took out two gold coins.

"Anything he needs brother. This may help."

"Above all, my son, remember the sixth commandment, *'Thou shalt not kill.'*"

Caena murmured an oath and Begiloc grunted. Halfway down the corridor Begiloc stopped and went back to the infirmarian where he shrugged off his pack and untied his hearpe.

"Take it," he thrust it at the monk, "give him this. He has a fine voice, he can learn to play."

The monk's eyes smiled, "Indeed, a generous gift – what Meryn needs."

"I can make another," came the gruff reply as he turned without glancing back. The malevolent maiming of Meryn, for him, annulled the sixth commandment.

Outside the monastery, he sat on a tree stump, head in hands. Caena hesitated, decided against pointless words and settled down on the bank at the side of the track.

In vain, Begiloc tried to rid his mind of the horror of Meryn's ordeal. Unwanted images of searing iron and pain made him want to strike his head with his fists. Why Meryn? Why the quick-witted, rascal with a ready smile on his lips? One that might seldom return. A world of darkness.

*'What kind of God let this happen? May the Devil take Abbess Cuniburg for her summons. To hell with all churchmen! What Fate wove the sweetness of life in Wimborne only to unpick the thread?'*

Blindness, lust, infidelity, cruelty, vengeance, futility, grief: a cascade of emotions tumbled through his mind.

*'I'll go mad unless I can shut them out.'*

Futile – nothing could restore sight to Meryn. A small voice resounded, that of the infirmarian, resonating calmness: *'Only time can help'*.

The tension in his neck sent silver stars shooting behind his eyes when he rolled his head. His fingers ran backwards and forwards across his forehead to fight off the threat of headache. How was it possible he lacked for air in the woodland? Breathing in, he savoured the fragrance, though its purity could never compensate for the evil in the world.

He calmed enough to join the Saxon who scrutinised him for a long moment, saying nothing then nodded. They walked a short way before Caena spoke.

"I want to say... it was ... and ..." he curtailed the effort, changing to "... on to Rems, then?"

They discussed this. Caena wanted to go straight to the palace to slay the bishop whereas Begiloc protested it would not be easy to murder a well-protected prelate. A saying of his father came to mind, so he shared it: " *'Rashness is the bedfellow of Rage.'* We would be wise to wait and plan."

Caena deferred to Begiloc.

"We Saxons are famed for acting with haste," he muttered, conceding that Meryn was more than a friend to the Briton. First, they would hunt down Aldebert, afterwards, they would return to scheme and exact vengeance on the Bishop of Rems.

The evening closed in as they came to Tours, so they found an inn for the night. Caught in a hailstorm followed by heavy rain, they were relieved to sit near a log fire to dry out. The tavern served fresh poached shad cooked with garlic: the cause of Caena's cursing.

"This shit is more bone than flesh!"

"Ay," Begiloc said, "like drowned hedgehog turned inside out!"

The next morning their questions drew a blank until they found a man leaving a tiny church. His cousin's wife, he told them, suffered with pains in her chest and a saint who preached at a cross by a spring near a place called Bouzy had cured her.

"They say folk flock to his preaching, he performs miracles every day. An hour away on foot."

Convinced they scented Aldebert, they hurried lunch. Sated, they took the road to Bouzy. Some time later, they spotted roofs and smoke but as they approached the settlement a grim sight met their eyes. Their approach scattered carrion crows from a corpse dangling from a tree. The remains of the man's face was a hideous bluish-grey colour and they, used to the aspect of dead men in battle, turned away disgusted to hurry past.

The village boasted a stone church. Ignoring the few women who interrupted their chores to stare, they entered the building where a priest knelt before the altar. Was it right to disturb a man of God at his prayer? Begiloc hesitated, but the sound of their footsteps cut short his orison to cross himself before facing them.

Their request for information produced a tirade.

"This false priest, this blasphemer! May Saint Basle intercede to end the ills afflicting us! The people here are no more than a rabble of pagans. They believe in anything: witches, magicians and the power of the old gods ..." he paused for breath, crossed himself again and continued, "... that a storm is the work of a sorcerer ... a charlatan can lure away my flock by pretence–"

"Father, you are right," Begiloc interrupted the gush of words, "Abbess Leoba sends us in search of this Aldebert at the behest of Archbishop Boniface. We must seek him. Else there will be no end to his preaching."

The mention of ecclesiastical authority had the desired effect. The priest smiled and spread his arms.

"The Lord be praised! Our patron, Basle, answers my prayers. My sons, of course, I will help you. These are terrible times. Yesterday there was a hailstorm–"

"Ay, it soaked us. Heavy was it not?"

"Indeed, it destroyed the blossom on the fruit trees." Pausing, his face twisted into a grimace, "Do you know what the wretches did? Dragged poor Gararic from his hearth with accusations of sorcery – of invoking the storm – blasphemy! The Godless louts hanged him from the 'sacred' oak at the entrance to the village. Sacred oak! Pagans! I've a mind to chop it down myself. Baptised every one of them and yet they cling to superstition and ignorance!" A shake of his head. "Nor will they let me cut Gararic down and give him a Christian burial. They say his corpse is to be an example to other weather-working sorcerers and witches–"

"Father, we shall haul him down and bring the body to you," Begiloc nudged Caena.

"Thank you, my son, but no, if I bury Gararic they will wait till you have gone before desecrating the grave. Who knows? They might vent their fury on his widow and that must not happen. I know these sinners. Time and new blossom will placate them and I will collect the bones of Gararic and inter them. For now, I must comfort the grieving family."

"Father, this Aldebert?"

Patience was needed with the garrulous priest but in a roundabout way came forth what he knew of the heretic.

"Two days ago, he preached at a place near the river to the east, three hours on foot. If you set off at once you will arrive before dusk."

They left the small church and when they came to Vallis Dominica had no difficulty getting news of the preacher. The place was abuzz with talk of his miracles.

The women, in particular, all were fervent followers of the so-called saint, but a man full of reverence bestowed on them the privilege of holding a light-brown lock of sacred hair, commonplace to their eyes like any other hair, but miraculous, the man swore.

"It's cut from the head of the apostle," he said, "I paid him a whole silver piece for it. I could have bought finger nail parings, but hair's better, more powerful, see?"

The saint, he protested, was a holy man who used all monies received to build oratories.

"They are erecting a church in the blessed name of Aldebert near a spring between here and Louvercy, nearby, two leagues to the east on the River Vesle, but you'll find it in the countryside before you reach the village. Many of our people are going to hear the preacher at noon, tomorrow."

Begiloc and Caena decided they would go with them.

"In that case, you are my guests tonight."

Grateful, they ate his cabbage soup and slept on the floor either side of the hearth.

The man rose with the dawn to work the land but he urged them to rise later. The villagers who intended to go to the service would leave, he pointed at the wall, when the sun was in that direction. Half-asleep, Begiloc managed to hand the man a coin with profuse thanks.

Mid-morning, a crowd made up of women, several children and one or two men gathered, some extolling the virtues of Aldebert. From the excited chatter, Begiloc and Caena learnt of the humility of the preacher, the way he walked, his modest dress and speech, a simplicity the people liked, for he preached a way of life similar to the apostles and lived that way himself, not like the priests and the bishops thereabouts.

Some called him a living saint and one woman told how the holiness of Aldebert healed an inflammation of the eyes of a neighbour's husband. Not only, the woman said, and everyone hung on her words, "While in his mother's womb the saint was filled with the spirit of God and born blessed. Before his birth, his mother dreamed a calf emerged from her right side and informed her he had received grace while yet unborn. From her *right side,"* the woman stressed, "like Christ sprang from the same side of the Virgin!"

After two hours, the procession came to a spring beside which rose a solid wooden cross and close by stood the shell of an unfinished church. In front of the building congregated an excited crowd from a nearby village and in the distance, Begiloc noted another group approaching.

Soon, the people of three villages crowded together before the house of prayer. Begiloc gauged four score worshippers and Caena was about to share the same assessment when the babble of voices hushed as an unkempt figure dressed in a long, white, linen robe belted at the waist emerged from the unfinished church. Aldebert raised his arms and his voice. "Brothers and sisters, let us pray. In the name of the Father, the Son and the Holy Spirit," he made the sign of the cross, "Amen. Our Father Thou who sit on the seventh throne above the cherubim and seraphim, hear our humble prayer. Oh Almighty, who promised Thy servant Aldebert whatsoever he asks of Thee, give him renewed grace to do Thy blessed will. Lend to Thy servant the support of the angels Uriel, Raguel, Tubuel, Michael, Adinus, Tubuas, Saboac and Simiel..."

Begiloc nudged Caena and protested under his breath, "We can't remember all those names!"

The Saxon shrugged and shook his head with "Well if *you* can't, *I* can't!".

"... Amen." The prayer ended and with the flourish of a magician Aldebert held aloft a parchment.

"Good people, on this day you are twice blessed," he waved the document, "I hold before you in my unworthy hand, a letter from Our Lord Jesus Christ Himself ..."

Gasps from the crowd accompanied his words, "... this document fell from heaven at Jerusalem, where the Archangel Michael discovered it near the gate of Effrem, delivering it into the hands of a priest named Icore, whence to a series of priests, one named Talasius in the town of Geremia ..." the preacher paused for effect, raised the manuscript again and shook it, "...Talasius gave the missive to Leoban who lived in a town called Arabia. Leoban sent it to Macrius in a city called Uetfania and Macrius forwarded the letter to Mont Saint Michel where the archangel bore the letter off to Rome ..."

Begiloc growled with exasperation, "The Abbess can't expect us to remember all this nonsense."

"We could take the letter from him," Caena whispered, "but say, Begiloc, I'm not a learned man and I know next to nothing of this religion thing, but I get a feeling what the fellow's spouting isn't quite... not ... oh, I don't *know* what I mean—"

"Ay, he's a fake all right. But we cannot take the document and risk an affray! We'll tell her what we can."

"... and in Rome, the twelve dignitaries who are in that city fasted, watched and prayed for three days and three nights ..."

The voice of Aldebert droned on, with the faithful clinging to his words. As the chosen bearer of the letter, he told them, his merits were such as to be of service to the people. Through the communion of saints, his supernatural powers endowed him with infinite wisdom.

"I don't need to hear your confession because I can see into the heart of every person here before me. I know your sins and so, I absolve you here and now."

He raised his arms aloft, asking whether they did not feel the grace of the Holy Spirit flowing through him into them?

"Since I am equal to the apostles, I will lay my hands on whosoever is in need of healing. And if anyone is inspired by the Holy Spirit to leave an offering, however small, for the building of the Oratory of Saint Aldebert ..." he indicated over his shoulder, where one of his followers had a basket.

"Come on," Begiloc nudged Caena, "We've heard enough of this pigswill."

"Now that I agree with," said Caena, "what I was trying to explain before ... like about this preacher ... is he's not right in the head. In our village, they scared us children half to death with tales of the *drycraeft* – spells cast by words and lists of names – well this sermoniser strikes me as doin' that, see?"

"You might be right. Whatever. The swifter we report back to Abbess Leoba, the quicker we get back to Rems and the sooner I get to separating Milo from his entrails."

# CHAPTER 10

*Anno Domini 736, June*
Bewildered, Begiloc sought Father Robyn. Two days Caena and he had waited for a summons from the abbess. Did she not wish to know the outcome of their assignment to Neustria? In church, he found the priest standing beside a wooden statue of the Virgin in the nave.

"Ah, Begiloc, well met. I can't decide whether Our Lady should stand to the right of the altar or in the corner on the left for offerings and prayer."

The statue, a finely sculpted and painted donation of a nobleman from a nearby farmstead, wore a golden crown and blue mantle. Father Robyn, to the accompaniment of noncommittal shrugs from the Briton, opted to place the dazzling figure by the altar. The honed muscles of Begiloc aided the clergyman to lift the statue in position. Stepping down to the nave, they surveyed their handiwork. The priest made the sign of the cross and instructed his helper, "Repeat after me, *'Ave Maria, gratia plena ...'*

The *Hail Mary* over, Father Robyn genuflected and rising, said, "I'm not sure whether you are troubled or impatient, Briton."

"Father, why does our Abbess not send for us? Odd, she always summons us at once, but this time after two days–"

"Can you think of no reason why this should be?"

A hint of accusation in the voice? Begiloc scrutinised the priest's face.

"Why, what did I do?"

"Examine your heart, my son. Nothing to confess?"

Plenty weighed him down but was locked inside without hope of release.

"Nothing."

The word rang false and Father Robyn smoothed back his red hair in a gesture of exasperation.

"As you will. I shall speak to Abbess Leoba."

Aware of the hardness in the eyes of the man whom he considered a friend, he mumbled a half-hearted thanks and left the church.

Within an hour, the priest ushered Caena and Begiloc into the presence of the Mother Superior. The abbess greeted the Saxon with a warm smile, but ignored the Briton. While she listened outraged at the news of Meryn, he worried about her anger with him. Her cousin, Boniface, she told them was at present in communication with the Holy See on the matter of the Bishop of Rems and his crimes. Given her mood, he decided to give her no inkling of his desire for revenge.

The abbess passed on to what they had learned about Aldebert. News of the so-called letter from Jesus drew nothing other than a sneer and an exchange of glances between her and the priest, but she questioned them about Aldebert's prayer, about the invocation of angels. Could they not recall even one name? She tapped her foot and clenched her delicate fists. Well, there was Michael of course, but that name failed to impress her "... between the two of them ...?" to his surprise Caena said, "Ay, one was Simiel, it reminded me of the bloo–, erm ... beggin' your pardon, My Lady ... the castrator, Shmuel, and for the same reason Uriel, but otherwise ..." he shook his head.

Begiloc said, "Tub-something."

"Tubuel?" she asked, eagerness evident.

"Ay, that's it."

"Demons! Others you say but you can't recall the names?"

"At least another two or three," his comrade said, "but the man spoke so fast ..."

The abbess bestowed her loveliest smile on the Saxon.

"You have done well, Caena. Quite sufficient for my letter to the archbishop. I am most pleased with you. You may go."

They turned to leave.

"Not you, Begiloc, stay!"

The eyes of the Briton met those of the Saxon reflecting his own bemusement. His gaze shifted to Father Robyn, but found him inscrutable.

Caena bowed and left.

*'What does she want of me? Not going to send me away again?'*

"You will excuse me," Leoba passed through a door to a vestibule. Begiloc turned to the clergyman but the priest frowned and stared at the floor.

The abbess returned wearing a mitre, cope and carrying her staff of office. The effect was startling. Her hard stare made his heart sink, for this woman, whose regalia so intimidated him, read it like one of her volumes.

"As our church father Jerome wrote, *'A woman's reputation is a tender plant; it is like a fair flower which withers at the slightest blast and fades away at the first breath of wind.'* Do you know why I tell you this?"

In a grave error of judgement, he shook and lowered his head. This feeble reply did not anticipate the ferocity of Leoba's response.

Lifting her staff, she drove it down on the stone floor.

"Fornicator! On your knees!"

He knelt at once.

*'She knows about Aedre!'*

Unable to meet her glare, he lowered his chin to his chest.

"Aedre has confessed her sins and repented. The Church has embraced her enabling her to take her vows; instead, you betrayed your wedding oath taken before God, your wife, the trust of your abbess and show no sign–"

"I did not mean–"

"Silence! You *will* hear me out. Impropriety of this nature, were it to become common knowledge would ruin the reputation of our community. The lay support upon which we depend for our life of monastic devotion would flee." Her voice blade sharp, "Important as it is, this is not my main concern. Most of all, I fear for your eternal wellbeing. When the chance came, you hardened your heart and failed to confess to Father Robyn." She pointed at him, "A wise man would not consider the beauty of the body, but of the soul. Turn your wanton gaze from Aedre, lest you conceive evil in your breast. She is to be a bride of Christ and love of her must exclude you from that of the Father."

"Ay, but–"

The staff slammed down again, "No *'buts'*..."

Under a half-raised brow, he peered at her. The stern beauty below the mitre overawed him so he bowed his head once more.

"Are you willing to do penance for your sins? Look at me!"

His gaze followed the rod of office upwards and moved to fix her hazel eyes. This time, he met them without flinching, ready to accept the punishment he deserved.

"That's better. Confess to Father Robyn and remove the weight from your heart. From Prime for one hour every day until I decide otherwise, you will stand in front of the church with your arms raised level to the ground. In that position, you will reflect on the suffering of Our Lord on the Cross. Your sin is part of His dolour. Lower them during that time and you will repeat the penance for one hour before Vespers, do you understand?"

He found the strength to say, "May God forgive me."

In strong contrast to her formal attire Leoba smiled.

"Ay, Begiloc, He will. As a loving Father, when we give our hearts to Him, He fills them with joy. Beware, repentance must be sincere."

With that, she turned and disappeared into the vestibule.

At dawn, a novice came to the lay dorter to fetch him. The bell chimed for Prime as they walked along the south wall of the church, where they positioned themselves under the sundial set high, carved out of a square block of stone, contained within a double circle. At the centre, in the style hole, a wooden peg cast a shadow in a weak but lengthy line along the first of the canonical hours to mark Prime.

The novice gestured and Begiloc raised his arms level with the ground. The postulant sat with his back against the wall and drew up his knees while a procession of monks filed past on their way from the dormitory to the service. They did not stare but kept their heads bowed, hands clasped in front of them. Soon afterwards the same happened as the nuns glided beyond him. Among them, he glimpsed Aedre, who did not raise her head either.

Grateful for their humbleness, Begiloc concentrated on his own humility. He felt better having confessed to Father Robyn. Absolution through penance granted, he still felt guilt for his betrayal – especially of Somerhild, but the priest warned failure to forgive himself was the sin of pride.

*'If I suffer enough in atonement might I absolve myself?'*

At first, easy to keep his arms raised but as time passed the aching began. The shadow on the sundial crept but remained far from the next line.

Jesus hanging on the Cross: the Lord had a crown of thorns, his hands and feet transfixed by nails and a wound in his side. What was his suffering compared to that? This thought did not stop beads of sweat forming on his brow and the fire in his shoulder muscles. Resentment prickled at him but he remembered the priest's warning, *'the human heart is often selfish, resentful, cold and restless. Recognise the counterforce working against you, your spiritual adversary, the devil, if you want to make progress as a believer in Christ.'*
The diabolical in him had brought him to this need to purge his soul.

The monks trooped out of the church followed by the nuns. Once again nobody looked his way.

*'Is it pride that makes me thankful? Is sinning second nature to me? What did Leoba say? Aedre confessed her sins and repented. She will take vows. Not the woman I know. Did she have a choice? Is it a sin to think? What I'd give to be in Wimborne where life is less complicated.'*

The shadow had run three-quarters of its course when he glanced at the dial. Could he resist? The burning in his arms and shoulders, the stiffness in his neck told him not. Teeth gritted, he baulked at the notion of coming here before Vespers. How to distract himself? In addition to his feelings of unworthiness, everyday thoughts invaded his attempt at praying for Somerhild and Ealric.

*'Sure, God has no time to heed a sinner like me'.*
The voice of the devil? The voice of experience? Insidious, it insisted he had lost his parents, his family and his friend blinded.

*'Why believe these priests and nuns? Aren't they the cause of my suffering? Or are these the murmurings of a demon? Where's the voice of God in all this? Why can I never hear it?'*

This skirmish in his mind brought him no closer to a resolution but served a purpose. To his surprise, the novice called, "Time's up! You may lower your arms." The shadow ran straight along the next line of the dial. An hour had passed. Aching, he rolled his shoulders and turned his head. When he looked up the young man was heading to the nuns' quarters. The novice was to report to the abbess – no surprise. After a while he strolled back.

"Tomorrow morning," he said before ambling away. Begiloc grinned in relief. Each day would be easier and he would never have to stand like that before Vespers, but for how many days?

The question was answered on the third morning when Father Robyn came out to speak with him after Prime, perhaps halfway through his penance.

Glaring at the novice scrambling to his feet, the priest directed his gaze at the penitent.

"Our Lord endured terrible pain on the Cross."

"Ay, that much I've learned."

"Have you acquired humility, my son?"

"I've been doing a lot of thinking, but I'm still full of doubts and short of faith."

The cleric smiled. "Then our Lady Abbess is right to send you to Rome–"

"Rome?"

*'Rome! Rome, he says the word like it was second turn left down the cart track.'*

Father Robyn's smile widened. "Ay, you and your band of Saxons. You'll escort Denehard and a couple of monks there on Church business–"

"I must go to Rems–"

"Careful, Begiloc. Penitence implies obedience!"

The eyes of the priest were ablaze with challenge. He met and held them, but there the clergyman read acceptance or hopelessness. Unsure which, he continued, "The abbess says your penance is to last until Denehard arrives, so pray he makes good speed. I believe he set off three days ago. Würzburg is two score and three leagues away, so my guess is another two and you will be released from–"

" Father, about Rems. It can't be right that the swine who passes for a man of God gets away with blinding my friend. I swore an oath to Meryn ... and she ... she ..." No explanation was needed for who *she* was. "... can't have any of the feelings, passions, yearnings of mere mortals like us! So she is punishing me for my trespasses but who decides what is sin? Who reigns over that! Is it God or her? I'm thinking it's Abbess Leoba chastising me for an act she–" In time to prevent blasphemy, he stopped short but he was enraged, indignant, besides himself at the thought of the pain tormenting poor Meryn."

Father Robyn pursed his lips, "Old friend, I understand your grief, but vengeance cannot bring back Meryn's sight. As you know well enough, a man hangs for the murder of a prelate. Retribution is best left to God – His mill turns at no great pace but how fine the stone grinds! Milo is one of the reasons for your trip to Rome. I wish ... *never mi*–... keep that arm up!"

Father Robyn turned on his heel and strode toward the portal.

Rome! Rome was the other side of the world. Was there no limit to what they wanted of him?

*'Damn the Church to Hell!'*

At penance on the fifth morning a nun stood in front of him with a list of implements to be acquired from the blacksmith. At least it took his mind off his aching arms by forcing him to memorise the items. Two sheep shears, five wool combs, three ladles for greasing wool during combing, six weaving batterns, four harbricks, two tweezers and two score needles in eight different sizes. The elderly nun made him repeat the lot by heart until she was satisfied, by which time the novice called time on penitence.

Each carrying two iron bars, Begiloc with Caena and three of their men set off from the monastery to the smith's forge. The smith, a giant named Dagobert, listened to the Briton repeat his order while scratching lines on the wall of the smithy under various suspended objects. The new scratches were below others crossed out. Caena spoke next, reciting a shorter list, two blades for scythes, four for sickles and a score of fish hooks of different sizes.

Gazing round, Begiloc saw two slaves, but what caught his eye was a steel blade, long thirty inches and wide two, double-edged and fullered. Down the central groove ran a serpent. Intrigued, he strode over and grasped the sword by the tang. Even without hilt and pommel the feel of the weapon in his hand impressed him, light and with the promise of a good balance. He must have it. Another serpent writhed in the hollow on the other side of the blade. Set apart on the bench ready to be riveted, the crafted knob was in the form of the head of a bear, but the sword lacked a hilt.

"This blade. Has it an owner?"

Dagobert grinned and showed more missing teeth than not.

"The first nobleman as sees it, I 'ope."

"This leud, how much will he pay?"

The smith threw back his head and bellowed, "More 'an you'll ever touch in your lifetime!"

The Saxons gathered round the two men curious to hear their exchange.

"How much would that be?" Begiloc asked.

Dagobert stared at the Briton, his smile fading to be replaced by an appraising look.

"That sword there, I couldn't sell it for less than one solidus. Know 'ow much work 'as gone into that? Just the pommel? The blade alone – ten days."

"Ay, and what about the hilt?"

"Well, that's up to whoever buys it. 'Orn or bone or then again, I can weld an iron one."

"Horn's good."

Incredulous, Dagobert stared at the Briton, at the Saxons and, beard upraised, roared out his amusement. Castration was a profitable business and Begiloc had the money taken from Shmuel in Rems. Rummaging in his purse, he drew out a gold piece, a solidus minted in Treves. A flick of the coin and the begrimed hand of the smith closed around it in mid-air. The blacksmith stared in disbelief from his clenched fist to the Briton. The huge hand opened and he turned the bright piece over for inspection.

"'Orn it is then. The sword will be ready to collect before sunset."

Begiloc strode over to seal the affair with a handclasp.

The chatter on the way back to the monastery was animated. Testimony to the famed skill of the Frankish smiths in these parts, the blade was a fine piece of workmanship. Alfwald took his chance. Sidling up to Begiloc, he clapped him on the back.

"With your splendid sword, you won't need that one anymore."

The Saxon jerked a thumb at the weapon in the belt loop of the Briton, the one taken from the floor in the castrating room in Rems. Truth be told, a decent blade but not a match for the one just bought.

"Ay, about right, better than that old seax," he teased.

"I'll take it off your hands then."

"Ay, you will that ... if ..." he let the word hang.

"... if ... ?"

"If you find me a good piece of yew to fashion a hearpe."

"I'll get the wood in exchange for the sword," Leofric cut in.

"Hey!" Alfwald turned and shoved him, "Keep your damned nose out!"

The younger man raised his fist but Caena stepped in front of him.

"The matter is settled," he said. "Alfwald will find the yew and get the blade. What say you, Leofric gets your seax? It's better than his."

"Done!" Alfwald held out his hand and his comrade took it. The older man said, "Unless you help me find the wood, no seax!"

They passed through the monastery gate in companionable chatter and headed for the refectory in the hope of a drink before lunch.

As Begiloc entered the room, his smile died. Three men sat opposite the door each clasping a jug of ale: two monks and a priest. The face of the latter, strong-boned, under his thinning blond hair, seemed carved out of the cliffs of his native Dorset: the nose the beak of a raptor on a crag. His eyes, the pale blue of goshawk's eggs, lit up at the sight of the Briton and his thick, fleshy lips curled into the half-smile half-sneer that he associated with him. Denehard!

The priest, in his early thirties, stood and spread his arms in welcome, his broad shoulders tapering to lean waist and hips. The Briton halted, causing Ina to shunt into him and the other Saxons to still their banter.

"You don't seem happy to greet an old friend, Begiloc."

"Friend!" the warrior spat the word. "What kind of a friend is it that frees a man from slavery and then enslaves him again?"

"How so?" The cleric lowered his arms and sat. Pulse pounding, Begiloc took two steps forward into the refectory.

"You know right well. If not for you, why am I here, far from home? More than three years since I saw my family."

The curious smile returned, "Enslaved? The opposite. Thank me, I fetched you to do God's bidding. Exult man! What you do helps free your soul. What are a few years in this vale of tears compared to an eternal life of purity and joy?" Denehard raised his jug and took a swig of ale, never shifting his gaze as he studied the emotions the other man displayed.

Indignant, Begiloc strode over to the table and placed both hands flat leaning towards the clergyman. The Saxons, boisterous once more, followed him to pull up chairs and call for ale. The Briton ignored them.

"God's bidding? Ay, and killing pagans is only part of it. It's the so-called Christians that bother me...Meryn blinded by a...*bishop*...!" his voice broke on the last word and Caena hushed the Saxons.

"Meryn? Blind?"

"Ay."

"Where is he? Here? I must go to him at once." Denehard made to stand.

Straightening, Begiloc said, "Not here. At Verzy. Want my opinion? I'd say he'd sooner the Devil visited him."

Face haggard, the priest slumped down, voice hushed.

"What can I do for Meryn?"

"You can let me take him home to Dumnonia."

There was a long silence in which Denehard put his head in his hands and one of his companions placed a gentle hand on his shoulder.

"I can't do that," the cleric frowned, "there are orders, you, I, your men, these brothers...we leave for Rome at sunrise."

"Rome! You see?"

Begiloc crashed a fist on the table causing the jugs to jump and the monk in arrival with a tray of ales to quail. "The difference between us is you've chosen your life as a priest while I'm enslaved to the Church. Your family is dead, mine is alive – we should each go and join our families!"

Denehard leapt to his feet. "Enough!" He pointed, "How dare you! Show respect! Remember this, we must all serve someone. Need I remind you of your position? I had hoped for old times sake...as it is, I see you hardened your heart to the Lord and to His servants."

Leaving his ale untouched, Begiloc spun round and walked away.

"I haven't finished. Come back! That's an order!"

Damned if he would obey, he strode out into the fresh breeze and tried to calm his rage. Gazing skywards, he spotted a falcon, its feathers ruffled, letting itself be carried along below the scudding clouds until, with a sudden beat of its wings, it wheeled and swooped on its prey. Ay, Begiloc grimaced, that's it. I must spread my wings – and soon – if I don't want to be swept off to Rome.

The next hour he spent chopping logs for the ovens as an excuse to work off his anger, but also as a chance to plan the future. Was there no way he could defy the Church and gain freedom?

*'I'd flee to the pagans but for Somerhild and Ealric.'*

The novice who had overseen his penance interrupted his thoughts. He lowered the axe and stared at him in anxiety. Had he come to inflict more torture for disobeying the priest? The youth brought the abbesses' summons and he must present himself forthwith. The axe, he planted in the chopping block before hastening to the nun's quarters.

To his vexation, Denehard and the two monks from the refectory were waiting when he was admitted into the presence of Leoba. Relieved the abbess was not wearing her mitre or bearing her staff, he supposed there was still time for them; in fact, her first words were tart. "Begiloc, can it be you learnt nothing from your penance? Well ... ?"

"My Lady," he bowed his head, "I understand something of Our Lord's pain ..." – then came an inspiration – "... and I discovered loss and suffering strain the way a man can love and trust God ..." he peered at the abbess from under lowered brow. Was it a smile? It was!

"You learnt far more than I supposed although you did not assimilate the concept of obedience. Still ... Father Denehard spoke to me of your loss and suffering since first we met in Wimborne and I came to a decision. Nerve-racked, Begiloc waited. "You will accompany these three brothers to Rome and bring them safe home ..." he gritted his teeth "... but, I give you my word, when you return you shall go back home to your family in Wessex with my blessing."

The warrior dropped to his knees, "Thank you, My Lady."

She bestowed on him her angelic smile.

"Your penance is over, but I must insist, you will obey Father Denehard on the way to Rome and back, is that clear?"

"I give you my word, My Lady."

The Mother Superior stepped forward, "Go with my blessing. *In nomine Patris ...*"

Blessing concluded, she ordered him to stand and began to speak but halted in doubt before engaging him with a long stare.

"I suppose, you will want to know why you go to Rome. In Neustria, with Caena you heard the heretic preach, it is precious testimony. The other reason is more complicated," she sighed, touching her cross, "Archbishop Boniface is pressing the Holy See for the removal of Bishop Milo since his crimes are repugnant to God and man ..." The abbess held up her hand to stay his words. "It is hard. His brother is Count of Hornbach and his sister, Chrotrude, Duchess of Austrasia. In these troubled times, the Church needs their support and that of the Mayor of the Palace. Yet," she raised her chin and her eyes turned heavenwards, "we must strive to deliver the people from the snares of Satan, the fowler, and from malicious and evil men, so that the word of God may have free course and be glorified."

"What is it I must do, My Lady?"

"Be steadfast in defence of my messengers," her hand swept to take in the priest and the two monks. "Be wary. Milo has a web of spies and will not hesitate to confound your mission. Most of all, bear witness to the Pontifex Maximus...," her voice grew as sharp as the whetted edge of his sword, "...to the barbarous blinding of Meryn."

Only after a moment did he stop gaping at his abbess. Speak to the pope, he, a simple ceorl!

Dismissed, his head was in a whirl. Meet the Holy Father, see Rome, he must find his confessor. With a light heart, Begiloc sought out Father Robyn. In his present mood, the beds of purple-flowered hyssop appeared lovelier than before – useful plant – grown for curing coughs and for making honey more aromatic. A monk gathering the flowers told him the priest was in the small chandler's workshop. Begiloc hurried there pushing open the creaky door. At the sound, Father Robyn looked up from braiding cotton strands for a wick. He smiled at Begiloc before passing it to the monk who dipped it into molten wax.

"Come to make candles, my son?"

"Father. How far is Rome?"

"All roads lead there they say, but also some rivers, so it depends. Why this sudden keenness? Last time we spoke I thought..." he paused, confused at the huge grin on the face of a man who seldom smiled. "...Why, what is it?"

The beaming smile widened.

"Father, our Lady Abbess says I can go home to Wimborne! To my wife and son! As soon as we return from Rome. So, I want to know how far it is. We leave at dawn."

The cleric scratched an ear.

"Let's see, it's the end of June. Three moons and you're in Rome." He ticked off three fingers. "There'll be business to take care of there," another tick, "then there's the three months back..." the priest swapped hands ...

A worried expression replaced the grin of Begiloc.

"Back in January then?"

"Can't cross the Alps in winter," Father Robyn frowned, "mid-April before you can depart Rome, so mid-July before you arrive here."

The sudden scowl with the jagged scar above the left eye of the Briton transformed the earlier exuberant countenance to one of abject misery.

"That's more like your old self," the clergyman said. "Be of cheer, it will be summer when you set off for Wessex and you'll be home to celebrate Christ's Mass with your family."

A semblance of a smile flickered for an instant on the face of the warrior.

"Ay, there's that to it. Thank you, Father."

The priest watched him leave and sighed at the pain and loneliness of the man, separated far from his family, his soul tormented, accepting the Lady's command with heavy heart. The sacrament of wedlock was quite clear: *'those whom God hath joined together let no man put asunder'* and yet in the case of the Briton, the Church was without doubt blameworthy.

## CHAPTER 11

Begiloc strode to the village with a spring in his step. The prospect of returning home, albeit a year hence, a hope that had died to a glimmer surged anew. This, with the expectation of wielding his new sword, raised his spirits from the depths where they dwelt since the shock of Meryn's blinding. He would have plenty to tell Somerhild and Ealric when he got back to Wessex. Rome! The Alps! Had anyone told him he'd see either when he tilled the Near Field in Wimborne, he'd have named him a madman.

The blacksmith, at Begiloc's shout, halted his hammering. Dagobert, arms slick with sweat, laid down his tool, greeted him and beckoned. The heat from the furnace blasted as Begiloc advanced into the smoke-filled smithy, where one of the slaves worked the bellows while the other flung a shovelful of charcoal on the blaze.

"Don't like to think what yon abbess'd say, I just started on 'er order. Been at yon sword all day," he said with a conspiratorial tone. The smith punched Begiloc, but his idea of a light blow sent the Briton staggering. "Ha-ha! Let's see what yer think of 'er. Mind, I made a change, a 'orn 'ilt's all well an' good, but if it breaks you're wielding a useless weap'n. Can't 'ave that! I've inlaid a bronze coil. Pretty job an' there's no way yon'll break."

Steering Begiloc deeper into the forge, he picked up the sword. The nimble Briton leapt back as the craftsman thrust it at him.

"Ha-ha! See 'ow I've polished 'er. 'Ad to grind 'er down a bit, balance wrong, see? Welded copper eyes fer the bear – nice contrast an' look at that 'ilt!"

"I will, if you shift that ham of a hand!"

"Ha-ha!" The smith threw his head back and roared. "Be as quick wi' your arm as wi' your tongue, an' ye'll slay a few with 'er!"

Dagobert lay the sword on the bench and Begiloc admired the beauty of the finished weapon. The smith basked in his approval but grabbed his wrist.

"Not yet. Need to know all about 'er first. Swords are like women, take some understandin'. See 'im o'er there?" A thick finger indicated the sturdier of the two slaves and Begiloc noted his skin was dusky; little wonder he hadn't noticed in the smoky, dark smithy with both men work-blackened.

"Captured four years ago after the defeat o' the Moors – he be one of 'em. Long story... found out 'e was a smith ... got 'old of 'im ... money well spent ... best day's work I done. Know a thing or two these Arabs!" The hairy finger rose again, "Ibn al-Naghira – 'son of the 'ot-tempered woman' – ha-ha! That's what he says his name means. Got a 'ot-tempered woman myself! Fact is, this sword's made wi' *my* an' *'is* knowledge together. Young Ibn waited for a balmy night to temper the blade, see? Passes cherry red from the fire ter the quenching wi'out suffering the chill from the air. Get it? Little things! They're important."

The sword clasped in his fist, he propelled Begiloc over to a workbench.

"This contraption 'ere. It's a post vice. Moorish invention. Clever lot! Ye can bash away at anythin' wi' yer 'eaviest 'ammer. The post takes the shock, see?"

He clamped the blade in the vice, "Watch this!" He grasped the hilt and bent the weapon in a breath-taking arc.

Begiloc gasped. "Stop ... don't ... !"

The smith let go and the sword flashed into the opposite trajectory and back and forth till coming to a halt in a vertical position.

"I thought it would snap–"

Dagobert planted his hands on his hips and glowered under lowered brow, "*It* ... *?... It... ?* It's a *she* I'll 'ave ye know! An' *ye* must have faith in yer woman an' in yer smith. Love an' trust 'er an' she'll be loyal to ye for the rest of yer life."

Unclamping the blade, he nipped the pommel between two fingers before passing it to Begiloc, who weighed the sword in his hand – light, perfect for battle. Precise balance – he swept it through the air – ideal for combat.

"Well?"

The warrior looked into the expectant, blackened face. "I love *her*," he said.

"Ha-ha, I knew it. Ibn! 'E loves our sword!"

Ibn al-Naghira laid down his pincers and bowed to him. The Briton in reply raised the weapon and kissed the flat of the blade.

Back at the monastery, the warrior, old sword in hand and new at his belt, found Alfwald playing dice with Leofric between the granary and the goose-pen.

"Have you two nothing better to do?"

"After an hour's combat training with Caena a man deserves a rest!" Leofric said, "Hey! Isn't that the new blade?"

Dice forgotten, they leapt up and he let them admire and wield his weapon. Alfwald contemplated the sword in the left hand of Begiloc.

"We shall have to search for that wood, Leofric, so the Briton can make good his word."

"My word holds, Alfwald," he said, passing over the sword, "it's yours, but at dawn we leave for Rome. There'll be no time to seek out yew."

"Rome?" the Saxon gaped.

"Caena has said nought of it?"

Alfwald shook his head, "Nay, the great bear has not. By Heimdall's horn, we're off to Rome!"

A range of emotions showed on his face as he eyed the weapon.

"I'll get the yew as soon as I can, Begiloc. We all miss your tunes." A hand rested on the shoulder of his leader, "My thanks for the sword."

The resentful scowls at Wimborne seemed a lifetime ago. Now they entrusted their lives to him.

*'A pity Meryn isn't here to share in this companionship. A true friend who is distant can be closer than one at two paces.'*

He turned away with a wry smile as Leofric resumed his bickering over the dice.

That evening a messenger was sent to Amorbach, a newly-consecrated Benedictine house, to advise of their arrival. The monastery, a stopping point on their way to the river Rhenus, lay eight leagues to the east in dense forest. Back in Würzburg, Denehard had chosen two of the missionaries with an eye to the journey. Brother Dignovar, a monk who had taken his vows at an abbey in the Alps, devised the plan to reach Vormatia and travel by boat to Basilia, the first stage of his task to guide them over the mountains. Instead, *Frate* Tanolfi, a Lombard, would lead them from Agusta to Rome.

Arrangements made, the priest, two monks and nine warriors set off next morning. Where the track permitted,

Begiloc marched beside Caena comparing the ease of progress with the fatigue of previous experiences. Overhead a cover of beech produced little undergrowth below and since it had not rained for days the hard ground meant good speed.

Both the monks were thin and wore a black habit but the similarity ended there. The Swiss was in his late thirties with hooded, intelligent eyes, long hooked nose, large ears with a strange, pointed lobe. A sound judge of character, Begiloc liked Dignovar from the start. Was there something of himself in the serious disposition, the few words from the thin-lipped mouth? In contrast, the younger Lombard had black hair, a flimsy moustache and beard restricted to the cleft in his chin. Frate Tanolfi with his large eyes, sunken cheeks and long, straight nose and ready smile might have smitten many a maid but for the otherworldliness of his demeanour. Time enough, thought Begiloc, for him to warm to the monk given what Brother Robyn had said about the length of the journey.

The low sun indicated the hour after Vespers when they arrived at Amorbach. The fields outlying the monastery testified to the hard labour of felling, clearing and tilling of the monks over the past years.

Abbot Amor, still full of missionary zeal, replied to the thanks of Denehard for his hospitable welcome, by quoting St Benedict, "Let all guests who arrive be received as Christ, because He will say: *'I was a stranger and you took me in.'* Matthew 25:35*,*" he added the citation with relish.

Ablutions completed, the warriors were conducted to a table in the refectory set apart from the monks. The abbot placed Denehard at his right and further along, at the corner of the high table, sat the dean, Prior Leuthard. Having taken an instant dislike to the pinched-faced monk whose eyes were ever in movement, Begiloc found himself seated close to him.

Monks brought a platter of unleavened bread served with roasted fowl on top to the delight of the tired travellers. The aroma sharpened their appetites. Rising, they bowed their heads for grace.

*"Benedictus benedictat per Jesum Christum Dominum Nostrum. Amen."*

The sign of the cross, then they were hacking at the flesh. Enhanced by herbs, the succulent meat melted on Begiloc's tongue.

A discussion began at the table behind him about the bird set before them, the monks agreeing it was teal. This led to a more lively exchange.

"Teal springs from the rotten wood of old ships," one monk affirmed.

"Not so," cried another, "they spring from the gum on fir trees!"

"Nay, they are born from a freshwater shell like unto oysters!"

Frowning, the abbot leapt to his feet, clapped his hands and called for decorum.

With Caena next to him deep in conversation, Begiloc sat in silence. It meant he caught Denehard's query that the prior was not of these parts.

"No, indeed," said the abbot, "Prior Leuthard is a Frank from the Abbey of St Matthias at Treves."

The hand of Leuthard clenched under the table until the knuckles whitened and Begiloc noted the hasty disclaimer.

"Oh, but I was there no time at all, a few weeks. Before I spent twenty years in Catalauns at the monastery of St Valerian as claustral prior."

He touched his nose and shuffled in his seat.

Denehard made a polite remark and the conversation changed. Begiloc frowned. What? Impossible! This religious house was new, at most Leuthard had lived here two years, plus a few weeks in Treves and yet he claimed to have been the claustral prior at Catalauns at the very time they were there. They had met Prior Walcaud with his crooked nose and lantern jaw.

*'Back in Dumnonia we say 'lies have short legs.'*
The prior's lie had been overtaken straight away.

*'What does he wish to hide? His time at Treves? Treves – of course! Bishop Milo!'*

In natural discourse, the insistence of the prior on knowing their route and on the purpose of their visit to Rome would have seemed no more than polite conversation. To the forewarned Begiloc it was blatant prying. Had not Abbess Leoba warned them of a web of spies?

No surprise therefore when Leuthard rose, excused himself and slipped out of the refectory. A moment later he too stood to follow the monk. The prior strode along the cloister out at the end of the arch-flanked walkway. Up to the door ran Begiloc and in the gloom spied the figure of the monk as he disappeared into a building to the right. A glance through one of the windows revealed rows of desks with bottles of ink and quills and parchments in various stages of completion – the scriptorium. The prior lit a candle and bent over a desk to write. Epistle ended, the monk blew sand from a small piece of parchment, which he rolled and tied up with thread. A message! The Briton dodged round the corner of the wall while the monk shaded the flame of his taper as he walked toward the church.

Leuthard turned the iron door ring to the bell tower and vanished inside leaving the door ajar. Begiloc dashed over to follow him. Footsteps echoed on the stairs beyond the bell rope and the light of the candle grew feebler as the prior ascended the spiral steps.

The staircase led to a simple structure with a wooden platform at the top of the tower, where a bell hung from a beam in the planked roof. The belfry was open except for the columns created by the four narrow, supporting walls. Through the hole in the floor Begiloc saw Prior Leuthard tie his roll of parchment to an arrow.

*'A message!'*

In the corner of the bell chamber, a bow was propped against the wall alongside white-fletched arrows. The villain had prepared everything in advance of their arrival and was moving the candle to and fro at chest height, clicking his tongue until he saw an answering glimmer of light beyond the walls.

"At last!" the prior murmured then bent to put the taper in the corner and reached for the bow, notched the arrow and hauled the string back with more strength than he would credit to a monk, to send the message arcing into the dusk.

Begiloc sprang on the platform and his adversary spun round. In the same instant, he grabbed another arrow. The Briton was on him, seizing Leuthard by the wrists before he could raise his bow, which fell to the floor as the two wrestled. The intent was to bring the monk to his knees, but the ease with which the prior had drawn back the bowstring should have been a warning. Stronger than he had reckoned, the prior at once broke his grip. He saw the fist coming, spun away, still clinging to the other wrist and his momentum pulled his foe off balance. Ten yards above the ground they staggered, teetering together on the edge of the open platform in a macabre dance. The intention of Begiloc was to save them both, but Leuthard brought his fist down hard on the hand grasping his wrist.

Crying out, he let go and with a warrior's instinct skipped aside light-footed as the prior aimed the expected shove at his chest. Finding no resistance, the monk wailed as he pitched off the platform and hurtled to the ground.

Grabbing the taper, he hurried down. Nobody could survive such a fall. In fact, he found the neck twisted at an unnatural angle when he held the candle over the corpse. He cursed for his double foolishness, for neither had he prevented the monk from betraying their movements nor had he forced answers out of the wretch. Nothing to show except what he knew: the Bishop of Rems was an ever-growing menace.

The investigation was brief since the finding of the bow and arrows in the bell tower concurred with the account provided by Begiloc. With hindsight, Denehard recognised the excessive zeal of the prior in ascertaining their movements and therefore the need for a change of plan.

Abbot Amor led Father Denehard, Brother Dignovar and Begiloc into the Chapter House, far from any eavesdropper, where he made a suggestion once the candles were lit.

"You planned to head straight to Vormatia and the vile Leuthard will have revealed this knowledge."

The abbot said, "Did you know less than seven leagues to the south there is a brother house consecrated the same month as our own? At Mosbach. From there," he glanced at Dignovar to check he knew the place, "it's not far to Sinsheim and the Old High Road that runs through the oak forest, you know the place?"

The Swiss monk smiled, "...and from there unless I'm mistaken, we can soon reach Spira on the river Rhenus."

"Father, by boat how far to the south is this town from Vormatia?" asked Begiloc.

The abbot stroked his beard.

"Fear not that your foe will find you. Acting on the information sent by Leuthard–"

"... and remember the enemy believes we know nought of the spy... excuse me, Father Abbot!"

The monk acknowledged Denehard, "... they will search to the east for you. Spira is seven leagues to the south, so they must scour many acres of forest or wait for you to board ship, but at the wrong place."

"We shan't pass them on the waterway if they are waiting at Vormatia," Dignovar said, "we will be well to the south." Everything agreed, they went to Compline before retiring for the night.

A hard day's march brought them to the monastery of Mosbach, in appearance, the twin of Amorbach. There the abbot outdid his monastic neighbour in welcoming, citing the command of St Benedict and "Galatians 6:10 ... *'and to wayfarers let the greatest care be taken, especially in reception of the poor and travellers, because Christ is received more specially in them ...'*"

The abbot, a plump, jovial monk true to his word, announced the next morning the fame of Abbess Leoba's love of reading had reached Mosbach. He gave Denehard a copy of *Dicta Abbatis Pirminii*, extracts from the Single Canonical Books, written by their founder, making the priest promise to consign it into her own hands on their return from Rome.

The rest of their journey to the river went well, the sight of the cathedral cheered them and their mood improved seeing the waterway, at least two furlongs wide, flowing past. They took a waterside inn, a hovel so filthy Begiloc refused to undress for the night and slept in his clothes.

By the riverside the next morning, Begiloc and Caena tried to find a boatman willing to take them upriver, but met with blank stares and shaken heads. No-one wanted the fatigue of a three-day trip against the current. The Saxon pulled his comrade aside to suggest asking for a one-day passage when a stocky, swarthy-skinned man with a forked beard approached.

"I hear you seek a boat to Basilia. How many of you?"
Begiloc scrutinised the stranger, whose face and manner did not please him, but this was the first boatman to show interest in the venture.

"We two, and eleven others."

"Thir'een! An unlucky number! Bein' as there's my men to add on it makes no diff'rence, right? O'ny thing is, it's three days out and two days back. You pr'pared to pay for five days?"

"Depends on the price," Begiloc said. After haggling for a while, they clasped hands. The boatman went off to fetch his craft and crew while the Briton sent the Saxon to bring their comrades.

Earlier the Briton had noticed the curious gaze of a fisherman sat mending his net on an upturned boat. Wandering over to the man, he smiled at the weather-beaten face. The fisher nodded and continued with his task, which slowed to a halt when Begiloc took a silver piece from his purse and held it between finger and thumb.

"I'm after an honest answer."

"Ask an honest question."

"The boatman we were talking to – can he be trusted?"

The fisherman lowered the net on his knees and stretched out a hand. The warrior dropped the coin into it and, swift as the strike of an osprey, it disappeared from sight.

"An honest reply," he picked the net up and tied a knot, "is that he don't be from hereabouts. Never seen him afore. An', bein' as we're talkin' about honesty, myself, I wouldn't let him anywhere near my purse."

Suspicions confirmed, he hurried away from the quay in the direction of the inn and found Caena.

"What's up?"

"I've been sniffing around and I don't like the smell. The boatman's not from these parts."

The Saxon tugged at his thick moustache.

"In the pay of Milo? Best forewarned."

"Could be."

The anxious faces of his men appraised him, waiting for orders.

"In the boat be ready. Anything strange and let me or Caena know."

Back at the quay, the crew hove a broad shallow-bottomed vessel into sight. Begiloc studied their approach. The swarthy-skinned boatman stood in the prow and the steersman brought their number to ten. All the men carried a sword.

The boatman sprang on to the wharf and tied a rope around a wooden block.

"You all ready?"

"Ay," Begiloc looked around his party and met each man's eye, sure of their attention. "How come all your oarsmen be armed?"

The reply rolled off the tongue but the eyes were wary.

"River pirates. Can't take no risks, 'specially upstream. Man has to defend his prop'ty. Are you gettin' in or what?"

"Ay," said Caena, "I'll go first," and he led them down into the boat.

They pushed off and soon the muscular oarsmen had them moving at a steady pace against the current in mid-stream.

Discounting the monks and the priest, they were ten against ten if these were enemies. Strange, no foe in his right mind would choose to be evenly matched, Begiloc reflected and edged closer to Caena to find the Saxon shared his unease. Everything seemed regular. The boatman strolled to and fro urging on his oarsmen and they were making good progress. Each craft that approached downstream the Briton eyed with trepidation, but none carried armed men – and it rang an alarm bell – did they not fear river pirates? Other than a vague suspicion, they had no reason to attack the crew, in any case, their fears might prove unfounded.

After some time, Eadwig, the youngest of the Saxons, moved over to him. Sensible and of few words, he spoke in a low voice.

"Do not look until I get back. On the other bank are armed horsemen following us."

Aware the boatman's stare was fixed on him, Begiloc did not move until, satisfied, the swarthy-skinned man turned away. With no sign of haste, the Briton faced the other way and sought movement on the far side of the river. Sunlight glinted off a helm, so that was it! Any moment, the boat would veer to the shore and they would be outnumbered.

"It's time!" he hissed, sword flashing, blood spurted from the throat of the nearest oarsman before Caena yelled, "To arms!"

Oarsmen jumped to their feet and drew swords, heedless of the danger of capsizing as men sprang over benches to strike at each other. The cramped space impeded normal combat, so the front three of Begiloc, Caena and Wybert fought with the first three oarsmen. On both sides, those behind struggled to keep their feet in the rocking boat. Next to Begiloc, Wybert slithered on the blood of the slain enemy and the deathblow that ended his life came swift and merciless. Enraged, sword locked with that of his foe, the Briton redoubled his strength throwing his adversary off balance to be shocked at the ease with which his new weapon sliced into the man's thighbone. At his side, Caena drove his seax into the breast of his enemy. Ina, who had taken the place of his dead companion, howled in triumph as his seax cut deep into the sword arm of Wybert's slayer.

Bloodlust up, the huge Saxon, an awesome avenger, forced the leader of the boatmen back on the man behind him. The confined space did the rest. The boatman fell over his comrade and Caena pounced. His seax carved into the neck of the swarthy-skinned man. The steersman, the farthest enemy from the fighting, had seen enough. Throwing his sword overboard, he followed to swim for the shore. Another dived after him as Begiloc cut down his adversary. The last enemy standing fell to Ina, the boat ceased its wild rocking and Caena howled a savage victory cry.

"You could have left one for me," Alfwald complained, "I didn't strike once with my new sword."
Their laughter was grim: the loss of Wybert too raw.

The vessel drifted with the current downstream. Alert, Begiloc gave orders to throw the enemy bodies into the river and sent Alfwald to the steer-board while the other Saxons manned the oars. The new helmsman decided on a landing place, their first task to bury Wybert in the soft ground near the bank where Father Denehard led prayers for the dead man over the grave.

Ceremony ended, Begiloc called, "Brother Dignovar, over here!" The men gathered round curious. "The foe follows on the other bank. To be rid of them I need to know the course of the river."
The monk hesitated.

"How many miles to Basilia, how many towns on the way?"

Dignovar furrowed his brow and looked from one to the other. "How far upriver did we come?"

Caena shrugged. "Three leagues?"

"At least three," Father Denehard said.

"Then there are forty to Basilia. There is one settlement at sixteen leagues, Strazburg, and four villages. Three of them after the town."

Begiloc located the position of the sun, "It's nigh on noon. Here's what we do," he reassured the expectant faces, "we travel for two hours, stop to eat and rest, row for another two and halt till nightfall. After dark, we journey through the night past Salzburg until an hour before daybreak when we hide the boat and camp among the trees. To confound our foe, we move at night – unless there's a better idea?"

Smiles and shaken heads answered him.

"Father Denehard, Brothers, you will be our eyes. Keep them peeled for movement on the far bank and be wary of the river traffic. Alfwald you take the steer-board and I'll relieve the first weakling at the oar!"

Gadwalls burped overhead and their shrill cries mixed with those of mallards and coot. To Begiloc's delight, among the purple moorgrass meadows the occasional orchid blossomed. When a monk pointed out a flash of metal from the far bank, it did not bother him since his plan relied on the cover of darkness.

The combination of new moon and scattered clouds provided the obscurity they needed to set off in silence. Deep in the night, disaster almost struck mid-river close to the small church of Brisiascus, where lay an island. Frate Tanolfi in the bows saved them from running aground otherwise the plan worked to perfection. In the early hours of the third night, Brother Dignovar came up to Begiloc.

"It's my guess," he said, "we are a league from Basilia. If we are to avoid the town, we should seek a place to leave the boat."

Alfwald steered them to the bank to rest until the weak light of dawn gave substance to the shapeless surroundings. Half-asleep in the bows, Caena unhitched the rope from a branch and sought a suitable place to hide the craft. Soon, they found a reed bed half a mile upstream where the harsh cry of an indignant bittern followed the call of a marsh harrier alarmed at the invasion; otters and water voles dived and scampered in outraged flight when the bows ploughed into the silt of the bank. Nearby, a purple heron stood imperturbable, a frog kicking in vain in its bill. The Saxons cursed as they slithered free of the cloying slime and Caena, the first to solid ground, hauled his companions out of the mud. Next, they made fast the boat before gathering large stones and laying them by the tree line in a distinctive pattern so they might find the vessel the next summer.

The local knowledge of the Swiss monk helped them skirt Basilia and by noon the town lay at their backs. A steep climb, packs and shields weighing them down, brought them to a village where they camped for the night. After only six miles on the second day in the mountains, they came to the monastery of Moutier where they found the comfort of a bath and a meal after much time sleeping rough.

Eight days later, they reached Lake Leman having first marvelled at mounts, waterfalls, lakes and tarns, a large graveyard and a place with an ancient bridge where three rivers met. The sight of the huge lake filled Begiloc with awe. What wonders he would recount to Ealric around the fire on a long winter's night!

The shore led them to the foothills of the Alps, past a ruined villa and a large cemetery, to the ancient Roman road and the steady ascent along the River Rottu. At the end of the valley, they reached Octodurus, the gateway to the Pass of Poeninus. The Romans had controlled the defile from this place and they shared amazement at the ruins of the amphitheatre, temples, canal and thermal baths and not least at the peak of the white mount that loomed immense over the village. However, the biggest surprise came early the next morning.

The monk led them through the settlement to a farm, where a number of mules grazed in a field. Brother Dignovar strode over to the house of the high-pitched roof to batter on the door, "Heyno! Wake up old bear, the winter's over, you can come out!"

"Who's that at this ungodly hour!" a deep voice rumbled. A moment later, the door swung back and a dark-skinned giant roared, "Dignovar!" and enfolded the monk in a hug worthy of any bear. Greetings and exchange of news over, the monk struck a deal for the muleteer to lead the group over the pass down to Aorta.

Barrel-chested Heyno marched up to Caena and stood in front of him feet apart. Only he could look the Saxon in the eye without raising his head.

"Sure you can do this? It's no place for faint hearts."
The warrior folded his arms, leaning forward so his nose almost touched that of the other.

"When I need a new heart, I'll cut me one out of the first bear I chance upon. Best not upset me!"

The muleteer rocked with laughter and clapped him on the shoulder. "Thing is," he looked around at the attentive faces, "we go up to over eight-thousand feet, but don't worry," he smiled, "the beasts know what to do. If we set off straight away, we can spend the night at Burgus Sancti Petrus. It's four leagues away, but it feels more like forty!"

The men from Wessex settled into the saddles of the docile but agile mules and began to enjoy views of the magnificent snow-capped peaks. They followed water courses along valleys and asked themselves whether Heyno had teased them about faint-heartedness, being mounted proved a relief from the tramping and rowing of the last two weeks.

In a small village, they set up camp and the muleteer took them to an inn he knew. Mid-evening, Begiloc stepped outside for a breath of mountain air under a night sky ablaze with pulsing stars and planets. The heavens seemed closer than ever.

"Light was created on the first day. It wasn't until the fourth day that God fashioned the stars." Surprised, he whirled round, having heard no footfall. Brother Dignovar smiled, "Think Begiloc, the sphere, the *primum mobile* carries round all these stars and above that is another sphere that rotates, the *empyreum* where the angels live. Think how bright it must be there!"

"Alas, Brother, I fear I was born under Saturn's influence."

"Cold and dry of nature, melancholic?"

"Ay."

The monk considered the Briton, a shrewd expression on his face.

"*In tears amid the alien corn*, is it? Or in this case amid the alien peaks. Truth be told, Begiloc, I sought you for a reason. On the morn, we climb about three thousand feet. We'll see no life until we reach the settlement of Saint Remy where Remigius of Rems baptised King Goutron."

Begiloc sniffed.

'*Monks bring religion into everything!'*

Impassive, he waited.

"Our ride takes us through a high and most remote land where evil men lurk to prey on pilgrims. The shame is many pious travellers undertake the journey to Rome bearing offerings to a favoured shrine and they make rich and defenceless pickings."

"Robbers, up there?"

The monk headed back towards the inn before half-turning to say, "A man forewarned is a man forearmed. Linger not to brood. I'll wager you're a child of the third planet."

"Third planet?"

"Ay, Mars. You're a warrior, aren't you?"

In front of the inn at sunrise, before going to the stables to collect the animals, Begiloc warned his men to be vigilant among the peaks.

Ina was incredulous. "What! Robbers up there in that godforsaken place? What sort of thieves make the effort to skulk up there?"

"Desperate men." The tone of Brother Dignovar brooked no argument.

To the eye, the houses dwindled to the size of boxes for monks' fish hooks as they followed a ridge and climbed ever higher. Frate Tanolfi halted first. White-faced and trembling, he cried, "I cannot go on! May the Lord forgive my lack of faith, but my head spins and I fear I shall fall."

How Begiloc understood him, for his stomach had clenched more than once on the ascent. What were they to do? Worse to turn back than to press on.

"Steady Brother," Heyno called, "leave it to the beast, he never puts a hoof wrong."

From behind him, Dignovar called, "*Fratello*, you must have crossed these mountains before. What you did once you may do again."

Agitated, the Lombard shook his head. "I left my homeland by sea. For Pity's sake, I can't go on!"

The muleteer dismounted. "There's only one thing for it," he tugged a length of cloth from his tunic, walked over to Frate Tanolfi and blindfolded him. "Leave it to our four-legged friend."

He clapped the monk on the back and they set off once more. Begiloc almost wished for a blindfold, because at moments a hoof slid on loose stones or the track narrowed threatening a fatal plunge, but as the day drew on and the sure-hoofed animals proved their worth, the Lombard monk found his courage and removed the cloth from his face.

Soon afterwards, they dropped down into a defile where stones showered down. An attack! One struck Heyno's mule on the flank causing the beast to rear almost unsaddling him. Another hit Leofric on the arm and Alfwald parried a rock with his shield before it could strike his head. Begiloc drew his sword and, shield raised, dismounted. The Saxons followed his example. Used to fighting on foot, they knew this land was unsuited to mounted combat. The hail of rocks on the advancing warriors continued relentless while, out of range, the monks and Heyno rounded up the terrified riderless animals and led them to safety farther down the defile.

With his shield Begiloc parried a stone. Too late, his assailant snatched up a cudgel from the ground, as the Frankish blade sliced deep through the shoulder into his chest. A rock flew past the Briton's face as he pulled back to wrench free his sword. In a rage, he scrambled over to the concealed thrower and sidestepped a club that pounded into the limestone rock. No armour protected the attackers, no leather jerkin, so the fury of his thrust transfixed the robber and he needed to place his foot against the body to slide out the blade.

Screams and curses echoed around him but the hail of stones ceased. Over to his left, Alfwald stood over the body of a foe. Skirmish over, the Saxons returned, on each face an expression of grim exultation, except for Caena, whose was anxious.

"Where's Ina?"

His name echoed around the mountain but there was no answer. Sigeberht, the cousin of Ina pointed.

"I saw him chase one of them up the side of the gorge, but I had to stave off an attacker and I lost sight of him."

Scrambling up the side of the defile, they reached the ridge, two paces wide. Far below the steep rock face two broken bodies lay on a ledge. The Briton cursed and Caena raised his eyes to the skies.

"We must leave him to the eagles. Fucking ruffians! Ina was worth a thousand of them bastards."

"The pilgrims they sought to plunder," Brother Dignovar said, "bared unsuspected fangs."

For his part, Begiloc admired the purple-tinged mountains, waterfalls, lakes, animals, trees and flowers and mused whether they, rather than Man, did not better embody the essence of God.

The sombre group rode into the village of Sce Remei.

# CHAPTER 12

The descent from Saint Remy to Agusta tested not only the mettle of Frate Tanolfi.

"Father, tell God I'll light a candle in the Lord's name if we reach yon church down there," Begiloc called to Denehard, wiping the cold sweat from his brow.

"Tell him yourself!"

"Damn it! He doesn't listen to my prayers."
The mule slithered and he clung on gasping in horror as a stone flew into the void. An eternity passed before it crashed below. Relieved, they rode into Agusta and Caena brought his mount level. The Saxon pointed to an amphitheatre rising near a ruined Roman temple, "I'd sooner fight savage beasts in there than come down that mountain again."

"Ay, this fellow's earned a good meal," Begiloc stroked the rough fur between the mule's ears as
Father Denehard cantered up.

"How strange to see these people at work after the vastness of the peaks."

"Keep your peaks Father, give me a flat field any day," the Briton said.

"Now you are on level ground, remember your vow. Over there, behold the church. Frate! Who's it dedicated to?"

"Ursus. The saint who gave clogs to the poor, an Irishman. Imagine being barefoot in the snow here in winter! We should be grateful too, for next to the house of prayer stands the hospice of St Ursus founded for travellers. Tonight we stay there."

Glad to be on his feet once more, Begiloc paid off the muleteer. While the others settled into the accommodation, he slipped away to buy his candle.

*'God keep Somerhild and Ealric and grant me a safe journey to Rome. May this pilgrimage to the holy city absolve my sins.'*

Would God hear his prayers? The usual hollowness inside assailed him when he left the church along with a sense of foreboding. Including himself, nine men had set off with the priest and monks. Wybert and Ina they had lost of the dozen who had departed Wimborne, Meryn was blind, and Hrothgar and the treacherous Paega were dead. Somehow he had more belief in the strength of his right arm than in candles and prayers.

*'Can't do any harm,'* he muttered, shrugging as he mounted the stairs of the hospice. He knew his was a faith in preparation, not moulded or complete like the monks, nuns, abbots and the rest: when uncertain he resorted to intuition.

West of Agusta, as the shadows lengthened the next day, they drew close to a magnificent Roman aqueduct. The central arch spanned a gorge where far below rushed the crashing, foaming water of a torrent. All told, the bridge stretched for more than fifty yards. Their guide, Frate Tanolfi, turned to Begiloc, "We must cross it. Over there the entrance."

Following the trail, they made for the tall, narrow, rectangular entry to an inspection corridor.

*'Was that the clash of metal against rock?'*

Spinning on his heel, he scanned the terrain but there was no sign of life. Was his imagination overwrought after the attack in the mountains? Dismissing his reaction as fancy, he led them into the passage where small, oblong windows ran along both sides, not opposite each other but staggered to cast light on the facing wall between any two openings. The corridor, the height of two men, had the same arrangement high overhead resulting in brightness set like gems dappling the walls amid patches of blackness. Hard on the eyes, he did not discern the figures of armed men sitting against the wall in the obscurity, who sprang up when he was halfway down the aqueduct. In that instant, the voice of Caena rang out from the rear, "Foe at our backs!" He cursed, so he had not imagined the clash of metal.

*'Fool not to trust my hearing!'*

A perfect trap as another half-dozen men closed in. They shrugged off their packs, unslung their shields and drew their swords.

"Father, Brothers, to the middle Alfwald, Sigeberht, Cynefrid to Caena! Leofric, Eadwig to me!"

Even as he shouted these orders, he realised the defect in the enemy plan. Hope surged in his breast. The corridor was wide enough only for single combat, so the assailant had rendered his greater numbers useless. Bless the candle in Saint Ursus Church! With Caena as the last man and he the first, the foe would rue his error.

Franks! There was no doubt about the enemy, nor, in his mind who had sent them. The knee length tunic with short-sleeved mail shirt over, the short cloak, the conical helmet with cheek guards, the oval shield with iron boss – and this vision hurtled towards him. Too fast. Begiloc, a veteran of conflict, knew it. As the Frank raised his arms, he knelt and let the onrushing enemy impale his groin on his sword. Screams...clash of steel...howls at his back, in this confined space the clamour waged war with his eardrums.

The fallen man writhing in agony at his feet made an obstacle for his next adversary. Not only had he time to set his guard but he could appreciate the roar of triumph from the Saxons behind him telling him Caena had slain his foe.

From the first exchange of blows he recognised his next assailant to be a seasoned warrior. As soon as their shields locked he felt the might of his adversary. This he used against him, letting his shield arm go limp, causing the Frank to pitch forward so, from behind, the seax of Leofric carved into his throat. Begiloc shrugged the body of the enemy off his thigh where he had fallen. Stepping over the other dying man, he locked on the frightened face of a youth in warrior's armour.

*'Never show fear to your foe.'*

Rage suffused him that one of six and ten years must face him. No time for pity. Tender years or not, his attacker wished to slay him.

*'Had Keresyk not met his doom at the same age?'*

A deft feint deceived the Frank.

*'Too easy!'*

A reverse sweep sliced between cheek guard and neck mail through the ear and into the great vein. Blood spurted. The light faded in the eyes of his foe who sagged and toppled. Distraught at the memory of his brother's death, Begiloc stepped back.

"Leofric, your turn!"

The Saxon sprang past him like a wolf on its prey and blade on blade he forced the next Frank to retreat.

Chest heaving after his exertion, Begiloc leant against the wall. Eadwig pushed through and he reached to grab him, but thought better of it. For the moment, he had done his part: three dead of the six foes were down to him. Gazing around, he noted the scared eyes of Frate Tanolfi, beyond Father Denehard to where Alfwald battled a Frank using Begiloc's old sword.

*'Where's Caena?'*

Sigeberht and Cynefrid were poised to step up if needed.

*'He can't be slain!'*

The whoop of Eadwig distracted him for a moment – another down. He stared back down the aqueduct where Caena stepped out of the dark shadow, hauling his two companions aside as they cheered the fall of Alfwald's adversary.

*'Thank God!'*

Relieved, he closed his eyes.

*'Who'd have thought I'd grow fond of the great bear?'*

Another hoot caused him to turn and seeing murder in the face of Leofric, he shoved him aside, hauled back Eadwig, ignoring the curse of the young man. He wanted to take the last enemy standing alive.

*'Parry the onslaught. Feint a strike. Up go his defences and it's done!'*

With all his might he slammed the edge of his shield to the point of the enemy's chin, before taking sword, dagger and shield from the prone man and striding over the dead foes. He shouted to Ealric, "Don't touch him! I want him alive! Strip the mail off him. Help him Leofric!"

In unison, the roar of the Saxons reverberated in the narrow confines of the gallery.

Silence.

The day was won without loss. Alfwald stared at him, his mouth turned down.

"Caena slew four of them. Once he's drawn blood there's nought for the rest of us."

"I saw you down one of them."

Encouraged, the Saxon recounted blow by blow how he had overcome the mightiest Frank ever to wield a sword. When he'd finished his tale, Begiloc surveyed the carnage. The enclosed space oppressed him.

"Let's get out of here! Pick up those three shields, they'll serve as spares. Caena, since you haven't done much, you'll have the strength to lend a hand with this one."

He bent and grabbed the wrist of the unconscious man while his comrade took the other.

"I'll wager I slew more than you, Briton!"

"Not if you include this one."

Fleeting respect flashed under the bushy eyebrows. Together they dragged the man along the passageway and with a sigh he stepped into the open sunlight. They flopped down on the grass and Leofric stared across the gorge.

"That's one hell of a bridge, that is."

When laughter erupted he stared nonplussed. They laughed until even Leofric joined in the deserved release – a battle won without a scratch in exchange.

"How high do you think it is?" he asked, which set them off again. "About 200 feet, I'd say," he said ignoring them.

The captive stirred at which the laughter stopped. Begiloc rose, unstopped his water skin to douse the man's face, who spluttered, shook his head and opened his eyes, wider when he saw the surrounding Saxons.

The Briton drew his sword and relished the fear it induced in the prone captive.

"Do you wish to save your worthless life?"

There was no reply. The terrified eyes darted from one face to another.

"Well?"

The man blanched.

"So, who sent you to kill us?" If possible, his terror increased. "I can slaughter you with mercy. Or I can make it long and slow. Or I can spare you. I don't care which. Want to live? All you need to do is give me a name."

The man closed his eyes. His lips worked, but with no sound. At last, he said, "Milo, Bishop Milo."

The Saxons exchanged glances and Begiloc frowned at the rush of words.

"We followed you on horseback along the river. Over the mountains. They told us you were not to reach Rome ..."

The eyes implored, never leaving the sword, but the warrior lowered it.

"Father, over here. You, kneel!"

The man hesitated, on his knees? A beheading? No choice but to obey. Yet weapon sheathed, Begiloc took out his carved cross sparkling in the sunlight and handed it to the priest.

"This rood is shaped from the thigh bone of Saint Ina, he invented. Swear before God upon this holy relic you will come to Rome, not try to flee and not betray us."

"Upon my oath."

"What the fuck's goin' on!" Caena looked on in disbelief, "We finish off the enemy and show them the pity they'd show us!"

Undeterred, Begiloc ignored him, "Kiss the sacred bone."

The ivory cross, he tucked back into his tunic and smiled at his deceit...and yet, he reflected, he had proved unworthy to bear the splendid gift. Again he hoped Rome would bring redemption. Eyes on him, he struggled back to the present.

"Give the spare shields to the Frank. He will carry all three to Rome as penance."

Both monks gasped.

"I must have missed your ordination. How long have you been a priest?" Father Denehard asked.

*'Churchmen! They're trouble.'*

Begiloc stared at the sky.

"Priests not laymen decide penance. Given your valour today I shall overlook your presumption." He handed his shield to the man and gestured to the monks. "The penance is confirmed."

The Frank slung one on his back and hoisted the other two on his arms. Begiloc's lip curled. Long hard days ahead for the man who had tried to kill him in combat. Gazing back at the aqueduct, he said, "We should hurl the bodies in the gorge lest travellers raise the alarm. Anyone wanting a Frankish sword helps himself." The face of Leofric lit up and Begiloc clapped him on the back.

"We'll drag the corpses here and throw them under the last arch. The Lombards won't find them down there."

The expected protests from the priest were not forthcoming; Denehard's silence, he took to mean that for a Christian burial one should not attack clergymen.

Task completed, they followed the Roman road along the valley of the Dora Baltea to Everi for two days and another two to Vercel in the plain of the Po.

In Vercel, Father Denehard began the first of a series of pious visits which taxed the warriors to the extreme. Frate Tanolfi said to the priest, "Our king, Liutprand is devout and has embellished many fine cathedrals, like this one. Rome and Ravenna are his inspiration. Wait till you see the mosaics, they're breathtaking."

Begiloc, who had paid little attention to the conversation, reacted to the word 'mosaics' with interest. Pictures made of bits of coloured stone, these he had never admired and neither had Denehard, because he, Begiloc, had heard him ask the monk what were 'mosaics' and the explanation. The road brought them into the centre of the town and they stood in front of the cathedral.

The priest again asked, "Who is the church dedicated to?"

"Well, at first to St Theonestus a martyr, but now to St Eusebius, a martyr and bishop saint who affirmed the divinity of Jesus against the heretical Arians ..."

The monk droned on and Begiloc yawned and swatted at another of the biting bugs that infested this area. *Infested,* he thought back with fondness to his life before its infestation by abbesses, monks, priests and nuns. In turn, this made him think of Aedre and her body. So, ridden by guilt once more, he entered the cathedral and was overawed by the beauty of the golden mosaic in the apse. Contrite, he fell to his knees and addressed the two saints who flanked the Lord in Glory.

*'Saints Eusebius and Athanasius, help me curb my lustfulness, keep me faithful to my Somerhild and guide me back safe to her arms. Amen.'*

They rested for a day in the *Three Kings Inn* not far from the cathedral and around the hour of None, while they supped their ale, a man entered with leggings caked in dried mud that flaked off as he walked. The fellow propped a pole with a looped net against the wall. In his other hand, he carried reeds with five frogs threaded on each.

"Ah, the *granocchiaio*!" The innkeeper thrust his hand in his apron to jingle coins. Begiloc wondered what frog tasted like. The idea revolted him. At mealtime, he wiped the last of his fish soup in his bowl with a piece of bread and smacked his lips.

"Ah, you like my frog soup, sir," the landlord said. Later, over an ale, Caena clapped him on the back, "Your face was a picture when you found out, fair turned green as a frog, it did!"

The squalor of the inns and the poor food characterised their march across the valley of the River Po. One day, they met a group of Bavarian pilgrims headed for the Alps, who told them there were many monasteries, nunneries and churches in Pamphica, the Lombard capital. Full of fervour, they told Denehard they had visited the tomb of St Augustine in the Church of St Peter. They were less forthcoming about Rome because they had to press on before nightfall.

"I can't wait to pray before the shrine of St Augustine of Hippo," the priest said.

Frate Tanolfi rubbed his hands together, "*Sì, sì,* I have been blessed to do it many times. Do you know the story of the saint's translation?"

"Nay, do tell."

Begiloc listened, even priestly chatter relieved the boredom of the long march.

"Well, of course, St Augustine was buried in Hippo Regius cathedral at the time of the Vandals. The body was moved to the island of Sardinia ..." he wondered who the Vandals were and about the strange place names.

*'I don't suppose I'll ever go there, but I never thought I'd eat frogs – odd taste frog.'*

"...by the Catholic bishops whom the Arian Vandal Huneric expelled from Africa. The remains were redeemed from the Saracens by the uncle of our present king, Peter, Bishop of Pamphica, made saint."

*'... something between fish and chicken, I reckon. I wonder what Wimborne frogs are like? I might try them when I get back.'*

"And the church where Augustine is buried is named after this Peter?"

"Ay, the king had it renovated, they finished it fifteen...nay, let me see ... seventeen years ago."

*'For Christ's sake, don't these bloody monks think of ought else?'*

In Pamphica before Vespers, though they were tired after the march, Denehard insisted on a visit to the shrine of St Augustine. Begiloc's was not the only voice raised in protest.

"Offer up your tiredness to our Saviour," said the priest and there the matter ended.

They made their way to the Citadel in the northern quarter and to the church. So keen was Denehard he arrived first. In front of the building, he weaved past the beggars who cried out for alms to survive. One of them reached up and grabbed his alb. "Father! For pity's sake, spare a coin for a poor cripple."

The priest fumbled in his tunic for money and the rest happened in the blink of an eye. The false invalid sprang up. A flash of steel. The captive Frank leapt forward and the dagger aimed at the heart of the clergyman embedded in a shield. Leofric impaled the would-be murderer on his sword and beggars screamed, dragging themselves away. Others, curious, gathered round gaping, while Begiloc's frantic eyes scanned them for any sign of weapons.

The Saxon wiped blood off his blade.

"I've christened my new sword ... sorry Father ... didn't mean to say *chri–*"

"Blast your right arm Leofric!" Begiloc said. "Now we'll never know why."

"Of course, we know *why*," Brother Dignovar said. "Who does not want Denehard to reach Rome?"

Begiloc stared at the blood-soaked corpse: "Milo! How did this spy know to wait here?"

"All pilgrims from the north visit the shrine of St Augustine. The false beggar waited for a priest, two monks and a band of Saxons led by a Briton to come by. No hard task to identify us. We shall have to be more alert. The evil of the Bishop of Rems and Treves has a long reach," the monk sighed.

The Frank laid the shield on the ground and stood on it to pull the dagger out with both hands. He grunted twice and it came free, turning, he made to hand the knife to Begiloc. "Wear it at your belt," he said. Gratified, the man smiled. "How are you named?" he asked.

"They call me Otto, son of Bero."

"Otto, son of Bero, I owe you my life," Denehard cut in, "But...but why did you save me?"

"Because I swore to God not to betray you." The man bent to pick up the shield, but the priest hauled him up. "Stay," he picked it up. "I shall carry this."

"And I this one," Brother Tanolfi said, taking the other from him.

"And I this one," the other monk stepped forward.

"Come, Otto, we will pray as brothers at the shrine." Denehard took the Frank under the arm and steered him into the building.

*'I wish I could believe in my cross as much as he. The Devil take me for a fool!'*

Consolation for the leg-weary group, the abbey was attached to the church, spirits lifted further when they learned their next stop was another nearby religious house. The monastery of Santa Cristina stood only four leagues to the east – an easy day for once. Afterwards, they marched to Placentia where Denehard worshipped at the tomb of Saint Antoninus the soldier martyr. Another abbey, further across the plain of the Po to Floricum, yet another and on to Sce Domnine where they learned Saint Donnino, an officer of the Emperor Maximian-Hercules who was dismissed for his conversion, was chased to the Stirone Torrent and beheaded. Of course, the priest prayed over his remains in the oratory dedicated to the saint.

Caena tugged at Begiloc's tunic, "Take courage Briton, I overheard the Lombard telling yon other monk tomorrow we start up the mountains. There can't be any flamin' martyrs up there, can there?"

"What, you've never heard of the Roman sport of hurling Christians off a crag?"

"Eh? Oh right! Ha-ha!"

Before nightfall they reached the Hospice of St Mary, constructed at the foot of the Mount Bardon Pass to accommodate pilgrims. At mealtime Frate Tanolfi said, "The defile leads us over the Apennines and thence to the hills of Tuscany."

At these words, the prior of the hospice warned, "Once over the pass, beware innkeepers. They're all scoundrels. They overcharge the poor traveller, that is when they don't steal his purse. Murders too, they say. Hell is full of evil hosts."

"Which is why we try to stay in monasteries Father Prior," said Brother Dignovar, words indistinct as he chewed.

"Wise, most wise, my son. They are not like we Lombards." He jerked a thumb, "Over those mountains is another world. Rogues the lot. The sooner Our Lord returns in Majesty the better." With those pious words he gave all his attention to the problem of perch bones.

The road climbed over three thousand feet up the Apennines, a grim march for Begiloc from the outset. An hour into their journey, without so much as a glance at an irritation on his arm, he rubbed it. A large bee dropped to the ground. At first the pain and swelling were commonplace and he ignored them, but after a while his throat closed, his tongue and lips swelled making breathing hard. Head spinning, he felt sick.

*'I'm damned if I'll let a bee sting slow us down,'* he gritted his teeth and continued to place one foot in front of the other.

"That'd be a good crag to shove Christians off." Caena nudged him and pointed to a place where the rock face overhung a precipice. "I said that'd...hey, you all right?"

They halted and inspected his arm. Nothing could be done to treat it in the mountains so they decided to rest. Begiloc moved away from his companions to vomit. Caena brought his water skin, "Must have been Milo's bee, yon, full of evil and spite. You'd do well to drink, wash away the poison. See, you're brought down by a bee *and* I'll wager your scared of spiders... call yourself a man!"

Grateful to rinse away the sourness of bile, he swilled his mouth. Hard to swallow, he forced the liquid down and handed the skin back to Caena who checked the position of the sun and said, "I reckon we'll top this pass soon. The day's young, we can all get some rest. Besides, you never know with the sting of bees. I knew one who got stung when picking blackberries and a sunset later he'd gone, no longer with us!"

"I'm not a maid, Caena," he'd enough of Caena's homespun wisdom, "I'm all right. Let's march!"

He put on a bold front but he felt queasy and weary.

*'To Hell with it! I can do this. I'll rest at the inn.'*

Stubbornness, not sense, took him to the top of the pass. Dizzy, he surveyed the descent following the course of the Magra plunging from the mountains, foaming and crashing through winding gorges. The river could not be swifter to the valley than his thoughts centred on the village of Funtrêmal below.

Once rounded a buttress of rock, the welcome sight of the town lay beneath them in a narrow dale. Frate Tanolfi pointed to the bridge.

"The *Pons Tremulus*," he said, "the Romans built it, but when you cross over, the Magra is so fierce you can feel it tremble. No more mountains before Rome."

The first inn did not have room for eleven travellers, a group of Lombards, pilgrims on their way back to Pamphica, arrived an hour before them. The apologetic host suggested the *Lion* the other side of the river so they crossed the ancient bridge in search of it. Begiloc was not impressed. The innkeeper wore a white apron, but the Briton had seen more white on a crow. A sallow-faced man with close-set eyes, an unskilful shaver too, the stubble on his chin grew around scabs. This charmlessness heightened for Begiloc when he dry-washed his hands when speaking to him. At least the varlet knew their language, though he spoke with a strong accent and hesitation.

The landlord led Begiloc to a large dormitory, where the warrior wrinkled his nose at the dust under the rushes and the grimy bedding. The thought of going elsewhere in his present state made his head ache. Besides, there was no choice of another inn. They agreed a price for Begiloc to pay from his bulging purse.

Weapons and packs stowed in the dormitory, downstairs the men found places at table and beckoned their host. Begiloc joined them but, still queasy, he decided to forego drink. The skinny innkeeper appeared, dry-washing his hands once more.

Caena gave his order, "A faet of fresh ale, landlord. And it'd better be an improvement on everything else in this shit-hole!" The landlord squirmed.

"Sir, we serve no ale," his eyes shifted everywhere not meeting those of the Saxon, "sir, we have red wine. The best in the Lunigiana. Shall I bring half an amphora?"

Caena, swift to lose patience, bellowed, "What! No ale and you insult me with an old maid's measure!" His anger rose, "Half? We don't do halves."

The Briton noted the shifty eyes light up.

*'Greedy son of a hog.'*

"Drunkenness is a sin," Frate Tanolfi said, his tone mild, he the first to reach for a cup.

Begiloc marvelled when he learnt the drink was not watered as of custom at wayside inns. The Saxons were hard drinkers and the wine strong so he was content not to join in. The effects of the sting had calmed, he felt better but exhausted. Once his comrades' speech slurred he slipped upstairs to lie down. Not much later, by the dim moonlight shining through the window, he saw them stagger in. The moon was nigh on full, but the sky was scattered with clouds, so the light came and went like flashing fireflies. His comrades dropped on their pallets and soon the dormitory sounded like a blaze of dragons had taken it over, not a group of Saxon warriors.

*'Not natural. The prior warned against innkeepers! Did he mean this one?'*

Then it struck him.

*'He's drugged the lot!'*

Pilgrims risked not only money but also their lives to retire in a woeful hovel like this. He'd had a bad experience of dormitories before, at Werham Priory with the weasel-eyed Paega – years ago – he should be prepared. He reached for his dagger.

*'I'll stay awake and ready.'*

The hard day took its toll and he drifted into sleep.

Waking with a start, in the feeble light he saw a wight-like figure flit to where Father Denehard lay. It rummaged through the priest's clothes and there followed a chuckle and the clink of coin. The scoundrel muttered, *"... e adesso dov'è il britannico?"* Though he could not speak the language, he knew what *'britannico'* meant.

*'He's coming for me the cur-dog!'*

The warrior feigned snoring like the others and a hand began to grope over his chest and down to his belt. He seized the wretch by the wrist who cried out in shock. In that instant, the blessed moonlight lit up the villain's blade destined for his heart. Twisting away, he thrust upwards with his hand-seax.

*'Fool, there was no need for the dagger. No need to die.'*

The others awoke with headaches. Whereas the drug had left its vileness in their bodies, he felt no after-effects of the bee sting. The mood of the men worsened when their dulled senses registered the corpse among them.

"Bishop Milo again?" Cynefrid asked.

"Check your purse Father."

Denehard's hand went to his belt and the cut leather thongs. Begiloc bent down and fumbled inside the tunic of the dead man, pulled out the bag and tossed it to the priest.

"Self defence, I did not want to kill him," he tilted his head toward the dagger stuck deep in the pallet.

"The coward met his rightful end," Caena said. "Hospitality is sacred where I come from."

"Ay," two or three Saxons concurred.

"The next inn we stop at, we make the host drink with us if I have to force it down his throat," Caena said, pressing his hands to his temples.

Later, in a foul mood, they set off as grumpy as men who have quaffed an amphora of drugged wine. The hour did not matter because they had an easy descent of the Magra valley that brought them to Aguilla.

"It's a new village, built by Margrave Adalbert I of Tuscany. Observe the castle? He constructed it to host pilgrims travelling on the via Francigena," said the Lombard monk.

A few days' march, breathing the salt air along the Apuan coast and two nights in inns that supplied a choice of ale or wine (all but Frate Tanolfi avoided the wine) where the bewildered hosts were obliged to sample the drinks under scrutiny, brought them to Campo Maggiore on the Via Cassia. There they stayed at the Abbey of St Peter and did not have to worry about innkeepers.

Past Luca and its famous stonecutters' workshops, their journey took them between a swamp and a lake, where Begiloc and his comrades were forever swatting at biting insects. Several days of dense forest full of deer gave them the chance to hunt. At last they came to the pilgrim post of Seocine and thence to Sce Quiric where Frate Tanolfi relished his role of guide and spiritual shepherd by halting and pointing to the town. "We shall go to the baptistery, of course," he said, his countenance beatific, "The place is named after the child saint Cyriacus also known as Saint Quirico in these parts."

The traffic of travellers and merchants on the Via Cassia made their days more interesting. The road skirted the crater Lake of Sca Cristina, where the priest paid a boatman to take them to the Island of Martana to visit the relics of Saint Christine and to the Island of Bisentina to admire the old frescoes in the Chapel of the Crucifix, before they resumed their march to the town of Sce Valentine.

Caena nudged Begiloc, "Bloody monks! We should have drowned the three of them in the lake. I'm pissed off with worshipping this and honouring that! No time for it! If they make us visit another bloody shrine ..." The threat was left hanging, but unbeknown to them worse lay ahead.

The next day, still on Via Cassia, they marched along the shore of Lake Vico and on to Suteria. "I have something wonderful to show you here," Frate Tanolfi said and he led them to a cliff opposite the town to the south, to a church hewn in the rock. "This is a sacred place," he said, "a Christian shrine dedicated to the Madonna of the Parturition." In the dim light of the interior, they discerned a step down and a baptismal font. "Barren women come here," said the frate, "and Our Lady often answers their prayers with the gift of a child." Lowering his voice, he said, "Before becoming a church it was a Roman temple, a Mithraeum to the pagan god Mithras, and earlier still a necropolis of the ancient Etruscan people."

Begiloc considered this and joined Father Denehard on his knees.

*'This is a good place to pray. More chance here – Denehard's God, Mithras and the gods of the Etruscans, one will answer my prayer. I don't care which as long as one does.'* Again, he prayed to return safe to his family, finishing with a sly smile at Denehard.

A couple of days after Suteria through dense woodlands of oak and hazel they climbed to the top of Mount Mario.

"You can't call this a mount!" Caena said to Frate Tanolfi, *"*Mount's an odd name for a hill four hundred feet high. I might be a simple soldier with no learning like you monks, but it's a bloody hillock, this is!"

The monk's eyes sparkled. "Over there! Through the trees to the south-east. What do you see?"

Begiloc stared, before him lay a city, its thick stone walls faced with russet brick. He counted at least seventeen towers and three gates in the arc of wall in sight. The whole embraced countless houses, churches, and ancient ruins.

"A town with fortifications. What name does it go by?"

"*Roma Felix*, Begiloc. We are arrived at last."

# CHAPTER 13

The city perimeter wall of huge stone blocks faced with red brick hugged Rome in a protective embrace.

"Eleven miles of walls," Brother Tanolfi said, "built by Emperor Aurelian five hundred years ago, because the settlement outgrew its old ramparts so everything erected outside was defenceless. What interests us," he turned to Father Denehard, "is Roman law forbade the burial of the dead *intra muros*, so they interred our martyrs in deep graves alongside the roads leading out of Rome."

Not caring about martyrs, Begiloc turned to Caena, "It'd take a mighty host to storm these walls."

The Saxon blew out his cheeks. "Ay ... yet they say it's been done."

The two men stared in awe at the fortifications and the Flaminian Gate ahead. Droves of pilgrims, merchants and countrymen, who descended along the Via Flaminia likely shared their wonder. One who did not, Brother Tanolfi, warmed to his discourse, "In fact, the blessed Emperor Constantine built the basilica over St Paul's grave on the Via Ostia, within Aurelian's walls."

Guards halted them between two archways to wait their turn to reveal their business and receive directions. When they emerged from the shadows of the round towers flanking the archway to a busy thoroughfare, Brother Tanolfi quashed hopes of refreshment and rest, "Here to the left is the tomb of St Valentine martyr."

Sleep eluded Begiloc in the Schola Anglorum, a hospice built by King Ine of Wessex to house English pilgrims. Their marches brought the gift of oblivion as soon as his head settled on his folded cloak. Not tonight. Resentment kept him awake. In his mind, he ran through the events, beginning with the image of a sick woman with matted hair wrapped in a blanket, her face a mass of sores, moaning before the shrine of St Valentine. Enough on its own, but on they went, east to the Church of John the Martyr, where Diogenus martyr was buried and in another cell Bonifacius martyr and below ground Sistus the martyr and the Blastus the martyr and further down Longuinus the martyr..., he tossed and turned on his pallet. What was it the monk said ...?... "We honour them in honour of He whose faith they witnessed. We honour the Master by means of the servants."

All well and good for priests and monks, but did he and Caena and the others need to endure the sight of the desperate sick on litters before these shrines praying for a miracle? Or witness scenes the likes of which had shaken him at the tomb of St Blastus, a youth possessed by unclean spirits – the poor wretch gnashing his teeth, rolling his eyes, foaming at the mouth and writhing on the ground? Eyes squeezed tighter closed, he hoped never to be prey to demons.

*'How to end this torment? What to do about Denehard? In the morning, I'll put a stop to these visits if it's the last thing I do. As for that ... that ... nay, no vile words Tanolfi lest a fiend enter my body.'*

The blanket twisted under his shoulder, he tugged it and turned on his right side. Not content with *two* churches full of tombs ten paces from the Gate, the damned priest had bought a Book of Martyrs from a toothless vendor.

*'So he has a guidebook now!'*

Rolling back on his left side, Begiloc drew up his knees. Down Via Salinaria to the Church of St Ermes, with the shrines of virgin martyrs and Ermes himself. The others whose names he did not recall, except Victor, an easy name to remember, then down the same street to another martyr, down twenty-four steps, like going down to Hell, but no fire only dust and bones...he drifted off to sleep.

In a black mood, he ate breakfast in silence punctuated by grunts when one of his companions spoke to him. They took the hint and let him alone.

As arranged, they met Father Denehard and the two monks after Terce in front of the hospice.

The priest greeted them with a blissful smile, "This morning we shall go to the Cornelian Gate," he waved the Book of Martyrs, "to visit the Basilica of St Peter. The saint, the rock on which Our Lord built his Church. Lead on Brother Tanolfi!"

A peremptory voice rang out, "Enough's enough!"

Father Denehard stopped and spun round. Everyone stared at Begiloc in surprise, for on the familiar amiable face there was a scowl, "Father, we've marched from Bischofsheim over the Alps, the length of this country all the way here. Don't you think we deserve a day's rest?"

"You do not wish to visit the tomb of the apostle ... ?" The priest seemed pained, "... the first Bishop of Rome?"

"Ay, I do. Some other time."

"We are going today."

"Why? What's so pressing? Is the Day of Resurrection nigh?"

"Beware!" The well-known sneer appeared, "Lest you stray into blasphemy!" He stabbed a finger toward Begiloc. "It is your duty to accompany us, to lead the men and ensure our protection. Let me remind you. You are sworn to obedience."

In Denehard's tone and manner, he identified the harsh, unbending, ritualistic face of the Church he found most difficult to accept. Sweat consumed in working on the land; blood and tears shed in combat; even the immoral violation of another man's wife – these were part of a warrior's existence. His life. Denehard's smirk, his contempt, his arrogance, his hiding behind threats of blasphemy – all these Church values were ... what was the word they were so fond of ... *anathema* ... to him.

"Father, there are sufficient men to guard us and we shall all go to the tomb of St Peter." Brother Dignovar said with engaging pragmatism, "Begiloc is weary and see, he regrets his rash words, born of tiredness. Ever the dutiful and faithful servant, he deserves one day's repose. A rest and he will be a new man."

The mild tone of the otherworldly monk and his open, honest face full of expectation had an effect on the priest. The fury in his eyes gave way to doubt and then to consideration.

Begiloc did not observe this since he directed his attention to a man lingering on the other side of the street. Instinct warned him the stranger was too interested in them. When their eyes met the man hurried off.

"Very well! Caena, you will lead the men today. Begiloc, I will see you in church at Vespers. I expect you to thank the Lord for this consideration."

Leofric shot him a glance worth many words and winked.

Thanks to the Swiss monk he was alone. No blessed martyrs, no cursed priest, he was free to do whatever he wanted. What? No idea came to mind, his anger had passed to be replaced by guilt. Once again he had broken a promise to Leoba – to obey Denehard all the way to Rome and back. Comrades and duty abandoned, he had turned his back on the most important of Christ's apostles. The thought made him smile. Had not St Peter thrice denied Our Lord? Therefore, the priest, the abbess and the saint could forgive him. There and then, he vowed he would go and visit the tomb of the apostle before he left Rome.

For some time, he wandered around the streets, his senses awhirl. Lurid odours mingling with incense from open church doors. Never had he seen so many people dedicated to the religious life gathered in one place nor so many whores, beggars and street traders. A stallholder offered him a drug made from the seeds of the poppy, *'... to banish painful memories – drop it into your wine.'* For a moment he was tempted, but his reminiscences were not harrowing, quite the opposite, what distressed him was separation from the source of his fondest recollections.

"Pssst!" The hiss stopped his musings.

The man he had seen facing the hospice beckoned him from the doorway of an imposing building. Lost in his reflections, Begiloc had not given it a glance. More impatient, the fellow waved again with the air of one who did not wish to go any farther. The Briton, who did not take kindly to being followed meant to confront his pursuer, so he strode back.

The man slipped into the darkness of an unlit hall. Was it a trap? Bishop Milo? Curiosity lured him. Drawing his sword, he stepped inside, stood still listening until his eyes adjusted to the dim light. There was a staircase ahead otherwise the rest of the ground floor contained barrels, sacks and boxes. Body tensed, a sudden sweat on his brow, his grip on the hilt tightened.
Mounting the stairs, he came to a landing where the man stood with folded arms.

"There's no need for that," he indicated the weapon, "there are no foes *today*."
The emphasis did little to reassure Begiloc.

"What is this place?"

"The Rome residence of the bishop."

"The Bishop of Rems?"

"Wrong prelate, the Bishop of Benevento. Since he is not here, he hosts his brother in Christ the Bishop of Mentz, who told me you may gain advantage from this meeting."

Begiloc studied the features of the man before him. By his portly build and chubby hands no warrior. For sure, he'd never wielded a weapon. A priest then? And yet his manner indicated nothing priest-like.

"A cousin to the Bishop if you're wondering. A friend, an advisor, messenger, servant, in short anything he wants of me." Begiloc sheathed his sword, pondering how he was known to the Bishop of Mentz.

"That's better. This way."

The factotum led on through a splendid chamber where servants bustled with brooms, bundles of fresh rushes, new tapers, baskets of scented petals, cloths and pails of water. A large oak table dominated the centre of the room, flanked by benches of the same wood. Imposing, at the head of the table, raised on a small dais stood a throne-like chair, incised with gold and purple scrolls.

"Farewell meal this evening. Opulent occasion. Hessians must hold their own with Romans, don't you think?"

The man's explanation served to heighten his sense of anticipation.

They left the chamber by one of its five doors and passed through an ante-chamber into a smaller room, where scribes, silent at their desks, prepared letters and maps. His guide threaded past them and knocked.

"Come!" The deep, authoritative voice penetrated the solid oak. The bishop's man waved him in.

"The Briton, Your Eminence."

The door closed and he looked back to see he was alone with a giant of a man who rose behind a table before striding over. Unprepared, he tried not to gape, but this was a warrior, not a priest. Yet, the hand extended to him bore a ruby ring, the insignia of a bishop, blazing insistence on homage.

"A Briton with a fine Frankish sword ... !"
The tone was jovial, but the eyes hard, twin purveyors of menace. In the evening, the prelate was to offer a sumptuous meal but gluttony was not among his sins, not an ounce of fat on the muscular frame. Here was a foe to be respected not only on the field in a skirmish but also in a battle of wits.

"... one skilled in its use by all accounts," said the prelate with nose straight as an axe blade, chin firm and clean-shaven, and above all, penetrating grey eyes, cold as Rhenish winter skies.
Aware of the attempt to intimidate, Begiloc waited in silence.
The bishop also bided his time, his stare never wavering from the eyes of the Briton. At last, the bishop gestured to a seat.

"Sit! We shall talk."
The prelate moved, light on his feet for such a big man, and raised a solid wooden chair from behind the table to swing it one-handed to the floor – an impressive display of arm strength. The Bishop of Mentz sat with his knee close to that of Begiloc.

"You will wonder why I sent for you, Be-gi-loc," sounding the syllables of his name as if sampling the quality.
*'So he knows my name. What else does he know about me?'*
Begiloc waited.

"My, my, a man of few words. I like that." The edge of the mouth, which had not smiled since they met, twitched. "I wish for you to enter my service. I shall make you a wealthy man. You will be Captain of the Guard. Heard of Mentz?

*Mongontiacum* – founded before the birth of Our Lord by the Roman general Drusus. A soldier like you. A fine important city, Briton. I offer you a post of importance. What do you say?"

Begiloc held the iron gaze. "I say there is a price to pay for such an honour and I would know– " The warrior stopped short, reproaching himself, marvelling not for the first time at the rudeness of his speech when dealing with an eminence. Time seemed to wait in suspension for the cleric's reply.

The bishop smiled but not with his eyes and clapped a bear-like hand on his guest's thigh causing Begiloc to wince. Two pats and the hand withdrew, "Of course there's a price. A light one for you, for it is in your nature. I desire you to be a man of *no* words."

"How so?"

"Consider why you are brought to Rome. Heed me well, what is done cannot be undone. No-one but God can restore sight to the eyes of your friend.

*'He knows about Meryn!'*

"In exchange for your silence I have made you a generous offer. When the Holy Father asks you about the Bishop of Rems, you plead ignorance. The next day you leave for Mentz as Captain of the City Guard. Are we agreed?"

The only thought that crossed his mind was whether as Captain of the Guard he would have a better chance of slaying Milo – and what if he threw in this bishop for good measure? He kept an inscrutable countenance.

"What if I should refuse?"

For the second time he had traded with the bishop: he a man of no education save the learning of life passed down by humble parents, no land to talk of – an honest man but unused to such exalted company.

*'True but why should it stop me from testing a bishop? David slew Goliath!'*
The prelate feigned astonishment, "Why this folly? Throw away the chance of a lifetime and for what? Bishop Milo has powerful friends, not least the Mayor of the Palace." His voice dropped and he spoke with deliberation, "Fail me in this and you gain two enemies, the Bishop of Rems and Treves and the Bishop of Mentz. There will be no place for you to turn in Austrasia." Again the hand squeezed his thigh. Spiteful. "It need not come to that. Think, the respected commander of the Mentz Guard."

Lithe as a lynx, the prelate stood and moved to the door, wrenching it open, "We are done here." The hand seized him, this time he pressed his thumb into the shoulder of Begiloc. "Ponder your choice Briton – prominence or oblivion."

Back on the street he swore under his breath. His thigh and shoulder ached, a reminder, no doubt, not to court the enmity of the Bishop of Mentz.

*'Captain of the Guard has a ring to it. The Devil take me should I break my oath to Meryn.'*
With no direction in mind, he walked on past the ruins of the ancient forum, his thoughts far faster than his feet.

*'There's no sense to this. Milo has powerful allies, so why fear my words? Why involve the bear of Mentz?'*
No response came, but the certainty of having a new and implacable enemy chilled him to the marrow. Confused, he dwelt on his situation, one of a humble man who had made an unthinkable journey as yet unfinished. How may he best serve his wife so far away? How to honour his pledge to Meryn? How to confront his nascent spirituality with the guilt for his lustfulness that had overwhelmed him not long ago?

After a tavern meal, he struggled to find his way back to the hospice. Rumination and distractions had caused him to ignore his whereabouts – an injudicious mistake in such a city. Only when he had the idea of gaining the walls and following them round to the Flaminian Gate did he regain his accommodation. Back in the Schola Anglorum after Vespers, Father Denehard approached him.

"Did you find the peace you sought this day, my son?"

"I'm not sure." The priest frowned, "But I vowed to visit the tomb of St Peter. I - I'm not sure I made the right choice. I mean, not to come with you today."

Moved by his words the cleric said, "You were tired, overwrought. There will be time to explore the basilica of the apostle. We shall go there together."

"Father, it's not that ..."

"You are troubled?"

"Ay."

"Can I help? Shall we pray?"

"Father, do you know of the Bishop of Mentz? I met him today."

"And this meeting bothers you?"

"Ay, you can say that."

"Well, I know nought of him. There's one who does and he awaits us. Come, I'll take you to him."

Denehard led him to a room reserved for encounters where they found a monk of noble bearing. His tanned, weather-worn face belied his age. On closer scrutiny, he was in his late thirties and his manner of speech and refined features confirmed his high-born origins.

The Saxon priest introduced Begiloc and they embraced although the fame of Willibald of Wessex whose travels had taken him to Constantinople and Palestine had bypassed the Briton.

"Begiloc," he said, "The Pope convoked my abbot of Monte Cassino. I travelled with him and praise be, the Holy Father requested a private audience to learn about my seven-year pilgrimage." He took him by the arm and led him to a bench by the window.

"I shall take the opportunity to request an early convocation for you and Father Denehard. First, I want to hear in person of your dealings with Milo of Rems."

The monk listened with deep interest, interrupting on occasion to clarify a point or ask a question. His face grew grave and pained when he heard of the blinding of Meryn and he tensed upon the Briton recounting his meeting with the Bishop of Mentz. Turning to Denehard, he shook his head, saddened.

"This is worse than Boniface feared. The Lord be praised the archbishop arrives in Rome soon. We must appraise him of these facts." He rested a hand on the arm of Begiloc, "My son, be strong in the faith, shun temptation and speak the truth to the Pontifex."

"What man is this Bishop of Mentz?"

"Gewilieb? A murderer! His father, bishop before him, departed this life in single combat with a Saxon. What did Gewilieb do? Sent a servant to the enemy camp to search for his father's slayer to arrange to confer. They met at the River Weber and the Saxon, suspecting nothing, rode into the ford to meet him. Treacherous, he plunged a blade into his heart, crying *'Behold the sword with which I avenge my father!'* – *qualis rex, talis grex* – as is the shepherd, so are the sheep. If the leaders of the Church are degenerate, what can be expected of the lesser clergy? The sins of the Bishop of Mentz are innumerable." Willibald bowed his head and murmured, "Our task is onerous. For Gewilieb to come to Rome the waters are murky."

A smile replaced the anxiety on his face.

"You are blessed to meet the Holy Father, my son. He is a great man – a Syrian. When the late Pope died, Gregory stood amidst the Roman people mourning the death of his predecessor, just one of the crowd – but to God he wasn't or to the people who recognised the holy man among them. They swept him away and clamoured for him to be the next Bishop of Rome." Voice lowered in reverence, he said, "Begiloc, we are privileged that we shall stand in the presence of such a man."

They took their leave of Willibald. Denehard ushered him into the street and they stayed quiet for some time before the priest spoke, "There is a war to be fought within the Church. It is more important than our mission to convert the pagan. The pity is Milo and Gewilieb are not the only ones. There is an abbot in Neustria who holds the sees of Rouen, Bayeux and Paris, amassing a private fortune." A bitter laugh. "Irish preachers wander the countryside and teach false doctrine. Heretics abound. Bishops and priests are in wedlock, hunt boar and deer and practise falconry. Milo ignores the rules of St Benedict, the order to which he belongs: I'll wager he knows not who the saint was!"

Denehard pondered on this and Begiloc was preoccupied too. Through no fault of his own he found himself caught up in momentous events and had made powerful and loathsome enemies. Without doubt there was a way out, but it meant disloyalty, deceit and dissolution of his soul – in truth, for him it was not a matter of faith, of religion, it was a question of honour.

"What man is this Archbishop Boniface?"

The priest halted, taking the arm of the warrior to steer him around to retrace their steps.

"Our leader in this fight. Boniface is a man of unblemished character and untiring energy. Humble, he calls himself the 'Servant of the Servants of God'. He has founded monasteries, built churches and organised...but you do not know about Gaesmere ... !"

Begiloc shook his head.

"Gaesmere is near Fritzlar and there stood an oak sacred to the thunder-god Thunor. To show the pagans how powerless were their gods, Boniface took an axe and they looked on aghast, expecting Thunor to destroy him with a thunderbolt, but he felled the tree and had a chapel built out of the wood. Many of the heathens converted. How brave is Boniface!"

"Ay," said Begiloc, "but he had armed men with him."

Denehard cast him a reproving glance, saying, "The Church has more than its share of martyrs as you cannot fail to notice. The pagan is not loth to spill Christian blood. I dare say there will be many more martyrs before the Word is spread to all corners of the world."

Nine days passed during which Begiloc and his companions accompanied the priest to the shrines of the virgins Rufina and Secunda and the tombs of Marius and Martha and their sons. It did not weigh on them as before because they were rested and had more time to visit the city and its taverns.

However, on the ninth day his life changed forever. A group from Wessex arrived that morning, seven monks and five nuns, but he had not encountered any of them.

Denehard sent for him so he strode to the same small room where he had met Willibald. This time, the priest stood beside a shorter man in his fifties. Strands of auburn showed in the grey hair though the colour could better be seen in the eyebrows. Begiloc assessed the man in front of him. The impression the stranger made was one of immense strength and yet his frame was slight. Doughtiness of character for certain. Was there such a thing as power of goodness? If there were, in this case it resided in a stern uprightness showing in the haggard lineaments, the set of the jaw and the soulful visage.

"Begiloc, greet Archbishop Boniface."

Once more he kissed the proffered ring, found himself in the embrace of a man of God who again led him to the window bench.

"I know of your work for the Church," the archbishop said, "and I know the price you paid."

There was sorrow in his voice. What did he wish to tell him?

"I received a letter. You are sure to remember my cousin, the Abbess Cuniburg ... ?"

*'Can I ever forget her? I'm here thanks to her.'*

"... the Lord called her to Him this winter past. She was taken by the ague."

"I'm sorry," he murmured, but this moderate reply belied his true emotion, noted at once by the other man.

The large brown eyes roved over his face and the prelate said, "Do not be. Rejoice! For Christ will soon come in glory. Death is joyous, full of hope of resurrection to eternal life. The same ague took your wife and son."

The blow was hefty as it was unexpected. A fluttering in his stomach began, he swallowed as his gorge rose. A fear never felt in battle gripped him and wrenched at his heart. Denehard spoke to him, but he did not absorb his words as though an invisible veil between the world and himself prevented it.

*'Somerhild dead? Ealric? Never to see them again. Not true. Why does he tell me this?'*

As in a dream, he saw the mouth of the archbishop move and forced himself to listen.

"... 'my father's house has many rooms; if that were not so, would I have told you that I am going there to prepare a place for you?'..."

"Has the Lord prepared a place for them?"

His tongue felt as though it did not belong to him.

Boniface took his hand and held it between his own. Begiloc stared into the dancing flames of the gem on the ring and could not wrench his gaze away.

'Fire consume me! Burn the pain!'

"... and you will see them again," the archbishop said, "when at last the Lord deems your hour is come."

'See them again ... Somerhild and Ealric? In heaven?'

The flames danced one last time as the prelate released his hand.

Begiloc stood and allowed his feet to lead him from the room. Numb, he walked out into the street and leant against a wall. He did not sob but felt the tears run down his face and, angry, wiped them away with his sleeve.

Four men passed him. One made a comment about the heat and another replied laughing. Though it was absurd, he was grateful. He needed people around him but he wanted them to talk to one another, not to him. To avoid the chance of an encounter with anyone he knew, he began to walk. A useless fury consumed him.

'Who's to blame for the ague? God? Had I been in Wimborne I could not have saved them. Died with them. It were a mercy. Too cruel. Living on without family at the bidding of churchmen but what meaning is there to this suffering? I'll ask Denehard. Rather it were Robyn.'

A thought came to him as he walked on.

*'I wonder when she died? Of course ...!'*

He laughed like a madman and the heads of passers-by turned to stare.

*'I didn't betray her with Aedre, at least, not while she was alive ...'*

Sobs wracked him and he went down on his haunches, back to the wall, where he buried his head in his hands and wept.

At the hospice, he sought out Denehard. The priest was praying before a statue of the Virgin and Child. Begiloc waited until he crossed himself and rose.

"I prayed for you and your family, Begiloc."

"I thank you for it."

"How are you?" The question verged on mockery.

A surge of rage swept through him, but he kept his voice flat, "I would know the meaning of my suffering. Why does God punish me? Is it for my sins?"

The priest ushered him away from the statue and towards a crucifix on the wall.

"Gaze on that. God does not chastise you Begiloc. We all suffer. The significance of our wretchedness is here, in the Cross of Christ where the greatest of evil happened – the murder of God. Out of it comes the most prodigious good that ever occurred – redemption. Do you see? God used the force of the Devil's malice to defeat him. We can endure sorrow because we know we will be redeemed." The brow of the priest wrinkled as he stared at the warrior. "Ask God for strength in your grief. Find faith. Lead a good life and rest easy you will see your family again in heaven."

Later, Caena found him lying in the dormer. "I heard," he said and sat on the edge of the bed, "brother, I want to say we're all sorry." His voice was gruff. "I'm not skilled with words and the like nor does death bother me but ..." and sympathy for his friend's plight welled up, "... but you have a friend, Briton. If you need me, ask." He lumbered out the room. Through a veil of tears, Begiloc lay staring at the roof beams.

The days ran into one another and he lost track of time. The pain was raw, but he recognised madness would take him unless he thought of other things. His comrades had left him in peace, respecting his grief and he was grateful, but he needed distraction. So he asked Father Denehard to help him keep his vow. On the way to the basilica, the priest confided why Boniface had come to Rome. The prelate was weary, he explained.

"Troubles have worn him down. The Bishop of Colonia laid claim to part of the district under his jurisdiction and flouts his authority. You see, it strengthens the false priests. The archbishop came to plead with the Holy Father to allow his resignation."

"Resignation?"

"Ay, he wants to go to the Saxon lands as a simple missionary to convert the pagans."

"Somebody needs to sort these bishops," he said through clenched teeth. As well the priest could not read his mind.

They entered St Peter's basilica. "Come," said Denehard, "I wish to show you the oratory of John VII." They passed paintings narrating the life of the saint on the nave walls and Begiloc smiled at the image of the cock crowing; textiles decorated with pictures hung between the columns and bedecked the altars. Adorned with gifts, incense burned in front of statues as offerings, making the air thick and heavy. They came to the oratory where Begiloc gasped at the resplendent mosaic before him, some ten feet tall and twice as long. Framed by colourful foliage, it shone in golden splendour.

Above the altar, the panel blazed scenes from the life of the Virgin and of Christ, which surrounded a large central image of Mary at prayer.

"In the niche," the priest said, "the *Theotokos* – the Mother of God. Think how She suffered, Her Son nailed to the Cross. St Paul wrote to the Romans ..." and he quoted the apostle, " *'I consider our present sufferings are not worth comparing with the glory that will be revealed unto us.'* You do see, Begiloc?"

The mosaic filled him with awe. In truth, he did understand. His heart might ease in time for the loss of his family, but his soul demanded vengeance and no-one, nothing, neither priest nor icon, would ever assuage his fury – no mercy on his part for the Bishop of Rems and Treves.

# CHAPTER 14

Father Denehard sent an urgent summons to the infirmarian of the nearby monastery. The weak-chinned, ingratiating monk lent over Caena, careful to avoid breathing in his tainted breath saying, "The fever rages, an imbalance in humours or he inhaled a bad smell ..."

From the first, Begiloc disliked the brother, whose indecisiveness rankled, confirmed by his words, "... we must observe him if the burning passes but to return he must be bled, it is the Roman fever."

Aghast, Begiloc and the priest exchanged glances. Without medical notions of his own the warrior had an ingrained suspicion the wiccan women of Dumnonia, with their herbs and magic, were more effective than monks and nuns for all their prayers and blood letting.

The monk continued his inspection, "It's not so much the lancing, the brute has veins like ropes in those muscular arms and my blade is sharp-honed, more the staunching and closing of the wound is a problem ... so much blood ..."

The hot, humid summer had taken its toll. Pilgrims died of the disease and the Bischofsheim party did not escape the scourge. To the consternation of Begiloc, Caena became the first to show the symptoms.

"It's just sickness. Do you think you can be rid of me, Briton! Not a chance!" he said, but his headache and nausea worsened. A day after his 'sickness' appeared, he boasted of being too strong to be smitten by the ague and since there was no sign of illness it seemed he was right, only for him to be stricken on the third day, when Father Denehard summoned the healer.

Later that day, Alfwald and Sigeberht took to their beds with the same symptoms. Both had purple insect bites on their arms. Begiloc hastened to Father Denehard. "I don't like it. People are dying of this fever throughout the city. The infirmarian wants to stand by and watch and he's talking of bleeding."

"The priest sniffed. "The brother knows his job. Do you think to pray for them?"

"Will you, Father?"

"Of course."

"I'm glad of it. If you don't need me, I'll search for a physician."

"Are you without belief in our infirmarian? No faith in prayer?"

"In *your* prayer, not mine. As for the monk, well, it's not that ... what I mean is ... it's ... I met a physician once who cured my men and I wish to seek one of his ilk."

"We should talk about your relationship with God."
Begiloc ran his hand through his hair.

"Not now Father. I'd best be off."

"As you will. I'd leave these matters to the infirmarian–"
Before the priest changed his mind, he hurried away.

From previous visits to the city, he recalled a synagogue by the river. For some reason, the smallness the temple reassured him yet he hesitated before its doors. An armed gentile entering a sacred building might not be acceptable. A wall opposite the structure afforded him a seat where he waited for a Jew to appear. The coin prepared for the encounter proved unnecessary.

"Yoash Gerbi will not take silver for information, friend. Not from one on a mission of mercy." The man bowed. "You seek a Jewish physician? Alas! Ours is a small community without a doctor." Begiloc pursed his lips and clenched his fists.

"But come! My family avails itself of one Qutuz al-Zafir. An Arab, a worthy man. I'll take you to him."

In the maze of narrow streets, the shade of the buildings gave respite from the sun if not from the insects drawn by excrement and urine. The Jew pressed his hands together and took his leave before a modest house.

A boy answered his knock, his stare never leaving the sword at Begiloc's belt, but did not reply to his question about the physician. A few minutes passed causing a debate in his head while he glared at the stout wood in front of him; wait longer or batter on it with the pommel of his hand-seax? The doctor, seeing him hand on dagger when he opened the door, leapt back and flung it shut. Only Begiloc's quick reaction stopped it from closing.

"Stay! Doctor, I mean no harm."
Pushing the door open, he found the man holding a broom.

*'He means to defend himself with that against a warrior!'*
Begiloc grinned and the physician seeing the absurdity of the situation relaxed and laughed. The white teeth contrasted with the olive skin of the man's face. Under a turban of rolled, wound cloth, he wore a white, sleeved collarless shirt beneath a mantle of yellow sewn at the shoulders. Camel leather sandals completed his dress. Puzzled, Qutuz al-Zafir scrutinised the face of the Briton.

A swift explanation, a drawn-out wrangle about the propriety of a Muslim entering a Christian hospice, dissension over the fee, coins pocketed and he led the healer, his medicine satchel over his shoulder, to the Schola Anglorum.

The physician was busy at a side table mixing powders and salts in a mortar when the infirmarian found them.

"What is the meaning of this?"

The monk pointed at the turbaned figure.

"Qutuz al-Zafir is a physician," Begiloc said.

"An infidel! An infidel cure a Christian? Poisoner!"

His rapid move for the door thwarted, without removing his hand from the monk's chest, Begiloc pulled out his hand-seax.

"Stay here and learn! My friends won't die for your ignorance."

"Blasphemy! My abbot shall hear of this."

"Dead men tell no tales."

The tip of his seax went to the throat of the monk.

*'It won't be penance this time. Qutuz al-Zafir get this wrong and we'll hang as murderers.'*

The doctor turned to them, pestle in one hand and a small leather pouch in the other.

"This is the secret of the cure and the reason it is so rare. Gold dust."

A glistering cascade into the mortar caught the sunlight.

"Fetch water and a drinking vessel," said the Arab.

"Brother, do not try to flee or on my oath, I shall spit you like a suckling pig."

"May God smite you, heathen!"

"That's my task. *I* smite the heathen for *God*. Bring what he needs," said Begiloc, following on the infirmarian's heels. The physician took the vessels from the monk who by his expression might have been handing them to the Devil. Pouring his mixture into the bowl, he stirred in water before raising the head of Caena aiding the trembling man to drink. Twice more, he repeated the operation with the other Saxons.

"The fever will be gone by morning and will not return." Qutuz al-Zafir smiled at Begiloc. "Hark Brother," he said, addressing the infirmarian, "there may be other cases of the ague. Take all the ingredients including the gold dust, for I am well paid for my services. Heed me well, for these are the proportions of the medicine ..."

The seax pressed against his ribs stifled the fledgling protest and Begiloc forced the monk to repeat the prescription twice until Qutuz al-Zafir was satisfied.

"Do you wear a cross?" the Arab asked Begiloc.

"Ay."

He pulled out the ivory rood.

The Muslim addressed the brother, "Take an oath on the cross, sacred to you: agree to wait until morning and to denounce the Briton only if the fever returns."

The monk glanced from the dagger to the eyes of the warrior where he found no hesitancy nor mercy.

"I swear to God."

Father Denehard came into the dormer the next morning to find Begiloc and the infirmarian deep in conversation. The Briton had pushed coins at the monk, ostensibly as an offering for the purchase of more substances for medicines, but in reality to buy his silence. The ease of the transaction confirmed he had read his man well. Final recommendations made on the matter, the priest arrived and both men fell silent.

"How are your patients, Brother?"

"They are asleep with no fever. The Lord be praised!"

"Rejoice! My prayers are answered."

"Ay, my new treatment works wonders. God has inspired me. Let me show you, Father."

The infirmarian led the priest over to the side table and took the pouch of gold dust in his hand. Begiloc exited the dormer in high good humour.

The cure left him grateful but troubled.

*'The Church didn't save them. Others possess superior knowledge and Abbess Leoba recognises as much. How many such as she reside in the Church? What about the other certainties they would have us believe? I want to trust them. I'd lose my mind without hope of seeing Somerhild in Heaven.'*

Later the same week, Archbishop Boniface, Brother Willibald, Father Denehard and Begiloc received the papal summons to the Lateran Palace. Every step up the Caelian Hill to the building, saw his ill ease grow. He felt naked without a weapon and such exalted company inhibited him. The three clergymen spoke among themselves whereas he remained in silence trying to interpret his emotions. To meet the Head of the Church, he, a ceorl, a former slave and a sinner, in the presence of an archbishop left him under no delusion as to his unworthiness, a sensation underscored when they reached the Archbasilica of St John in Lateran. An inscription in Latin between the entrance and the doors of the adjacent palace caught his eye. The archbishop followed his gaze and translated, " *'Most Holy Lateran Church, of all the churches in the city and the world, the mother and head.'* This is the oldest in the West, Begiloc."

Boniface guided them through a door into a darkened hallway where stairs rose before them. The archbishop knelt and crossed himself. Had he misheard the words of the prelate?

"I shall mount the Scala Santa on my knees."

When Denehard and Willibald also began to climb the steps in this ungainly and wearying way he supposed he ought to do the same.

*'What's the point? Three, four, five ...'*
Arriving at the twenty-eighth marble step his joints and sides
pained him. Denehard, who had gained the top offered a hand
and hauled him to his feet.

"Father, why did we do that?" he whispered, not wanting to
show his ignorance to the other two men. Willibald caught his
words and said, "My son, this staircase is from Jerusalem. The
one Jesus of Nazareth ascended in front of the Praetorium of
Pontius Pilate to be tried."

"How came it here?"

"Saint Helena, the mother of Emperor Constantine had it
brought to Rome and reconstructed in this sacred place."

The landing served as an antechamber with six chairs lining
the far wall. Boniface knocked and after a short exchange with
a figure indiscernible in the gloom, the archbishop called to
Willibald, "Brother, the Holy Father grants an audience to you
alone. We shall wait."

To Begiloc's left hung a painting, a picture of Christ on
wood. Convinced the brown eyes of the icon were studying
him, he could not detach his gaze but the work also enthralled
his companions. In an awed voice, Boniface said, *"The
Acheiropoieton.* The word means *'made without hands'.*"

"How can it be?" Begiloc asked.

"They say St Luke painted it with the help of an angel."

*'Could be. I don't like the way it stares at me. It knows I'm a
sinner.'*
Averting his gaze, he refused to look in that direction.

For the warrior, an eternity passed before the summons into
the presence of Gregory III. Willibald stood smiling as they
entered. The Pontifex rose from his bowl-shaped throne and
they knelt before him. The heart of Begiloc pounded and he
wished himself anywhere but here.

They kissed the papal ring and received the command to stand.

"How goes your mission to the Alemans, Boniface?"

*'So the Pope speaks our language.'*

A long speech concerning of tribulations in Alemania and neighbouring Bavaria, of adulterous priests and obstreperous bishops, caused Begiloc to lose interest and to study the Holy Father, a Syrian, whose bronze complexion confirmed as much. A white mitre with cloth of gold at its base rested on a fringe of grizzled hair.

*'It's shaped like a helm. He's going grey but he's seen fifty winters.'*

The sleepy-looking eyes did not deceive him.

*'As sharp as my blade .. .ah, my sword – first time without a weapon since Wimborne.'*

The severe tone and the stern face of the Pope interrupted his musings.

"Request not granted. The Saxons will come to Christ in due time." The voice quickened, "Return to Bavaria as my vicarius with three letters: the first, commanding the bishops to provide you with all the assistance you require; the second, to the nobles and people of Germany ordering them to obey you; the third, insisting on an assembly twice a year at Augsburg under your authority."

"As you wish Holy Father," Boniface bowed his head.

*'No resigning. No fleeing the will of the Church.'*

The Pope turned to Denehard for news of Aldebert. The priest related what Begiloc and Caena had discovered in Neustria and the Pontifex, grave-faced, looked at him for confirmation. Thus far the warrior had coped by nodding but Gregory asked a direct question.

"Other than what you remember, by chance did this self-styled apostle also mention Raguel, Adinus and Sabaoc?"

They stirred a memory, he frowned, but remained unsure.

"Holy Father, they are familiar ..."

*'Did Aldebert utter them?'*

"...forgive me, so many names and much time passed."

The Pope stared at Boniface, "The presumed letter from Our Lord is harmless while these are names of archangels. He sets up crosses at fields and springs? Should these be fallen angels, the blasphemy of demon worship and witchcraft underlies this litany. We shall be attentive to this Aldebert. Reports reached us of another, a wandering Irishman, a licentious false prelate who preaches in the same region." The pontiff shook his head, "These are troubled times and the Evil One cast from Heaven wreaks harm among the unbaptized, the ignorant and the unwary."

Pope Gregory turned to Begiloc. "My son, we received word of your grief for the loss of your family and our heart goes out to you. Fear not, God holds them in his infinite love. The cruel separation has a sense, for Our Father in Heaven brings you here with a purpose that will soon become clear. Tell me of the Bishop of Rems."

Leaving out no detail, he recounted the events in Neustria. Account ended, Boniface begged leave to speak.

"Holy Father, this false bishop, this Servant of Satan must be deposed for flouting your authority and working against the true Church. His wickedness knows no bounds."

"Time ago, we received messages," said Gregory, "the Lord took Theuderic, king of the Franks, to his bosom with no successor and Charles Martel styles himself *'Prince'*. All Christendom is in his debt for the defeat of the Muslims at Tours and his power waxes. Rome needs the support he provides in Burgundy and Neustria; moreover, Milo is a scion of a powerful clan. We must proceed with caution. It is no easy matter to depose the wifebrother of Charles Martel."

In spite of the sacred surroundings, Begiloc could not hold back bloody thoughts.

*'Holy Father you can't unseat him, but I can kill him.'*

The Pope turned his attention to Brother Willibald.

"My son, you are informed of the problems faced by my legate. Boniface needs your exemplary conduct and indomitable spirit. Leave the abbey of St Benedict and proceed to the country of the Franks."

"Holy Father, I must ask permission of my abbot, according to the prescriptions of our Rule."

Pope Gregory smiled, an indulgent father on a wayward child, "If I am free to transfer Petronax to any other place, he has no power to oppose my wishes. Obey without a qualm of conscience."

"Your Holiness I shall carry out your commands, wherever in the world you are minded to send me."

The Pope turned to Boniface.

"Where will our brother best serve the Lord?"

"In the north of Bavaria stands a small church ringed by pagan lands," said the archbishop. "Named Eistedd. Thence we penetrate Thuringia."

"Willibald," said the pontiff, "you will travel there and progress our Ministry. Wisdom gained as a pilgrim will inspire others. We desire a monastery in those parts." Gregory paused and scrutinised the warrior. Never detaching his gaze from the Briton, he reflected for a while, then said, "Begiloc, the missionaries will need our protection."

"Holy Father, my muscles and sinews are at the service of the Church."

*'What choice is there?'*

Challenging his thoughts, the Pope said, "My son, a strong arm will not be your salvation. Let God enter your heart."

He lowered his head.

"You are a stalwart of the Church and demonstrate your honesty. You refuted officer rank in the City Guard at Colonia. Resistance to temptation is the measure of a man. We appoint you Captain of our forces in Bavaria under the command of Archbishop Boniface."

Unexpected emotion rocked Begiloc.

The Pope addressed the prelate again, "Raise troops with the help of our loyal son, Duke Odilo. Eradicate the heretical tenets and pagan customs adopted by ignorant priests scarce able to read or write." The Holy Father rose to his feet, indignant, "My advisers relate of pastors in Bavaria who hold services for Christians and offer sacrifices to idols for the heathen. This cannot be! Boniface, Denehard, Begiloc we dispatch you with Willibald to Eistedd, there to destroy the graven images. Be fishers of men as Our Lord commanded. Kneel for my blessing!" The Pope laid his hand on the head of the warrior who swore a stillness and power, a quiver bright as gold, surged through his body; although he never confided it to another.

Upon their exit, they entered the adjacent basilica. The priests and the monk prayed kneeling, eyes closed, while Begiloc contemplated the momentous events of the morning. Gregory III, was a charismatic and compelling man. What an honour to be blessed by him and to receive a prestigious rank.

*'Captain of the Church forces in Bavaria. How far I have come from slave in Wimborne to officer in the papal army!'*

The archbishop, of late a stranger, was his commander. His family dead, alone, he had new kinsfolk if he could but embrace them. Therein lay the problem. The Holy Father had told him to let God into his heart. How?

*'The blackness in my soul is born of murder in my heart.'*
He would rather risk Hell and not seeing Somerhild than break his oath to Meryn. The Church was to take him farther from Rems. Eistedd? He must consult a chart.

*'The captaincy means a delay. But, I'll hunt down Milo to slaughter him like a boar.'*

# PART THREE

## CHAPTER 15

*743 Anno Domini, April.*

Time, reflected Begiloc, like a wolf-pack in the forest, hurtles headlong, gathering speed towards an unknown destination. Too late for the onlooker when he realises he is the prey, the pack snapping at his tendons.

Not the case of Willibald who wasted no time in Bavaria and Thuringia. Far from him to plunge into converting and baptising, yet the pagans flocked to him, inspired to become Christians. When he arrived nothing rose there but a small church with heathen settlements all around, so he and his small band slept inside its wooden walls. Within six years he built a magnificent double abbey of stone, where visitors flocked to learn of his pilgrimage and of monasticism. As a result of the success of his unique missionary style, Boniface ordained him priest, then consecrated him bishop.

Notable events, like the wolf pack, flashed past the trees of this remote forest – the death of Charles Martel, the division of the Frankish lands between Pepin and Carloman, the demise of Gregory III, the enthronement of Pope Zachary and the coronation of Childeric III.

To an onlooker in the wilderness – as Begiloc regarded himself – these occurrences held little importance. Only the news of the deposition of Gewilieb, the Bishop of Mentz, and his death months later in circumstances unknown, roused him from his torpor.

*'Time passes. The bear is dead. What of the other false prelate? What of Meryn? I wear my oath tucked away like my ivory cross.'*

At the head of a fighting force of three score men provided by Duke Odilo, he won honour and coin repelling pagan Saxon raiders. With his standing high and Caena a more than an able leader of men, the time had come to plead with the bishop.

*'I must get to Rems. What reason can I give to leave? How to convince Willibald?'*

Providence intervened. The prelate came to him.

"Begiloc, there has been a synod at Soissons."

"A synod?"

"Ay, a meeting of archbishops and bishops. I can tell you Boniface is the new Archbishop at Mentz?"

*'A thousand times better than the bear.'*

"Gladdening news!"

"Praise the Lord! Heed me well: as the representative of the see of St Peter, Boniface has been charged by Pepin, the Mayor of the Palace, to restore faith and morality to the Church in Neustria. All our might must be directed, with God's help, to extirpate incest, fornication, the practice of magic and the removal false priests."

"Such as Bishop Milo?"

"Indeed, Milo! At the behest of Boniface and the bidding of the Holy Father, the Synod deposed him, but he clings to office supported by the arrogance of certain nobles. A war is waged in the Church..."

*'I've heard those words before.'*

"...and heresies abound and prosper. A letter from Boniface arrived this day wherein it states one by the name of Aldebert and another, Clement, preach heresy in Neustria. The Synod condemned both and the archbishop entrusts you the task of arresting them. The last news of Aldebert is from the forested area of the Ardennes where he preached in a place named Valmy."

"Valmy?"

"Ay, near Sanctá-Menehilde. I believe you know of the place and I remember you heard him preach."

"It is true. Of this Clement I know nought."

"A blasphemer! The son of a murderess! An Irishman, a wanderer who married his brother's widow! Even though he has two children born during his false episcopate, he claims to exercise the functions of a Christian bishop. He rejects the teachings of the holy Fathers and despises all synodal decrees. Take him alive and bring him to me!"

"Where do I find this Clement?"

"Boniface writes he is at Sparnacum six leagues south of Rems..."

*'Close to Rems!'*

"... though he wanders from place to place. From his mouth issues vile doctrine as a spout gushes foul water. At the harrowing of hell, he sustains, Christ led not only the virtuous but also all others out of perdition, so no man remained." The bishop exclaimed, "What then? Is Hell a place in the sole possession of demons? That cannot be!" Willibald sighed and shook his head, "Begiloc, this heresy must be eradicated."

Doctrine did not intrigue the warrior. Any notion of God, he found in nature, in such moments when the sun unveils the suspended web of a spider in glistening dew. Heresy interested him inasmuch as it might lead him closer to Rems and nearer to fulfilling his oath to Meryn; otherwise, more practical matters occupied him.

"My Lord Bishop, how many men can you spare?"

"Take all your men." The prelate acknowledged his fleeting surprise, "The pagans have not ventured this far south for more than a twelvemonth."

"Is it wise to leave the monastery undefended?"

"Undefended? Our Father in heaven will watch over us while our guardians are away. Rest easy."

*'Were Leoba here, she'd say the same.'*

He realised the pointlessness of discussion.

"Very well."

"Another thing ... Aldebert builds churches and erects crosses at the sites of pagan practices, these are an abomination. Burn them! Prepare for your journey, you leave at sunrise."

Later, Caena found him walking enthralled, ticking off fingers.

"What ails you, friend?"

Setting aside thoughts of Sanctá-Menehilde and travel time, he reported his conversation with Willibald.

"To Rems is it? At last! Six years since they brought us here and how oft have I reminded you of our oath to Meryn?"

"Thirteen moons in a year and for each moon, you remind me fifty times – *many!"*

The Saxon guffawed and said, "Cannot we do something about it?" The determination on the face of the warrior mirrored his own and they clasped hands in silent accord.

The overland journey west to Sanctá-Menehilde lasted six weeks, with four days lost to bad weather. Thrice challenged by riders sent by the local leud whose land they passed through, the letter of Willibald sufficed to let three score and seven armed men proceed unhindered.

Once across the River Meuse, Begiloc thought it best to send Caena ahead with the missive to Sanctá-Menehilde to advise the Comitis of their peaceful intentions. They received a cordial reception from the dowager comitissa, who sought tidings of Leoba, but Begiloc disappointed her with only second-hand accounts of the abbess. Instead, the Lady Albemarle and her son pressed them for details of the work of Willibald and of his pilgrimage to the Holy Land.

When at last a chance came to seek news of Aldebert, Lord Girard conceded the heretic had been at Valmy but reports indicated his preaching had taken him farther off to Auve.

"Is it not the village of the *'need fire'* blaze?" Caena asked.

"Of Ingitruda, maybe?" said Begiloc, a lightness in his voice.

Next day, they marched to the settlement. On their way, they burned wooden crosses each the height of two men. The third of these they found in Auve erected at the spring, the source of the river.

Approaching along the stream, they sighted the cross before seeing the crowd. Amid the throng stood the self-styled apostle recognisable from his wild gesticulations, unkempt appearance, once-white tunic and, Begiloc had to admit, charismatic presence. The numerous people assembled around the preacher confirmed Aldebert continued to draw believers to his sermons throughout the countryside.

Their advance went unnoticed. The country folk too enthralled by an account of God seated on the seventh throne above the cherubim and seraphim to notice them. At this point, the stream flowed no more than a yard wide so Begiloc split his force, sending half under Caena to the other bank. They would take Aldebert in a pincer movement and to this end, he waved both groups wider to encircle the congregation. The arrest of a holy man was sure to inflame the righteous anger of the villagers, and although Begiloc doubted the depth of their piety, he would take no chance of bloodshed.

Encircled and confronted by drawn swords and shields, the men in the crowd reacted with oaths and bunched fists, some women hysterical pulling their hair and screaming.

Aldebert, cried out in protest. "Does Pilate send his guard to arrest Our Lord's apostle? If it be the will of the Father I shall drink of this bitter chalice!" A wild light flared in his eye.

The mob grew truculent and one reckless youth bent to pick up a stone, but Amalric, the elder of the village, grasped his wrist and cuffed his ear.

"What avail stones against armed warriors?"

"Bind him and tight!" Caena ordered, "accept no resistance." He addressed the crowd, "No harm will come to this man."

The angry murmuring hushed and the people strained to hear the voice of the new speaker. Holding up his hand, Begiloc said, "I crossed the highest mountains in the world," and with these few words captured their attention, "on a pilgrimage to Rome." The ensuing gasps encouraged him. "I met the Holy Father, Pope Gregory in person ..."

"The Antichrist!" Aldebert cried.

All eyes turned to the preacher, but Begiloc said, "Spurn not your bishops and priests, be not deceived by this imposter! To call the pontiff 'Antichrist' is blasphemy. Our charge is to take him to the vicarius of Pope Zachary in Neustria and there he will be heard–"

"Did they hear Jesus? Nay, first they clothed Him in purple; then they twisted a crown of thorns, thrust it on His head ... and when they had mocked Him, they took the purple off Him, put His own clothes on Him, and led Him out and nailed Him to a cross of wood!" Aldebert yelled, spittle flying.

Begiloc pointed at him, "See, he likens himself to Christ, but he will not be crucified, he will not be harmed at all. The archbishop desires to speak with him, but those who refute the summons of the Church leave no choice, obedience must be enforced and we will escort this man to him. Would any here defy the authority of Archbishop Boniface?"

The challenge issued, the crowd deliberated.

Whether the silence and acquiescence were due to his words or to the brandished swords mattered not to Begiloc. In the hush, a word rang out: "Caena!"

Everyone turned to stare at a young woman wrapping her arms around the tall, blond warrior.

"Ingitruda!"

Weapon in one hand, shield in the other and in between the woman attached to him like a limpet to a rock. Staring up into his face, she breathed words none but he could catch. Whatever she said, his face softened and his sword arm encircled her.

Smiling, Begiloc ordered five men to escort Aldebert to Sanctá-Menehilde there to await his return. Once they departed along the stream, he commanded the crowd to disperse and called for Amalric. Inconsolable women wept and wailed, believing the preacher to be a healer because of his holiness and some of the men, wary of the Bavarian swords, struck a sobbing wife into submission dragging them off home. A few men remained to discuss the events.

Amalric joined Begiloc, "Well met friend. I never did like the sermoniser. He claims to be a saint but I've seen some of our women come back rumpled after an hour at his hut. 'Orat'ry' he calls it, but I got another name for it–"

"Enough!" he interrupted, "there are more pressing matters to attend to. Can you spare bread and cheese for these men?" To forestall objection, he raised his hand, "I'll pay."

After their meal, he oversaw the burning of the cross and though Amalric maintained "... never did like it ..." he waited until it was past saving before he summoned his men with the intention of striking out into the forest towards a place called Juvinia, which the village elder confirmed as on the way to Sparnacum.

No sign of Caena until they found him near a barn where, in a gruff voice, he said: "I'm coming, aren't I? What's all the fuss about?" Taken aside and taxed by Begiloc on the reason for this delay, the warrior grunted, his shiftiness clear.

"I'll tell you when I'm ready."

In the forest, the charcoal burner gaped at the column of armed men. A league of woodland further on, Caena turned to Begiloc, "Ingitruda told me ..."

"*Ingitruda*, is it?"

"Let it be, man! She said your cure worked on the pigs. Remember, the one for the mange?"

"It took her some time to tell you that, didn't it?"

The Saxon muttered, relapsing into silence as they strode along the forest trail. Curious to know what was on his companion's mind, Begiloc smiled but determined to torment him first. At last, the Saxon blurted, "I shall take Ingitruda for wife. I told her so and now, you know of my intent!"

With a cheer, Begiloc seized Caena and in consequence halting the whole column of men. Over the years, shared hardship had brought them close now they embraced as brothers.

"Water is poor fare to drink to your joy this night in the rude comfort of a forest camp!"

"No matter, for my bliss will be shadowed till Milo lies dead before me. I told Ingitruda only then shall we wed."

Tight-lipped, Begiloc shook his head, "Of this, we'll speak in good time."

Forced to toast Caena without strong drink, nevertheless they sang and recounted tales around the fire while Alfwald spent the evening whetting his double-edged axe, a recent purchase in Eistedd.

Next day, mid-morning, they broke from the cover of the trees and sharp-eyed Eadwig hurried over to Begiloc.

"See there! On the hill. A lone rider."

Following the direction of the outstretched finger, he spied a motionless horseman, a league off. To their surprise, the rider galloped towards them. Five hundred heartbeats later and the man drew up in front of them before leaping from his mount to bow.

"Begiloc the Briton, my lord bishop Bladald sends you greetings. Know you this, the road into Juvinia where the bridge crosses the river is beset by the men of Milo in wait among the trees lining the banks."

"A trap! How many?" he asked.

"Six score. Twice your number."

"Does Milo lead them?" Caena asked. Would that we finish off the sinner sooner than we thought!"

The messenger shook his head, "The bishop is in Treves."

Begiloc and Caena both cursed.

*'Milo again! But this time not personal. To thwart Boniface and his reforms.'*

"How did they discover we were coming to Juvinia?" asked Begiloc with furrowed brow.

"How did my Lord Bishop learn of their movements? Trees have ears! Clement the wandering preacher is near Sparnacum, perforce you pass through the village."

"What does his eminence advise?"

The messenger pointed, "To the south, you will reach the Marne. Follow the river valley and it will take you to Sparnacum, it is a longer way to the town. Be warned, the enemy is charged to slay you and on no account let you take Clement." The man paused and frowned, "May I speak my mind?"

Begiloc studied the messenger's face and gestured to continue.

"When you fail to show the foe will make all speed to thwart you. I fear they will reach the preacher first and set another ambush."

"We heed your words and thank you for them."

The messenger inclined his head in respect and mounted to return to Catalauns. While he rode over the hill Begiloc used the time to think. Outnumbered, with a longer route to gain Clement, the situation dire, he found no sense in the bishop's well-meant counsel, but Bladald was not a warrior-prelate.

"What then?" Caena asked. "How do you mean to get out of this!"

"We can't evade them for long. South leads to the river and that way we shall go – but not far." Begiloc noted the troubled faces and gathered his men round to explain the only hope of victory was to benefit without delay from the split in the enemy force.

From the plain to the south, they crept into the woods, each step along the trail taken with care not to alert the enemy to the sound of a snapped twig or a trip and a curse. Begiloc regretted not bringing spears for ease of travel, a decision he knew might prove costly.

Time passed before they sighted the enemy who were directing their attention to the road. Keeping to the plan, with a score of men, Caena, detached from the main force, began to sweep around the foe to reach and try to hold the crossing point. They waited from behind trees and bushes till the tall Saxon and his men mounted the bridge, when Leofric sounded the war horn they charged the backs of the lurking men. Their adversary carried no spears! An exultant and fearsome war cry burst from the throat of Begiloc, taken up at once by his Bavarian warriors, the woods resounding to the din.

Alfwald, first into the fray, axe flashing like a scythe at harvest, carved a swathe in the enemy ranks. Their numbers were well matched, but the onslaught was ferocious.

Begiloc singled out their leader upon hearing the fellow bellow orders to stiffen resistance. Agile in spite of his thickset frame, the squat, muscular warrior impressed the Briton with the might of his arm as soon as he parried the first blow with his shield. Eyes locked, they circled, seeking to anticipate the ploy of the other. After a fierce exchange of blows, Begiloc realised none of the feints and tricks he deployed in combat was of use against this man. Face taut with concentration, he blotted out the clash of steel, roars and screams around him, since he faced an adversary capable of ending his life in a moment, at the slightest distraction.

The Frank stepped forward and attacked inside Begiloc's sword arm but sprang to the left and feinted to the head obliging Begiloc to parry. The fatal instant upon him, too late he realised his misjudgement, the warrior's blade pierced under the arm and would have entered his heart had instinct not urged him to twist aside. He fell, shocked and hurt. The Frank inverted his weapon two-handed for the final blow. Embracing death, he closed his eyes and did not see Alfwald bury his axe into the neck of his unsuspecting foe.

Aware the hot dampness under his arm meant loss of blood, Begiloc drifted in and out of consciousness. At some point, he felt rough hands strip him of his tunic.

*'The day is lost. They're stripping the corpses. Why don't they finish me?'*

Instead, they placed a swab over his wound and raised him to bind it tight around his chest. When he came round the voice of Caena greeted him.

"Thank the stars! For one minute I thought we'd lost you, old beast!" He continued "... they'll bring more men from Rems. We must hasten where they can't follow."

"... and Clement?" asked the querulous voice of Leofric.

"Hang Clement! The important thing is to take Begiloc to an infirmary. We need the Briton alive! The sly fox knows a trick or two, without him, we'd be lost."

"So Sigeberht and the others died for nothing?" Leofric's voice rose.

*'Sigeberht's dead? The others?'*

Begiloc tried to sit up, but a pain seared through his side preventing him and he groaned.

"Well, I'm going after this Clement. Who's with me?" Leofric blazed in defiance.

Caena glared around the men, but the recalcitrant faces were Saxon. On closer scrutiny, Alfwald's expression was sullen, not truculent, so he addressed his remarks to the older man.

"If we chase after the preacher and seize him, do you think we can return to Sanctá-Menehilde before the Franks are on us? Speak! Are you dumb or stupid? How you try my patience!" Alfwald lowered his head. Ignoring the Bavarians murmuring agreement, Caena stared at the three doubtful Saxons in turn.

"Risking his life," he pointed at Begiloc, "won't restore Sigeberht to us and the Church can deal with Clement. We've got the other sermoniser for them and we've paid a high price in blood."

"He's right," Alfwald scowled, "they've taken flight to Rems, the curs, to seek more men and they'll slay us if they find us. Then there's Begiloc, if we wear him out hunting for the preacher, he'll die."

Caena spat on the ground, "If he dies, on my oath, I'll flay that bastard, Milo, alive."

"I'm not going to die," Begiloc said through gritted teeth and to his own ears the words croaked. Two branches held together by cloaks – Frankish, he guessed – formed the litter he lay on. In an attempt to prove his determination, he tried to rise, but the severe pain in his side caused him to fall back with a groan.

Caena leant over him, noting the pallor, "Hang on Briton, we'll get you to the monastery, it's two leagues hence. I'll not let the Devil take you yet."

The litter jostled and bumped up to the religious house in Catalauns, where – before joining the other men at Sanctá-Menehilde thence to escort the heretic Aldebert to Bishop Willibald – they consigned Begiloc to the infirmary, the flame of his life little more than a spark.

# CHAPTER 16

Eleven weeks of the infirmarian's hen broth remedy, Begiloc reflected, would kill all but the hardiest of fighters and he gave thanks the rheumy-eyed monk's faith extended to the healing properties of red wine and bread but the combined intake proved a violent and daily emetic, disgorging any beneficial effect and prolonging his recovery. Wounds and hard knocks accompanied his life as a warrior but this shredding of his stomach lining made him fear for his existence.

In early convalescence, when the fowl gruel snatched him from death's door, his elderly carer informed him of God's mercy in guiding the enemy blade so it did not penetrate the lung but instead chipped and broke two ribs. Scrupulous attention to cleanliness and he admitted this virtue in the monk, prevented the wound from festering.

Time to leave the monastery. Before thrusting his sword into his belt, he chewed on a morsel of stale bread washed down with wine. Unsteady on his feet, his head spun but the pain in his side had ceased days before. The journey to Eistedd daunted him, but he refused to contemplate drinking another drop of hen broth.

The battle of wills with the infirmarian over, effusive thanks, a visit to the almoner, frugal supplies and he departed.

Twenty-four hours trudging through the forest, breathing pure air and toning his leg muscles did not restore him to fighting fitness, but for the first time in months, he felt well. The idea of going to Rems crossed his mind since nobody expected him at Eistedd. Determination is the offspring of a combination of factors, in this case, he lacked strength of arm, not of purpose. Accepting this, he kept to the track leading to the charcoal burner's clearing.

Occupied, the ragged, soot-blackened ceorl did not hear him approach. Bent over a heap of logs, he gathered and carried them to a well-ordered stack. Intent on reaching the village in the valley, Begiloc did not slow but greeted the man in passing. The charcoal burner started, dropped his wood and began to shout, waving his arms. The Briton ignored him, continuing on his way but he turned at the sound of running steps. To his surprise, the fellow dared to seize his arm, gabbling incomprehensible words. Were there colours other than black under the grime, they drained from his face when the warrior's hand went to his sword. Releasing Begiloc's forearm as it were one of his ardent branches, agitated, he pointed at the stack of logs. The coarse Frankish dialect and the man's speech defect made it impossible for the Briton to understand him. Did he mean to force an armed warrior to pick up the wood? How?

The charcoal burner beckoned to him, his pleading eyes convincing him not to walk on. Calmed by this acquiescence, the ceorl's speech slowed enough for him to interpret "...wait for the woman ..."

*'Woman? Who?'*

Try as he might, unable to distinguish the words, he brought his ear close enough to be repelled by the man's foul breath. In turn, frustration made the woodlander shout and quicken his speech so he understood less. Intrigued, he sat on a tree stump since the day stretched ahead of him and he wished to discover the identity of the woman.

The charcoal burner hurried over to his store, coming back with a bundle of straw clutched in his burn-scarred arms. Carrying it over to his smouldering kiln, he laid it on the ground whence he dashed to the shack and emerged with a pail of water to dampen the stalks before flinging an armful into the fire. At once a column of white smoke rose into the air as the water turned to steam. Pointing, he uttered one word: "White!"

"A signal?" asked Begiloc, the man grinned, adding more straw before taking a tin and striding to the goat to squat and milk the nanny before bearing the vessel to him, a kindness the warrior appreciated since he had managed on a piece of bread and cheese at dawn. For a meal, he relied on the hospitality of Amalric in the village or in the unlikely event of the elder's absence, on buying food. The warm, smooth milk he drank with relish but careful not to finish it, he offered the can to his host. However, the woodsman shook his head, indicating to drain the vessel. From a second series of gestures, it appeared the ceorl would leave him and return. Throwing the last of the straw into the kiln, he hastened among the trees as the white smoke thickened.

Soon the shambling unkempt creature of the gap-toothed grin returned, pointing into the woods and Begiloc caught the words, "... woman's coming."

No clue hinted at her identity when she appeared carrying a wicker basket, for a hood hid her face till she threw it back and greeted him.

"Ingitruda!"

The young woman stilled his curiosity with an impatient wave.

"They await you in the village," she said, face tense, "they plan to hang you, Begiloc."

"Who? Who are they?"

"Bishop Milo's men know you are on your way from Catalauns."

"How do they know?"

"Spies in the monastery or near it." Ingitruda sighed and frowned. "One of them said with you wounded it would be a child's task to take you since the only way for you to reach Sanctá-Menehilde is along the river. The forest is dense where it stretches up to the plain lying before the castle and the maze of trails confound an outsider. So they wait, sure to seize you here at Auve."

"I must turn back?"

"Hark, I have a plan," Ingitruda reached in her basket to pull out bandages.

"A leper house receives at Verden, so should they overtake you, they will chance on an untouchable. Leave your sword with Hartmut here—"

"Never! I will hear out your scheme but I cannot be separated from my weapon."

"We shall strap it to your back."

The empty tin drained of milk lying by her foot she handed to Hartmut, "Fetch water!" With equal forcefulness, she pointed at Begiloc, "Strip off your tunic!"

Pausing only to run her fingers over the raw red scar at his side, she secured the sword by bandages around his chest and back. The warrior dressed and she studied her handiwork.

"Well, if they don't come too close, it will pass. Make a fist, no, the other hand."

Left hand bandaged to resemble a stump, she made him unlace the thongs of his shoes, stuffing them in his pack then proceeded to bind his feet.

"I can only hobble," he protested.

"Lepers hobble."

She took the tin from Hartmut and set it on the ground by the basket from which she took a small flat piece of wood. On this, she shook flour from a packet and mixed it into a paste with water. Using her finger, she smeared it in circles on Begiloc's face and bare arms.

"Clay from the stream," she said shaking earth from a bag, again drizzling water. She painted the brown sludge with care on the round marks, leaving only white edges visible.

"Fetch a clout, Hartmut!"

When the ceorl returned with a filthy rag she gave him instructions and he hastened over to the goat. Confused as to why the charcoal burner began to pass the cloth with vigour over the animal's fur, violence sprang to Begiloc's mind when Hartmut started to rub the malodorous rag over his tunic.

"What in the devil's name ... ?"

"Lepers smell of goat," said Ingitruda, "and now for your hair!"

"My hair?"

A short knife appeared from her basket and he shied away.

"You choose," she glared at him, "better the corpse of a vain Briton or one alive with cropped hair?"

After hacking at his locks and she stood back to survey her handiwork.

"A pity you can't see yourself, I'd run a league if I chanced on you. Remember should anyone come near you, keep the thumb of your right hand tucked in. Lepers have claw hands. Hartmut will lead you through the forest beyond Auve to set you on the way to Sanctá-Menehilde."

She picked up the empty basket and put the knife into it, "I'll gather herbs so my return will not be greeted with suspicion. When they grow uneasy at your not coming to my village they will ride out and find a leper, a pariah. Farewell! Begiloc ... " she hesitated and blushed, "greet Caena for me."

"I suppose I should thank you," the warrior said, his expression so downcast Ingitruda laughed and Hartmut sniggered.

"Hold fast to that mood and none will doubt your disguise," she said.

Forced to shuffle along the road shamming illness moved him to pity for lepers. Shamed and humbled, he thanked God for being sound of limb. Time passed and he began to feel weary from the effort of hobbling but found it impossible to sit for a rest with his sword strapped behind him. Thus, fear mixed with relief when hoof beats thundered behind him. He made a claw hand.

A band of riders reined in well before reaching him. Their leader pointed with a sneer of abhorrence, "A God-forsaken leper!" To the man next to him, he said, "Dismount and question whether he has seen the Briton."

Begiloc's heartbeat quickened. The horseman sprang down and led his mount toward him.

*'What of the skill of Ingitruda? Artful enough to deceive close inspection? God help me! Run into the forest? Nothing more than a shamble along the road! My sword unusable and trees aplenty to hang a man.'*

At the soldier's relentless approach, he swallowed hard.

*'What's this? Does his advance slow?'*

The warrior halted four paces away, his aversion writ clear on his face, and he wrinkled his nose.

*'Bless the goat!'*

A moment passed – one of the longest of Begiloc's life as the horseman scrutinized him from his tuffets of hair to his blotchy face and down to his bandaged hand and feet.

"Go you to the leper house at Verden?"

Begiloc, fearful of betrayal by his foreign tongue made a sequence of throaty sounds and bobbed his head. The man narrowed his eyes and shouted to his companions, "A leper! The poor bastard can't speak! And he stinks to high heaven!" Turning back, he said, "Did a warrior, a Briton, pass you on your way?"

An idea leapt to mind and he uttered more sounds, indicating the trees with his claw hand.

"The forest!" the Frank clenched his fist, "Of course, the sly cur! He saw us coming and slipped into the woods, am I right?"

Pointing with his bandaged stump back down the road, he grunted incoherently.

"How far? Not far!"

Vague assenting gestures with both hands by the leper and the warrior remounted. Before re-joining the others he called, "Get you hence to the lazar house. No place in the world for the likes of you!"

Milo's men wheeled their horses to gallop off into the trees. Time for a grim smile of satisfaction and a blessing for Ingitruda before hobbling on towards the castle of Lord Girart. The horsemen did not reappear and evening drawing nigh, he stopped. Free of bandages, he risked the cool air of the fading day to plunge into the river, still in his tunic, in the hope of ridding his clothes of the reek of goat and his flesh of fake leprosy.

By the time he gained Eistedd, with autumn well advanced, his hair had grown back.

On his arrival, to his vexation, Bishop Willibald apprised him of Aldebert's escape from under their noses.

"I know not how," said the prelate, "we suspect a serving woman drugged the guard at night and freed the heretic who was last seen in the north of Hesse. Caena led his men – I mean *your* men – to flush him out, but like a cunning fox he eluded them."

"When?"

"After the goose fair. After Michaelmas."

"Two moons past. Do you want me to pursue him?"

The bishop shook his head.

"Winter is coming. The days grow short and the weather turns for the worse. The false prophet will keep until Easter when for sure he will spring up anew as a weed among the green shoots of true believers, for it is in the nature of blasphemers to betray their whereabouts. The Devil speeds the spread of sacrilege."

Willibald left him with this thought, but Begiloc found it hard to shake off resentment. He had risked death for nothing. Milo had prevented him from seizing Clement and they had let Aldebert slip from their clutches. He took stock of his situation: he had lost his wife and son, his friend blind and unavenged, the Church had robbed him of what should have been the best years of his life and the enemy he had sworn to kill prospered a hundred leagues away. Indignant, he ground the heel of his shoe into the turf and determined come the spring everything would change, and with it the situation of Caena.

During a milder winter than usual, Begiloc regained strength through weapon training. When the fieldfares flew north, with the appearance of the first snowdrops then purple crocuses among the trees he sought an audience with Bishop Willibald.

From their first meeting in Rome, he esteemed the noble monk from Wessex and had seen him progress in the Church. Were this prelate not to accede to his request, he felt sure no other would. Encouraged by a benign welcome, he began without more ado: "My Lord Bishop, twelve springs ago Caena and I set sail from Wessex at the bidding of churchmen," the prelate's brow creased and Begiloc's heart sank, but he continued, "we have given our all in service–"

"And now, Begiloc, you wish to leave us?" tone icy, the prelate interrupted.

"Not so, Your Eminence, I would you release Caena."
The cleric's forehead unwrinkled and his features softened.

"How so?"

"In a village by Catalauns, his bride awaits him but duty wrenched him from his betrothed. The woman as saved me from the noose on my journey here."

"A brave young woman – and will he wed her?"

"With your consent," said Begiloc.

"Shall you want for a right-hand man?"

"Alfwald is older, less headstrong, he'll serve."
The smile of Willibald removed a thousand cares from his face.

"In that case, Caena will receive my blessing to marry his beloved. Send him to me, Begiloc."
The warrior sank to his knee, took the bishop's hand and, though he loathed this sign of servitude, he swallowed his pride and kissed the ring with sincerity.

"What does the bishop want of me?"

" I can't imagine."
The puzzlement on Caena's face pleased him as much as the huge smile on the face of the Saxon when he emerged from the audience. It uplifted his spirit.

The next morning, Begiloc stood at the monastery gate with Alfwald, Leofric, Cynefrid and Eadwig, making five of the original thirteen warriors who left Wimborne twelve years before. It meant he would be alone, for he held Caena a friend while the others old comrades. Determined not to reveal his true feelings, for fear of showing weakness, he clasped hands with the tall Saxon, making light of the circumstance and eliciting a promise from the warrior to carry the leper's thanks to Ingitruda.

"Make fine children for me to play my hearpe to one day."

"Ay, were you ever to shake off the hounds of the Church. Which reminds me, Auve is nearer to Treves. There's my oath to Meryn and Ingitruda knows I–"

"Stay!" Begiloc seized the oak branch of an arm, "Meryn is my friend and my word holds. In the name of friendship, I beg you to wed your love and leave the deed to me."

The Saxon stared for an age into the eyes of the Briton. He acceded, "This is what will happen: you will delay no longer to visit doom on Milo, thereafter go to Meryn and then to me. If word arrives of your death, I set out on the instant to slay the bastard."

They clasped hands and embraced before Caena saluted each of his companions. The rock of a man disappeared into the woods and though Begiloc remained imperturbable, Eadwig coughed and wiped a sleeve across his eye.

A messenger from a monastery in north-eastern Hesse arrived to distract them from the crater in their ranks caused by the departure of the rock. Willibald sent for the Briton and gave him his orders.

"This brother comes with instructions from Archbishop Boniface to take your force to the house of St Benedict at Haerulfisfeld. It stands seventy leagues hence. Your time in Bavaria is ended and I thank you for all you have done." The weather-beaten face became grave. "Remember, Begiloc, let God into your heart. Do not stray from the path of righteousness and your reward will be beyond imagining. Now go! Prepare your men. You will all receive my blessing after Prime."

Pensive, he obeyed, aware his life was about to change once more and Bishop Willibald had counselled him with the words Pope Gregory had used as though both cast a light into the dark corner sealed against God. With the circumstances of Caena resolved, it appeared his own stood to worsen.

*'One day at a time ... I will be ready ... but leave I must.'*

Sturm, another high-born Bavarian missionary, ordained to the priesthood, established the monastic settlement at Haerulfisfeld. On their arrival, pleasantries over, the priest explained, "The archbishop sends us to the solitude of Bochonia to judge whether the place is fit to dwell for the servants of God. As a result of his petition, the Mayor of the Palace, Carloman, gathered the nobles of the area and requires them to cede the land I shall choose. The Lord be praised for their eagerness to consent! Among them are those who would send their sons when the monastery opens its doors."

The persona of the priest intrigued Begiloc. Not only had his tonsure grown out, but his curls, the colour of his own, cascaded over his shoulders.

"So," he asked, "the land lies open to the pagans, an outpost for missionary and military work among the heathen?"

"Lull told me you were strong of arm but also shrewd," Sturm smiled.

"You know him, Father?"

"We studied under the late-lamented Abbot Wigbert at Fritzlar – may his soul rest in peace. Lull spoke to Archbishop Boniface on your behalf."

"On my behalf?"

"It is so, but first we must travel to the wilderness. I cannot say more."

With preparations to be made for the exploration of a thickly-forested region, Begiloc thought no further on the matter. Sturm opted to ride on an ass and bring two other of the beasts with him. One to be used as a pack bearer to carry essential tools, two-handled lumber saws, hammers, nails, and chisels.

Protected from predators by a palisade, they slept on the bare ground under a canopy of stars, but the glorious night sky that so fired Begiloc's enthusiasm did not seem to inspire Sturm, not an easy man to please. His demanding eye found nowhere suitable for a monastery so to solve the problem he fasted, sang psalms and prayed. In spite of this, they made two expeditions in vain, but one day they came upon a man with a horse who knew the area. He, the first living soul they encountered since leaving Haerulfisfeld, told them of a place in the forested hills nearby where the purest water spouted from springs. Below them in the valley, he said, a small river flowed into a wider one called the Fulda.

When they reached a clearing with a spring, Sturm turned in his saddle and ordered the men to build a palisade for the night. Trotting over with a mounted monk, he brought the third ass for Begiloc.

A short way upstream, Sturm halted and dismounted at a place where fallen stones, many overgrown with weeds, indicated to Begiloc's warrior instinct an ancient camp destroyed. The priest fell to his knees and prayed. A sign at last, had he chosen? Apart from the ford across the river, Begiloc considered it no better nor worse than many of those discounted. The cleric rose and pronounced himself satisfied, adding, "In the name of the See of St Peter in Rome, our Holy Father Zachary, the Archbishop of Metz, I Sturm of Lorch take possession of this land to here construct a convent according to the rules of St Benedict and it shall be known as 'Fulda'."

In the following days, Begiloc and his men with a handful of monks felled trees and removed stones from the soil. Small huts rose for temporary shelter and to the curiosity of the Briton, under the direction of one of the brothers, they constructed a lime kiln. One day he would witness the use of mortar, for Sturm designated the house of worship to be the first masonry building. Prayers the priority, they erected winches and a crane to put up a simple wooden church next to the planned site of the stone one.

Sturm sent out monks to search for ironstone and limestone. While the quest went on, the warriors built a forge since they would have to make their own tools. Under the priest's directions, they constructed timber buildings for stonemasons, carpenters, wood turners, basket weavers, potters, roofers, broom makers, textile workers, and rope makers. They put up pens for sheep, pigs, and goats, and a chicken coop, and beehives. A herb garden for the kitchen and for the healer's plants followed. Where the monks to fill these buildings were to come from bewildered Begiloc until one day, months later, a familiar figure appeared and proceeded to hug Sturm. Surrounding the newcomer were four score brothers – Boniface had arrived.

Begiloc was sawing through a trunk with Alfwald when a monk came over to tell him the archbishop awaited him.

To the surprise of the warrior, the prelate embraced and kissed him, asked about his wound, before mooting the reason for their meeting.

"Alas Begiloc, they made me the keeper of the vineyards: but mine own vineyard have I not kept. I dug about it, I brought to it a basket of dung, but I did not guard it. When I looked that it should bring forth grapes, they were but wild."

The warrior scratched his temple and bit his lip. Was he supposed to understand the meaning?

"I speak of the heretic, Aldebert, of the negligence that allowed him to shake off his shackles and flee." The archbishop sighed, "Ever I pray to be delivered from the wiles of Satan, the seducer, and from malicious men such as this false shepherd who pretends to dispense the gospel but beguiles his flock, *multitudinem rusticorum*, from the laws of God. The Holy Father has pronounced anathema on him and on Clement."

Begiloc recalled the word but not its meaning.

"Anathema?"

Surprised at the question, the archbishop explained.

"Deposed, suspended from the functions of the priesthood and excommunicated, destined to perish in eternal flames. I am advised he preaches near Franconofurd twenty leagues hence. It pains me to weary you anew, but go, Begiloc! Arrest the blasphemer and bring him to Fulda. Go in the name of Christ."

With his four Saxons and six other chosen Bavarians, he tracked the heretic to a village some leagues before Franconofurd. Standing beneath a towering wooden cross, the preacher, as described by Boniface, addressed a multitude of country folk. Many of the crowd were women and some of these cried out like hysterical prophetesses. In his opinion, the fake, Aldebert, was a skilful manipulator of minds, a sorcerer, a perverse representative of the Almighty who imprisoned poor gullible peasants and ensnared them in their own ignorance. The vast number of the throng troubled him as they approached. Calling a halt, he said to Alfwald, "Unlike at

Auve, I fear we shan't be able to use reason with no friend in the crowd."

The Saxon frowned and pulled out his sword, "Straight in. Seize him, straight out."

Wanting no blood spilt, Begiloc scowled, bowed his head and closed his eyes.

*'More hot-blooded than Caena!'*

"We retreat into the forest."

"What! Why?" asked Alfwald.

"Women and children are among the gathering. We wait till the end to take him."

Eadwig had the first watch while the others broke their fast. The odd word of the false apostle's raised voice carried on the breeze, "...the Angel Uriel, the Angel Raguel, Angel Tubuel...". Mention of Tubuel brought Leoba to Begiloc's mind.

*'How does she fare? In a way, I miss her, not that severe zeal. More her beauty and the power of her presence. Did she not say Aldebert invoked demons? Tubuel is a demon,'* Begiloc shuddered, *'the sooner we remove this heretic the better for everyone. Who knows what the criss-cross of shadows among the oak trees conceal? We marched past an ancient standing stone in the forest, with evil spirits sure to be near it.'*

Touching the rood under his tunic, he prayed, *'Let no demons lead me and my men astray on our return. Unseen perils lurk in the world, imps, wights, witches and werewolves. If God and his saints fail to protect us, I hope my ancestors and their gods will.'*

Cynefrid, his turn on watch, called them over. "The long-winded son of a sow's finished. He's selling to the people. Not so many around him. Most are off home."

Begiloc peered from behind a tree to see a man handing a trussed hen to the preacher, the bird clucking and struggling. A number of women still surrounded Aldebert, but better not to delay.

"Put your swords away, shields only and fists if need be. We don't want women bloodied. Clear?"

Amid startled screams they rushed out from their cover.

"Eadwig, he's making a dash for it! Stop him!" Begiloc called. "Shields up, men! Stones!"

Faster than Aldebert, Eadwig overtook the preacher pushing him to the ground. Two comrades joined him, pinned the arms of the false apostle behind his back, bound and hoisted him to his feet.

Alfwald covered his head with his shield, crying, "Get back to your hearths, bloody whores!"

In spite of the seriousness of the situation, Begiloc laughed as five women tried to land puny blows with their fists on a warrior who in the past had cut down men thrice their size.

"Ah! Fucking wildcat!" Cynefrid's hand went to a scratch down his cheek as he pushed a spitting wench away.

"Close up around the madman!" Begiloc ordered and shields raised, the wails of the women pursued them as they forged into woodland where nobody dared follow. Marching past the menhir, he crossed himself and wished for an amulet like Meryn's to protect him from malign spirits.

No wraiths hindered them, they made good speed to consign Aldebert in Fulda ten days after their departure. Sturm catechized the heretic and placed him in solitary confinement.

Word circulated within the monastery Boniface considered the sermoniser a misguided madman, but locked in his hut, Aldebert became of no concern to anyone. On the orders of the prelate, Father Sturm visited him each day to instruct him in the tenets of the faith and after a month obtained permission from the archbishop to allow the excommunicated preacher to attend services, but not to partake of the body and blood of Christ. At three-hour intervals, he appeared throughout the day and night until they took his presence for granted.

The years slipped by and the monastery grew. The stone church neared completion. On one of his annual visits, Boniface named Sturm the first Abbot of Fulda. The orderly life of monastic ritual provided cadence to the passage of time broken only by Saxon raids repelled by Begiloc and his men.

One night between Matins and Lauds came the cry: "Begiloc, Begiloc! Wake up!" A monk shook him by the shoulder, "What the Devil ... ?" The Briton, through sleep-heavy eyes, peered up at a brother, his face distorted in a demonic mask by the weak light of his candle.

"It's Aldebert! He's gone. No-one saw him at Lauds and when we checked his hut, we found it empty. Father Abbot says to take your men and hunt him down since he can't be far away."

Furious, Begiloc gathered his Saxons.

"Rouse the Bavarians! Alfwald, you'll lead half of them. The heretic may be a madman, but he is not mad enough to venture into the forest alone at night, not with wild beasts or worse ready to devour the foolhardy. He's bound to follow the river. Take your men downstream and hunt him down. If you find him sound two blasts of a horn. We'll go upstream and do likewise."

Sky ablaze with stars and a three-quarter moon affording its creamy light, still they needed torches to prevent mishaps underfoot. A league from the monastery they came upon an area of sodden ground and Leofric, a torchbearer, halted them, "Look! I've found fresh footprints here in the mud."

Eadwig sounded two long blasts and they followed the marks left by Aldebert's shoes. At one point, the prints showed farther apart.

"Here, he heard the horn and started to run," Leofric said, "so he can't be far away."

They hastened their pace to where the footprints veered towards the trees.

"He feels our breath on his neck," Begiloc said, "he's making for the woods. Quick! Form groups of three, each with a torchbearer. Leofric to me and you," he grabbed the nearest Bavarian.

"Fan out, you to the left, you over there," he pointed, "there, there and there!"

The crashing sound of their feet on the fallen leaves and branches gladdened him. It should drive off wild beasts. With demons and wights, they had to take their chance but it proved to be a mortal of whom they should have been wary. A figure stepped out from behind a tree delivering a ferocious blow with a woodcutter's axe on the unprotected head of the Bavarian warrior. His falling body crashed into Begiloc, pitching him into Leofric. Seizing his opportunity, the killer dashed into the woods.

"Poor Bastard! Didn't have a chance. The madman's taken an axe from the monastery!" the Saxon said, steadying Begiloc. They drew their swords and rushed after him, soon overhauling the preacher whose fitness was no match for a warrior.

The flickering light of Leofric's torch lit up the mad glint in the eyes of Aldebert and the swinging arc of the steel axe head. The sermoniser turned and began to spit out exhortations from Ezekiel and Leviticus while Begiloc, who knew little of Old Testament prophets and law and cared less, never took his gaze from the hands of his adversary. The dim light of the moon under the leaves with the torch casting deep shadows meant the slightest miscalculation even against an untrained assailant might prove fatal, but deft as ever, he skipped aside when the strike came. In truth, he could have urged the false apostle to lay down his weapon or disarmed him with ease, but his anger at the death of the warrior and at all the trouble the madman had caused him hardened his heart. Had the Holy Father not pronounced anathema and what were the words of Boniface? '... *he will perish in eternal flames'*. Torn between duty and vengeance for an instant he stalled and Aldebert, seeing the hesitation, launched a mighty blow. Ready, he stepped inside the arc of the axe and lunged. The blade of his sword sliced the throat of the heretic all but separating the head from the body.

"May the cur rot in Hell!" Leofric said, "It's a deed well done."

They dragged the body to where the dead warrior lay, where Leofric blew three sharp blasts for the men to gather. In turns, they hauled the bodies to the monastery at Fulda.

Abashed, Begiloc explained the events to Sturm but the priest absolved him, saying, "Nonetheless, the Church cannot be seen to have inflicted this end on the heretic. We shall spread the tale he fled the abbey and murderous thieves set upon him in the wild. Far better this way."

The warrior shrugged. He cared nothing for ecclesiastical politics but felt guilt at the death of Aldebert. It lay heavy on his conscience. Daylight broke but with unnatural weariness, he dropped to his pallet and fell into a restless slumber.

Some days later, unbeknown to Begiloc, Boniface arrived on a visit to Fulda. The next morning, a monk woke him at the first sign of dawn. With sleep in his eyes, Begiloc stared at the brother.

"What is it?"

"Come Begiloc, Archbishop Boniface desires your presence forthwith."

What did this call mean at such an early hour? Fear consumed him the archbishop had yet another mission into the wilderness: neither in mind nor body could he withstand further demands of this nature. But, as he cast off sleepiness, a troubling thought occurred, did this audience concern a certain Denehard?

# CHAPTER 17

*Anno Domini 753, October*

The rose-hued dawn tinted the dew on the grass wetting Begiloc's boots. This summons, he conjectured, might after all concern the death of the heretic rather than Denehard. In spite of the madman's blood on his conscience, he did not foster regret, entering the archbishop's hut in no mood for penitence, he stood in defiance before the prelate.

As expected, Boniface asked him to recount the fate of Aldebert but tale ended, to his surprise no censure came. The archbishop spoke with sorrow.

"That the heretic was mad and capable of wanton murder is beyond dispute. Twice he was warned and God the Father said *'thou wilt give them warning. When I say unto the wicked, Thou shalt surely die,'* and, *'he shall die in his iniquity, but his blood will be required at thine hand.'*" A thin smile did little to reassure Begiloc, but the prelate's next words comforted him.

"Suffer not my son for the deed. Be stony of heart, because your adversary the devil, as a roaring lion, prowls, seeking whom he may devour."

For a fleeting instant, the battle weariness appeared graven in the noble face of the elderly prelate otherwise so full of energy and determination.

*'My enemies are of flesh and blood, but his are unseen and tireless.'*

The archbishop smiled, "Be easy, nothing to repent and to absolve. Instead, I wish to speak of the son of a thane of Wimborne who has your wellbeing at heart."

"Lull, Your Eminence?" Remembering the words of Sturm – '... *on your behalf* ...' – Begiloc's pulse raced. What did Boniface wish to impart? A change of luck after his deprivations and devotion to duty?

"The venerable Lull spoke well of you Begiloc. He exhorts me to release you, who are steadfast in the face of sufferings and faithful though racked by hardship, from service to the Church. After deliberation and prayer, I believe the time is right so I accede to his request if it be your will."
The face of the archbishop remained impenetrable. The longed-for moment come, Begiloc stood dumbfounded, his thoughts awhirl.

"Of course you need not give your response in haste," Boniface said with solicitude.
"My Lord," he dropped to his knees, "I beg you release me."

"You are a free man." The prelate pronounced in solemn a tone. "I shall have a document prepared for you that you may travel unimpeded within Christian lands. My son, be not barren in faith, walk in the ways of the Lord Jesus Christ and never be lost through despair of forgiveness. Let God into your heart." The brown eyes softened, "Go with our thanks and blessing," he placed his hand on Begiloc's head, "may the hand of the Lord guard you, beloved and honoured brother in Christ, unharmed against all adversities. Amen."

Later, Sturm brought the document bearing the seal of Boniface, regret in his voice, he said, "Farewell. God be with you."

"Set Alfwald in charge of the men, Father, for he has their respect."
The abbot embraced him and Begiloc took his leave before strolling to the library and scriptorium. There he found and

studied a map of the Frankish lands. Satisfied, he called for his Saxons.

When they gathered by the gate, he said, "Sword-comrades we fought and suffered together for many years. The time has come for me to depart," he laid a hand on his breast, "we shall not meet again unless after death, but you are ever with me."

Taking Alfwald aside, he said, "Think hard before you act, henceforth you decide for your comrades."

Heaving his pack over his shoulder, he did not look back.

Begiloc had lain restless the night before, the words of Lord Girart so long ago returning to mind: *'He insists on being alone to finish off the beast. That's the measure of your foe.'*

The memory elicited the germ of an idea, leaving him torn between desire to head straight for Treves to slay the false bishop, Milo, or to return to Bischofsheim to bid farewell to Leoba. In truth, he wished to greet her, but did it cloak the hope of seeing or gleaning news of Aedre? At last, before sleep overwhelmed him, he opted for Bischofsheim, although it meant lengthening his journey, as it would also give him more time to plan the slaying of Milo.

The third day out from Fulda towards evening and deep in the forest, Begiloc sought a site to camp for the night. Two clearings lay close by each other, ringed by oak trees. Aware of summer's end and this a cross-quarter day: the time of year when the veil between the world of the dead and that of the living is at its flimsiest, one glance at the huge tree in the centre of the larger of the glades made him choose the other. Far wiser to stay away from the majestic oak lest malign elements were drawn to it after dark.

The small clearing sprouted ferns so he cut a wide swathe around his chosen spot, gathered and laid them out as a pallet for under his sheepskin. In the bracken, he found dark-capped cep mushrooms and cleaned two for a meal with his cheese. A few others he placed in his pack. With his spear, he traced a circle in the earth and eight equal spokes to his bed, creating a charm learnt as a child from his father – protection from mischief-working sprites.

Weapons aligned next to his bed, he lay down to study the sky with its waning moon and gazed at the rising Sifunsterri pulsing like seven sisters – the rainy stars, foretellers of plentiful crops. Awestruck, he marvelled at the immensity of the universe.

*'Is this reality my imaginings? My senses can never penetrate the mystery of divine being ...'*
Inspired, he sat up on his sheepskin to improvise a haunting melody on his hearpe. The music comforted him and, drowsy, he lay back to sink into sleep.

On a sudden, he woke. What had disturbed him? How long had he slept? The moon had moved around the clearing. It must be midnight and – what? No doubt – voices! Sounds coming from the glade with the oak at its centre. Catlike, he swooped for his weapons and slunk to the edge of the trees.

Around the majestic oak, gathered a score of women of different ages naked to the waist, faces painted white. Borne by the only man among them, a single torch lit the darkness. Dressed in purple but for a cloak of black feathers draped over his shoulders, the gothi, the sorcerer-priest, held a bowl in his other hand. A pagan rite! In the flickering light, he peered at four tethered billy goats, grazing. Startled, he noticed shining eyes near the ground, reflecting in the darkness. Cats' eyes! The sorcerer walked to the centre of the half-circle and offered the bowl to a maiden, who took it in both hands.

The celebrant began to chant:
*"May the Goddess, The Lady of the Moon*

*And the God, Horned Hunter of the Sun,*
*Bless this place, and this time, and I who am with You.*
*On this night of Samhain, I mark your passing..."*
On she went with the intonation, on and on, ending with:
*"... Teach us that in the time of darkness there is light."*
The gythja, the priestess, he supposed. Chanting, she strolled around the half-circle moving from one worshipper to the next, they taking the bowl and eating. The cats rubbed against her ankles, mewling and spitting at each other to gain position. The gothi strode over to a goat, untethered it and led it to the first woman who hoisted her skirt, straddled the beast, grasped its horns and kicked her heels. Riding it! The strong male animal rushed into the trees with the rider clinging on using her knees. The chant continued:
*"... O Wise One of the Waning Moon*
*May the energies be reversed:*
*From darkness, light!*
*From bane, goodness!*
*From death, birth!"*
Another two sped off on the back of a goat and then disaster! The fourth animal rushed straight towards him, he swore, but the gothi saw him. Burying his spearhead in the ground, Begiloc put his sword through its belt loop.
*'There's nought to fear from a priest and a gaggle of wenches.'*
The sorcerer raised his torch and came over.
"Well met on Samhain stranger, welcome to the night of the Crone, of the owl, wolf, crow and raven."
His hair braided in pigtails to his waist, long beard and face painted black in sharp contrast to the women, the gothi seemed to Begiloc at one with the creatures he named. Odd as this apparition appeared, his words came more curious, "Fru Freke

sent you for she took the souls of your loved ones in her cat-drawn chariot. Hasten hence to Sessrymir in Folkwangr to embrace them. Come!"

He let himself be led to the gythja.

*'What are these strange names? Is it possible? Can these pagans reunite me with Somerhild and Ealric on this, the night of the dead? I'd give an arm to see them again if only for a moment.'* On the ground, cats in their laps, the women rocked and moaned, their eyes big and black in their white faces.

The priestess held the bowl out to him, "Eat!"

"Mushrooms! I ate them tonight," Begiloc said.

"Eat!" the gythja repeated.

He took three or four, chewed and swallowed them.

The sorcerer led him over to the fire. "Sit!" said the ...

*'... crow-feathered, black-faced, long-haired – What's happening? His hair is glowing golden and it's growing as I watch!'*

The gothi took out a bag and into his hand sprinkled white crystals with the appearance of salt but larger-grained. These he cast into the fire. Flames sprang up, deep, rich purple.

"Stare into the blaze and think of your loved ones!"

The voice, warped, resonant and awesome from a distance, penetrated his consciousness.

*A field lay before a great hall. On the grass gathered men, women and children of different ages, silent and pale. 'Wights, all!' He wanted to scream. Somerhild must not be a wight! His legs would not obey him when he tried to run away. A voice called to him: "Begiloc! Begiloc!" and another, "Father! Father!" Somerhild and Ealric! They had not changed and were not pale, not wights! But, as he remembered them: she smiling at him, her arms wide, tears of joy rolling down her cheeks. Ealric running, throwing himself at his leg clinging on tight, the mane of blond hair begging to be ruffled. He obliged and his heart leapt for gladness. His wife fell into his embrace, soft, emanating the scent of rosewater blended with smoke. He wanted their kiss to last for eternity ...*

Except it did not.

A raging thirst woke him, his dry throat made it difficult to swallow and his head spun and ached. Through half-closed eyes he peered at the shimmering form of the gothi sitting cross-legged beside him. In the glade, they were no longer alone: four tethered goats grazed, cats prowled around the women, some of whom were sleeping including the gythja, others looked like he felt, the white paint, he supposed, covered equally pallid faces.

The black visage drew close to his, the white of his eyes in unsettling contrast. "You were with your loved ones?"

"I know not," said Begiloc, voice hoarse. Had he seen them? An illusion? A dream?

"They await you, but your doom is not upon you. What is your wyrd, stranger? Let it be revealed." The gothi drew pieces of strangely-carved wood from inside his cloak.

*'What are these symbols? What can I learn from them? Why am I comfortable with this? Am I a pagan?'*

The sorcerer peered at him through narrowed gaze, "The runes. I'll cast them to divine what fate brought you and where your path leads." With a twist of the wrist, he strew them on the ground where they fell at random.

"Choose, stranger!"

The will of the gothi loomed and engulfed Begiloc whose hand moved to pick a rune as though under the control of an outside force.

"Rad! Hark! Heed me well! Rad gives strength to he who travels the high road on a stout horse. The roving is inner and outer. Be brave, for the roaming will be hard but with vast rewards. Move on with good heart! Is all!"

"I have no stout mount," Begiloc said, only to conceal how these words touched him. The pagan gave him a thin smile and his expression showed he was not deceived. Resting a hand on the Briton's shoulder, he said, "Go, stranger. Fulfil your doom."

Recovering his spear, pleased to leave the glade, back at his pack he drank as much water as his stomach could bear. Sleep! The only way to deal with this headache. So he laid out his weapons once more, ignored the distant howl of wolves and gave in to the balm of slumber.

The sun striped by fleecy clouds shone above the treetops when he woke. The events of the night before were a haze, but the image of his holding Somerhild and of Ealric clinging to his leg was as clear as the brook where he bent to fill his water skin. The water gleamed, skipping and swirling over the stony bed of the rivulet. The music of the water and the hues painted in its spray by the rays of the sun spoke to his soul. In all this, was no explanation of the divine essence: the sublime, marvellous order revealed in Nature enounced God, but he, Begiloc, could not hear Him. Or had their forefathers the right of it? Had he penetrated the mantle between this life and the afterlife? Were there spirits in the stream, in the oak and in the stone of the river bed? In the name of Jesus Christ he had fought pagans and destroyed their idols, yet the fiend he hated most was a man of the Church.

The days passed bringing the end of his journey nearer. The ordered vineyards announced vast changes at Bischofsheim. Word had spread of the importance of this wine-producing area and its wealth. The sight of the watermill by a tributary of the Tauber underlined it. Around the monastery, a stone wall replaced the outer palisade of wood. Where once grew thick forest lay a village surrounded by fields. In one, smoke rose where men burned stubble, elsewhere, amid a swirl of crows, others sowed beans and a youth beat a drum to scare the scavengers away. In a third field, children weeded between furrows.

Within the abbey, time had wrought changes. Of the nuns, many had the bearing, speech, and fine features of young noblewomen; an imposing new scriptorium caught his attention, but he was not surprised, knowing the abbess's love of books. Passing the church, he glanced ruefully at the sundial displaying half an hour before None and hastened his step. Before the service, he needed to find Father Robyn, instead, the priest's voice greeted him.

"Begiloc! Is it you?"

They embraced, the clergyman laughing, "Look at you, is it grey hair I see at your temples?"

"Father, envy is a sin," he smiled, "the abbess should change your name. Once a red-haired priest lived here. Now there is an old grizzled bear: Father Beorn!"

The priest's gaze roved over the spear, sword and hand-seax, "Still armed to the eyebrows, eh? Come, let's drink together. There's time before afternoon prayer. Give me news of the pagan lands."

How good the Bischofsheim ale! The glow of contentment, owing more to the ease of old friendship renewed and cheering conversation – as when he learnt the fame of Leoba's wisdom and piety spreading beyond Alemania. With pardonable pride, Father Robyn told him she was the only woman allowed into the single houses.

"Father, do you think the abbess will have time for me? I know she's busy."

The priest feigned a sorrowful countenance and the crestfallen expression on the face of his friend delighted him.

"Begiloc, you'll believe anything," he laughed. "I should think she'll call for you as soon as she learns you are here. I'll tell her myself at the service, I must leave you now."

After None, Begiloc stood before Abbess Leoba and two nuns in her room and appraised the subtle changes in the lady. The nun never lacked confidence but now she exuded authority and her winsomeness was replaced by – how could he describe it? – a mature grace adding to her comeliness. The hazel eyes swept over him with the same thoroughness as his over her. They lingered on his scarred arm and rose to meet his own but without judgement, her whole expression one of quiet pleasure. He relaxed.

"Welcome Begiloc, I find you well."

The abbess pressed him for details of his exploits on the edge of the wilderness and of the fate of Aldebert. Not wishing to dwell on the end of the heretic, he stated he had died in the forest, but her query gave him the opportunity he sought.

"My Lady, what of the other preacher, Clement?"

Leoba frowned at the name and said, "The Synod at Mentz ruled he be stripped of his episcopal office, excommunicated and condemned by the everlasting judgement of God as anyone who agrees with his sacrilegious teachings. The Irishman will not trouble the Church further."

The moment come, he swallowed hard. The abbess noted the hesitation and raised an eyebrow. Voice kept flat in spite of his keenness, he said, "Bishop Milo, My Lady?"

She sighed and put her hands together. "What can I tell you? He prospers – a thorn in the flank of the Church. Our cousin Boniface, whom you know, is in contact with the Holy Father about him. In response to his appeal for advice against Milo, Pope Zachary counselled leaving him to divine vengeance."

She bowed her head and Begiloc's jaw clenched.

*'He prospers, is that it? The Church is powerless.'*

"All is conflict without and anxiety within," the abbess said, "it is wearisome to be occupied by the deceiving wiles of the devil and worn out by the cunning assaults of his ministers. Other than false priests, Begiloc, last year alone, pagans burned or demolished thirty churches in the Frankish territories." Leoba smiled and her voice brightened, "Oh, but come, what a poor welcome to burden you with our problems!"

"Serve our guest," she ordered a nun standing behind her, "a beaker of wine?"

"My Lady," he said, accepting the drink, "in Hessia on my journey here I encountered paganism in the forest."

The hazel eyes blazed, features taking on a hardness worthy of a statue of a Roman goddess.

"The Devil thrives on ignorance. There are dual faith presbyters who offer sacrifices to the pagan deities and to the saints..!"

Begiloc savoured the red wine, rolling it around his tongue. Leoba affected him like the drink, a little more of her powerful presence and his head would spin.

The abbess continued, "... the synods are resolute in condemning sortilegium and maleficium also imposing a fine of fifteen solidi on those engaging in pagan rites ..."

Discomfited, Begiloc did not meet her eyes. Swirling his wine in the beaker, he pretended distraction.

"... we must thwart the Devil by compiling, copying and diffusing the sacred canons to ignorant priests. An informed cleric can instruct the people in Church law to ensure an educated Christian community. It is one of our main duties."

Her face lit up with enthusiasm, "Begiloc! Did you see our new scriptorium?"

"Indeed, I passed it, My Lady."

"Come, finish your wine. We shall accompany you there to see the wonders of our toil."

The abbess paused and pursed her lips, almost as though changing her mind but, said, "There you will meet..." again the hesitation, "... an old ... acquaintance and you will bid farewell."

He frowned.

*'Who does she mean? Talking about old acquaintances ...'*

"Lest I forget, My Lady, what news of Meryn?"

The face of Leoba brightened once more, "Meryn! Good tidings! A miracle, Begiloc."

Hope sprang in his chest, "Can he see again?"

"You will, of course, visit him on your way home?"

"God willing."

"Witness it with your own eyes, I shall say no more!"

The abbess led him to the scriptorium. Back-to-back desks whose flat working surfaces sloped upwards to meet, ranged beside the windows either side of the room. On one side sat monks and across the central aisle on the other side, nuns. Absolute silence reigned save for the scratching quills or an occasional cough.

Filled with enthusiasm, Leoba pointed out the work of the first nun, engaged in the patient copying of canon law. The sisters displayed unwavering concentration and precision confirming the rigorousness of their Mother Superior. The calami left black trails on the parchment in loops and circles he did not understand. It was humbling.

A blaze of coloured ink attracted his attention at the centre of the aisle, where a nun devoted herself to the decoration of a large letter, adorning the figure of a beast over a colour wash.

"A page of the Gospel of St John," the abbess said. The sister did not break her concentration for a second. "This work will require many months of patience to produce a precious volume."

They moved forward, where a nun dabbed gold with a fine brush on the halo of the Virgin. The scene depicted the Mother of God receiving the crown of heaven on her death bed. Like the sister at the previous desk, she did not raise her head until the abbess said, "Take a moment to say your farewells, Begiloc."

The nun caught her breath at his name but did not lift her head. When she did her astonished face grew paler.

*'Aedre!'*

Leoba and the sisters moved away.

"Aedre it is you! Can you do this? These splendid drawings?"

The sincerity of his admiration matched his amazement. And this served to calm her.

*'She's aged, of course she has, but she's still a pretty woman. She's changed. She's more ... more serene.'*

Aedre blushed and whispered, "Here I have peace of mind. I renounced the sins of my youth." Cheeks flushed a deep red, she said, "God has taken my heart. This labour I offer with love to His Glory every day. And you, Begiloc how are you?"

"Well, I thank you. I'm a free man but know not what the future holds ... I must see Meryn and then ..."

Hard to catch the words as her voice hushed further.

"Go ... go to Dumnonia, to your people. Find one of your own and marry. The Lord will bless you with babes."

Begiloc stared at Aedre. What did he hope to find when he came to Bischofsheim? True to his disposition, he had hidden his feelings – from himself. At this point, better leave them buried.

"I shall never marry," he said with conviction.

The smile of Aedre was sorrowful, tender, and a tear welled.

"Go with the Lord. Seek consolation in the love of God. Find faith, Begiloc."

On impulse, he took her hand and kissed it but she pulled it away like one stung by a hornet.

"I'm sorry," she breathed.

"Farewell Aedre."

Outside the scriptorium, he took leave of the abbess. A sense of wretchedness griped at him at turning his back on a solemn part of his life. The consideration he would never see Aedre, Leoba and Robyn again weighed on him. Driven by a score to settle, insistent, constant, his doom summoned. After embracing the priest, he left the monastery for the lower hamlet by the river.

To the deafening sound of hammering, Begiloc entered the forge where he found Dagobert alone. The giant did not see or hear him arrive, leaving time to study the smith. More changes! The mane of black hair and bushy beard bore grey with streaks of black while the bulging sweat-sleeked muscles remained as unchanged as the infernal smithy. The blacksmith halted his blows to turn over a ploughshare.

The smith started at Begiloc's cough, "Briton! Upon my life! 'Ow many years gone by?"

"Too many, old man! Where is the son of the hot-tempered woman?"

"Ibn al-Naghira? I set 'im free last year. On'y right. I'd learned all I could from 'im. Sucked all the juice and spit out the pips!"

Sure Dagobert had treated Ibn al-Naghira as a brother, Begiloc grinned into the grimy face he'd taken a liking to from the first.

"The other one died years ago. Dropped a white hot bar on 'is leg and the wound festered, poor fellow. Hey! By chance, d'ye seek work? A 'and in the forge'd come in 'andy. It's too much fer one man."

"It's more toil I bring you."

The blacksmith blew out his cheeks and the warrior followed his gaze down to his sword.

"'Ow's she be'aved?" he asked, "Never let yer down, I'll wager."

They engaged in a long discussion on the weapon as though *'she'* were a living person and Dagobert had to hold *'her'* to make some imaginary thrusts and cuts. At last, they came to the explanation of his needs, followed by the smith taking a measurement of the girth of his spear. Clasping hands, they arranged for Begiloc to collect and pay for the work after noon the next day.

The inn the smith suggested was half-decent, its food surpassing the acceptable ale. The shin of boar in nut and garlic sauce cost more than usual but he made a swift end to it. The room did not please him, but used to sleeping rough, the uneven straw mattress and the din from below of sots raging and threatening murder over dice games did not trouble him.

The next morning, he spent whetting his sword and hand-seax before buying salted meat, bread, dried pears and raisins for his journey. In his mind, he went over the map he studied in Fulda. If his calculations proved correct seventy leagues stretched before him. Wondering whether he'd manage five a day, he remembered the words of the sorcerer – *'Rad gives strength to he who travels the high road on stout horse.'* Of course! It fitted his plan and would make travelling less arduous.

The innkeeper described a farm three leagues down the river valley where they reared horses for the local leud. Twenty-four scillingas bought a man a mount in Wessex. If needed, ten times the amount jingled in his purse to persuade the breeder.

A man of his word, Dagobert was honing a curved blade to treacherous sharpness when Begiloc sauntered into the forge.

"There Briton," he said, "I wouldn't test the edge 'less yer want to lose a finger."

An oiled cloth wrapped around it, satisfied, he placed it in the centre of his pack, paid the smith, clasped hands and made his farewell.

Following the river downstream, Begiloc came to the farm with a field of grazing horses. The breeder, a stocky man, had a devious face whose shrewd eyes roved down to Begiloc's sword where they lingered on the pommel to judge the worth of the weapon. The Briton decided to be bold and state his knowledge of the cost of the animals.

"I'll pay no more than fifteen denarii," he said, cursing himself for a fool when the man spat on his hand and held it out.

In spite of this misjudgement, when the breeder strolled over to a dun mare grazing apart from the herd, Begiloc called, "Not that one. Bring me the grey!" No dullard regarding horses since he grew up accustomed to Dumnonian ponies, he noted the reluctance in the man's mien confirming the soundness of his choice. The farmer placed the bridle in her mouth and led her over. She walked well over the uneven ground and he liked her strong hind quarters and the angle on her shoulders. The hooves were even and, for closer inspection, he approached from the side to pat her neck. Lifting the upper lip, from the teeth, he judged her a two-year old. The breeder was vaunting the merits of another horse, which only strengthened his resolve. Ignoring him, he took the reins, led the mare in a circle and shoved her hip with his shoulder. The animal staggered, but regained her balance and, satisfied, he petted her and spoke to her in a soft voice.

"She's the one," he said.

A sly expression crept into the farmer's face.

"I should charge you more. She's the best mare and the comitis wants her."

"Content yourself," Begiloc said, "for we clasped hands and I need to buy a saddle and straps for my spear. I'll add another two denarii. Does it suit?"

It did. The mare bore him away at a canter.

"Carry me to the final reckoning!" He patted the mare's head, "I name you Doom."

# CHAPTER 18

Every hoof beat brought Begiloc closer to the act of retribution smouldering repressed for years. Christians, like Leoba, insisted vengeance belonged to God but Milo thrived impenitent and the heart of the Briton ached for justice. Under no illusion about the fearsome retaliation the Bishop would mete unless he destroyed him utterly, he rode Doom into Treves.

In town, he reined in before a tavern. *'The Apple Press'* sign tallied with a youth outside pouring apples into a wooden press and the bustle of customers promised decent fare.

Lucky to find a seat in the tap-room, he partook of a jug of fermented juice lighter and sweeter than the scrump cider of Dumnonia. As soon as a place emptied opposite him, another filled it, one with the weather-beaten face of a man used to working outdoors. The ceorl struck up conversation.

"Stranger to these parts?"

"A Briton on his way to Saxony."

"Saxony?"

"To fend off pagan raiders for the Church."

Better to stick to experience. Although talkative, unlike himself, his new companion was not inquisitive.

"They tell me the Bishop of Treves likes a hunt?"

The man looked uneasy – *did I glimpse hatred in his eyes?* – "His title is *Arch*bishop..." Begiloc scowled "... and you're right. The chase is one of the archbishop's pastimes."

How to tease out information without causing the man to clam up?

"Ah, he likes sport?" he asked, raising his jug.

The fellow did likewise, wiping his mouth with a sleeve.

"No offence, Briton, but in Treves best not to be loose with words about yon," voice lowered, he said, "The hunt and falconry are not his only pleasures," and wary, his eyes swept around the room, "... gold and women – I said too much!"

"Fear not, mine is but curiosity."

Reassured the countryman conversed on familiar matters – the harvest, yield and weather before Begiloc steered the conversation to family. The ceorl's sister married two months past, the argument touched a raw nerve.

"The brother of my sister's husband is the woodsman of the archbishop, so Milo wed them in the cathedral. A real honour!" Sarcasm and revulsion in his tone, "Leastways, would've been if the ram had not set his eyes on the bride. The tup forewent chastity payment forcing her to pay in nature on her wedding night." His eyes narrowed, "We're simple folk – what can we do? When one such as he decides on tupping a ewe there's no stopping him." The ceorl's eyes roved over the face of the warrior. "Swear you'll never breathe a word. Must be cider gone to my head!"

"On my honour." His hand went to his heart. "Tell me what name does this woodsman go by?

"Wulfhard."

"A fine name for a forester," he smiled, "I wish to meet him."

The fretful expression reappeared so Begiloc hastened to soothe him, "Let be the evil priest! No concern of mine. Of woodland lore, I would speak with Wulfhard."

Sincere, gullible, the fellow's relief was palpable. The art of loosening tongues was the preserve of Meryn, but in his absence, cider proved effective. Soon, he discovered the location of the woodlander's hut, in the forest of Meulenwald where Milo preferred to hunt. Resolved to find Wulfhard the next day, he settled down to repay his new friend, Unroch, regaling him with tales of the Alps and Rome over a meal, drinking till late and parting as might old friends.

The next morning, Begiloc waited by the woodsman's dwelling. An ox of a man carrying a two-edged billhook appeared. Wiser not to surprise him, he thought, springing to his feet to hail the fellow from distance.

"I come in peace in the name of Unroch," the warrior said. "I would speak with you on a matter of importance."
Intrigued, the ruddy-cheeked forester led him into his home. The blinding of Meryn and his plan for vengeance was a slow, cautious tale in the telling. The Briton ensuring Wulfhard would not betray him. Unlike Unroch, this man kept a close check on his reactions guarding them with a generous dose of suspicion. The warrior studied every subtle expression in the round face. Over the woodsman's salted meat and fresh spring water, he discovered an honest man whose desire for retribution matched his own.

The afternoon dawdled into evening and still they sat and planned. Time to leave with all arrangements agreed, Begiloc tried to press a gold coin on Wulfhard. When the forester stared into his face, expression wounded, he recognised a man like an oak, not to be swayed.

Early next morning, he found him leaning against his doorframe. Tethering Doom, he clasped the hand of the woodsman who said, "The sun'll burn off this 'ere mist wi'in the hour. Come, ah'll take yer to the 'nest'."

They followed a trail under the dripping leaves where his guide pointed out a pine, bark stripped away in a girdle. "Boar yon be. Rubs agin the tree ter get the resin out. Kills off 'ems parasites as bothers 'em, see?"

At each of the forks in the track, Wulfhard cut a short branch and planted it in the ground as a marker until they came to a glade.

"Here's the spot," said the woodsman, "where ah'll lay the lure."

"What will you use?"

"Fermentin' strawb'ries is best, but if not, overripe marrow will do as well."

Pressing on they came upon a corpulent toad, body pulsing. "Yon's a brave un," he murmured, "near a boar's nest an' all. Tasty snack for a boar 'em is."

The woodsman held out his arm to halt their advance.

"Better not get too close. Not that yon'll be 'ome. Smelled us comin' a mile off."

A tilt of the head indicated a hole in an area of thick underbrush. "O'er there! Yon's 'is way in." He pulled Begiloc to his left. "Nah then, you'll get rahnd the back this way. Come on!"

By a tortuous route, he led him behind the nest.

"'ere," he began to chop with his billhook, "Gi' us an 'and!"

With reluctance, he hacked the plants with his sword, swearing under his breath. After this, he would have to whet the blade for hours. They hacked away the undergrowth until Wulfhard stopped him.

"You'll force through yon easy 'nuff now. Don't want ter alert the boar or the ram for that matter!"

"Unroch named Milo that too! Are you sure he always makes the kill alone?"

"Allus! The Devil take 'im! Yon's one as allus wants ev'ythin' for 'issen."

Everything in place, Begiloc allowed himself a grim smile. Back at Wulfhard's hut he strode over to Doom and reached into the pack at the saddle, pulling out a leather bottle and grinning at the woodsman. In an hour, they emptied the contents. The last of the cider, he divided between the two wooden cups before glancing up.

"How shall I know when to come?"

"The ram allus sends a servant the day afore he wants ter hunt. Then ah lay the lure an' points 'em in the right direction. 'Em solit'ry boars allus run fer their nest. Ah'll send our Unroch ter warn yer afore'and."

Three days of bad weather made Begiloc restless, but the fourth broke cloudless and fair. In the late afternoon, the ceorl sought him out.

Sitting at his table, Unroch ignored him for a while. The warrior approved. No-one must link the countryman to him should the plot go awry. After some time, in a hushed voice, the farmer said, "I know all, Briton. May God guide your hand! Tomorrow the ram hunts. Wulfhard says be there at dawn."

That evening, Begiloc avoided drink to keep a clear head the next day. Soon after supper, he retired.

Thoughts of vengeance and sleep are bad bedfellows. Milo's sins assailed his mind: the blinding of Meryn, Aedre at Rems, the castrator at Verden, the battle at Juvinia, the sister of Unroch and all the other virgins the prelate had deflowered. For sure, he would not regret sending the ram to eternal damnation. Sleep eluded him.

*'What can go wrong? I've been over this a thousand times.'*
At last, he fell into a deep slumber. Out of habit, he woke before dawn.

Away from the woodsman's hut, he hitched Doom to a tree. As for the case of Unroch, no-one must connect him to Wulfhard if his plan went amiss. Concealed in the trees, he took his spear and exchanged the head for the murderous blade forged by Dagobert. Ready, he followed the trail, turning at each peeled branch until he reached and passed the boar's nest where he took up position and waited.

Tension, stiffness, concentration, anxiety, doubts – sensations and emotions engulfed him, all testing his patience. With exercises, he tried to keep his muscles flexible to pounce at the right instant, but at the same time, remained aware of the need to focus and maintain silence. An uneasy thought penetrated the blankness imposed on his mind.

*'Will the ram show? All these years – and if he doesn't come?'*

The sun hung high to justify his worry. The shadows shortened with no sign of the hated foe. The only sounds, birdsong, the buzzing of innumerable insects and the gentle rustling of leaves overhead.

*'Damn! I've wasted my time. This was a good plan! What to do now?'*

Forced to wait years for vengeance for his scheme to go awry. Not so, minutes later, rhythmic hoof beats accompanied by terrified squeals resounded along the trail.

The sounds loudened when a boar sped into the grove chased by a man on horseback. Through the foliage, Begiloc saw the ram thrust his spear behind the shoulder of the beast – the perfect blow from an experienced hunter sending the animal shrieking to slump to the ground in its death throes. The Briton sprang out of the underbrush startling the horse, which reared, its rider fought to stay in the saddle while Begiloc swung his spear in an underarm slash, slicing the blade deep across the inside thigh of his foe. Milo crashed to earth, his femoral artery severed at an angle. The steed bolted leaving the Briton little time before it alerted the hunter's companions and servants. Dashing over to the prelate, leather strap in hand, he hauled it tight round the top of the thigh, under the groin, to slow the loss of blood.

No attempt to save the life of Milo, but to gain time to look him in the eye, so the false priest should regard his killer before descending into Hell.

"Remember me?"

The warrior grinned into the face of the stricken prelate. Even now, in death, the archbishop's hand groped for his dagger but Begiloc pulled the weapon from the belt of the cleric and tossed it to the ground.

"Your days of evil-doing are ended!" He thrust his face into that of the clergyman. "You blinded my friend, Meryn, remember? You named him a spy to excuse your wickedness. A life of darkness, he lived these long years. By rights, I should rip out *your* eyes. But the beauty of it is this ... the blade that carved away your body from your rotten, stinking soul is in the form of a boar's tusk." Wild, the eyes of the prelate moved around the face of his assailant.

"What an unfortunate accident, Your Em-i-nence!"

Realisation dawned in the stricken face and Begiloc's heart leapt with joy; he released the pressure of the belt.

The lifeblood of Archbishop Milo of Treves, Bishop of Rems, pumped away. The dagger, Begiloc replaced at the cleric's waist.

*'Nothing to arouse suspicion.'*

On the tusk of the fallen boar, he smeared gore, the blood of the prelate, keeping alert for the slightest sound: apart from the rattle in Milo's throat. Standing over the corpse, he said, "Meryn, I kept my word. This is for you ..." as an afterthought, he said, "... and his other victims."

Satisfied, he searched around.

*'No, nothing to give me away.'*

Voices from along the trail alarmed him. Dashing behind the boar's nest he stole away from the scene of his revenge. Fate forced him to wait for so long that he wanted to shout for joy and relive the fatal blow with the whole world, not hide in silence and quieten his elation.

Collected, he sat on a tree stump to detach the vicious, tusk-shaped blade from his spear. Disgusted, loth to touch the shank, still wet with the blood of the demon-prelate, he separated the curved metal from the ash pole, dug a hole in the woodland soil and buried it. Wiping his hands, he covered the spot with sodden leaf litter before replacing the spearhead.

The hour of Prime, at the inn, the air reverberated with tolling bells announcing the demise of the archbishop. The death knell rang sweet to his ears otherwise battered by the clamour of voices. Men shouted to drown those of fellow imbibers in keenness to surmise how a hunter, with many kills, might fall to his prey. These things happened – God's will. Amid the din, Begiloc did not fail to notice the joy bubbling under a surface of feigned sorrow. Folk began to speculate about a new archbishop – one who might lower taxes – one of a saintly life worthy of his calling.

Unroch, Wulfhard and another entered the inn and took seats at a table. In the corner of the room, Begiloc waited while they bought cider, noting the ceorl peer at him from under lowered brow. With casual air, he made his purchase before strolling over to stand opposite them.

"My friend! How are you? Ah, you are in company. Forgive me!"

He made to move away.

"Stay!" the ceorl said, "Meet my sister's husband, Durand, and his brother Wulfhard. Join us, won't you?" and he pulled out the empty seat. Nobody paid them any attention, the drinkers besotted by the day's event ignored lowered voices amid the raucous din.

"When them found yon body and yon boar," Wulfhard said, "them saw yon wound and bloodied tusk. Only one thing to think, wi' no sign of no-one nor nuffin."

All four shared a grim smile. Durand said, "We owe you more than you imagine. My Bertha cried with happiness." Reaching under the table, he brought forth a wicker basket, pulling aside a piece of linen to reveal bread and a handful of ripe, purple plums nestling between two earthenware pots.

"She sends you a fresh-baked loaf, some fruit and conserves for your travels."

They drank into the night and so too did most of the men in *The Apple Press*.

Staggering into his room, he set down his food basket with undue care before collapsing on his pallet, oblivious to the world.

Eight days later, saddle sore, dusty and weary, Begiloc reined in outside the monastery at Verzy. Greeting Meryn after many – too many – years, set his heart pounding in his chest like that of a courting youth. His bounden oath fulfilled, he arrived with honour. The great oak door of the religious house loomed but he did not knock. Too sweet the moment not to be savoured.

*'How shall I tell him? In a matter-of-fact voice? Drop it into the conversation? Or tell the tale blow-by-blow and leave nought aside?'*

A thought occurred, *'What is this miracle is the abbess talked of?'*

A couple of hard raps and a monk opened the door.

"I'm here to visit Meryn."

"Brother Meryn?"

"*Brother?*"

"Ay, the Chant Master?"

"*Chant Master?*"

"I'll take you to him."

The brother led him into the church where they mounted three steps into the nave. When his eyes adjusted to the dim light, he beheld two figures in habits of undyed wool. On a bench midway from the door to the altar, one sat upright and the other stooped over a parchment, candle in hand.

"Brother Meryn! A visitor!" the monk called, his voice reverberating in the near-empty church and this time without Begiloc's echo. One of the monks rose to his feet.

*'Meryn, a monk! Am I dreaming?'*

With care, the other monk put his script and taper on the bench and helped the blind man into the aisle.

"Who seeks me?" Meryn asked, his head moving sightlessly. At the sound of his voice, Begiloc's heart skipped a beat. The warrior, who had crossed the Alps and faced the Holy Father in Rome, he, the slayer of pagans, heretics and a false bishop, sought the courage to address his oldest friend.

"Well met! A wending way brought me to you."

A moment's silence, one of disbelief, followed by a cry of joy distilled in one word: "Begiloc!"

Arms stretched, Meryn stepped forward to receive a ferocious embrace.

"Steady! This, brothers, is what you get when you mate a bear with an oaf!"

With some reluctance, he let go.

"I'm glad you're your old self again."

"My old self? The last thing, I am! If you came to see me more often ..."

Disconcerted, instead of the expected bitterness, Begiloc heard lightness of tone, no resentment but teasing.

"Well, you've shed the beads in your beard and gained a tonsure."

"Ay, and *you* are to thank for it."

"Me?"

"Well, to be fair, God and you."

"And my part in this?" Begiloc asked.

"'Twas you who left me your beloved instrument. I learned to play better than you ever did. Pardon me! Vanity is a sin. Did you bring a new one? I'll wager you've forgotten how to pluck ... we should harmonise together!"

"I did, and there's time for that. Tell me, is there the danger of a tonsure if I strum my hearpe?"

Meryn's laugh resonated in the church. Bless the sound! One he thought never to hear again.

Of a sudden, his voice grew earnest.

"Music brought me to God, Begiloc. It opened my heart and love entered. I changed to what I am today ..." – the flippant tone returned – "... a paltry sinner instead of a huge one! I'm the Master of Chants. Did you know?"

"A brother told me."

"We are working on Psalm 48, *'Great is the Lord and greatly to be praised in the city of our God!'* " Meryn waved a hand, "This brother is marking the text on my instructions to indicate the rise and fall of the voice ..."

*'This is what Leoba meant by a miracle!'*

"... ah, but it needs days of practice. You will come to Sext, won't you?" Without waiting for a reply he said, "We're changing from the Gallican to the Roman chant. It will soon be the same all over. The brothers are like old dogs, they cling to their habits and I don't mean the ones they're wearing! You understand the difference, of course – in chants, I mean?"

"Hold!" Begiloc said, overwhelmed by the flood of words. "You can explain another time. We have urgent matters to discuss. In *private*."

Shrugging off offers of help from the two brothers, Meryn led him to his cell.

"Memorising the steps and how I lean my body – before you ask."

"Are you a mind reader as well as a monk? Any other surprises?"

"Well, what about this." His friend went over to a corner and picked up Begiloc's old hearpe and began to play. One of the tunes from many years ago on the Seine.

"Remember?"

He started to sing leaving the warrior awash with memories.

*'O Meryn, Meryn, where did the years go? We were full of hope and light of spirit in Wimborne.'*

The linen-bound face bobbed to the tune. Which reminded him – time to tell his news.

"Cease! We must talk."

Sitting on his bed, Meryn laid the hearpe beside him and waited.

"Old friend. Yesterday, I fulfilled my oath."

"The difference between the Gallican and the Roman chant is the former is more florid..."

*'Has he heard me? Is he mad?'*

"...like this – *ah – aah –aah* – on each syllable in an upward pitch where– "

"Damn the Gallican chant! Did you hear me? I said, I fulfilled my oath."

The blind man sighed and stood. Crossing the room, he groped for a small box, removing Talwyn's brooch and holding it out to his friend.

"Take it!" he said, voice sorrowful, "this is a constant reminder of my sinful past. Indeed, of the heaviest sin blackening my soul." His tone changed to one of reproval, "Had you come but once to find me, I should have released you from your vow."

"What!" – *'He has gone mad!'* – "Why? Milo stole your sight, bedded other men's wives, virgins! Had men castrated, plundered the Church..." Begiloc ground his teeth.

*'Why doesn't he say something?'*

"... I couldn't come to visit you. They sent me to Rome, to Bavaria, to the wilderness of Saxony–"

"Did you find *yourself* in any of those places?"

"What?"

"Only God can judge sinners. I'm saddened we bear Bishop Milo's death on our conscience–"

"Meryn, he blinded you!"

"He did...and I'm grateful to him."

"Grateful!"

"Back then I had sight yet I was blind. Begiloc, you have eyes but you cannot see!"

"Damn you Meryn! Damn the Church and Damn God for that matter!"

In a rush of blood, later regretted, he strode to the door and as the Master of Chants cried, "Begiloc, wait!" he slammed it behind him.

More than once on the way to Auve, he wanted to turn back to set everything to rights between them but ire fought with remorse conquering good intentions, spurring him to gallop to the ferry where a gentle canter might have saved a friendship.

Before nightfall, he dismounted near the spring at Auve to let Doom drink her fill.

"By the stars! It *is* you Begiloc!"

Back to the speaker, he did not turn, pretending deafness. A smile spread across his face.

*'Caena!'*

How good to hear the deep, resonant voice once more.

"Begiloc!"

Not so much a greeting more the bellow of an enraged bull. No use continuing the pretence. Grinning, he spun on his heel. The bull charged, altering mid-charge into a bear clasping him with almost spine-snapping force – *this* was what he called a welcome!

"Come!" The Saxon gave him no choice, clamping a hand on his arm, the might of the warrior concentrated on one direction, towards the houses.

"I'd feared never to look on your rough face again – not in this world! You good-for-nothing, you old beast! Did I say 'in this world'? Well, damned if it'd be the land of the blessed! With all the sins we've chalked up. More likely down in Beelzebub's palace! There'll be a feast tonight! Begiloc you shall try my ale. I learnt to brew it! Do you like pheasant? There's one hanging and we'll lard and stuff it!"

The Briton stood firm forcing Caena to halt his torrent of words and his stride.

"Pheasant, is it? No need to drag me, I'm more than willing to come!"

The Saxon smiled and desisted, finding fodder for Doom and stabling her but grew impatient while Begiloc wiped her down.

"What ails you?"

"Come! A surprise for you! Well, two to be honest."

They made their way to the house and to the Saxon's agitation, they encountered Amalric, his greeting almost as crushing as Caena's. Rapid arrangements for the feast made, the Saxon reached to seize the Briton again, who evaded his grasp.

Caena flung back the door and a girl with blonde hair and pale blue eyes rushed to him – "Father!" – she skidded to a halt, eyes widening.

"Gisela, meet my friend, Begiloc." He turned to his guest, "She's six, aren't you Ella?"

The girl, a female version of the warrior in miniature, buried her face in her father's cloak.

Begiloc bent down, pulling a large, shiny chestnut from his pack.

"Here, Gisela, these are sweet. Try one. Peel it first, mind." Nut consigned, he straightened. "How did an ugly brute like you beget such a blossom? What of Ingitruda?"

"At her mother's. 'Spect she's feeding Hrothgar."

"Hrothgar?"

"Our babe. I named him after –"

"Our comrade."

"Gisela, be good, run and fetch mother."

Alone, Caena pointed to a chair.

"The deed is done?"

"Ay. Like you, I am a freeman. I rode here direct from Verzy."

"How is Meryn? He's crossed my mind more than once in recent days…"

Begiloc weighed his words.

"Well, and contented. There is more, a tale that bears keeping."

"Yet, you live to tell it. That in itself is worth the hearing. As I said, I never thought to see you again."

"It's best told over an ale and roast pheasant. An appreciative glance at the bird hanging from a beam. Taking the hint, Caena stood, unhooked it and began plucking. At the same moment, his wife came in bearing a squalling red-faced babe.

"Behaves like his father, but looks like his mother. Well met, goodwife!" Begiloc laughed.

Conversation punctuated by baby cries, the Briton spoke of the seven years passed since Caena left Fulda while Ingitruda prepared the food and served ale. Joined by her parents, they completed the meal in high spirits.

The children bedded and the women retired, Begiloc began his account of the demise of Milo. The two men heard him out, the Saxon conceding that a lingering death, which he craved for the prelate had not been possible. Indifferent to the fate of Milo, Amalric pointed out Auve lay under the jurisdiction of Bishop Bladald, a good man, but conceded Begiloc had rid Rems and Treves of a servant of Satan leaving the world better for it.

"What do you know of bishops and right and wrong?" Caena reproved his wife's father, "It's thanks to me we have a church in this village and the priest comes once a moon to bring us communion. Up to you, we'd all be heathen."

A heated argument, followed by protestations of innocence, led on to Meryn's acceptance of monastic vows.

"Well," said Caena, "as to vows, the poor fellow has no problem with poverty and chastity. Attempting to lighten the mood, he said, "it's a surprise, though, I thought it easier for me to become a monk than him!"

As bemused as his old comrade regarding the conversion of the Briton, he added, "How can you thank someone for blinding you? No sense to it. I've never got my head round all that church stuff...and you say he would have released us from our oaths? Are you sure he's not lost his reason?"

They sat in silence pondering the imponderable: Meryn the

monk.

At last, Begiloc said, "There were no beads in his beard either. He's not mad, you know."

*'I shouldn't have stormed out on him.'*

With the excuse of checking on Doom, he stepped into the chill autumn night. The stars confronted him in a silent chorus. Intimidated by the heavens, he idled over to the stable, admitting he no longer knew who or what he had become: a man with no purpose other than to kill or be killed? A man whose ire obscures his reason?

*'Meryn's right. I never found myself.'*

Propping an arm against the wall, he stared at the ground, reflecting on the course of events. Caena possessed everything he, Begiloc, had lost and more. Not that he begrudged him the joy of his wife and children, in fact, his heart sang for his friend. The Church had dragged the Saxon around half the world too, but in this village, he was the guardian of the Faith. His wyrd, he thought, as for each of us on Earth, was writ distinct from his own – as it should be. In spite of his affliction, Meryn opened his heart to God and discovered joy. A *'blessing'* he called it. Aedre had vowed poverty, chastity and obedience and found serenity in her purpose, her beauty as luminous and severe as her illustrations. Did she too not let God into her heart...the advice he had received from the Pope, Archbishop Boniface, Bishop Willibald, Abbess Leoba and from the examples set by Meryn and Aedre? Why did he not follow them on the same path? Not for pride. Nor did he believe himself above his neighbour – on the contrary. A pagan? Not so, but he found God in Nature...neither did he hate the Church, in spite of having reason. In honesty, his heart contained dark secrets. First, he needed to open it to his own inspection, then unbar it to others before baring it to the scrutiny of God. How to begin?

Irresolute, he sighed and slid down on his haunches. Free, but with no idea of what to do with his life. For many years, he thought to destroy Milo, with the deed done he was nought but an empty shell.

*"A man with no purpose,"* he repeated. In his forty-sixth year, he stumbled in obscurity. Was he able to prise open the vault beating in his chest? He rose and surrendered to the splendour of the universe.

The constellations whispered to his soul of a quest for wisdom and faith, of a search for one as bright as the Dog-Star. One such lived at Bischofsheim. Come full circle, he would depart at dawn to seek an audience with Abbess Leoba.

# CHAPTER 19

*'In his lifetime, a man can count true friends on the fingers of one hand,'* his father told Begiloc and since destiny granted him longer life than Gerens, he knew this to be true. Fate decreed much time should be spent far from Father Robyn, yet their easeful companionship renewed whenever they met. He basked in anticipation of the pleasure his reappearance would enkindle since their subdued parting, neither expecting to see the other again.

A monk directed him to where the frate pergamentarius reigned over a world of parchment, whipped egg whites and powdered chalk. The production of vellum, the cleaning, bleaching, stretching on the herse, scraping with the lunarium and abrading fascinated Begiloc, but less than the argument flaring between the priest and the monk when he entered the room unnoticed.

The frate stood feet apart, arms folded, "... and I tell you, the abbess designated five calfskins to the scriptorium and I'm one short–"

Father Robyn, face ruddier than usual, shouted, "... and I tell you, she assigned two skins to the school–"

"She wants the Gospel finished by Christ's Mass," a thumb jerked at the herse, "this goes to the scribes, make an end to it!" The Briton announced his presence with a respectful cough and the wrathful expression of Father Robyn turned to joy, "By all that's holy! Begiloc! Weren't you supposed to be across the English Channel? What brings you here? No, don't answer!" A baleful eye turned on the frate, "First, persuade this pestilential monk to spare three leaves of vellum – at sword point, I mean."

"Brother pay no heed," Begiloc laughed, "The passing of the red hair begets no mellowing of the temper!"

A temporary truce established, they left the parchmenter to his work and walked through the drizzle to the cloister where they sat for Begiloc to explain the reason underlying his return.

"An audience with the Abbess?" Robyn said. "Difficult."

"Is she so busy?"

"Never too occupied for you, friend. Leoba's not here. She's gone with the half-sister of the king to found a convent in Bavaria. Our Mother Superior received a letter from a comitissa – how the Holy Spirit moves in mysterious ways! – well, this lady was standing on the ramparts of her castle when the wind swept away her bejewelled scarf of purple silk. The fortress is high above a valley, so she vowed to build a cloister where it landed."

The lines at the corners of the priest's eyes grew deeper with his smile.

"They recovered it otherwise our abbess would not be away," Begiloc said.

"Indeed," said the clergyman, "a shepherd called Chizz took it back to the comitissa. Not only a reward did he receive but the lady named the spot, where the abbey rises, after him, 'Chizzingim'. Now, Hadeloga will be the first abbess–"

"The king's half-sister?"

"Ay. There'll be a good magistra in Thecla, the learned nun from Wessex, advanced in years. Leoba is free to return to Bischofsheim. I heard she wishes to arrive for Christ's Mass. You'll not wait long for an audience."

They sat in companionable silence. Robyn scrutinised the warrior, not pleased with what he saw.

"May I ask? What troubles you, Briton?"

He considered the priest with his warm, open countenance, not only his confessor but his friend. If he must reveal the secrets of his heart, who better to confess to than Robyn?

The tale of the death of Aldebert poured out.

The cleric listened without interruption before saying, "Disarm him and take him alive? A madman, who slew your comrade and assailed you with an axe? What is done with rabid dogs?"

Begiloc met his long, hard stare. "In the end, you rid us of a grave problem and the Church can absolve you."

Fearing less simple absolution, he winced, spurring the cleric to ask, "Is there more?"

Silent and indecisive, he appreciated Father Robyn's stillness that encouraged him to recount the murder of Archbishop Milo. Self-loathing poured forth from his mouth like a breach in a ditch, his tale the stagnant water. Finished, Begiloc felt lighter, relieved, but the fleeting solace vanished seeing condemnation on the face of the priest whose sigh weighed as heavy on him as the Rock of Agony.

"Justice without love is no longer just, but vindictive," Robyn said.

The warrior considered this and dismissed it: his confessor must understand and forgive him then decide for exoneration to let him move forward with his life, to embrace a new reality, else he would die inside.

"Milo was evil, repugnant to the Church. The Pope himself unable to unseat him. The fiend laughed when he blinded Meryn. What right did he have to be living in wealth, abusing his power to satisfy his lusts?" As he spoke, he regretted his pleading tone.

*'Why can't he understand?'*

The face of the priest showed no sign of comprehension.

"You ask as the prophet Jeremiah," the clergyman said, *"'Why does the way of the wicked prosper? Why do all who are treacherous thrive?'* You are a man made in the image of God, born of his mercy. The law is the instrument of justice, a man may not arrogate it whether it be human or divine – as you did. Were your act judged by man, you would hang. What you seek, I cannot confer. God sees all and to pardon a mortal sin would ..." He paused and frowned, "... unless–"

" unless... ?"

"... you join a pilgrimage to the Holy Land to beg forgiv–"
Begiloc leapt to his feet, "Jerusalem? Don't you think I've tramped far enough in the name of Christ? A lifetime dedicated to your Church burdening my soul to cut out the blight in her stem so she may bloom, ay, e'en in the wilderness! All I seek is absolution. Grant it without a journey of–"
His words died as Father Robyn stood, face contorted and red.

"You know nothing! Less than nothing! You reject God, forging the chains of sin wallowing in loneliness, remorse and inner turmoil. These are the worst punishments of transgression. Accept your penance but do not absorb yourself in human law lest you forget Divine Judgement. Death and Fate belong to the Lord and we have no right to intervene. Go on pilgrimage to Palestine!"

"I shall not," Begiloc folded his arms. "I'll await the return of Abbess Leoba and seek her advice."
He glared at the priest. The clergy, he decided, chose which personality to adopt according to circumstances. Robyn was a friend, an equal, a confidant when he so elected and he spoke the language of friends. Come an issue outside those boundaries and he invoked the wrath of God.

The ire on the visage of the clergyman changed to pity. "Begiloc," his voice softened, "Do not refuse the grace of the Holy Spirit. Go! Go pray and seek forgiveness. The love of Our Father in heaven overflows and exonerates our sins although we still stand under divine judgement, He alone can remit them if we repent."

Father Robyn half-smiled, half-raised a hand, but dropped it to his side and turned away with another sigh.

At first, angry with the priest, he railed about false friends and the Church. To assuage his rancour, he wandered outside to the river. On the bank, he regarded the flowing water. One of *'inner turmoil'*, the clergyman described his disposition. Exact. For certain, he felt remorseful and lonely, given that the person he most wanted to find at Bischofsheim was the one he had raged against.

The greyness of the day matched his mood, but as he meditated on the drizzle mingling with the stream his temper eased.

*'What is it about water? Pure, clear and calm. O to cleanse my soul to be innocent as a child.'*

Ignoring the seeping dampness, he contemplated the water sliding past. His thoughts flowed with the river imagining it widening on its journey to the sea. In the same way grew his resolve.

*'I did well to open my heart to Robyn. Seeing the hollowness inside he spoke as a true friend. And I, in my self-obsession, wounded him.'*

Determined to defer to the higher authority and wisdom of Abbess Leoba, Begiloc rose. Father Robyn had paved the way, whatever the decision of the Mother Superior he would abide by it, even a pilgrimage to the Holy Land. Walking back to the monastery he reflected on his relationship with the priest who served as calm water in a lake wherein to study his own reflection.

*'He knows all about me and still he cares for me.'*

Nobler thoughts drove him back to beg forgiveness, into the

embrace of his confessor and a world of devotional compliance.

Unaware of changes within himself, the period of waiting for Leoba, coinciding with Advent, marked an imperceptible acceptance of the need to love and serve others. Willingness to work in the fields during bad weather, to wash clothes and repair fences around the monastery with never a complaint, indicated an assumption of moral responsibility, likewise, his avoidance of contact with Aedre.

On the Feast of St John the Evangelist, the abbess returned from Bavaria, she and her travel-wearied nuns retiring into the depths of the convent. Aware his wait must continue, nonetheless he reminded Father Robyn of his desire for an audience.

Three days later, a monk beckoned Begiloc from digging up winter turnips to the presence of Abbess Leoba. They appraised each other as old acquaintances after an absence. To his eyes, she appeared paler and more delicate. Not surprising, given the demands of her position and although the skin around her eyes stretched tight from weariness, her beauty still enthralled him.

With scrupulous honesty, he repeated his confession in its entirety including the priest's suggested penance. For the second time, he bared his soul to another without reservation.

"My Lady, I am a free man, Dumnonia called me but after ... after my gravest sin, I believe God lead me to seek your spiritual guidance."

What did her expression portend? Condemnation like Father Robyn? The identical sigh came, heavy to his overwrought mind as the gale that threatened to toss their ship on the Wessex headland, years before. He dreaded her wrath.

"Begiloc, you committed a terrible sin," the hazel eyes spoke clearer than her voice, mixing love with pity, "but among the multitude of sorrows in my heart, the death of Milo can find no place." Leoba stretched out a hand, "God forces no man to adore and serve Him; but when we refuse His invitation, we must sup the bane of impenitence to the dregs. Only in God's grace shall we find our peace." The countenance of the abbess became serene, her eyes distant before regaining sharpness, accompanied by a radiant smile. Hope sprang in his breast.

"I will not impose a visit to the Holy Land upon you, for I know not what, but God has a purpose for you ... I believe it has ever been so." She opened both hands before her, "Come! Take my hands and feel the grace of the Father–"

*'She wants me to take her hands!'*

Hesitant from a sense of unworthiness, the Briton stepped forward, obeyed the noblewoman sinking to his knees. Overcome, his eyes filled with tears and all else he felt, later, defied description. Deep in his heart, the way opened for his soul to be healed.

Abbess Leoba raised him. "Go Begiloc! I must pray for guidance so you may shrive yourself. When God reveals your atonement, I shall make it known to you."

The Mother Superior recommended prayer, blessed and dismissed him.

To mark the baptism of the Saviour, he shared in the solemnity of Christ's Mass and the celebration and joy of Twelfth Night. In the gloomy days of winter, work aplenty occupied him, undertaken with an inner lightness that bloomed in a constant smile and a ready greeting to those around him. Alas, no word from the abbess began to disturb his equanimity.

The passing of January stole his serenity. In spite of efforts at prayer, doubts about his purpose in life returned. Everyday tasks such as the mixing of dung with marl to spread on the fields, pruning vines and mending hedgerows did not distract him, his composure leaching away, replaced by the familiar hollowness within.

Early in February, a party of monks distracted him from warfare against moles in the vegetable garden. He noticed the abbess greet the elderly brother at the forefront of the newcomers and at supper, learnt Boniface had arrived from Mentz.

After the meal, Begiloc gleaned more about the visit from one of the guests. The monk, full of self-importance, proved keen to share his tidings.

"The archbishop intends to call an assembly after Prime. Matters of import ..." he whispered obliging the warrior to lean close, "... Boniface is in dispute with the bishop of Colonia and enlisted the aid of the Holy Father."

"Why do they quarrel?"

The brother shrugged, "Over pagan lands," a hand waved, "I dare say we shall learn more at the gathering tomorrow...but take my word for it, friend, it comes down to *animosity*. Archbishop Boniface is Saxon and the Bishop of Colonia is Frankish, need I say more?"

The assembly, restricted to those of high ecclesiastical rank, did not include the opinionated monk. Begiloc was convened to the chapter house where his amazement soared to new heights. The middle-aged prelate who proffered him the episcopal ring and embraced him was Lull, last seen twenty or more years past. The son of a thane from his late wife's village, become a bishop! Bewildered by events, he let himself be drawn to a seat next to the cleric while Boniface stood to address the council.

"Reverend brothers and sisters, I, Boniface, legate in Germany of the universal Church and servant of the Apostolic See, appointed archbishop without the claim of merit, offer greetings of the most humble affection and most sincere love in Christ."

Since their last encounter, Begiloc reflected, the man had aged but emanated energy although the burden of more than three score and ten years weighed on his shoulders.

*'How well he speaks! But why am I here?'*

The archbishop, dressed in the habit of a monk, turned to Lull, "Reverend bishop, I resigned the see of Mentz and on my recommendation our beloved Holy Father confirmed you as my successor. I commend you solicitude for the faithful and zeal in preaching the Gospel, preserve the churches we built and above all, I bid you, venerable brother, to complete the building of the monastery at Fulda."

Enchanted by the speech of Boniface, Begiloc wondered at the tone.

*'He knows he's going to die.'*

The legate's next words confirmed as much, "Remove my body thither after my death to await the Day of Resurrection."

From the tail of his eye, the warrior witnessed the emotions on the face of Lull change like spring weather. The moist eyes of the new archbishop explained his lack of reply.

Gravity and sorrow lined the faces of the senior monks, the abbess and her attendant nuns.

*'This man alone wrought vast changes in our lives.'*

Next Boniface turned to Leoba, "Beloved handmaiden of Christ, never grow weary of the life you have undertaken, extend the scope of your labours and pay no heed to your weakness. Never count the long years that lie before you, nor hold the spiritual life to be hard nor the end difficult to attain, for the years of this life are short compared to eternity and the sufferings of this world are as nothing likened to the glory that will be made manifest in the saints."

What was this man? One who spoke in this way to the person he, Begiloc, most admired? What authority, what assuredness! And she, stricken in countenance, clung to every word.

The prelate turned to Lull and admonished the senior monks to care for Leoba with reverence and respect and to the amazement of them all, said, "After her death, place her bones next to mine in the tomb, so we who served God in our lifetimes with equal sincerity and zeal shall await together the day of resurrection." In awe, Begiloc looked on as the archbishop, with solemnity, removed the cowl from his habit and handed it to Leoba. An unlearned warrior, the Briton understood the immensity of the gesture.

*'Why me? Why am I here to behold such wondrous events?'*

"God called me," said Boniface, "to resume the mission of my youth. At dawn, we leave for Trecht, whence to the pagan lands, that our Lord and God Jesus Christ, who will have all men to be saved and come to the knowledge of the Father, may turn to the Catholic faith the hearts of the Frisians, and that they may escape the snares of the devil, by which they are held bound."

Boniface, with an air of weariness, sat amid heavy silence.

The Briton marvelled that a man of advanced age should wish to risk his life taking the Gospel to a forsaken wilderness.

Distracted, he did not notice the Mother Superior rise to her feet, but in the fathomless quietude, one word – his name – like a thunderclap. "Begiloc!" He started. The abbess, the cowl of Boniface draped over her shoulders, drew near.

"God revealed your penance to me."

A warrior scarred and hardened by battle, he had to resist the urge to cower at her approach. Mortified at talk of atonement and of his sins before an exalted gathering, he did not meet her eyes, mumbling, "My Lady."

"Are you disposed to accept your penance and receive absolution?"

She drew the cowl over her head, but the raised chin did not obscure her intense piercing stare.

Intimidated, he would consent to anything and muttered, "I am."

His was a mortal sin, he did not expect clemency but the severity of the penance shocked him.

"You are no longer a free man. Instead, accompany Archbishop Boniface to Frisia. There you will command his troops, obey his every order and serve him faithfully. Do you so swear?"

*'Accept and lose my freedom?'* a diabolical voice resonated in his brain, *'I know how sweet it is. Throw it away for a mad venture into the wild? A slave once more? Refuse!'*

Everyone in the room assessed him, including the archbishop, intrigued as to his response. No fool, he quelled rebellious thoughts, aware of the penalties of incurring the wrath of the Church. In any case, he dwelt on what he had heard in this chapter house and on the admiration he bore for Leoba. The fact she deferred to this elderly prelate settled the matter.

"I do, My Lady."

Satisfaction showed on the face of Boniface and the hazel eyes of the abbess softened – and it was done.

"Kneel, Begiloc!" She intoned: *"Ego te absolvo a peccatis tuis in nomine Patris et filii et spiritus sancti"*, drew the sign of the Cross above his head and blessed him. He arose unblemished, physically bound to the Church but spiritually free.

Lull, swift to embrace him, whispered in his ear, "Keep Boniface safe, Begiloc. Defend him with your life and may God preserve and guard you against harm."

Dawn afforded poor light amid the driving rain. Surrounded by eight monks and the former archbishop, in the gloom, they loaded an ox cart with three small chests containing sacred relics and holy books. Boniface called to Lull sheltering next to Leoba in a doorway, "Beloved brother, I forgot, pray have a shroud fetched wherein to wrap my mortal remains."

Lull protested before dispatching a novice to fetch the winding sheet. Taking the folded linen from the postulant, the elderly monk carried it to the ox cart himself. The anguished face of the prelate moved Begiloc.

*'Tears not rainwater coursing down his cheeks!'*

With this ominous portent, they bade farewell and the cartwheels slithered along the muddy ruts on the short journey to the Tauber from the monastery, whence they were rowed into the River Men, its water flowing grey as molten tin. Overhead, the clouds were a shade darker. The wind as keen as a whetted blade filled the sail and their craft sliced up the river.

What Begiloc assumed would be a voyage as depressing as the weather proved otherwise. Brother Boniface, now a simple Benedictine monk, sought him to exchange tales of their youth. The warrior spoke of Dumnonia and the monk of Wessex the brutal conquests of the great warlord, Caedwalla.

"When I was a lad, Caedwalla took the Isle of Wight, the last heathen stronghold in England. The monarch massacred the population. Horrible. No mercy in those dark days."

In the eyes of the missionary, Begiloc read the unsettling depth of his passion, "I was sixteen when Caedwalla abdicated and announced his pilgrimage to Rome for baptism. The hardest hearts can be softened by the Word, and we – you and I – will convert the pagan Frisians also by force if need be."

The unease of the Briton grew at the light burning deep in the eyes of the elderly brother, underscored by the direness of his words. No doubt the sinews of his sword arm would be strained to the full and this conviction was confirmed at their destination.

The Abbot of St Martin's at Trecht, a disciple of Boniface named Gregory, accorded them a warm welcome. Amid preparation for the mission that followed, Begiloc occupied himself with the recruitment and training of men. Trecht was not a poor diocese and the chorbishop, Eoban, another follower of Boniface like Gregory, made his task easier by a generous contribution to the purchase of arms and pay as an incentive to volunteering. Soon, Begiloc commanded twenty sturdy men, half of whom he rated as seasoned warriors.

He noticed the bishop's appraising glances on more than one occasion. Twice a spectator at his training routines, Eoban slipped away before they ended. When the prelate waylaid him in the cloister, he suspected the encounter was not casual.

"A Briton are you not?" were his first words.

"I am."

Begiloc noted the auburn curls and green eyes of his middle-aged interlocutor as he drew him to sit on the low wall.

"It is common to us. My parents raised me in Wessex since they came there from Brega by ill chance when rebels deposed and exiled Fogartach mac Néill as king. Later, he returned to reassume his birthright, but the voyage ended in disaster in a terrible storm when two of the three ships were lost. As a child I sailed on one of the doomed vessels. The gale swept it on the coast of Dumnonia ..." The bishop smiled in confirmation of Begiloc's startled expression, "... ay, Gerens saved my mother and I, laying down his life for us! In the village afterwards, we discovered his name before seeking out your mother – we were but *buachailli* yet I remember you – a boy of six like myself. Here I am to warn you, I would not our wyrd be entwined."

"Warn me?"

Moved, Begiloc, grown up worshipping his father as a hero, stared at the prelate. Before him, the child his father saved, become a man – a good man. What were his feelings? Not resentment. More a kindred spirit with this person, but what did he mean to say?

*'He would not our wyrd be entwined? Not the words of a Christian bishop! No man may avert his destiny ...'*

The clergyman scanned the cloister to ensure they were quite alone.

"What I say must remain between us. Your word on it?"

His eyes met those of the prelate, "I can't believe the Lord's servant means harm to any man, you have it."

Eoban flushed, "Harm, the opposite. At worst, a disservice – to one who is more than a friend."

"How so?"

"Leave Friesland now. Return to Dumnonia. Go home!"

The prelate raised his hand, "Hear me out. I must thank Boniface for my elevation to bishop and am grateful to the man I repute most holy and an example to follow. Yet, within him burns a relentless ardour. The late lamented Willibrord saw it as an all-consuming fervour. Many years ago, they had a dispute over it and Boniface left for England and thence for Germany." The urgent tone of Eoban slowed, sure of Begiloc's attention. "Instead Willibrord converted the Frisians by the strength of his meekness and by example. True, he changed the heathen temples into Christian churches, but only after the people were baptised. The infidel King Radboud later undid his work and now the pagan ruler is dead, Boniface intends to press into North-West Friesland where the tribes are untouched by Christianity."

Eoban held up his hand again, "Hold, I beg of you, another moment's patience. Boniface talks of destroying the temples as he did Thunor's oak in Hessia. He believes challenging their gods by acting with impunity will convince them to convert. It is not so simple. Would that it were. Frisian law is explicit: whosoever destroys an image of a god shall forfeit his life by beheading or drowning–"

"Why do you intend to follow him?" Begiloc asked.

"I gave my life to Christ and swore obedience. The most I can do is seek to convince through argument. With Boniface, my poor words are in vain whereas I hope they will not be with you."

The sincerity of the Irishman moved him, he replied with equal frankness, "I fear so, I too vowed submission. Sin lay heavy on my soul and in return for absolution I vowed to follow and protect Boniface. I may not break this oath. In return for your concern, I offer you my hand, for our lives are ravelled and our wyrd inexorable. Brothers in the death of our fathers, likewise let us be brothers in life and leave the rest to fate."

Eoban rose, his expression unreadable, but the bishop clasped his hand, pulled him into an embrace and in a hushed voice said, "What we call wyrd, the Church calls divine providence and declares that God knows what is going to happen, not the contrary. Either way, brother, let us prepare to wear the martyr's crown."

# CHAPTER 20

*Anno Domini 754, March*

Doleful, Begiloc scowled at the desolate landscape. Lichen oozed water on rocks isolated between pools dank with moss and mould. Rivers gorged by ceaseless rain flowed seawards creating marshland and swamps.

Frisians managed to live there, hardy or foolhardy folk. Wild reindeer and aurochs roamed undisturbed on the geest since lack of bushes and trees provided no hiding place to stalk them. How the people grew tall with little sustenance mystified him. The Frisians lived on terps, raised mounds proof against storms and surging seawater where they cooked over fires fuelled by the dry dung of the few animals they possessed.

Begiloc and his men, Boniface, Eoban, deacons and monks, soaked and cheerless, squelched towards the coast from terp to terp.

*'I understand why Boniface wishes to bring the news of eternal life to this forlorn outpost. If ever a people needed the prospect of paradise with the promise of sunlit, flower-strewn meadows, it's these marsh dwellers.'*

Stumbling over a rotting branch, mildew-like fibres crisscrossing its surface, Begiloc swore. No time to consider why a log lay among the sedges because their Frisian guide pointed ahead. Above the reeds rose another mound, without huts, different. The sound of voices from a congregation drifted down amid the swaying stalks. The splendid building atop the terp defied the dim light of the sodden March day.

"Spread out! Charge!" Begiloc ordered.

Women's screams mingled with the cries of unarmed men as they fled.

In moments, only one person stood his ground, defiant, arms aloft – a man with long plaited blond hair, face and limbs daubed with purple pigment. A cloak of woven rushes hung over his shoulders while on his brow, tucked into a band of twined seaweed, sprouted quills of black and white gull feathers. Over their heads, twelve columns with a lamina of beaten gold supported a shining roof plated in silver. On each column hung trinkets and amulets of the same precious metals – treasure in a land of craneflies.

"Halt, lower your weapons!"

The monk faced the heathen who pointed at him. In a strange tongue yet resembling English, the sorcerer cried, "Turn back! Risk not the wrath of Fosite!"

Glaring at the pagan, the white-haired brother folded his arms, "Demon-worship! We come in the name of the one God, the Creator Omnipotent..." with a gesture at the temple, he said, "...to prohibit divinations or drawing of lots, auguries, phylacteries, incantations and all your unclean usages. Repent! Abandon the demon Fosite, embrace the true faith!"

The sorcerer raised a hand holding a veined stone. He began to turn it, his eyes narrowed and intoned in a malevolent voice, "O mighty Fosite, son of Baldr, Lord of the Deep, as the dead are powerless and still, so make this desecrator, his feet, his hands, his body!"

In defiance, the monk made the sign of the cross and raised a crucifix above his head, "Servant of Satan, repent! Kneel before Jesus Christ, the Son of God. Agree to be baptised in His name. Save your immortal soul!"

The pagan spat at Boniface and again called upon Fosite to strike down the monk. With a heavy sigh, the missionary turned to Begiloc, "Behold an impenitent whose vileness springs from the Evil One. Slay the idolater!"

The warrior stared from the face of the man who had spread Christianity through the German lands to the sorrowful countenance of Bishop Eoban. Had he heard aright? End this man's life without compunction? The Irishman nodded. Begiloc blinked, drew his sword and not letting hesitation stay his arm, sliced deep into the throat of the baleful heathen.

As though in a trance, he regarded the death throes of the purple-faced sorcerer without registering the words of the guide who, impassive, explained how the adornment of the temple represented Glitnir, the home of Fosite.

"Strip the gold and the silver," Boniface ordered, "we shall use it to raise a church on this site. Do not destroy the pillars and the roof, they will serve for the new construction."

The monk looked with distaste at the body.

"Throw the corpse into the swamp!"

Still the Briton stood motionless.

*'Is this the way of the God of Love we follow?'*

A tug at his sleeve and he stared at his men prising the gold leaf and the silver plate from the wood, Eoban said, "Do not sorrow. The Lord guided your hand for the greater good of these people. Harsh as it is, there can be no sorcerers or magicians to lead the people into impurity and sin."

The roof of the temple afforded shelter for the night but dry fuel for a fire. In this way, they avoided the waterlogged ground below. When drizzle began to fall they huddled together in the centre of the covered space to evade the damp.

The murder of the sorcerer in the name of duty oppressed him. Being in the wilderness was supposed to absolve him from sin; yet the slaughter remained a vile deed in the name of whatever deity. Did the pagan deserve his cruel end met weaponless with bravery or ingenuousness, confronting twenty armed men in the name of the god of his forefathers? Would not Begiloc's own ancestors likewise have defended their sacred groves?

*'Eoban is right, there can be no sorcerers if the people are to accept Christ.'*

Rational thought proved no relief from inner turmoil. In the following days, he soothed his mind with blind acceptance. Overcoming the hostility of the Frisians at the death of their priest and the defilement of their sacred site was not his task but one suited to the charisma of Boniface. The force of his personality, the energy he radiated at an advanced age, the conviction behind his words, penetrated the resistance of the pagans, conquered their resentment and opened their hearts to Christ. The irresistible power of his oratory uplifted Begiloc too, and in him the germ of certitude in the righteousness of their mission began to grow.

Baptisms followed apace and the converts were edified by the words of their evangelizer: "Listen, brethren, and consider well what you renounced in your baptism. You repudiated the devil and all his works, and all his pomp. But what are the works of the Devil? They are pride, idolatry, envy, murder, calumny, lying, perjury..." he said the words in a slow recitation, at each transgression his voice rose with accusatory venom, "...hatred, fornication, adultery, every kind of lewdness, theft, false witness, robbery, gluttony, drunkenness, slander, fight, malice, philtres, incantations..."

No end to human perfidy wondered Begiloc as the list went on, "...lots, belief in witches and werewolves, abortion, disobedience to the Master, amulets. These and other evil things are the work of the Devil, all of which you forswore by your baptism, as the apostle says: *'Whosoever doeth such things deserves death, and shall not inherit the kingdom of heaven...'* But as we believe, by the mercy of God, you will renounce all this, with heart and hand, to become fit for grace, I admonish you, my dearest brethren, to remember what you promised the Father Almighty."

Spring changed the aspect of the land, in spite of the rotting foliage and creeping vapours from the bog, the pestilential gnats and flies, Begiloc began to appreciate the elemental beauty of his surroundings. Flowers appeared, kingcups followed by marsh violets and with them the first butterflies so his spirits soared with the piping curlews and snipe.

They continued to destroy the *fana deluborum* as the monk called the shrines in the language he, Begiloc, would never understand. Not one remained intact, they felled hollow trees for passing cattle through and demolished shafts with strange carvings at the meeting of three roads, eliminating any manifestation of paganism wherever they ventured. Plundered timber served to make frames for the wattle and daub construction of two churches while reeds abounded to thatch the roofs, all done before the appearance of the tender water forget-me-not in May.

Conviction grew in Begiloc that the belief of Boniface in the readiness of Friesland to embrace Christianity was justified. When some of the ethelings, the men the monk called *nobiles* converted, they brought the *frilings* – the free men –who in turn coerced their tenants and slaves tied to the land. In a short time, the number of baptisms surpassed expectations.

In May, one of the fervid ethelings unsettled Begiloc's newfound certitude. The nobleman arrived at a church with a captive. The lordling addressed Boniface, "Brother, I seek advice on what to do with this man. You preached of our responsibility to stamp out poetry praising the old gods and the lore associated with their worship." Perplexity greeted his words, "The prisoner is a bard and stands accused of singing the saga recounting how the war god Tīw lost his right hand to the wolf, Fenrir."

Appalled at the hypocrisy, Begiloc disdained the etheling's self-righteous denunciation of the songster.

*'How often has he enjoyed a good tale sung by the fire on a winter's night?'*

In the name of an adopted religion, he stood before Boniface asking what to do with a man whose 'crime' was to sing a traditional poem. A question of a fine? The other day they fined a man twenty-eight thousand denarii for hitting a free woman in child.

*'The poor woman died. A song can't cost much coin.'*

He strove to understand the injustice in their lives.

*'How can silver compensate the loss of life?'*

The elderly monk, forefinger curled over his upper lip, heard out the accusation. The brown eyes flashed as he threw back responsibility on the plaintiff, "Heathen poesy is the work of the Devil. What do you suggest to silence this purveyor of paganism?"

The nobleman did not expect to make a decision, but a sly expression crept onto his face.

"What does the Church advise?"

Begiloc stared at Boniface. How would the monk react?

"Bring the bard to me."

They pulled the captive in front of the missionary.

"My son," admonished Boniface in a low voice, "are you prepared to be saved and come unto the knowledge of the Lord Jesus Christ? Will you not use your God-given gift to sing His praise? Come, eschew the eternal flames. Renounce the demons of your verse!"

Hope writ in his visage, Boniface waited but dismayed, Begiloc noted the narrowing of the bard's eyes followed by a shake of the head.

*'This is not a matter of a few coins.'*

By now, he was used to Boniface's swift changes of mood. Ire replaced expectation as he turned to the etheling, "Here stands a peddler of sacrilege, uncontrite. Let us crush this sin. My son..." he addressed the nobleman with earnestness, "...we are both united in the same cause and an equal obligation is imposed upon us to care for the Church and the people. I beseech you, let God inspire you with wise counsel on how to silence the utterings of the heathen."

Once more the oratory of Boniface had effect. The light of fervour entered the eyes of the etheling who ordered his men to hold the bard while he drew a dagger from his belt.

*'Will he murder him in front of us?'*

As a solution, it might have been more merciful. Stomach clenching, Begiloc saw the Frisian insert the blade into the bard's mouth, slicing the frenulum thence up through the tongue. When he pulled the weapon out, the bard retched in excruciating pain and upon an inhuman howl from the throat, half the bloodied organ fell to his feet.

The Briton turned away disgusted from the songster who would never sing again. The bard's body would heal but not his spirit. Walking into the church, Begiloc stared comfortless at the cross fashioned from the silver of the temple of Fosite, dwelling on the blinding of Meryn. Where was the difference? The agents a saintly monk and a sinful bishop but the same end – the maiming of a man.

*'Good and Evil as one?'*

He bowed his head, prayed for enlightenment but in his agitation no stillness came. Turbulent thoughts troubled him.

Was their coming to Friesland to bring the Love of Christ or to destroy traditions and culture?

No answer came in the emptiness of the house of prayer or from the hollowness within.

The next day, they left the church. On their way, voles and shrews scurried among the hemlock and marsh pennywort encouraged by the warmth of the June sun. Avocets and oystercatchers on the shore counterpointed the progress of the mission along the coastal *morra* – the wetland with its lustre of green. The waders, to Begiloc, represented the seasonal changelessness of nature; in contrast, their quest an upheaval aspiring to change the spiritual landscape of Friesland.

They followed the tidal river, Bordne, and pitched tents on its banks. The next day, the fifth of the month, the converts received an invitation to the great feast of Pentecost. The religious party of Boniface, Bishop Eoban, three priests, four monks and three deacons were to administer the sacrament of confirmation to the baptised.

As every morning, Begiloc rose with the sun. Sweeping aside the flap of his tent, he breathed in the scents of the new day. The droplet-pearled grass glistened under a sky filled with birdsong.

*'The voice of God is heard at dawn.'*

The early risers, monks apart, were his veteran warriors like himself, hardened in battle and indifferent to comfort. In the centre of the encampment, the tethered ox grazed not far from its cart. Resting on its shafts, it stood laden with sacred books and parchments, candles, images and other religious trappings. Eyes wandering past it to the edge of the trees where yellow-hearted purple irises bobbed in the breeze, Begiloc closed them to take another deep breath of the late-spring air. He opened them to a horde of men with spears and shields surrounding the camp. The cries of alarm, the dash of men to arms, were to no avail, and Begiloc knew it. Eoban had been right to warn him to prepare for the martyr's crown and that day had come. The pagans meant to avenge themselves on the Christian missionaries who dared demolish their shrines.

Begiloc drew his sword as the Frisians rushed into the camp and striding to meet them Boniface shouted, "Sons, do not fight! Lay down your arms. Overcome evil by good!"

*'Damned if I will! Die like a wolf not a sheep.'*

In battle, faced by an onrushing spearman, Begiloc would sidestep to deliver a counter blow. But this day, three charged him leaving no escape. The force of the spear threw him backwards to the ground. As the fallen warrior had so often done to an adversary in the past, his foe thrust a foot against his body to retrieve the weapon. Head spinning, the pain unbearable, he had a vague awareness of his disinterested assailant driving on to seek another victim.

Amid the clash of steel and screams of dying men, the white-haired monk, kneeling, held a black book aloft as though it were a shield to fend off the enemy blade. The beheading was swift, Boniface martyred, witnessed by the fading sight of Begiloc.

Soon, in his fiftieth year, he would join the monk. Tranquillity of thought, the certainty of death conquered, were these but the folly of a dying man? Whatever, he prayed, ending with two names, his last words: "...Somerhild and Ealric."

Reaching inside his tunic, he drew out the ivory cross, pressed it to his lips and thought of Leoba. Blood seeped through his fingers as he hoped for personal victory in defeat.

The low sun cast the long shadow of his kneeling form in front of him and the outline of another behind him brandishing

an upraised sword. Enthralled, he watched it swing downwards
to his neck.

#

# APPENDIX

There can be no certainty about the exact year the letter was received by Abbess Cuniburg. In *The Purple Thread* I have chosen a possible early date of 733. As can be seen from the letter, the young freedman, Begiloc, was summoned to join the missionaries along with his companion named Man. I preferred to call the latter Meryn.

## A letter from Denehard, Lull, and Burchard (732-42)

Dominae dilectissimae Christique relegiosissimae abbatissae Cuneburge regalis prosapiae generositate praeditae Den[ehartus] et L[ul] et B[urghardus], filii tui ac vernaculi, sempiternae sospitatis salutem.

Agnoscere cupimus almitatis tuae clementiam, quia te prae ceteris cunctis feminini sexus in cordis cubiculo, cingimus amore: quod genitoris et genetricis et aliorum propinquorum nostrorum ob obitum ad Germanicas gentes transivimus, usque in venerandi archiepiscopi Bonifatii monasticae conversationis regula suscepti ipsiusque laboris adiutores sumus, in quantum nostrae pauperculae vilitas praevalet. Nunc itaque ex intimis praecordiorum iliis suppliciter flagitamus, ut digneris nos habere in tuae sacrae congregationis communione, et nostram lintrem procellosis fluctibus huius mundi fatigatam tuorum oraminum praesidio ad portum salutis deducere et atra contra piaculorum spicula parma tuae orationis protegere non recuses, sicut nos quoque, licet peccatores, pro tuae celsitudinis statu divino subfragio singulis momentis deprecantes sumus. Hoc vero, si corporibus praesentes fuissemus, flexis genuum poplitibus et salsis lacrimarum imbribus rogitantes diligenti petitione speramus posse impetrari; et nunc absentes hoc idem obnixis precibus postulamus. Illud etiam scire desideramus tuae sagacitatis industriam: quod, si cui nostrum contingit huius Brittanicae telluris sceptra visitare, quod nullius hominis oboedientiam et institutionem antea quaerimus, quam tuae benivolentiae subiectionem, qui in te firmissimam spem mentis nostrae positam habemus.

Similiter obsecramus, ut puerulos duos nomine Beiloc et Man — quos ego Lul et pater noster liberos dimisimus Romam destinantes et avunculo nostro commendavimus — pro mercede, animae tuae, et si liberi arbitrii sint et illorum voluntas sit et in tua potestate sint, nobis transmittere per harum litterarum gerulos studeas. Et si aliquis eis prohibere vellet iter pergendi sine iustitia, deprecamur, ut eos defendere digneris. Parva quoque munusculorum transmissio scedulam istam comitatur; quae sunt tria, id est turis et piperis et cinnamomi permodica xenia, sed omni mentis affectione destinata. Huius muneris magnitudinem ut non consideres, sed spiritalis caritatis amorem adtende, poscimus. Illud etiam petimus, ut rusticitatem huius epistiunculae emendes et nobis aliqua verba tuae dulcedinis non rennuas dirigere, quae inhianter audire gratulabundi satagimus.

Vale, vivens Deo aevo longiore ct vita feliciore, intercedens pro nobis.

MGH, *Epistolae Merovingici et Karolini Aevi*, 6, *S.Bonifacii et Lulli Epistolae,* ep.49

**Translation of letter:**
To their beloved lady, greatly devoted to Christ, Abbess Cuniburg, distinguished by the regality of her blood, her sons and compatriots Denehard, Lull, and Burchard send wishes for her eternal health.

Holding you above all women in the innermost vault of our hearts we desire your graciousness to know that, after the death of our parents and other relatives, we went to the people of Germany, were admitted into the monastic rule of the venerable archbishop, Boniface, and have become helpers in his labours in so far as our humble incapacity allows.

And now, we beseech you from the depths of our hearts that it will be your pleasure to honour us by communion with your holy congregation, and with the support of your prayers guide our small boat, battered by the tempests of this world, into safe refuge, and that you will not decline to shelter us against the cruel barbs of sin with the shield of your prayer, as we also pray for divine intervention every moment for the well-being of Your Reverence. If we were in person before you on bended knee and with floods of tears, we feel sure that our petition would be granted; so now, in our absence, we humbly beg this very favour from you. We also entrust to your care and wisdom that if any one of us should visit Britain we should not prefer obedience and rule of any man to subjection under your benevolence; for in you we place the greatest confidence of our hearts.

We beg also that you will send on by the bearer of this letter two young freedmen, named Begiloc and Man, whom I, Lull, and my father released on our departure for Rome and entrusted to my uncle for the welfare of my soul — if this should be their free act and if they are within your jurisdiction. And if any one shall unlawfully attempt to impede their journey we beg you to protect them.

Some small offerings accompany this letter: frankincense, pepper, and cinnamon — a very small gift, but given out of heartfelt devotion. We beseech you not to think of the measure of the gift but to bethink on the loving spirit behind it. We beg you also to correct this unlearned letter and to send some of your own sweet words, which we shall await with enthusiasm. Farewell, and may you live long and in happiness to intercede for us.

Translation - ©John Broughton, *2017*.

# GLOSSARY

**Monastic Religious Services**

| | |
|---|---|
| Matins | midnight |
| Lauds | 3 am |
| Prime | 6 am |
| Terce | 9 am |
| Sext | midday |
| None | 3 pm |
| Vespers | 6 pm |
| Compline | 9 pm |

**General Terms**

| | |
|---|---|
| wyrd | Anglo-Saxon concept of ancestral fate, destiny |
| leud | A Frankish lesser nobleman, vassal to a Duke |
| comitis, comitissa | Frankish count, countess |
| faet | Liquid measure probably translates as 'pot' |
| Sifunsterri | Anglo-Saxon name for the Pleiades |
| gothi | Germanic pagan priest |
| gythja | Germanic pagan priestess |
| Fru Freke | Germanic goddess, otherwise Holda or Diana |
| Folkwangr | Fields where the souls of the dead gather |
| Sessrymir | Freke's hall |
| sortilegium | Divination by drawing lots |
| maleficium | Malevolent sorcery |
| chorbishop | Greek Χωρεπίσκοπος and means rural bishop. |
| buachaillí | Irish Gaelic for 'boys'. |
| terp | artificial dwelling hill |
| geest | sandy heathland |
| morra | marshland |

**Place Names mentioned in Part One in order of appearance**

*Wherever confirmable eighth-century place name usage has been adopted.*

| Eighth-century place names | Modern Name |
|---|---|
| Dumnonia | Latinised name for the Brythonic kingdom between the late 4th and late 8th centuries, in what is now the more |

| | westerly parts of South West England |
|---|---|
| Bishofsheim | Tauberbishofsheim |
| Werham | Wareham |
| Corf | Corfe Mullen |
| Brunoces | Brownsea Island |
| Hamwic | Southampton |
| Neustria | Western part of the Kingdom of the Franks |
| Aanwerp | Antwerp |
| Quentovic | No longer exists, but was an important port located east of Étaples, France. |
| Champany | Champagne |
| Rems | Rheims |
| Meldi | Meaux |
| Catalauns | Châlons-sur-Marne |
| Austrasia | The north-east section of the Kingdom of the Franks |
| Sanctá-Menehilde | Sainte-Menehauld |
| Somepin | Sommepy-Tahure |
| Verden | Verdun |
| Glywysing | Gwent, Wales |
| Narbon | Narbonne |
| Arbūnah | Arabic for Narbonne |
| Comitis Villa | Coinville |
| Mentz | Mainz |

**Place Names mentioned in Part Two in order of appearance**

| | |
|---|---|
| Louvercy | Livry-Louvercy |
| Treves | Trier |
| River Rhenus | River Rhine |
| Vormatia | Worms |
| Spira | Speyer |
| Strazburg | Strasbourg |
| Basilia | Basel |
| Mustruel | Montreux |
| Rottu | Rhône |
| Octodurus | Martigny |
| Pass of Poeninus | Great St Bernard Pass |
| Petrecastel | Bourg Saint Pierre |

| | |
|---|---|
| Sce Remei | Saint-Rhemy-en-Bosses |
| Agusta | Aosta |
| Everi | Ivrea |
| Vercel | Vercelli |
| Pamphica | Pavia |
| Placentia | Piacenza |
| Sce Domnine | Fidenza |
| Floricum | Fiorenzuola |
| Luca | Lucca |
| Seocine | Siena |
| Mount Bardon Pass | Cisa Pass |
| Funtrêmal | Pontremoli |
| Aguilla | Aulla |
| Sce Quiric | San Quiricio d'Orcia |
| Sce Valentine | Viterbo |
| Sca Cristina | Bolsena |
| Suteria | Sutri |
| Flaminian Gate | Porta del Popolo |
| Colonia | Cologne |
| Eistedd | Eichstätt |

**Place Names mentioned in Part Three in order of appearance**

| | |
|---|---|
| Sparnacum | Épernay |
| Juvinia | Juvigny |
| Haerulfisfeld | Bad Hersfeld |
| Bochonia | Buchonian forest area |
| Franconofurd | Frankfurt-on-Main |
| Chizzingim | Kitzingen |
| Trecht | Utrecht |
| River Men | River Main |

## ABOUT THE AUTHOR

If you wish to find out more about John Broughton and his writing please visit my website www.saxonquill.com
or find me on Facebook www.facebook.com/caedwalla/

Printed in Great Britain
by Amazon